RING OF RUIN

A RELIC HUNTERS NOVEL

KERI ARTHUR

With thanks to:

The Lulus
Indigo Chick Designs
Hot Tree Editing
Dominic Wakeford Editorial
Robyn E.
The lovely ladies from Indie Gals
JMN Art—Covers by Julie for the amazing cover

CHAPTER
ONE

"My father is a goddamned sadist."

The words were muffled by the woolen scarf I'd wrapped around the lower part of my face, but they nevertheless seemed to freeze briefly in the air. It was damnably cold and would undoubtedly get a whole lot worse, given we were only a third of the way through a decidedly insane eleven-miles-round-trip hike up Ben Nevis, Scotland's tallest mountain.

In the winter.

In the fog and the rain and the occasional flurry of snow.

The figure immediately ahead of me chuckled. Like me, my brother was dressed from head to toe in waterproofs to keep out the weather, and multiple layers underneath to keep in the heat. He was also wearing a backpack filled with tea, water, and food. Strapped to the back of this was a black sword that, even though it was fully sheathed in a silver-coated leather scabbard, emanated dark fury.

It was the sole reason we were on this goddamn mountain.

We needed to safely get rid of the thing, and that meant handing it back to the old gods who'd made it.

Presuming, of course, said old gods were home and that one of them would deign to talk to me.

There was never any guarantee, because the old gods could be cranky old bitches and bastards at the best of times.

"You've got the 'god' part of that right," Lugh said. "But I think the only sadist here is you. It was your idea to risk the climb on such a shitty day; no one else's."

Despite the fact the wind was at our backs and should have been snatching his words away from me, I could hear him quite clearly. I'd created a small "weather bubble" at the beginning of our climb, not only to ensure that we could hear each other, but also to keep the three of us out of the very worst of the weather. Maintaining it tugged at my strength, but it also made moving through the storm easier, so it basically evened out.

"True," I replied, "but it wasn't like we had any real choice."

We'd already wasted two days waiting for the weather to clear, and the feeling that we were running out of time had grown so sharp, it felt like I was being knifed. I might have been a late bloomer when it came to second sight, but to date it had proven remarkably accurate. I didn't dare ignore the warning.

Thankfully, we'd pre-arranged a guide to take us up to the summit, and while he hadn't been too pleased about the prospect of a possible nine-hour trek in inclement weather, he'd also agreed that today was as good as it was likely to get for at least the next week. He'd charged us double for the inconvenience, of course. If there was one thing to be said about dwarves, it was that they never wasted an opportunity to make an extra buck.

But in this case, it was worth it. Holgan's people had called this region home eons before it became a national park, and they made a good living escorting hikers up and down the mountains.

The zigzagging path changed direction again, and the wind's ferocity briefly eased.

Holgan turned to face us. Unlike either Lugh or me, he wasn't wrapped to the nines in waterproofs, ski masks, and scarves, although he did have an oilskin on. His thick red beard—which had been artfully platted—was tucked inside the coat, but his sodden red hair was plastered to his skull. He didn't seem to care.

But then, his people did live under Stob Coire Easain, which was a "lesser" part of this mountain range, so he was no doubt used to these conditions. It wasn't as if there was much in the way of public transport or even roads in that particular area.

"If you be needing a drink and something to eat," he said, his voice seeming to come from somewhere near the vicinity of his boots, "it's best you do so now. There's not going to be much chance once we get onto the scree slopes."

Lugh immediately tugged off his pack and retrieved the thermos and three chocolate bars. Holgan refused the latter, so I grabbed it. We'd had a full English breakfast at the pub we'd been staying at, but that was hours ago, and my stomach was getting to that grumbly stage. Besides, I'd no doubt need the energy boost once we hit the more open areas near the summit.

Lugh handed me a steaming mug of tea. I took a sip and then asked, "How much further to the top?"

Holgan shrugged. "Depends whether the conditions ease like they're predicting or get worse. Either way, we can't go too fast because we'll run the risk of the wind pushing us into the gully."

The wind would do no such thing, and I'd make sure of it. I wasn't the daughter of a storm god for nothing. While my control of the weather could at best be described as minuscule right now, I was decidedly more proficient when it came to the wind.

Holgan accepted his mug with a nod, then added, "There's going to be zero visibility on the summit."

"There's zero visibility right now," I replied, "so that's hardly a surprise."

It didn't really matter anyway, because we weren't here for the views. While the summit held all the usual remnants of bygone eras—the remains of the meteorological observatory, a few memorials, and some cairns—it was also, according to Beira—who was a hag and one of the aforementioned cranky old goddesses—a confluence. Which in dictionary terms meant a meeting or gathering point, but in this instance meant a gateway junction between heaven and earth.

Apparently, such gateways rarely opened for humans or any of the other races that still inhabited our modern world, such as elves, dwarves, shifters, and the like, and Beira had no idea whether it would open for me, despite the fact my father was a minor storm god.

Or, indeed, what would happen if it *did*.

"Then what's the reason for this insanity?" Holgan said. "Is it the sword on the wee lad's back then?"

I couldn't help a snort of laughter. Lugh was a six-foot-six bear of a man with unruly red hair and frost-green eyes.

The term "wee" didn't even fit me, and I was eight inches shorter.

"I do believe we're paying you extra for no questions asked," the lad replied mildly.

"Fair enough," Holgan said. "But I'd appreciate forewarning if you believe anything unusual is about to happen."

"If anything unusual *does* happen," Lugh growled, "we expect you to stick around and ensure we get off the mountain safely."

Holgan smiled, but there was a decidedly steely glimmer in his brown eyes. "I never abandon a client."

Unless he was paid to do so. He didn't say that, of course, but there was a part of me that couldn't help filling in the unspoken blanks. It appeared my natural pessimism was doing its best to darken an already dark day... and I seriously hoped that's *all* it was.

I finished my tea, shook the remaining droplets out, then handed the cup back to Lugh. Once he'd repacked everything and slung the pack back on, we continued.

Holgan certainly hadn't been kidding about the ferocity of the storm on the scree slopes. While my weather bubble remained locked around us, it couldn't fully blunt the force of the storm. Going was slow, and we seemed to be trudging on forever. By the time we reached the highlands, my limbs were shaking with effort, sweat trickled down my spine, and the air was so cold, my lungs hurt. I was sure there were icicles hanging off my scarf, because the damn thing seemed to have doubled its weight. There were *definitely* ice crystals on my eyelashes, and that was a damnably weird sensation.

The only reason I knew we'd actually arrived at the summit was that Holgan stopped at what looked to be a cairn and said so. The world up here was nothing more than a sea of shifting gray, and there was a decidedly other-worldly feel about it.

I hoped it meant the confluence was accessible, but given I knew absolutely nothing about them, it was totally possible that otherworldly feeling was nothing more than imagination or even wishful thinking.

I stopped beside Lugh and Holgan and looked around. Though I'd studied several maps before we'd left, the shifting gray made it impossible to judge where exactly we were on the summit, or even which cairn we'd stopped next to. "How far away is the edge?"

"Maybe two dozen steps directly ahead of us." Holgan studied me for a second. "You planning to throw that sword over it or something?"

I half smiled. "Or something."

"Whatever that 'something' involves, can I suggest you put on the harness and rope the wee lad has been carrying? Better to be safe than sorry in these conditions."

"Oh, she's not going *anywhere* unless she's roped to me."

I wasn't entirely sure being roped to my brother would do any good if the confluence was some sort of portal to another dimension, but as Holgan had noted, better safe than sorry.

Lugh placed the pack on the ground, then handed me a harness. While I pulled it on over my coat, he carefully unlashed the sword. We both wore silver-laced silk under-gloves under our regular ones just to be sure we could handle the sword safely. While neither he nor I were mages, and therefore never likely to be a target for the unholy power that lay within the sword, we weren't about to take any chances. Not when the mere act of touching its hilt with unprotected flesh would not only unleash a siren's call to any evil that inhabited the area but doom our souls to the stygian—which was not, as human legend would have it, the river presided over by the boatman Charon. There was no actual river or even a boatman, and the stygian were simply the souls of those charged to bring fresh fodder to whatever dark god they served.

The jewel in the black sword's pommel chose that moment to come alive, and my inner unease strengthened. It shone with the same unearthly purple that had appeared when I'd unsealed the chest it had been hidden in, and while I wasn't sure what was causing the light now, there was a big part of me hoping we didn't find out.

"How do you want to play this?" Lugh asked.

"Cautiously."

I didn't see him roll his eyes, but I could practically feel it. "Now is not the time for levity, dear sister."

I actually thought it was the perfect time, given the shit might well hit the fan in a matter of minutes, but I refrained from saying it. I rubbed my arms, but it didn't in any way ease the inner tension.

"Once I grab the sword, I'll step away from you both and call the confluence. We can play it by ear from there."

He nodded and held out the sword. Tendrils of dark purple shot out from the jewel's eye, briefly illuminating the gray.

There were shadows in the gray.

Human-shaped shadows.

"We ain't alone," Holgan said casually. "I'm guessing you're expecting that, though."

"No, we certainly weren't." But the sword did call to darkness, and I guessed the souls of the dead could be classified as that. "I suspect they're nothing more than the ghosts of those who have died on this mountain."

And if luck was on our side for a change, these ghosts would be the only ones who answered the sword's call for help—because that's what I suspected the pulsing dark light was. At least there was no known dark gate around these parts, because the last thing we needed was another Annwfyn attack.

Of course, the Annwfyn were the whole fucking reason we were in this mess in the first place.

They were a distant branch of elves existing in a place alongside yet apart from our world, and they considered human, fae, and shifter flesh something of a delicacy. Their nightly hunting incursions into our world were brutal and bloody and were the main reason most of humanity feared walking through shadows.

The Looisearch—the people who'd stolen the Crown of Shadows from under my nose, and who'd almost succeeded in grabbing the sword—intended to use the three Claws to forever banish night from our world, thereby ensuring the Annwfyn could never again hunt here.

The trouble with their whole plan was the fact that, while the Annwfyn appeared to make every attempt to avoid sunshine and any form of artificial light, no one had any real data on whether it was simply a matter of preference rather than a real restriction. Given their culinary tastes, it wasn't like anyone dared ask.

"In all the years I've been coming up here, I've never seen the shades in such numbers," Holgan commented. "I take it the sword is responsible?"

"Yes," Lugh said before I could. "And let's just hope ghosts are the only things that appear."

"Does that mean I should be grabbing my axe?"

I glanced at him sharply. "Why on earth would you be carrying an axe?"

His brief smile crinkled the corners of his earth-brown eyes. "I rarely feel the need to murder my clients, if that's what you're thinking."

I raised my eyebrow. "The 'rarely' qualifier suggests that you indeed have."

"There's been one or two I would gladly have practiced my swing on, but before you start getting all stressed, lassie, neither of you fit the criteria." His smile flashed, revealing surprisingly white teeth. "And I'm talking about an ice axe; I always carry a couple in conditions like this."

I took a deep, somewhat relieved breath, and regretted it the minute the icy air hit my lungs. It might have been filtered through the scarf, but that barely took the edge off. Once I'd finished coughing, I sipped the water Lugh handed me and then said, "It would definitely be a good idea to keep a weapon handy, because we have no idea what will happen when I step into the confluence."

Holgan sniffed. "Fighting will cost you extra."

"I wouldn't expect anything else," Lugh said, tone dry. His gaze met mine. "You ready?"

"No." My lips twisted. "But let's do this all the same."

I reached out and took the sword. Though there were layers of silk, leather, and silver between my fingers and its blade, my skin nevertheless crawled. I could feel the darkness in it. Feel its power. Feel an odd sort of awareness that suggested perhaps this sword was far more than anyone—even the last woman to have successfully wielded it —knew.

I shivered but tightened my grip rather than let it go, as a good part of me wanted. Lugh roped me on, checked everything was sitting right, and then gave me a nod. He didn't say to be careful. He didn't need to. It was right there in his eyes and expression.

I took a dozen cautious steps forward, until I was surrounded by gray and the two men were no longer visible. Only the ghosts watched me, and their confusion—and perhaps a little anger—stained the air. Whether at me or the sword that'd called them into existence, I couldn't say.

I flexed my free hand, then metaphysically reached for the black stone tucked neatly under my left breast. Lugh had created a fancy "cage" necklace for it to enable me to wear it rather than shoving it under a boob, but the stone worked best when it was touching skin and the last thing I wanted to do up here on the mountain was to undo multiple layers of warmth in order to press the caged stone into my hand.

The Eye itself was a "seeker" stone that had been gifted to my family long ago by the goddess Eithne. Mom had used it to track and return missing relics to the old gods, though I'd not been aware of its presence in her hunts until recently.

Of course, she'd no idea—as far as I was aware, anyway —that the Eye was just one part of a triune designed as a means of fighting those who sought to raise the dark gods. That triune was foresight, protection, and knowledge, in the form of the Eye, the knives that were strapped to my thighs, and the Codex, a book that supposedly contained all the knowledge of the gods themselves.

Just under a week ago, I'd performed a blood-based cere-mony that had made me one with the triune. It had allowed me to call the knives into my hands even though they were miles away and had given me some measure of control over the Eye—at least to the extent that it didn't immediately sweep me into a vision the minute I touched it. I'd yet to use it in *this* particular manner, but again, I wasn't keen on stripping off my gloves or undoing any layers. Not with the cold, and especially not when I was holding the sword.

The Eye pulsed—something I felt physically *and* metaphysically—and its power swam through me, an energy that was rich and aware and as strong as that when I held the Eye in my hand. In my mind's eye I could see the lightning that cut through her dark heart, and it was the same unearthly color as the stone encased in the sword's pommel.

In this case, it was a reaction to the proximity of darkness. A warning to be wary, and one that was echoed by the knives themselves, though their pulsing was something I could feel rather than see.

As the Eye's response grew in tenor and tone, an answering echo came from the gray to my right. It was a low response, not unlike the deep resonance of a bell.

Tension—and more than a little fear—swept through me, but I held my ground despite the growing urge to back the hell away.

The ghosts drew closer, their insubstantial fingers reaching for me. I had no idea what they intended, but for now, the weather bubble kept them at bay. I hoped it continued to do so. Ghosts rarely had the capacity to interact or cause harm to humans, but these had been called here by darkness, so who really knew what was and wasn't possible.

The bell-like tolling continued, and the Eye's burning grew stronger. I had no immediate sense that she was, in any way, drawing on my strength, and yet my body trembled. I had the oddest feeling that I was once again standing on the edge of a precipice, about to step into the great unknown.

Darkness cannot enter this place.

The statement rolled out of the gray, the voice neither male nor female but so filled with power it hurt my ears.

This sword was created by the gods. It must be returned for humanity to remain safe.

Darkness created that sword. It cannot enter this place, the voice repeated.

Then what the hell am I supposed to do with the thing? I was told to come here by one of your own.

In darkness it was created, and in darkness it must be destroyed came the response. *You can enter. It must not.*

Well, fuck.

Amusement rolled around me. Which was good, because for one brief moment, I'd totally forgotten just who I might be talking to.

I glanced down at the sword in my hand and then did the only thing I could do—tossed it in the air. I wrapped the wind around it to ensure it stayed beyond the reach of ghostly hands but kept it within the overall protection of my bubble.

Then, with another of those unwise deep breaths, I followed the direction of the voice and stepped into... nothing. Everything. There was no sound, no wind, no darkness or light. No protective bubble and no icy cold.

There was nothing here but a vast emptiness that was utterly silent, and yet it was filled with all sorts of sensory stimuli.

No sound but there was music.

No flowers and yet I could smell the sweet scent of them.

No sunshine but it caressed my face and warmed the

chill from my bones.

It was unreal and beautiful, and it scared the hell out of me.

Someone like me should not be in a place like this.

This place is far more than you can see came the voice. *You are not, and never will be, equipped to see the full extent of it.*

Then why was I told to come here?

To control the storms, you must meet their master. Only he can grant you the skill and the means to control that which would otherwise destroy you.

So you're not this master?

Amusement filled the air, a rumble that was warm and oddly endearing. *I am merely the gate master. I accept all calling cards and ensure the appropriate god or goddess receives them.*

So that's what this is? A request for help rather than actual help?

And did that mean I had to go through the whole fucking journey up the mountain again to get a reply?

It is indeed a request came the response, *but you do not need to return. If your request is granted, the master will ensure you receive the necessary information.*

How?

That is not for me to divulge.

Meaning I just had to hang around and hope for the best? Great.

What about the sword? Is there someone who could advise me where to take it?

You already have the means to seek a fuller answer, young pixie.

With that, I was yanked out of the silent, beautiful darkness and in the full force of the storm.

Right into the middle of a goddamn battle.

CHAPTER
TWO

IT WASN'T THE GHOSTS WHO ATTACKED, ALTHOUGH THEY continued to tear ineffectually at my bubble. It was the weather, and it wasn't a natural ramping of the storm's ferocity, because there was dark intent behind the wind's actions.

There was a weather witch up here somewhere.

I swore and drew my knives. The wickedly curved silver blades pulsed a deeper purple, which meant the sword wasn't the sole evil here now, even if the only figures I could currently see were ghostly ones.

From somewhere ahead, almost lost to the swirling, bitter gray, came the sounds of clashing steel.

Which was decidedly odd. I mean, why steel? Why not use guns? There was no one up here to hear a gunshot, and it wasn't as if the sound would carry to the—

The top of my bubble tore open, and thick fingers of air reached in to grab the sword. I hastily pulled it down, then thrust those fingers away and resealed the bubble. It wouldn't hold for long. The witch seemed far more proficient than me at controlling the weather.

I took a step forward, and only then realized the rope connecting me to my brother was slack. Perhaps that was the reason I'd been suddenly yanked from the confluence—maybe some bastard had snatched the other end from my brother.

I sliced the rope from my harness to ensure it couldn't be used against me, then followed its trail through the shifting gray and the deepening vale of ghostly forms, using the sound of fighting as a guide and hoping like hell it wasn't being distorted by magic or even the storm. It'd be just my luck to be walking toward the cliff rather than away from it.

The gray briefly parted, giving me a glimpse of two figures—one tall, one short. Around them were the shadows of at least half a dozen people, though I had no idea if they were human or something else.

I shoved one blade back into its sheath, then gathered the wind around my fingers. But just as I was about to unleash her, the ghosts broke through my barrier and swamped me in a sea of insubstantial, cloying ectoplasm that blocked my vision even if it caused me no harm.

I swore and cast the streams of wind around my body rather than at the men ahead, spinning the ghosts away and clearing a path. More ghosts moved in, forcing me to keep the whirlpool close.

The bubble above my head fractured again. Again, I pushed the grasping fingers of air away, then grabbed the sword's sheath at the pointy end and charged forward. I might not be able to use the blade itself, but the damn thing carried a fair bit of weight and would make an excellent club. Especially given the size and weight of the pommel.

Two figures emerged from the gray and came straight at me. I swung the sword, keeping it low, aiming for kneecaps.

The first man leapt above it and slashed at my face with a knife. I raised mine to counter and, as the song of metal against metal echoed, spun away from him. Without stopping, I swung the sword again and smacked it against the stranger's skull, sending him staggering into the gray. The air whistled a warning, and I dropped low. The fist that would have smacked into my chin soared over my head instead. Before the second man could regain his balance, I twisted around and slashed the knife across his calves. The blade cut easily through material, flesh, and muscle, stopping only when it met bone.

My attacker screamed and dropped. I flipped the knife and smacked the hilt into the side of his face, repositioning his nose. He made an odd sort of sound in the back of his throat and fell face-first into a drift of snow.

I'd learned the hard way it was better not to pull your punches when it came to bad guys, because the bastards always made you pay for that leniency. If he couldn't get up, he couldn't re-attack.

Still, I didn't want him dead, so I shifted him onto his side to ensure he could breathe. Killing never worked out well for us pixies, thanks to a blood curse placed on us eons ago. It did have a self-defense clause attached, and that meant I should be safe from anything I did to our attackers, but it was always better not to risk it.

I scrambled to my feet and ran on. The wind continued to spin around me, but her threads were being torn away by the opposing force, weakening her even as it reached once again for the sword. If I didn't find the fucking witch and deal with him, he *would* end up with it. I didn't have the strength or the knowledge to stop him. Not when it came to the weather, anyway.

I slid to a halt and "reached" again for the Eye, this time

attempting to find my foe. Just for an instant, the image of a cowled man with a thick ginger beard standing behind what looked to be a rock wall rose, then the image fractured as something cannoned into my back and sent me flying forward.

I hit the ground on hands and knees, somehow managing to keep a grip on both weapons even though shock reverberated up my arms. Then a hand grabbed the hood of my coat and yanked me up. I swore and instinctively lashed back with my knife. The cretin dodged, laughed, and then grabbed the sword out of my grip.

I did the only thing I could do. Wrapped one finger of air around the blade to maintain possession of it, then spun the remnants of my fragmenting whirlwind at the bastard. It picked him up and tossed him away. Far away. Over the cliff away.

After ordering the air to cushion his fall, I caught the opposing slivers of wind that were tugging at the sword and "felt" for a direction.

The witch lay to my left.

I ran toward him, scrambling over the wet ground, pushing through the ghosts once again crowding me. The sword continued to feed their desperation to stop me, but all it succeeded in doing was ensuring the dark purple glow of both the sword and the knife was encased in a thick shroud of ectoplasm and invisible to anyone more than a few feet away. *I* could barely see them, and I held the damn things.

Dark shapes loomed out of the gloom. I wasn't entirely sure whether it was the ruined walls of the old observatory or another cairn, but either way, the weather witch stood behind it.

I couldn't see the bastard, just as he wouldn't be able to

see me, but that didn't matter, because we could both feel the other in the cry of the wind.

Her force increased, raging at me, trying to stop me. I thrust an arm sideways, holding the knife high even though it was only capable of stopping true magic, and pushed my wind in that direction.

The witch took the bait, swinging his weather attack around to meet mine head-on.

As the two forces clashed, I gathered speed, then leapt high, clearing the wall with inches to spare and landing hard on the other side.

The witch spun around, but before he could cast or do anything else, I grabbed a thick handful of his beard and pushed him, with all force I could muster, against the wall.

There was an ungodly crack, then his eyes rolled back in his head and he collapsed in a heap onto the ground. I swore and checked his pulse. Thankfully, he was unconscious, not dead. Whether he'd be able to give us answers as to who had employed him when he came to was another matter entirely. Heavy cracks on the head did tend to rattle the brain and memories.

But at least the force of the wind had dropped, and though the curtain of gray remained, its thickness was already easing.

It made the continuing clash of metal echo even more sharply across the peak.

I swore again and raced through the broken remnants of a nearby doorway. The ghosts continued their sad effort to stop me, but the sword's pulsing had eased, and light no longer spun from the jewel in the pommel. Perhaps with the witch unconscious, it realized it had lost this battle.

Most would have scoffed at the thought of attributing any sort of intelligence to an inanimate object, but when you were dealing with the relics of gods you never really knew. Hell, my knives had protected me multiple times from magical attacks without any sort of direction or input from me.

I raced from the old observatory toward the looming shadow that was my brother. Saw two figures launch at him and raised a hand, calling to the wind yet again.

She caught one and tossed him back down the mountain. The other, Lugh punched so hard that I could not only see his jaw break but heard the crack of it. As the man staggered back, Lugh kicked him in the nuts and dropped him.

I slowed and, as I neared, he turned, his gaze quickly scanning me and coming up relieved. "No major damage done, by the look of it, and you still have the sword—that would have to be a first in the scheme of things."

"We're not off this mountain yet."

I shoved my knife back into its sheath and handed him the sword so I could check my battered knees. My fall had torn both my waterproofs and jeans, but despite how much my knees hurt, it appeared I'd escaped with only minor scrapes. They were oozing rather than full-out bleeding, which made a nice change. Rather surprisingly, my knuckles had also escaped with only minor damage, even though I'd slid along on them as hard as my knees. Maybe the knife had somehow protected them. It seemed unlikely, but there was still so much about these knives—and the triune in general—that we just didn't know.

I straightened and said, "What about yourself?"

"One of the bastards caught my thigh with a knife, but the multiple clothing layers protected me from the worst of it."

"Says the man who called a broken arm a minor inconvenience."

He laughed. "Well, it was. I've suffered far worse on hunts, trust me on that."

Given he worked full-time as an antiquarian for the National Fae Museum in Deva—which basically meant he traveled to all sorts of remote and dangerous places hunting relics for their exhibitions—I had no doubt of that. I also didn't want to know all the gory details, because I worried enough about him as it was.

I motioned him to turn so I could check. He rolled his eyes, but obeyed. I carefully peeled away the layers of waterproofs, jeans, and thermals, and saw that while the wound was bleeding quite heavily, it really wasn't all that deep or long. I grabbed the first aid kit out of his pack and treated the cut as best I could before using the duct tape to reseal his waterproof pants.

"Thanks," he said.

I nodded and sliced off several strips of duct tape to fix the tears in my pants. "Where's Holgan?"

"Chasing one of the bastards that attacked us." Lugh's grin flashed. "Apparently, he knew the man and was most affronted he'd taken the job. Answers will be gotten, one way or another, I suspect."

"That's presuming his friend is actually capable of giving him said answers."

"There's not many pixies living up this way, and telepaths are expensive to hire." He nudged one of the four unconscious men lying around him with the toe of his boot. "But we'll find out as soon as one of these bastards wakes."

"If they all wake at the same time, it's going to be problematic." I could leash them with the wind, of course, but the weariness washing through my limbs suggested that might not be a good idea. We still had a long walk back down the mountain.

"Not if they're tied up." He paused. "You didn't toss the rope off the mountain, did you?"

"No. Just a man or two."

He raised an eyebrow, his expression suggesting he wasn't sure whether to believe me or not. I waved a hand. "They're fine. I cushioned their falls."

Lugh snorted, looked around for a few seconds, then stepped to the right and picked up the rope. It didn't take him long to tie his captives together and by the time he had, the man closest to me showed signs of waking.

I knelt beside him and waited. After a few seconds, his eyelids fluttered. He didn't open them, but he was pretty obviously testing the strength of rope around his wrists and ankles.

"You're not going to be getting out of them any time soon," I said conversationally. "They were tied by a man who loves his knots."

Which was true enough. One of the weirder things Lugh and his mates used to do when much younger was play a game that involved seeing who could tie the toughest knot to get out of. It was a game Lugh invariably won.

The stranger's eyes sprang open. "I can't tell you anything. I don't know anything."

"We'll soon enough see the truth of that statement."

Lugh walked over and stood behind me. I'm not sure what his expression was, but our captive looked decidedly nervous all of a sudden.

I touched the stranger's forehead and said softly, "You will answer all our questions and do so honestly. Understood?"

The latter was nothing more than a simple courtesy, because he really had no other choice. An ancient goddess had "rewarded" pixie women with the so-called six gifts of womanhood—beauty, a gentle voice, sweet words, wisdom, needlework, and chastity. Thankfully, we Aodhán women had not only missed the whole chastity thing—I mean, what in the hell was the goddess thinking gifting *that?*—but all the others except for "sweet words." It meant we could control people via voice and touch, and it worked on humans, shifters, and most of the fae except for the elves. I had no idea why they'd been exempted, but it was probably why I'd spent far too long in a relationship with a light elf who'd been cheating on me.

Of course, the serious lack of decent pixie talent in Deva also had a lot to do with it. It wasn't as if I hadn't known going in that light elves were rarely ever faithful, even when married.

An odd mix of consternation and annoyance swept across the stranger's expression. "Fuck, you're a damn pixie?"

"What is it about bad guys not giving their crews full information about the job at hand?" Lugh's voice held an edge of incredulousness. "It definitely seems to be a reoccurring theme lately."

"I guess it's easier to employ idiots if they're not given full facts."

"Hey, I resent that comment." Our captive sniffed. "I'm not an idiot, I just wasn't given full details."

Which basically confirmed the whole idiot thing. "You don't know who hired you?"

"Gratham did. I can't say who hired him to do the subcontracting, though, because as I've said, I wasn't told." His eyes gleamed. "Safer that way for us all, isn't it?"

Safer for the employer, perhaps, but only up to a point. "What does Gratham look like? Is he here?"

"Gratham?" The man snorted. "He's a desk jockey, not an action man. In this weather, he'll be holed up at home in front of a roaring fire."

Which probably made him the most sensible of us all. "And his description? Address?"

Our captive rambled off a pretty generic description of an elderly human male and then gave us both his home address and his office, even though I hadn't asked for both. "What were you supposed to do?"

"Retrieve a black sword and take it back to Gratham."

"And us?"

He shrugged. "We weren't told to kill, if that's what you're worried about. We were just meant to grab the sword and get the fuck out of here. Nobody mentioned the fact you were fucking pixies, and giant ones at that. Wouldn't have taken the job if I'd known."

I raised an eyebrow. "Why not?"

"Because you bastards are mean fighters." He sniffed. "At the very least, I would have demanded more money."

"Are your companions also subcontractors?"

He nodded. "I've worked with Benny and Jules a few times, but not the other four."

"Which ones are Benny and Jules?"

The description he gave matched the two men lying at the other end of the rope, and left us with one unknown man if we weren't counting the couple I'd tossed down the mountain.

"And the weather witch?"

"There's a weather witch?" Lugh said, surprised.

I waved a hand toward the old observatory. "He was hiding over there. I knocked him out."

Lugh immediately headed across, the sword gripped

like a club in his hand. The stranger sniffed again. "He was supposed to hide our entry and exit."

He'd certainly done the former very well, as I'd had no idea the storm had been enhanced by the witch until it was almost too late. It wasn't until he'd directed the weather to attack *me* that my knives had reacted.

"Do you know his name?"

"Johnson? Jackson. Something like that." The man shrugged. "Don't know, don't care. Better not to, if you know what I mean."

I did. And given how chatty this fellow was even without my magic's prompting, it was likely he hadn't been told anything for a damn good reason. "What's your name?"

"Jimmy. Jimmy Brown."

I touched a hand to his forehead again. He didn't try to avoid it—he obviously knew enough about pixies to understand I'd just order him to be still anyway.

"Jimmy Brown, you will head straight home once we release you, and you will never take a job that involves me or my brother or indeed any other pixie. Understood?"

"Yes, but it's not like I ever actually know if the job involves a pixie."

I half smiled. He did have a point. "Then you will always ask, and if they can't or won't tell you, you won't take the job."

"Well fuck, that's just mean. It's not as if there's a ton of work up here for subcontractors, you know?"

"Not my problem. Besides, it's better to be restricted than dead."

"Pixies can't kill. There's that whole curse thing you have happening."

"There's an exception to that—"

"There always fucking is," he cut in sourly.

I smiled, pushed to my feet, and moved on. The one Lugh had kicked had stopped writhing, but his expression remained pained—no surprise given the bruised nuts and the broken jaw. The latter meant he probably wouldn't be able to talk even if he did know something, so I simply repeated the orders I'd given the chatty man.

Lugh returned, and he didn't look happy. "The witch has gone."

I grimaced. "I'm not entirely surprised. The crack on the head would probably have curtailed much of his ability to produce weather magic."

"Don't suppose our prisoner knew his name?"

"It's Johnson or Jackson. I'm thinking he's probably not from around these parts."

Besides, weather witches were rare enough that they generally were in high demand and their services were appropriately priced, especially when it came to out-of-the-way places like this. Whoever had hired this one obviously had money to burn.

We questioned the other two men but basically got the same answers Jimmy had given. It was pointless keeping them here—aside from the fact they had no choice but to leave, it was too damn miserable for any of us to stay up here longer than necessary.

As Lugh began releasing them, Holgan returned.

"I take it you didn't capture your friend?" Lugh said.

"Oh, I got the bastard," Holgan growled, "but he couldn't give me much information because he wasn't told much. But I know who hired him—Biran Gratham—and we can go question him if you're still feeling up to it by the time we hike back down."

"Is there any point?" I asked. "Won't your friend have already sent Gratham a warning?"

"He gave me his oath that he hasn't and wouldn't, and no dwarf would dare break his word." Holgan sniffed. "It'll probably take us three hours to get back down now that the weather has eased some, but we should be leaving now, just in case those bastards you released say something."

"They won't," I said. "Trust me on that."

He studied me shrewdly for a second, then nodded. We hadn't told him we were pixies, but gossip got around surprisingly quickly in wilder regions of the world.

Which made me wonder why the chatty man and his friends hadn't been aware of exactly who they'd been attacking. Or maybe it was simply a case of him not putting two and two together. And we had been very careful to ensure the sword was always hidden.

We gathered the rest of our gear, strapped the sword onto Lugh's pack, and then headed down. It was far easier to walk down than it had been to walk up, but that wasn't saying much, given I was also closer to exhaustion. By the time we reached the visitors' center at the base of the mountain, the worst of the storm had passed, although the drizzle that remained continued to make the day unpleasant.

Holgan opened his four-wheel drive and motioned us to get in. I'd barely done so when he was reversing out and heading off. Dwarves were slow to anger, but you didn't want to be around them when they were. I suspected Gratham was about to find that out.

We headed for his office first. While the chatty man had insisted the contractor was probably home tucked in front of the fire, it was a working week for most people, and it hadn't yet neared five.

Holgan wound his way through the relatively quiet streets, then turned into one that was mixed use, the various residences and shops interspersed with each other. Gratham's building stood between a fish-and-chip shop and a sports bar, with a laneway running along one side. It was an unpainted four-story stone building that housed his shop on the ground floor and what appeared to be apartments above, and it was rather ratty-looking compared to some of the other buildings in the street.

I seriously hoped it *wasn't* ratty. I'd already had more than enough encounters with the beady-eyed little bastards over the last few weeks to last me a lifetime.

Holgan halted opposite the chip shop and switched off the engine. "Can't see any lights on, so he might not be there."

I undid my seat belt and leaned forward to peer through the front windshield. There was no obvious signage on the door or single window, the blinds were half drawn, and the room beyond dark. But if there was one thing we'd learned over the last few weeks, it was never to take things at face value.

"We should still check," Lugh said and reached back for the pack.

"Leave it," Holgan said. "It's safe enough in the car, and besides, the shop doesn't look all that large. The pack will just get in the way."

Lugh hesitated, glanced at me, and then got out. Holgan followed. I unfastened the sword from the backpack, then climbed out. While Holgan might be sure the sword was perfectly safe locked in the car, I wasn't about to leave it unguarded. Not when it could call to evil as easily as I called the wind. Besides, the weather witch had escaped, and it was possible this place was now being watched. I couldn't

27

see anyone obviously doing so, but then I wouldn't if they were in any way good at their job.

I called to the wind, wrapped her around the sword, and then ordered her skyward. It rose so fast it was little more than a shadowed blur. The witch might have recovered enough to make another attempt at snatching it from my grip, but at least I'd feel any attempt to do so.

I zipped up my coat and hurried across the road after the two men. A little sign on the front door said the shop was closed and would reopen tomorrow.

I stopped and shoved my hands into my pockets. A chill was running through me, and I wasn't entirely sure it had anything to do with the icy wind rolling off the nearby loch. "Any sign of pixie dust?"

"Pixie dust?" Holgan glanced at me. "Why on earth would there be pixie dust here in a place like this? This ain't one of your major cities, you know, but a simple country town."

A simple country town that not only possessed a shady contractor, but also a ton of subcontractors willing to do whatever was necessary if the pay was good enough.

"Yes," I said, "but if the person or persons behind the attack can afford a weather mage, they can afford to buy pixie dust."

There were actually two types—blue and gold. Gold was generally the refuse of the dust the two smaller pixie lines used to fly, and it could, in certain circumstances, be reshaped to make certain spells stronger. Blue dust was found in ancient forests under a special type of mushroom that only sprouted during a blue moon. It was generally used to replenish the dust trees from which both the Malloyei and Gadahn pixies—the two lines who flew—drew their power but could also be used as a spell augmenter and rejuvenator. It was definitely the deadlier of the two dust types, though few pixies dared use it with murderous intent because of that whole blood curse thing. It could also only be used by pixies, whereas gold dust could be used by anyone capable of magic.

"I'm not seeing any dust," Lugh said. "But that doesn't mean it's not inside."

Or that there weren't other spells set. He didn't say that, but we were definitely both thinking it.

He gripped the handle. The door opened.

"I'm thinking that's not a good development," Holgan said.

"No." I peered in through the window but couldn't see anything more than a few vague furniture shapes.

I moved to the door, ducked under Lugh's arm, and peered inside. The knives weren't reacting, but I nevertheless got one out. The silver blade glittered coldly in the darkness that held the shop's interior captive but otherwise gave no indication ill intent lingered within.

Lugh reached over my head and flicked the light switch. No lights came on. Another not-so-good sign.

Either that, or Gratham had decided not to pay his energy bills.

"Hang on while I go grab a couple of flashlights," Holgan said. "Easier than using your phones, and less expensive if someone leaps out of the shadows and whacks them out of your hand."

He hurried back to the car without waiting for an answer. I shifted uneasily from one foot to the other and, once my eyes had adjusted a little more to the darkness, said, "From what I can see, the place isn't very big."

There were a couple of desks, a few filing cabinets, and a half dozen rather uncomfortable-looking chairs. Obviously, Gratham did not want his clients hanging about too long.

"Which makes me think there might be a doorway along that back wall somewhere," Lugh said. "The building is definitely longer than this room."

Holgan returned with not only a couple of flashlights but also an ice axe.

I raised an eyebrow, and he grinned with an odd sort of relish. "Just in case things go south."

I took a flashlight, turned it on, and swept the beam across the darkness. No one was waiting to pounce, and there was no obvious glimmer of pixie dust. There was plenty of real dust, however. Gratham was not overendowed with the cleanliness gene, apparently.

"The door is at the back to your left," Lugh said.

I swept the beam over and saw it in the corner. I hadn't spotted it the first time because of the stack of opened boxes sitting on top of the desk in front of it.

I walked across and took a look, but they were all empty aside from the usual packing crap. I moved around the desk, then stopped in front of the door, bending to check the handle. Still no sign of pixie dust, but that didn't ease the inner tension. Maybe I was just being paranoid, but things had gone wrong for us so often recently that tension and paranoia were definitely warranted.

I gripped the handle and twisted it. Locked. "Holgan, you any good at picking locks?"

"I'm a mountain guide, not a damn thief," he said. "But these types of doors are rarely a match for a well-placed boot."

Said boot was employed, and the door promptly crashed back against the wall, sending plaster dust spinning into the air.

"You've done that more than once in your life," I said, amused.

"The missus has a habit of locking me out after I've had a few too many in the pub." He shrugged. "The boot is easier than the shoulder, and locks are easily enough replaced."

"I'm surprised she hasn't thought about getting a metal door or even a medieval iron drop latch."

I had one on the tavern's medieval front door, and it had stopped many a would-be thief or thug. It couldn't stop a witch or even a dark elf, of course, many of whom could control metal as easily as they did earth, but the alarm spells woven around the perimeter generally did that.

Holgan shone his light through the doorway, revealing a long corridor off which were five doors, then stepped back and motioned me to lead the way. I didn't immediately enter, instead pressing my fingers against the doorframe.

Pixies, like wood elves, had an affinity with forests and wood, and both of us could manipulate it to our will. Certain branches of pixies, however, could also hear the song of wood that no longer lived in the ground, wood that was used in furniture and in buildings, which caused no end of distress to youngsters until they learned how to control and mute the ability.

This particular frame was made of cheap pine, which was always harder to hear because of its relatively short life span, and it had been painted over often enough for its song to be almost muted. But in this case, it didn't really matter, as I simply wanted to use its connection to the structure of the building to "see" if there was anyone occupying the rooms ahead or the floors above us.

As the connection deepened, an interconnected network of power and music appeared in my mind's eye. I ran mental fingers along the golden arteries that bound the building together, but there was a big black hole when it came to the floors. The walls of this place were alive and strong, but the wooden flooring had been covered with so many layers of vinyl that its song had been silenced long ago. It couldn't tell me what might wait ahead.

"Anything?" Lugh asked.

"Dead wood."

"Ah. Shame."

We moved on. Three of the five doors were open, but a quick look revealed nothing more than an office and two storerooms. The fourth was locked and barred with an almost medieval-looking metal gate none of us was getting through. Which left us the final door and a set of rather dodgy-looking stairs leading up to the next floor.

But as we neared the final door, light flickered down the knife's fuller. I stopped abruptly. There was no dust on the door and nothing to indicate there was magic here other than that soft flicker.

I hesitated, then touched the knife's tip against the door handle. Nothing. I tugged one of my gloves from my pocket, pulled it on, then pushed the door open.

Revealing a ransacked office.

"We might need to call the cops," Holgan said. "This is looking like something we don't want to get involved in."

"Too late for that, I'm thinking," Lugh said. "Especially when we've already kicked one door down."

"Nah, Jimmy will understand that," Holgan said. "He knows I've a bit of a temper when someone does me wrong."

Jimmy was obviously a popular name around these parts. "How well do you know the local copper?"

"Meaning, how likely is he to charge us for breaking and

entering?" Holgan said, amused. "We grew up together. He'll be fine as long as we immediately report what we found."

"Do so then," Lugh said. "We'll check upstairs, just to be sure we're alone."

Holgan nodded, pulled out his phone, and then grimaced. "No reception here. I'll have to head back out to the street."

I watched him leave and then pulled out my own phone. No reception, as he'd said.

"Distrustful type, aren't you?" Lugh said in a wry tone.

"I think it's warranted in this type of situation. Besides, just because he didn't abandon us on the mountain doesn't mean he won't now."

The Looisearch might be the ones after the Claws, but there were other forces at play, forces that had stolen a huge cache of godly relics the light elves had been protecting. It was highly unlikely they'd decided to make a play for the Claws as well, but it wasn't something we dare discount, given we had no idea who was involved in *that* particular theft.

But we would find out.

They'd murdered Mom, and they *would* pay.

I carefully made my way through the mess to the other side of the desk. All the drawers had been opened—or forced open, in the case of one—and the contents tipped out over the floor.

"Wonder what they were looking for?" I bent and carefully sifted through the junk. "Gratham is a service broker and isn't likely to be holding anything of value in a place that's in essence unsecured."

"You're forgetting that iron-barred room."

"I wouldn't have thought Gratham would be dealing

with anything actually requiring that sort of security. Not in an out of the way place like this."

"Maybe he was a black market collector of valuables on the side."

I snorted. "In a small town like this, where everyone knows everyone else's business? Unlikely."

"Maybe he was a legit collector. There are plenty around, you know."

"I guess so." I wrinkled my nose. "Do you think they were looking for the keys to the grated door?"

"Possibly." Lugh shrugged. "It's also possible whoever hired him to attack us thought Gratham was holding onto the sword. We were supposed to go up two days ago, remember."

"Yes, but we weren't exactly hiding out in the hotel. If we were being watched, they'd have known we didn't head up there until this morning."

He carefully opened the top drawer of a filing cabinet whose contents lay strewn around his feet, then felt inside with a gloved finger. I wondered what he was searching for, then remembered the cabinets in Nialle's basement had had a wireless switch hidden in the back of them that opened a secret room.

Out in the hall, something heavy scraped across the floor.

"And I think that might be our door. Follow me, sister dearest."

I carefully picked my way back through the rubbish to the hall, and once again energy flickered down the knife blade. I paused, looking up, wondering if whatever it sensed lay upstairs. The response wasn't particularly strong, which suggested the evil or spell it was picking up was either days old or simply fading.

"Ha, right first time," Lugh said, snagging my attention again.

I hurried over. Both the barred door and the wooden one behind it were now open, revealing another storeroom. Rather than the open shelving the other storerooms had, this one was filled with sturdy-looking two-door security cabinets with mesh fronts. Inside the closet were a number of silver plates and gold statuettes, though from where I was standing, I couldn't see if they were antiquities or modern.

"I'm not seeing anything in the way of protection spells, which is odd," I said. "He's a services broker—he'd have to be aware that a dark elf or even a really good human thief could get in here easily enough."

Lugh shrugged. "Spells can be disarmed if you have the knowledge. Besides, he's got cameras and a point-to-point beam system installed. That makes things a whole lot tougher."

I'd seen the cameras but not the point-to-points, and they were so small it took a good bit of squinting at the skirting boards to see them. There were enough of them to suggest the floor was heavily crisscrossed.

"Do you think this is the reason why the power is off?"

"Possibly, but most of these systems have a battery backup. Unless you can deactivate that before you take the power out, you've little chance of getting in without being caught."

I raised an eyebrow. "And you know this how?"

He grinned. "Not all the antiquities I acquire for the museum are found in out-of-the-way, dangerously remote locations. Some of them are found in the very plush, supposedly ultra-secure safe rooms of black-market collectors."

As the sound of approaching sirens began to bite the air, I snorted and stepped back. "I suggest we check upstairs before the coppers get here. The knife is intermittently reacting to something up there."

Lugh glanced at the currently inert knife, then nodded and motioned me to lead again. The steps creaked as we made up way up, and the banister was silent. Not because of the multiple layers of stain, but because it had been made of recycled materials whose voice was lost long ago.

I reached the landing and stopped. Three doors lay before us—one to the left, one to the right, and one in the middle. All were closed, giving absolutely no indication of what might lay behind them. There was no sound other than the approaching sirens, and no odd smells—though I wasn't entirely sure why I'd been half expecting the latter.

The knife was reacting to the middle, but its response remained faint. I hoped that was a good thing, though I suspected the opposite might be true.

My pessimistic nature coming to the fore again.

I glanced at Lugh. "I don't suppose you want to go first?"

He raised an eyebrow. "I can, but you're the one with the knife that'll counter any magical attack."

I wrinkled my nose but nevertheless moved forward cautiously. After once again inspecting the handle for pixie dust, I pushed the door open.

A very naked, very dead-looking man lay spreadeagled on the bed.

CHAPTER
THREE

"Well," Lugh said. "That's totally not what I was expecting."

"No." The man on the bed matched the fairly generic description we'd gotten of Gratham, so it was probably safe to assume it was him. I glanced briefly at the knife. "I think it's safe to enter. Whatever magic was used here is almost nonexistent now."

Outside, the sirens stopped. We had a few minutes, if that, to find anything useful before the cops took over.

"You check the victim," Lugh said. "I'll do a quick search of the other two rooms."

I nodded and edged into the room. Gratham's clothes were all over the floor, suggesting he'd stripped off in a hurry. Had he invited a lover over? Was that why he was in bed at this hour of the day? I couldn't smell any perfume or aftershave to suggest someone else had been here, but unless they'd drowned themselves in scent, I probably wouldn't have.

I swept the light around the room. Aside from the clothes on the floor, the rest of the room was relatively neat.

There was no wardrobe and only one side table rather than the usual two. It was on the left side of the bed and was a simple open-shelf design. The torn-open condom wrapper that lay on top said my guess about the lover had been right. My gaze somewhat automatically jumped down his body. The condom remained in place, so he'd either died before ejaculation or just after, and his lover had gotten the hell out of here rather than report it or make any attempt to save him.

Which didn't explain the fading magic, or the fact instinct said this was no accident.

I tugged off my glove, leaned over the bed, and felt for a pulse. His lips had a faint blue tinge, which usually suggested either a lack of oxygen or lack of blood flow, but there was no obvious cause evident for either. No marks on his neck, no signs of a struggle, no bloodred eyes.

Maybe he'd had a heart attack mid proceedings, but again, there was little evidence things had been interrupted. I'd have thought his expression would have been horror more than pleasure had that been the case.

Footsteps echoed below, a physical sound rather than one heard through the inert floorboards. Three people headed our way. I shoved my glove back on, stepped away from the bed, then caught sight of something under it. As I bent for a closer look, the knife's pulsing sharpened.

Lugh glanced in. "Whatever you've found, grab it fast. I'll go report what I've found and delay them."

As he stepped away, I pressed the knife's tip against what looked to be a token of some kind. There was a soft retort and a brief shower of sparks, and the pulsing in the knife died. I reached in, plucked the token free from the dust bunnies, and then rose and tucked it in my jacket pocket. A minute later, two cops appeared in the doorway.

"I checked for a pulse but can't find one, and his lips are blue," I said calmly.

The biggest of the two cops—big being relative when compared to my brother—glanced back at his companion. "Find out where the ambulance is and call in the coroner."

She nodded, checked her phone, and then headed back downstairs. The larger cop stopped beside me, his gaze sweeping our dead man before centering again on me. He flashed his ID, revealing his name was James Reid and, I presumed, Holgan's mate Jimmy, and then said, "And what might your name be?"

I suspected he already knew that, given Holgan would have no doubt updated him on everything, but I nevertheless told him. He glanced back at Lugh, who dutifully did the same.

"Did either of you touch anything?"

"I pulled off my glove to check for a pulse, but other than that, no."

"What about that secure room downstairs? Holgan says it wasn't open when he left."

"It wasn't," Lugh confirmed. "But we didn't go in. I suspect the point-to-point beams remain active."

The cop raised an eyebrow, his expression sharpening. "And how you be knowing something like that?"

"I'm an antiquarian for the National Fae Museum."

Jimmy's gaze remained skeptical. "And the key to open the door? Hard to believe you could find it so quickly in the mess left in that room."

"There wasn't a key." Lugh explained the switch and how and why he'd found it, then added, "You can ring my boss and confirm I am who I say I am, if you wish."

"Oh, I will. In the meantime, you can both head downstairs. Isla will take your statements and contact details."

"We'll be heading home tomorrow, Officer," I said.

"As long as we have your contact details, that should be fine."

As he began to record the scene, we left the room and headed downstairs. Holgan was still there, which surprised me a little given his contract had technically expired once he'd delivered us back in town.

He must have seen my reaction, because he grinned and said, "With the fee I charged you, the least I can do is deliver you safely back to the hotel."

"It wasn't necessary but appreciated all the same," I said.

He nodded and leaned against the wall, whistling softly while our statements were taken. By the time we were released, night had well and truly fallen. Holgan led us out of the shop, only to stop abruptly on the sidewalk and start swearing.

After a second, I realized why. His car was gone.

He swore, spun around, and clomped back into the shop.

Lugh waited until he'd gone and then said, with an odd mix of hope and resignation in his voice, "I don't suppose...?"

I grinned. "I did indeed."

Relief flickered through his expression. "Well done, you."

"I do occasionally catch your unspoken orders."

"Yes, but you usually ignore them."

I laughed and leaned against the streetlight, doing my best to ignore the chill coming off the loch and half wishing I had someone warm and willing waiting for me back at the hotel room.

Although to be honest, a long hot shower would be just as good right now.

I glanced around as Holgan finally reappeared. "What's happening?"

"Jimmy's put out an APB. It shouldn't take too long to track it down. Not many roads in and out of this place." He sniffed. "You got anything valuable in that pack, other than the sword?"

"No," Lugh said. "Does Jimmy need us to file a report?"

"Nah, I've already given him a full description of the sword, but if he needs anything else, he'll be in contact."

Lugh hesitated and then nodded. "Thanks for your assistance up on the mountain today, Holgan."

The dwarf grinned. "As I said before, you were paying me a damnably good fee. Least I could do."

"True," Lugh said with a short laugh.

"Remember to look me up if you ever need another trip up the mountain," Holgan said, and without waiting for an answer, shoved his hands in his pockets and walked away.

Lugh caught my elbow and guided me in the opposite direction. I waited until we were well out of earshot and said, "Are you thinking what I'm thinking?"

"That the theft of Holgan's car is no coincidence?" He slanted me a sideways glance. "And that maybe, before Holgan called the cops, he called someone else?"

I nodded. Holgan had never really seen much more than the sword's hilt, and even then, not very closely, so he couldn't possibly have given *anyone* a full description. "You think he's working with the same people who attacked us? Or someone else?"

Lugh hesitated. "It's unlikely there's a second group after the sword, given how few actually know we have it. I

41

suspect he might simply have been their backup plan if things went south up on the mountain."

"It's not going to take them long to realize they've been duped, though."

"No, but I doubt they'll risk another direct attack right away. Aside from the fact you've already ordered the subcontractors not to take another job against us, word will get around that Gratham is dead. It'll make others more wary."

"I hope you're right."

He opened the hotel's door with a smile. "But suspect I'm not?"

"Pessimism seems to have settled into my bones lately."

He laughed and led the way up the stairs. Though I'd wanted nothing more than to grab a shower and then collapse into bed for a good twelve hours of sleep, we still had the token to deal with.

I followed Lugh into his room, walked across to the window—which faced the rear lane rather than the street like mine did—and slid it open. The wind whipped in, filled with ice and an odd sense of welcome.

I shivered and thrust a hand into the night, calling down the sword. Once it had thudded into my hand, I tossed it over to the bed, hastily slid the window down, then walked across to the small desk. After claiming the solitary office chair, I pulled the token from my pocket and studied it. Like many of these things, this one was an air-dried clay coin about the same size as a penny. There were multiple tiny symbols etched onto its surface, and I had absolutely no idea what any of them represented, though given the knife's reaction and our dead contractor, there was obviously ill intent behind the spell that had been cast upon it.

Lugh filled up the kettle, then walked over for a closer look. "*That* isn't your run-of-the-mill street token. It's been specially created for a specific purpose."

I raised an eyebrow. "How can you tell?"

He motioned to a squiggle that vaguely resembled a snake or a worm in a circle. "That's the symbol for an Eve spell, and they're extremely pricey."

"Eve as in Adam and Eve?"

He nodded. "It basically renders the wearer irresistible to a particular person. Not sure what the rest of the squiggles mean though."

"Even if Gratham was seduced via the use of this thing, wouldn't he have heard them downstairs? The walls aren't soundproof, and given the state of the office, they would have made a hell of a racket."

"Maybe that's what the rest of those symbols are— attention capturing or noise reduction spells."

"There are noise reduction spells? Seriously?"

He smiled. "You can buy a spell for absolutely anything these days. How well they actually work is almost entirely a matter of where you purchase them from and how much you pay."

Which is why tokens such as these had a street rep amongst humans for being more for tourists than anything else. The real deal was rarely found on the high street. "How long does an Eve spell usually last? And how do you even know about it?"

"Got caught by one once. Best six hours of my life."

"That is a rather sad statement, brother mine."

"Not when it was nonstop. I'd wager not even your dark elf could last that long."

I'd wager he'd go damn close. The man was sex on legs with the stamina to match.

Lugh straightened, wincing a little and absently rubbing his leg. "This one doesn't look particularly well made, so I doubt it would have lasted that long. Why?"

"The token was still active when we arrived, and that suggests we didn't miss his lover and whoever did the office search by very much."

"We might not have missed them at all. It's very possible they were scampering out a window as we were coming in the front door."

I frowned. "There weren't any windows on the ground floor in that back section, and the lane didn't have any external stairs. Unless they were spider or bird shifters, scampering out of a window would have been dangerous."

"Unless they had a man on the roof with a rope at the ready. Which they did. I saw it being hauled back up."

"I take it you mentioned this to the cops?"

"I did. You want a cuppa?"

I shook my head and pushed to my feet. "What time are we leaving in the morning?"

"The desk opens at six, so if you're happy to grab something on the road, we'll leave then."

I nodded and walked over to grab the sword. As tempting as it was to leave the bloody thing here for Lugh to guard, if a witch or someone else with dark intent came looking for it during the night, at least my knives would give me warning.

Though in truth, Lugh had plenty of experience when it came to sleeping with one eye open. Relic hunts didn't always go to plan, and though he rarely said anything, I knew well enough that he'd been betrayed by guides more than once over the years.

"Once we deal with *that* thing"—Lugh waved a hand towards the sword—"we need to concentrate on the ring."

I nodded. "I wished we knew what exactly the combination of the three Claws did."

"You have the Codex—why not ask it?"

"I might have to, given how little luck we're having finding answers elsewhere."

Whether it would answer was another matter entirely. It might hold all the knowledge of the old gods, but there was no certainty it would pass said information on to me.

But that was a worry for another day.

"Don't forget to set your alarm," Lugh said. "And make sure you lock the door."

I rolled my eyes at him, and he laughed. "You're just annoyed that I said it before you could for a change."

I couldn't deny that particular truth, so I pulled a face at him and headed back into my room. After locking the door, I leaned the sword against the wall, then pressed my hands across the small gap between the frame and old door. Thankfully, both were made of a good hardwood rather than softer, cheaper pine, and their song was unhindered by the layers of stain. I gently eased into the rivers of gold, caught multiple fibers, and then carefully wove them together, forming a bond between the two that wouldn't easily be broken. After repeating the process with the window, I stripped off, had a shower, then fell into bed.

Sleep hit quickly, but so too did prophetic dreams. At first, they were little more than fragmented images—an old tunnel hung with curtains of slime and shored up by wood older than time itself. A lake of thick black water surrounding an island with no trees. An old wooden chest protected by bony fingers of fluorescent green. As the night moved on, these images gave way to a chaotic mix that revealed little but seemed filled with danger, death, deception, and desire. The latter I understood, because hey, it had been four days since I'd seen Cynwrig, but the visions of deception and death worried me, especially when they were scant on details. It made for a restless night.

The alarm woke me just after five-thirty. I scrubbed a hand across my eyes in an effort to rub away tiredness, then sighed, climbed out of bed, and stumbled into the bathroom. After a quick shower that didn't do much to wake me, I got dressed and then separated the door from the frame. After shoving the sword back into the banner carry bag—the only thing we could find to easily hide its shape—I grabbed my purse and overnight bag, then went downstairs to meet Lugh.

He was in an annoyingly cheerful mood.

Thankfully, he'd had the foresight to google the nearest takeaways, and had discovered a McDonald's only a small detour away from the hotel. An egg and bacon McMuffin, several hash browns, and a large white tea later, I was definitely feeling more normal.

Which most would say was a relative term when it came to all things me.

Once we were on the road home again, Lugh said, "Care to explain the grumpiness? You're not usually so snarly in the mornings."

I grimaced. "Sorry. Didn't get much sleep."

"For any particular reason? Or shouldn't I ask?"

I half grinned. "It wasn't sexual frustration, if that's what you're inferring. Besides, I'm perfectly capable of dealing with that if necessary."

"Aren't we all?" he said sagely.

I gave him the look. "If you're still self-satisfying, you've only yourself to blame. Darby is ready, willing, and able—"

"Stop derailing the conversation," he cut in, obviously

not wanting to discuss Darby's state of readiness or maybe even contemplate his own. "What stopped you sleeping?"

"Mostly unclear dreams, but I did see what looked to be an old treasure chest sitting on an underground island surrounded by a jet-black, somewhat oily-looking lake."

"The location for the ring, maybe?"

"Possibly. We were talking about it just before I went to bed."

"If it's underground and shored up with wood, then we're possibly dealing with an old mine, especially given the oil."

"There's not that many unexplored mines left these days, is there?"

"More than you might think. Plenty are too deep and dangerous to explore."

"I'm betting that if what I saw *is* a mine, it'll be one of them."

He laughed. "It's likely the only way an old wooden chest would have been left untouched."

"I'm thinking the fluorescent green fingers might also have had something to do with that."

"You have your magic-killing knives, so that won't be a problem."

"Famous last words, I'm thinking."

He grinned. "I'll run a search once we get home. Between the mine research societies and the industrial heritage listings, I should be able to come up with a short list."

I nodded. "I'll check with the Codex when I ask it about the sword, though I can't imagine it's up to date with centuries of land developments."

He raised an eyebrow. "You haven't tried to use it yet?"

I grimaced. "It's not like I've had a whole lot of time to even look at the damn thing."

"That's an excuse, and we both know it. You're scared of it."

"And rightly so, I'm thinking. There has to be a reason Mom's ancestors basically erased all knowledge of the triune from family history. Maybe that reason is the price it exacts."

"You might have already paid the price," he said. "It did make you stab yourself in the guts to ensure you were bonded to the thing."

"You make it sound more dramatic than it was." In truth, I hadn't even been aware it had happened until afterward, and the wound had healed itself pretty much straight away. The old gods obviously did not want their earthly "agents" incapacitated for too long. "What worries me more is the fact that none of these things come with instruction manuals."

"You figured out the knives, you're figuring out the Eye, and I have every faith you'll work out the Codex." He paused. "Besides, how hard can it be? Vincentia was using it."

I snorted. Cousin Vincentia was a relic hunter who sold to the highest bidder and didn't particularly care if they were black market or museums. She'd also been the inside source for the Looisearch and the main reason they not only had the crown but had almost claimed the sword.

But Vincentia—and Aunt Riayn—had paid a heavy price for her betraying us. Not only had Vincentia lost her left hand and two fingers on her right when the mage she'd been working with magically exploded the gun Vincentia had been holding, but she and my aunt had been served the red knife by the pixie council. It was both a symbolic and physical cutting of ties and was the ultimate punishment for a pixie. Not only was she excommunicated from pixie society for a period of ten years, but their ability to hear and use the song and power of the trees had also been ripped from them. And, in a final act of retribution, they were both confined to the small acreage Riayn called home, unable to leave for anything other than a medical emergency.

And even then, the magic within the red knife—which could not be moved or touched by them—would notify the council, and a guard would be dispatched.

Only death could break the power of the knife, and neither my aunt nor my cousin was the type to self-harm.

They *were* the type who'd bide their time and seek revenge. But at least I had ten years to figure out counter-measures.

Of course, they weren't the only ones who'd gotten into trouble with the pixie council. Magicking kin was against the code, and I'd crossed that line when I done a deep mind meld with Vincentia. They'd yet to decide my fate, and while it was unlikely to be anywhere near as brutal as what they'd handed to Vincentia and Riayn, I would still be punished. The council would want to send a message to the wider pixie community that crossing the line was never acceptable, even if the reasons were well-intentioned.

"The Codex never fully worked for her, from what she's said," I replied.

"It worked well enough for her to beat me to several artifacts."

His voice was a mix of amusement and old frustration. I smiled. "Yes, but if it had worked properly, she'd have beaten you to them every single time."

"I guess."

His phone rang sharply, making me jump. He gave me a

"what the hell?" sort of look, then punched the answer button as it came up on screen. "Rogan, what's up?"

Rogan was Lugh's boss and a man who'd spent the better part of his life working for the museum, first as an antiquarian like Lugh then as director of operations for the Antiquities division.

"You've been uncommunicative for nigh on five days. What do you think is up?" Rogan's reply was dry. "Your wages are paid by the museum, remember, and we do occasionally need to know what you might be up to."

Lugh laughed. "I did send a text."

"It said—and I quote—got family shit to look after then off to Scotland to deal with the sword. To which I replied, what sword and why Scotland?"

"Didn't get that."

I raised my eyebrow at the lie. I'd actually been there when the reply had come in.

Rogan sighed. It was a long-suffering sound. "And the sword?"

"It wasn't part of the Claws as we'd hoped."

"And you confirmed this how?"

"Spoke to a light elf oracle who lives in the Coedwig Hynafol encampment. She did her 'communing with the old gods' thing and gave us the bad news."

"Was this Castell?"

"You know her?" Lugh said, unable to keep the surprise from his voice.

"I had dealings with her a long time ago. She's... different."

Different was definitely putting it mildly. But the edge in his voice suggested his dealings with her hadn't gone all too well, and curiosity stirred.

Sadly, Lugh had obviously either missed the inflection

or simply didn't care, because he said, "She's a light elf. Different comes with the territory."

Rogan grunted. "And the Ring? Any progress on locating it?"

"Not really."

"What about your sister? From what I've heard, her foresight has finally awoken, so it might be worth asking if she's seen anything."

"I have."

"And?"

Lugh hesitated. "There was something about a hoard of treasure, but there were no details as to where it was located or even if the ring was part of it."

"Unhelpful."

"Tell me about it."

"Are you going to grace the museum with your presence any time soon? We do have a new employee, remember, and you're really the only one who can update him on everything Nialle had been researching."

Said new employee was a rather lovely-looking pixie by the name of Eljin Lavigne. Lugh was already match-making—no doubt as revenge for all the years I spent shipping him and Darby—but given the dearth of pixie men anywhere near my age in Deva, I wasn't putting up too much of a fight. We'd had coffee a couple of times already and had plans for a dinner on Friday night—tomorrow, I realized with a start—but given my hormonal fixation on all things Cynwrig, there was a part of me thinking it was probably best to take it slow with Eljin.

Of course, there was another part saying, "What the actual fuck, woman?"

Which, given the abovementioned dearth of decently

aged pixie males in Deva, and the number of pixie women on the hunt for a husband, was a damnably good point.

"I'll be in tomorrow," Lugh was saying, "I've got some more researching to do anyway."

"So, you're on the way home now?"

"Yes."

"I'll expect a full update tomorrow then."

"Looking forward to it."

Lugh's voice was dry, and Rogan snorted. "Right."

Once he'd hung up, I said, "Why did you lie about the text?"

"Because someone set Nialle and me up by planting the singing bowl in the crypts, and that someone has to be working in the museum. No one else has access to that area."

"Rogan can't be involved—his life is the museum. It's all he thinks about, all he works for."

"Yes, but it's possible he's either an unwilling or an unknowing participant in treachery, especially given what has already happened to Mathi."

"Mathi's bit on the side was drugging him—does Rogan even have a partner?"

He'd certainly never brought a plus one to any of the museum events over the years and I couldn't remember him ever mentioning anyone. Granted, not everyone was as open and honest about their relationships as Lugh and me, but surely given how long he and Lugh had worked together, something would have been said, however casually.

He gave me a somewhat wry look. "I'm surprised you don't know. You're the scheming matchmaker in this particular outfit."

I grinned. "In ten years' time, when you're happily

married and have all these mini Lughs and Darbys running around your feet, you'll appreciate said scheming."

He snorted. "Darby might not. Especially if said littlies inherit my height and come out large."

An interesting comment, given he'd yet to do more than kiss the woman.

"Besides," he continued, "the only way we can find out if Borrachero or indeed a similar drug has been used on him is by blood tests, and even then, it fades pretty quickly in the bloodstream."

Borrachero—the drug used on Mathi—pushed you into a twilight zone between consciousness and unconsciousness, making you chattier and disinhibited while leaving no memory of events when you woke up. It was a banned substance but could still be purchased on the black market if you had the money and the contacts.

"Getting him to test will be the problem," Lugh went on. "He's not going to appreciate the inference that I don't trust him, either."

I hesitated and then said, "What if I have a word with Cynwrig? The council has instigated regular blood testing for all councilors thanks to the Mathi situation, so maybe they can widen the order to include the heads of all government departments to have one."

"The museum isn't a government department."

"But it is funded by them."

"I think it's highly unlikely to be approved, but I guess it's worth trying." He cast me a somewhat deadpan look. "I'm thinking you're just looking for an excuse to see Cynwrig tonight."

"Oh, I don't need an excuse, trust me on that. Which reminds me—" I pulled out my phone and tapped the text app. "Better contact the man and see if he's actually free."

The reply came back in minutes and was a simple, *your place or mine?*

I grinned and sent back *yours. Should be there around seven. Be naked.*

Only if you are too.

Is that a dare?

Yes.

Dare accepted.

He sent back a questioning emoji. *If you wander naked through the streets, you'll get arrested and that'll do neither of us any good.*

There are such things as Ubers.

No man with even an ounce of sexual drive left in his body is going to be paying attention to the road when you're sitting naked in the rear seat. Trust me on that.

I sent back a smile and a heart. He replied with a row of hearts and one hungry face in the middle. I laughed.

"I take it the man is available?" Lugh said, voice dry.

"He is indeed, and you can step on it if you wish."

"I am not going to get a speeding ticket just so you can satisfy your raging hormones half an hour earlier."

"What about Darby's raging hormones? Are you ever going to satisfy them?"

He rolled his eyes. "You know, in most families, a sibling's sexual life would be off-limit, conversation-wise."

"We're not most families. Besides, if more people were open about relationships, maybe there'd be less emotional hang-ups and problems in the world."

"I tend to agree, but that doesn't mean I really want to discuss the ins and outs of *my* relationships."

I sniffed. "It's okay. I can get all the gritty details from Darby."

He made a growly sort of groan sound but otherwise didn't reply.

We stopped for lunch at a chippy van, and I used the break to craft a small storm cloud in which to hide the sword. It would self-perpetuate for a week, which should give us the time to discover its birthplace. Once I wrapped it around the sword, I sent it toward the Irish Sea, where it would circle until I called it back in. Even if they hired another weather witch, it would take him ages to inspect every cloud in the UK. This was the United Kingdom, after all. Clouds and rain were the dominant weather features here, even in the summer months.

By the time we reached Deva, it was going on two. Lugh wound his way through the traffic until we neared the end of St Werburgh Street—the closest we could get to the tavern, thanks to the fact our section of Eastgate Street had become a pedestrian walkway—and then stopped.

"You intending to use the Codex before you see Cynwrig tonight?"

"Probably—why?"

"Do you want me there? Just in case something goes wrong?"

I hesitated, then shook my head. "I should be right. The worst that could happen is the damn thing won't work." I paused, but couldn't help adding, "Don't forget to ring Darby."

He gave me a deadpan look. "Shut the damn door and be gone, evil one."

I slammed the door shut, then walked around to the trunk to grab my overnight bag and the banner case. It now held a couple of Lugh's hiking poles in an effort to give it some weight and fullness. If we did still have watchers, it was better for them to believe I still had the sword. It might lead to another attack, but I was better equipped to deal with them on home turf. The building might be old, but the structure was strong and the wood song was rich and vibrant; it would tell me if anyone attempted to steal inside.

Of course, it couldn't stop magic, but that was where the protection spells that ringed the place and the knives came in.

Ye Old Pixie Boots—the name Mom had given the tavern when she'd taken over—lay in the middle section of the rows that lined the pedestrian part of East Street. Like most of the buildings in this section, it was heritage-listed, and consisted of an undercroft at street level, one floor at "row" level, and our living quarters above that. Aside from a few layout changes upstairs and the necessary modernizations, it was basically the same building that had stood on this spot since it had undergone minor remodeling in the late 1400s.

I pushed open the old wooden door and clattered down the steps to the main room. Like most buildings of this age, it was an intimate space, with five tables in this front area and four smaller ones and the bar on the far side of the stairs. Bright pixie boots of various sizes hung from the exposed floor joists and beams, some of them real, some of them not, but all of them a nod to tourist expectations. The background music of the oak frame sang through me, a noise as bright and warm as the happy chatter coming from the other end of the room. A group of eight had pushed a couple of tables together and were happily munching on free pretzels and peanuts while they drank their beers. A late business lunch, if their suits were anything to go by.

The barman looked up as I neared the stairs. Rik, like his older sister Ingrid—who'd been the tavern's manager for as long as I could remember—was a Gadahn pixie, though his curly hair was a deeper shade of green and his eyes golden rather than deep brown. He exuded the same sort of "I take no nonsense" air as her, though, and there were few patrons who risked getting rowdy when either of them was around.

"Any problems, Rik?"

"Been a bit slow, but it is winter." He shrugged. "It'll pick up tonight though—it's Jack's birthday, and Phil's arranged a surprised gathering."

Jack and Phil were a couple of old pixies who'd been coming here for as long as anyone could remember and, like many of the elders who lived permanently here in Deva rather than at one of the widely scattered enclaves, basically treated the Boot as a second home—and the fierce joy that radiated off the old oak beams in this place was part of the reason. It was as close as they could come to communing with nature in the old city without having to take public transport out to a public park or even an enclave.

Both Gran and Mom had petitioned Deva's fae council to do more for our elderly, but the low number of full-time residents meant the council didn't see the need to improve facilities beyond what already existed for humans. It was a cop-out, and everyone knew it, but there wasn't anything we could do other than support Jack, Phil, and all the others when and where we could.

"Ingrid's told him food is on the house and drinks half price for the first two hours, I take it?" I said.

Rik nodded. "Phil argued, of course. Said he didn't want to be treated any differently to any other paying customers."

I smiled. Pixies of all ages generally saw no harm in bending the rules or taking advantage of a situation if opportunity presented itself, but Phil was a man who played it straight down the line. According to Jack, this propensity for honesty had only happened once age had set in and he'd realized just how close to judgment day he now was.

"I take it he grudgingly accepted the offer after arguing with Ingrid for several minutes?"

Rik smiled. "As ever."

I laughed and headed up. Ingrid wasn't there—which no doubt meant she was coming in for the evening shift and the party—but both Jonnie and Zoe were, as well as the kitchen crew.

After I'd checked that there were no problems needing to be dealt with, I unlocked the door that led to my living quarters and then stepped through. After shoving the newly installed, heavy-duty door latch home, I bounded up the stairs, the wood creaking slightly under my weight. Its song was gentler, a little faded thanks to constant use.

It wasn't particularly large up here, even with the roof height lifted. There was a combined kitchen-living area and two bedrooms—one had been Mom's and was now mine, and the other one Lugh and I had shared as kids, and I now used as a spare. The bathroom was the second biggest room in the flat, but it had to be, given that, at one point, four oversized pixies had been using it. Gran had moved out when she'd handed the tavern's reins over to Mom, but she'd slept in the loft before then. It was only accessible via a loft ladder, which was the reason behind her decision to leave. Or so she'd claimed. Given Lugh and I would have readily swapped our shared room for the larger loft space, I personally thought she'd simply wanted to give Mom the space and freedom to run the tavern any way she wanted.

I slung the banner bag onto the sofa and hurried over to

the fireplace. After four days away and no fire burning, the air up here was positively frosty. I suspected the only reason there wasn't an *actual* layer of frost over everything was thanks to the fact that these old buildings didn't have a lot in the way of insulation, and the heat from the down-stairs fires drifted upwards.

I hastily lit a fire—saying a gentle prayer of thanks to the wood even though its song and life had long ago left—then walked over to the kitchen to put the kettle on. Once I'd prepared the teapot, I pulled open the pot drawer—a leftover from the days when we'd actually had an oven up here—moved a couple of pots and pulled out the Codex. While there were hidden "safe holes" built into the struc-ture's lovely old beams, I suspected too many people were aware of them now thanks to the fact Vincentia—who knew about them all—had been working with the enemy.

But I wouldn't leave it here. Not now that I knew we were still being followed. A thorough enough search *would* find it.

When I'd first found the Codex, it had been nothing more than a worn and very plain-looking leather notebook. The blood bonding ceremony had changed that, turning the old leather a glassy black. Light rolled across its surface as I moved it, reminding me of the lightning that cut through the Eye when it was active. It didn't have the same dangerous feel, though given I hadn't used the thing yet, that might be nothing more than an illusion.

I grabbed a block of Cadbury's Toffee Wholenut out of the fridge, then walked back to the coffee table, placing both down before pulling the Eye out from under my breast. It was as black as midnight and about the size of an oval-shaped marble. Which, given it had once been the eye of an old goddess, made sense. It reacted immediately to my touch, its surface lit by streaks of purple lightning, and a throbbing sense of power coming from its dark heart. Whenever I'd handled the Eye like this in the past, it had immediately swept me into a vision. That didn't happen this time, though I could feel them pressing at the back of my mind, waiting to be unleashed. Merging with the triune had at least one benefit, it seemed.

I put the Eye on top of the Codex, unsheathed my knives and placed them either side—for no real reason other than the fact it felt right—then spun and walked back to the kitchenette.

Once I'd made my pot of tea, I grabbed a mug, then moved back to my chair and broke open the chocolate. A couple of rows and one mug of tea later, I finally felt ready to tackle the Codex.

The light that rolled across its surface now matched the pulsing coming from the Eye, suggesting they were in sync. The knives remained inert, which I guessed was a good thing, given their talents lay in reflecting or destroying magic rather than enhancing it.

After a slight hesitation, I pressed a fingertip to the Eye. The thrum of power didn't change, but the light whirling through the Codex brightened.

I had no idea what to do next, so I asked, "Where was the Goddess Agrona's Sword of Darkness created?"

I waited for some kind of response, but nothing happened.

Neither the Codex's swirling light nor the Eye's pulsing changed in any way.

Damn it, why could nothing be straightforward for a change?

While I could blame Mom for my lack of knowledge when it came to the Eye—though in truth I understood why she'd been reluctant to burden me with the baggage that came with it, even if I found it frustrating—I couldn't blame her for my lack when it came to the Codex. She—like so many of our ancestors—had apparently been similarly clueless about its importance. Which made me wonder yet again what had gone so wrong in the past that all information about the triune's importance had basically been forgotten.

I slid the Eye onto the table, then picked up the Codex and tried again. Still no response, and the inner light seemed fainter.

Perhaps I needed to open the thing first?

I flipped it over and tried to do that, but the damn thing appeared glued shut. Or maybe it always had been. It wasn't like I'd really had a chance to examine it properly after we'd snatched it from Vincentia.

I grabbed another row of chocolate and munched on it while I contemplated the Codex. When I'd first used the Eye, I had to be holding it for it to work, but that obviously wasn't holding true here. Or was it simply a case of it not being designed to work alone, despite the fact that both the Eye and the knives were individually functional? It definitely had gleamed brighter when the Eye had been sitting on it.

I leaned forward, picked up the Eye, pressed it against the front cover, and then repeated the question.

Ghosts stirred through the back of my mind, tantalizing images that promised much and provided little.

Frustration stirred, but I leaned forward and scooped up the knives. If this didn't work, I was out of fucking ideas.

I dropped the Codex onto my lap, positioned the knives and the Eye on its surface, then pressed a hand across the lot of them and re-asked the question.

Light erupted from all three even as a whirlpool of power surrounded me. It swept me up and then swept me away, though it wasn't a physical departure as much as a mental—or perhaps spiritual—one. I could still feel the old leather chair under my butt, could still hear the building's song and the crackle of the flames in the hearth. But they were little more than whispers against the sheer noise coming from the deepening maelstrom of color I arrowed toward.

But unlike the first—and to date the only—time I'd connected the triune, I didn't fall straight through that storm but rather stopped in the midst of it. For several seconds, I did nothing more than watch as the maelstrom's spinning slowed, then settled into a multitude of different shapes. Long and tall, thin, or thick, some round, but most square or rectangular.

I blinked.

They were *books*. Books that glowed with an unearthly energy.

Ethine had told me—when I'd spoken to her via her stone monument—that the Codex held the vast knowledge of all creation. Given its size—or lack thereof—I'd seriously doubted the statement. And in many respects, I hadn't been wrong, because the Codex was actually a key that unlocked what basically amounted to a library. A goddamn godly library.

How in the fuck did we ever lose this resource?

It is a very long time indeed since an Aodhán pixie has graced the halls of this place.

The voice was neither male nor female, and held no warmth, hostility, or power. It exuded wisdom, knowledge, and an odd sense of welcome, and yet I had a deep sense that it could all change at the snap of a finger.

I hesitated, uncertain how to proceed, though I suspected it wouldn't be considered polite to simply ask my question. Good manners were a thing when dealing with old gods. They were likely to smite you, otherwise.

I'm afraid all knowledge about the Codex was lost—

It was not lost. It was a malicious and deliberate action by an ancestor after she and her offspring were banned for a period of three lifetimes for misusing this library.

A comment that made me think of Vincentia and the fact that she'd obviously inherited that ancestor's treacherous traits. *I don't suppose that misuse involved the theft of Agrona's Claws, did it?*

It was a guess, but a logical one given we'd recently learned it had been an Aodhán pixie—an ancestor of mine, in fact—that had stolen the Claws.

Indeed. What is it you wish? You should not linger here too long, young Aodhán—it could be fatal.

Which made me remember the shattered mess I'd been after the bonding ceremony. *The confluence's gatekeeper told me the Sword of Darkness must be returned to the darkness in which it was born. Are you able to tell me where that is?*

The glowing books whirled briefly around me, then one popped out and floated toward me, hovering in the air while the pages flipped open.

There were no words—or if there were, I couldn't see or understand them—but there were images. *A malformed limestone rock formation that stood high above a disused quarry. A jagged slit in the cliff face that swooped down into heat and darkness. A massive blacksmith's forge in which coals still glowed white hot, as if the smithy had merely stepped away only a few minutes ago. A hammer that glowed with an eerie light and bellows no earthly hand had ever used.*

The book snapped shut and whisked back to its place. I

took a deep breath and felt an odd sort of quivering stir deep inside and instinctively knew it wasn't excitement or even fear. It was this place draining my energy. My life force.

That was why the omniscient presence had warned against staying too long.

Can the Ring of Ruin be destroyed the same way as the sword?

What forged one claw forged the others.

Which was the long way of saying yes. Old gods rarely used one word when more were in the offering. I hesitated briefly, quickly sorting through the questions crowding my mind in order to find the ones we most needed answering. *Does possessing all the three Claws offer the user additional benefits other than their individual powers?*

That is the way of these things.

I waited, but when no further information came, said, *what might that be?*

Another book wheeled out of the shelving and hovered in front of me. After a few page flips, it revealed a series of moving images—*the crown immersed in waves of gray that were neither light nor day, but an odd combination of the two, sitting in a land that held no color or life. The sword steeped in a darkness so thick that the crawling dead made waves through the air. An ouroboros ring—in the form of a serpent devouring its own tail rather than a dragon—presiding over a land that was barren and empty. Then the page flipped one more time to show the three Claws being used at once. The sun fell from the sky, the darkness consumed all, and the earth rose up in a wave to destroy everything that stood on her, until the very world itself was destroyed by the energies that tore through her.*

Holy *fuck.*

I'd suspected the combined forces of the Claws would

indeed offer an enhancement of all three dark "gifts," but if this book were to be believed, the Claws united could *literally* destroy our world...

If you do not wish to believe what you see, then do not ask the question.

There was a hint of censure in that comment, and I swallowed heavily. *I did not mean to doubt. It's just... a lot to take in at once.*

It is your first visit, young Aodhán, so your disbelief can be forgiven.

Suggesting that in future sessions, I had best keep my emotions and doubts to myself—though that might be a tad hard when my connection to this place and the omniscient presence within it seemed to be a metaphysical one.

Not to mention the fact he could obviously "read" what I was thinking.

Can the powers of the Claws be reversed? Can it banish darkness as easily as it draws it down?

Another page flipped. *An image of the sun chasing the moon and the night from the sky. Rather than darkness, there was endless light in a land that heaved in dusty barren emptiness, until all was gone.*

In other words, we were right. The powers of the Claws *could* be used to forever ban night, though the end result remained the same.

I sucked in a breath and flexed fingers that didn't exist in this place to calm the rise of fear and trepidation.

We were told that only a mage can access the sword's powers, so is that true of the crown and the ring? What is the cost of combining the three?

The book hovering in front of me flipped another page. Obviously, unless you asked a specific question, you would not be shown all the information the library had.

A final image—*an androgynous being holding the Claws being consumed by the very powers they were unleashing.*

Although "consumed" was putting it mildly, given its flesh melted, its muscles turned to liquid, and its bones to ash, until all that was left were the hands holding the Claws. Then there was nothing. Nothing other than a crown, a sword, and a ring, gleaming in the destruction they had wrought.

The price of unleashing all that power was high indeed.

You should go, young Aodhán. You linger too long.

His words seemed to quicken the reaction within. Suddenly I could feel the frantic beating of my heart and a wash of weakness so strong it felt like my very being was wasting away.

I swallowed heavily and said, *Thank you for your help.*

That odd sense of dangerousness receded just a fraction. *We are here if you have further questions, young Aodhán.*

And with that, I was released.

The maelstrom faded and my consciousness or spirit or whatever the hell had gone into that place returned to my body. My heart was indeed racing, my breathing rapid and shallow, my chest on fire, and there were dozens of crazed miners drilling into my head. I released the triune and dropped my head into my hands, rocking back and forth for several minutes, trying to take deeper breaths in an effort to control the desperate racing of my pulse and heart.

Eventually, it worked. As the fire in my brain and my chest eased, I leaned forward and, with shaking fingers, poured myself a mug of now lukewarm tea.

It took another ten minutes or so before I approached anything close to normality. I carefully pushed upright. The room spun briefly, and weariness washed through my limbs. I glanced at my watch. Just on three. There was time before my date tonight to grab a bit of sleep.

I gathered up the triune, walked—staggered—into my bedroom, dropping both the Eye and the knives on my bed before moving back out and down to the end of the room. I swept my fingers across the paneling, pulled the hidden lever to release the loft ladder, and then scrambled up. The effort left me trembling and lightheaded. I breathed deeply for several seconds, then rose and padded down the dark and dusty room, the warm greeting of the old wood guiding my steps. When Gran had moved out, Mom had converted this area into a reading-chill-out zone. All her books—many of them centuries old—remained on the shelves exactly where she'd left them, along with the foot-high stack of to-be-reads on the table next to her favorite chair.

But I wasn't interested in any of the bookshelves—too obvious a hiding place—but instead headed for the small wood heater tucked at the back of the room. Or rather, its flue. The protective mesh around it was broken at the back, and it was just big enough to fit the Codex.

Once it was safely hidden, I made my way back down the loft ladder, stripped off, and fell into bed. I was asleep before my head hit the pillow.

Cynwrig's apartment was situated on the top floor of a three-story, double-fronted, very gorgeous old Georgian building that was one of many such buildings owned by his family within Deva. I all but ran up the front steps, my bootheels clicking softly on the lovely old tiles. I punched in the keycode and then opened the ornate glass and wooden door. The entrance hall was large, airy, and opulent, with doors to the two ground-floor apartments on the left and the right. An ornate and obviously original, red-carpeted staircase dominated the center of the hall, curving up to the next two levels. I walked over and placed one hand on the banister, feeling the warmth and joy of the song within as I moved up. My bootheels made no sound on the soft carpet, but my heart was beating so loudly, it sounded like a drum.

I reached the top floor and headed left. The apartment to the right belonged to his sister, who I'd yet to meet. And maybe never would, given I was just a fun time rather than a long time. Which, given he wasn't only a dark elf but the co-heir to the Myrkálfar throne, was understandable.

Technically, of course, there was no such thing as an elven throne let alone an elven king these days, as they'd been forced to swear allegiance to the "true" and very human royal line after they—and most of the fae—had lost the great war eons ago.

We pixies had sensibly kept out of that mess and, as a result, had basically kept all our rights and lands. But then, neither the Fae nor the humans had ever really considered us a threat, in war or out. Which, considering both the Aodhán and Tàileach pixies had once both been guards to the old gods, was rather strange.

I strode across to the door, but before I could tap in the keycode, it opened.

He was buck naked, and I couldn't help a delighted grin.

Unlike their golden kin, dark elves were neither slender nor delicate, and this man's powerful body was nothing short of magnificent. His chiseled features were sublime, and his body ebony perfection, from the well-muscled planes of his chest to his washboard abs and the happy trail of dark hair that drew the eye to his long, thick, and getting-ready-for-action cock. Even his damn legs were perfect—long and lean, holding the muscular strength of a runner rather than a weightlifter.

I lazily let my gaze drift up again to meet his; they were a smoky silver filled with heat. The kind of heat that urged me to rip off my coat and have hot and sweaty sex with the man right here in the doorway.

Which was only partially due to the deep and very sexual connection between us. Dark elves had an inbuilt magnetism that could make even the iciest maidens weak with wanting.

This maiden had never been considered icy, but oh boy, when he turned on the charm it hit like a club.

"See anything you like?" he drawled.

His voice was deep, velvety smoke, and fanned the fires of wanting to greater heights.

"Plenty, but he's hogging the doorway rather than being a gentleman and inviting me inside so that I can safely jump his bones without providing a show for the neighbors."

He laughed, a low sound that danced across my skin as sweetly as a caress, then stepped to one side and waved me through. "I cannot help a twinge of disappointment to see you clothed, but I do approve of the boots. Can I take your coat?"

"Well, it's definitely too bulky to be doing anything serious in." I handed him my overnight bag, then turned so that my back was to him and undid my coat's buttons.

He closed the door and placed the bag down. A heartbeat later, his fingers brushed the back of my neck, sending a light tremor of delight curling through me. He chuckled softly and slid the coat down my arms—so damn slowly that I wasn't tempted to tell him to just hurry up.

Some things were worth savoring.

"Oh, I do believe we're both flexible enough to get around—" The rest of the sentence ended in a sharp intake of breath.

Apart from the boots and the necklace that caged the Eye, I was as naked as he.

"Disappointment turns to elation," he murmured, and casually tossed the coat toward the sofa. It landed on the floor, but I didn't care, and I didn't think he did either.

He stepped closer, his breath whispering across my neck, sending a riot of delicious sensations rocketing through me even though he wasn't physically touching me.

And didn't, not for what seemed like ages.

He simply stood there, his breath caressing my skin while his intensity and desire swirled around me, a force so strong it ratcheted up expectation and left me quivering.

Then, finally, his lips brushed my ear and trailed down my neck to my right shoulder. I closed my eyes but couldn't stop a sigh escaping. It felt like heaven.

Felt like home.

He chuckled softly and repeated the process on the left. Dear gods, he'd barely even touched me, and I was already a melting mess.

His hands slid to my waist and gently turned me. Time stretched as we stared into each other's eyes, heat, passion, and longing burning the air around us.

Then he groaned and his lips met mine, his kiss an exploration as much as a statement, a fierce and demanding thing that left my head spinning and my body aching.

From that point on, there was no conversation and no stopping. We explored each other, caressing and teasing with lips and touch, leaving almost no part of our bodies untouched, until the need was so fierce that all I wanted, all

I could think about, was him. In me, filling me, completing me.

I wrapped my arms around his neck and pressed so close it was hard to tell where his skin ended and mine began. The heat of him, the hardness of him, sent my pulse into overdrive.

"Enough," I whispered. "I need you. *Now*."

He laughed softly, his breath warm against my lips. "I do love a woman who knows what she wants and is not afraid to ask for it."

"You're still talking."

He laughed again and slid his hands down my back, cupping my butt, then lifting me with little effort. As I wrapped my legs around his waist, he swung around and carried me across to the table, depositing me gently before stepping between my legs.

He cupped my face and kissed me—gently, sweetly—then slid his hands down to my hips, and held me still as he slipped all the way in.

I gasped, heated from within and without, filled with the power of the man and the joyous energies of the table under my butt. I gripped his shoulders, wanting more, *needing* more, and yet unwilling to break the magic of this moment.

He kissed me again, though there was nothing sweet or gentle about it this time, and then began to move. First with agonizingly glorious slowness and then with increasing urgency.

I slid my hands down his muscular back to his rump, cupping them fiercely as the force of his movements threatened to push us apart. My breasts were pressed against his chest, my nipples hard and aching. Every movement brushed them, tortured them, adding to the pleasure. I burned, tightened, until pleasure was so sharp and fierce that it felt like I would break.

Then I did break, my orgasm so fierce and intense that I couldn't think, couldn't breathe, couldn't do anything other than be swept away. Cynwrig followed me over that edge, crying out in pleasure as his body stiffened against mine.

He rested his forehead against mine, but for several seconds, neither of us moved, our breaths mingling, harsh and rapid.

Then he sighed, kissed my forehead, and stepped back. "So much for me doing the gentlemanly thing and offering you cheese and champagne before I got down to the business of seducing you."

"You can still offer all those things but later. One quick session of sex does not make up for the absence of it over the last five days."

He laughed and caught my hand to steady me as I moved off the table. "Does that mean you don't want to be fed just yet?"

I grinned. "It does, though I am of the view we should think practically and move to the shower."

He raised an eyebrow. "I have absolutely no arguments with this view, but I do wonder why you would consider a shower more practical than a bed."

"Because we can clean up the aftermath without actually moving."

He laughed and tugged me over to the bookcase that contained the lever for the hidden door that led up to his bedroom and work area.

Needless to say, over the course of the next few hours, the need was well and truly assuaged.

He handed me a flute glass full of golden bubbles and said, "Many would consider it foolish to be drinking at this hour—"

"I have no idea who this 'many' is of which you speak, but they are wrong. There is no such thing as 'too late' when it comes to fine champagne." And this certainly *was* fine—creamy soft and beautifully mellow, containing none of the "abrasive" characteristics so often found in lesser quality bubbles. "Though if you don't hurry up with that food platter, the alcohol might well go straight to my head and make me sleep."

Especially since I'd not had any dinner.

He laughed and immediately handed me a small platter containing a varied selection of sliced fruits, cheeses, and crackers. I put it on the sofa next to me, then crossed my legs and tugged my borrowed dressing gown over the top in an effort to warm my feet. He'd lit the fire twenty minutes ago, but the air still held a decidedly icy edge. If that didn't change soon, I'd be borrowing some wooly socks.

"Did you get any answers from the confluence?" he asked, sitting down opposite.

"Nothing more than a godly version of 'your message has been received and will be passed on to the appropriate division.'"

"Meaning the sword?"

"No. I was told the sword can only be destroyed in the darkness in which it was created. That's not the confluence, apparently."

"Did they happen to mention where it was created?"

"Of course not. I did, however, ask that question of the

73

Codex, and was given a few somewhat vague image directions."

"But not place names or coordinates?"

"What? And make things easy? Unlikely."

He chuckled softly. "I guess it is expecting too much. What about the ring?"

"The Codex said all three Claws can be destroyed in the same fires in which they were created."

"No, I meant did you ask where it was?"

I shook my head. "I did see glimpses of its location in a dream, though. Lugh seems to think it's an old mine of some sort and will check the records tomorrow. Or today, as it now is." I picked up a slice of triple-cream brie, dropped it onto an apple slice, and took a bite. Food heaven itself. "I did ask the Codex if possessing all three Claws offered the user additional powers, and the answer was a very definite yes."

"That's not entirely surprising. Godly artifacts do have a tendency to be ultra-destructive if they're linked and used as one."

And he'd know that better than anyone—except, perhaps, for Lugh. His family had been protecting the Tenebrous hoard—of which the Claws had once been a part—for centuries. There were two other hoards under the protection of the elves; the Éadrom hoard, which had been under light elf protection until its recent theft, and one other whose name I didn't know and which I presumed was guarded by both.

I took another sip of bubbles. "I still don't get why the Looisearch are willing to risk the destruction of our world just to ensure the Annwfyn never enter it again."

"People wrapped in grief often can't see through the veil of it with any sort of clarity."

There was an odd note in his voice that once again suggested he was speaking from experience. Curiosity stirred, but I held my questions at bay. Our relationship was surface-level and very new besides, and it wasn't my place to ask such intimate details.

Especially when he hadn't offered any explanations the first time he'd mentioned grief in this manner.

I picked up a strawberry and dunked it in the little cup of chocolate sauce. The man really did make a most excellent cheese and fruit platter.

"I guess we'd just better ensure we find the ring before they can."

Not to mention keep both it and the sword safe until we could find the means of destroying them.

"That might be a little hard when the descriptions you've been given are so vague."

"They're no more vague than the visions that led me to both the crown and the sword." I shrugged. "What about you? Get any more information out of Jalvi?"

Jalvi was a cousin of his, and her sister, Telyn, had been one of five lives lost in the Annwfyn attack that had started this whole Claws mess. She'd been actively working behind the scenes for the Looisearch, but her luck had finally run out when she'd murdered Jules Auclair, a historian Lugh and I had arranged to meet. We hadn't arrived in time to save his life but the description we'd gotten from the café's waitress had led us—or rather—Cynwrig—straight to Jalvi's door.

He grimaced. "She's not saying much at all."

"You've tried a truth seeker?"

He nodded. "All she's been able to give us is what we already know."

"Do you think her memories have been altered?"

"Possibly, though she's been well guarded since her capture and few but me and the IIT have been near her."

The IIT—or the Interspecies Investigation Team as they were officially known—dealt with all police events involving nonhumans and had both a day and night division. Which didn't mean that there weren't traitors within their ranks, of course, but I knew the two men in charge of both divisions, and they ran fairly tight ships. Ruadhán Dhār-Val—the light elf in charge of the day division and Mathi's father—did tend to stretch certain legalities when it suited him, and suspects had been killed in the day division lock-up recently, but the main suspect was a lawyer who up until that point had given the division no reason to suspect she might have been doing more than interviewing clients.

Sgott Bruhn ran the night division and was straight down the line when it came to the law. He'd been my mother's lover for well over sixty years and was the only father I'd ever known, having entered my life when I was barely two, but I wasn't viewing his actions through rose-colored glasses. Mom had been a powerful seeker. She wouldn't have spent so long with anyone who wasn't a decent and honest man.

"Her memories could have been altered at any point in time. They were well aware you and Sgott were looking for her."

He nodded. "They did call a pixie consultant—"

"Which probably wouldn't have done any good." Mainly because it was often difficult for one pixie to undo the commands of another, especially if more than a few days had passed. "I take it they've also erased any information about the location of her immediate family?"

"No, because it wasn't necessary. She rang them after

she disposed of Auclair and told them to leave where they were and not, under any circumstances, tell her where."

"She knew you were closing in."

"I made no secret of the fact I was hunting her."

"No." I loaded a few crackers with hard cheese and munched on them for a few seconds. "I take it you've searched the location where her family had been hiding?"

"Yes. Nothing was left behind, but then, that's hardly surprising."

Because they'd successfully traded in the black market for absolute eons and "leave no evidence" was undoubtedly a motto they lived by.

I sighed. "These people always seem to be two steps ahead of us."

He leaned back in the chair and studied me for a second. "Could Vincentia still be in play? I realize she's been confined, but the connection you formed hasn't been broken, has it?"

"The red knife should have severed it."

"And if it hasn't?"

I hesitated. "She only ever caught snatches of conversation, not my direct thoughts. The distance now between us should have nullified that."

"What about your aunt?"

I raised my eyebrows. "What about her?"

"She inherited the family second sight, did she not?"

I nodded. "It wasn't as strong as Mom's or Vincentia's though."

"Is it strong enough to track your location?"

I hesitated. "Second sight doesn't work on demand like that."

Scrying could, though, and it was an ability that ran strongly in our family. It was one I rarely used, but I knew the basics of it, having seen Mom and Gran use it many times over the years during the psychic nights they held at the tavern to gain a little more revenue.

"I'm not sure it's possible to stop her from doing it, though," I added. "And the red knife forbids any pixie contacting them."

"But it doesn't stop non-pixies paying a brief but threatening visit."

I raised an eyebrow, a grin twitching my lips. "You volunteering?"

"It would seem prudent, and they cannot manipulate me with touch as they could Sgott or one of his people."

"You wouldn't happen to enact a little bit of revenge, would you?"

He raised his eyebrow, expression all innocence. "And why would I want that?"

"They did attack us—"

"They did," he cut in, "but if such attacks were a primer for revenge-seeking, I'd waste my entire life doing it."

The exception being attacks on his direct family and especially his twin sister. Someone had foolishly done just that the night he'd landed unconscious in the river—which had resulted in my fishing him out and the bloom of our relationship—and to say he intended to visit hell on them was not an understatement. Dark elves could control stone, and a prison buried so deeply in the earth none would ever find them had been mentioned for the perpetrators.

And he hadn't been kidding.

I studied him for a second, seeing the amusement dancing lightly through his lovely eyes and the deeper, more serious intent behind it.

Not seeking revenge, my ass.

"You'd need the approval of the pixie council first."

"Easy enough to arrange."

Probably was for him, being heir to the throne and all. Personally, I was keeping well out of their way. While I doubted they'd forgotten about the whole punishment thing, I wasn't about to make an appearance and jog their collective memories.

I swished another strawberry through the chocolate and bit into it. But as I did, my phone rang, the sound sharp and somehow urgent.

It wasn't a phone call.

It was a warning.

Someone had just broken into my living quarters at the tavern.

CHAPTER
FOUR

I CHOKED DOWN MY STRAWBERRY AND SCRAMBLED UPRIGHT. Cynwrig was already on his feet. "That was the tavern alarm, wasn't it?"

"You've a damn good memory considering you only heard it the once."

"That once almost resulted in a fabulous ambush going astray. You'd better call Sgott. I'll head upstairs and call the car."

I nodded and walked over to my overnight bag. Once I'd dressed and strapped on my knives, I grabbed my phone and rang Sgott.

"Heard it," he said, the Scottish brogue in his voice sharper than usual. "On my way. Where are you?"

"At Cynwrig's."

"Good. Stay there while I deal with this."

I snorted. "How long have you known me? Besides, I can't. They'll be looking for the sword, and while it's not there, the Codex is."

"Why in the gods' names would you leave something like *that* there after all the recent break-ins?"

His voice held a resigned sort of disappointment rather than anger, and I always thought that was far worse. Not that he'd ever reacted angrily at anything we'd ever said or done over the years, but I *had* seen him unleash at those who dared threaten us. He was a fearsome sight in full flight, but then, he *was* a bear shifter. It came with the territory.

"I couldn't risk carrying the triune. Not when someone was keeping tabs on us in Scotland, and we were more than likely followed home."

He swore. "I take it you do have the knives, then?"

"And the Eye. Trust me, no matter how good the thief, if he is looking for the Codex, it'll take him a good while to find the damn thing."

"Unless it's a spellcaster or a sniffer. Those bastards could find the merest whiff of magic at fifty feet."

Sniffers were canine shifters and were called in on crimes where cause of death wasn't obvious. There weren't all that many of them in Deva and, from what Sgott had said over the years, the few that did live and work here were kept busy with legal jobs.

Which didn't mean they wouldn't take a shadier deal if the money was good enough, of course.

I glanced around as Cynwrig rattled down the stairs, fully dressed and phone in hand. "We'll be there in five."

"Meet you out the back."

I hung up, put my phone away, and then followed Cynwrig out of the apartment and down the stairs. A black BMW pulled up just as we walked through the front doors. A heartbeat later, the chauffeur—a tall dark elf with a sprinkling of silver in his hair—jumped out and ran around the vehicle to open the rear passenger door and usher us in.

While Cynwrig did have a driving license, he—like

many elves, light or dark—preferred to use a chauffeur within Deva's narrow and often congested streets.

"It didn't take long for your car to arrive," I said as the BMW accelerated smoothly away.

"He resides in an apartment around the corner." A smile ghosted his luscious lips. "Rent free, as part of his wage. We do keep odd hours."

"Really? Hadn't noticed."

My voice was dry, and he chuckled softly. "You, my dear, are a good part of the reason for those odd hours of late."

"Me *and* the bevy of beautiful women you have at your beck and call."

"I do not have a bevy."

I gave him my best "don't believe it for a second" expression. "I'm guessing your definition of bevy and mine are two very different things."

"A bevy is a number of at least ten. Even *I* couldn't cope with that many women demanding my attention. There'd be six—seven at a maximum."

His smoky eyes twinkled, leaving me wondering if he was joking or not. Elves in general had a voracious appetite when it came to sex, and the dark elves were particularly well known for their sexual "endeavors."

"Does this six or seven include the lovely Orlah?"

I couldn't help the very slight but very evident edge in my voice. Orlah was a tall, dark-skinned elf with long, curly black hair and a figure to die for. She'd briefly interrupted our dinner at the upmarket and very expensive Viridis restaurant recently and had made it patently obvious she intended to reignite their relationship.

He and I might be short-term rather than long, but the warmth in his tone and manner in which he'd greeted her suggested theirs had been more than *just* a sexual relationship. And I didn't want *ours* to end. Not just yet anyway.

He studied me for a long moment. "Is that the green head of jealousy rising once again?"

"No, it is not."

I said it firmly, but he nevertheless laughed. "I'm delighted, I truly am, but there is no need. As I said at the time, she was—and is—merely a bed companion."

"And as *I* said at the time, we're both free agents."

His dark eyebrows quirked upward. "Does this mean you have another date with the 'lovely' Eljin?"

The emphasis he put on "lovely" was somewhat derogatory, but I ignored it. "It does indeed. Tonight, in fact."

"And does he take you somewhere special?"

I met his gaze squarely. "When you tell me about your dates, I'll tell you about mine."

He laughed again, caught my hand, and kissed my fingers. "You delight me, Bethany Aodhán."

I wasn't entirely sure how to take that statement, so I ignored it.

It didn't take us long to get across to the tavern. The chauffeur drew up beside the lane that ran down to the tavern's rear exit. After telling his driver that he'd ring if he was needed again, we both climbed out and ran down the narrow but well-lit lane. I spotted one man lurking in the doorway of a small loading bay belonging to another shop, but suspected Sgott would have others out here.

He was, as promised, waiting near the rear door. He was a big man, with thick, wiry brown hair, brown skin, and a fierce, untamable beard.

"You need to be giving me the new door code," he said.

"It would save me time and you the trouble of always coming back here if something happens."

"I will, but you should also know that I'm never not going to come here if there's a problem."

"Aye," he said, in a way that spoke as much to sorrow as pride, "in that you are very much your mother's daughter."

I didn't reply but, just for a moment, my gaze misted. I hadn't truly grieved for Mom yet and was utterly determined not to until we caught her killers. But every now and again, a gentle comment had all the pain and sorrow rising.

"I take it you've people out front as well as the three down the lane?" Cynwrig said.

"Yes, so unless they left the minute they triggered the alarm, they have to be in there."

"Vincentia would have passed on the information about the alarm on the stair door," I said, quickly punching in the code. "She did, after all, trigger it herself."

"Yes, but let's be honest here," Sgott said. "The Looisearch haven't always employed the sharpest tools in the shed, and this break-in would have been hastily arranged if you've only just arrived back in town."

"None of which changes the very low odds of someone remaining inside." Amusement gleamed in Cynwrig's smoky eyes. "Trust me, any thief worth his salt would not only have a lookout stationed nearby but also a means of escaping if all the main exits are compromised."

"Speaking from experience again, I see."

I carefully pushed the door open. Wood song immediately greeted me but there was nothing in its music to suggest anyone or anything moved through the building. But there was a thread of pain running along the outer edges of the song, suggesting damage done to the wood somewhere within. It didn't take a whole lot of brain power to guess where.

There was also a slightly heavier cadence coming from the very top of the building. Something lay on the floor up there and it wasn't moving.

"Not anymore," Cynwrig was saying, "I gave up thievery ages ago."

"The family, however, has not," Sgott said dryly.

I smiled and moved quickly down the hall, not bothering to check the storage or bathrooms simply because the floorboards would have sung a different tune if anyone waited within. Coals still glowed in the hearth in the main room, providing enough light to see by. The freestanding chairs had all been placed upside-down on the tables so that the floors could be washed, and they cast crazy shadows through the otherwise empty room.

I paused near the stairs, unzipped my boots, and then padded up barefoot. This middle floor was darker, the fire having died down quicker and the streetlights barely illuminated the row—which was basically a series of first-floor covered walkways linking all the buildings in this street—let alone this inner section. Still, the room was obviously empty, and that was decidedly odd. Surely, as Cynwrig had already noted, a sensible thief would have lookouts, and not just outside.

I led the way around to the stairs leading up to my floor, the sharpening thread of pain that ran through the wood song telling me what had happened long before I actually saw the damage. The intruder had ripped the security door off its hinges and torn the frame in the process. I resisted the urge to heal it immediately and glanced back at Sgott and Cynwrig.

"I'm not feeling any movement, but there's an unidentified weight upstairs." I hesitated, cocking my head as I moved deeper into the cadence of the song, sorting through the various strands until I found an exact location. My stomach clenched. "It's in the loft."

"The loft?" Disbelief vibrated through Sgott's voice. "How the fuck did anyone spot the ladder release?"

"They wouldn't. Not without being told what to look for, anyway."

And *that* meant someone we knew—perhaps a friend of Mom's or Gran's—had shared the information. Or, more likely, had had the information forced out of them. The Looisearch certainly weren't averse to violence, that was for sure.

Sgott motioned me to one side. I obeyed, and he drew his gun, lightly and swiftly moving up the stairs. They didn't creak under his weight, but only because multiple generations of pixies had ensured they never suffered the shrinkage that wear, tear, and constant use caused over time.

Unless, of course, we actually *wanted* them to creak as a form of advance warning. I'd certainly done that more than a few times over the years, especially after Mom had disappeared six months ago.

I followed him up, Cynwrig two steps behind me. The living room was silent and the air cool, despite the coals that still glowed in the hearth. Sgott drew in a deeper breath, his nostrils flaring slightly, then pointed his chin toward the rear of the building and held up one finger.

One person.

Whether that person was intending to ambush us, was unconscious, or even dead was now the question needing an answer. I personally doubted the former would happen. No one, no matter how trained, could remain *completely* still for extended periods of time. They would have at least made some small adjustments as we'd entered the building, because despite our best efforts, neither Sgott nor I could walk as silently as an elf.

Sgott moved on. Cynwrig remained at the top of the stairs, but I followed, my bare feet warmed by the heat retained in the floorboards. The knives remained inert, which at least meant whatever the hell waited for us wasn't offering any sort of magical threat.

That didn't discount the possibility of some other kind of threat, of course.

The loft ladder was down.

Fuck.

Sgott stopped and looked up. There was no sound of movement and no indication that anyone other than that unmoving weight was up there, and its location hadn't changed.

Sgott motioned to me and then to the ladder. I nodded. The loft entrance had been designed to cater to pixies of a certain size—meaning Gran, me, Mom, but not Lugh, and definitely not Sgott. I could widen it enough for him to get in, of course, but it would take time and that wasn't practical in a situation like this.

I undid my coat, released the retention straps on the knives, and accepted the small flashlight he handed me. After a deep breath that did nothing to steady my nerves, I gripped a ladder rung and began to climb.

Once I neared the top, I paused, switched on the flashlight, then scrambled the rest of the way up, my pulse beating so loud it felt like a drum. Nothing attacked me. Nothing stirred except dust. I swept the light around, spotting lots of mess but no immediate reason for the weight.

I climbed fully into the loft and then stood, pointing

the light toward the location of the weight, which was close to Mom's beloved reading chair. The somewhat wonky crocheted rug I'd made to warm her knees when I was barely a teen—my first and *only* attempt at a crotchet rug—remained draped over the leather arm where she'd left it. Her pillow had been tossed onto the floor, though, its stuffing bursting through a new slash in the material. The pile of to-be-reads that had been sitting on the coffee table earlier were now scattered over the floor, and the table itself overturned. My gaze flicked over to the book-cases. Ornaments had been smashed, books had been pulled from the shelves, some torn apart. That was mali-cious damage, nothing more, as all the torn books resem-bled the Codex's original form. Obviously, they'd been checking each one to see if it was the right one, and then destroying them when they turned out to be wrong. Vincentia *had* seen the Codex immediately after the bonding ceremony had changed its form, but she hadn't believed it was the real thing. Her employers obviously didn't either.

Either that, or she'd simply not passed the information on to them.

"Anything?" Sgott said.

I glanced down and met his gaze. "Lots of mess, but no sign of anyone and nothing to explain the weight I'm feeling just yet."

"Are all the skylights locked? Because if they're not up there, and they didn't leave through either door or a window, it's the only other option of escape."

I raised the light and scanned the roof. Gran had added the skylights when she'd first decided to make the loft her retreat—though she'd done so surreptitiously, because the fae council had very dim views on anyone altering the physical appearance of heritage listed buildings, even if said changes couldn't be seen by the public.

The first two skylights were locked, but the third—which had a latch so unreliable that Gran had looped a bit of wire around the handle then tied the other end to a nearby crossbeam to keep it secure—was open.

"They've gone out through the roof," I said.

He grunted. "I'm coming up."

I nodded and moved left. That's when I saw the boots.

Boots that were connected to legs.

"Sgott, we have a body. It's behind Mom's chair."

His head popped up through the loft entrance, though the rest of him remained firmly on the loft ladder. "Unconscious? Dead?" He paused, his nostrils briefly widening. "Definitely the latter. I can smell the blood."

Thankfully, I *couldn't*.

I trained my light on the chair, but from his position wouldn't have been able to see the feet. I hadn't. "I'm not seeing any blood splatter."

"The killer might have cleaned it up or perhaps used some sort of containment magic. Do you want to go closer, or would you prefer to retreat and let us deal with it?"

"I'm not going anywhere until I know if it's a stranger or a friend."

Not to mention checking whether the Codex remained in place. The flue's secret compartment didn't look to have been disturbed, but it was hard to be sure from this angle.

"Be careful," Sgott said, and tossed a pair of silicon gloves at me. "And wear these."

I pulled on the gloves and warily moved forward.

"The boots look to be a woman's rather than a man's," I said. They were also deep emerald green, a color that had been favored by both Mom and Gran. It couldn't be either

89

of them, of course, but that didn't discount the possibility of it being a relative.

It *was* a bit of a logic jump, of course, especially given the destruction done to the door—something no reasonable pixie would have stood for. But I just couldn't escape the notion that there was pixie involvement in this break-in or the possibility of it being a relative.

It was unlikely to be one of *my* relatives—I had few enough of them left after all—but it could possibly have been one of Vincentia's, on her dad's side. He'd divorced Aunt Riayn decades ago, but I knew Vincentia had kept in contact with not only him, but her cousins, aunts, and uncles.

It'd be just like her to drag one or more of them into this mess. She might be intent on protecting the Looisearch's asses, but she wasn't dumb, and she wouldn't risk the possibility of them finding the Codex *and* another Aodhán relative who could use it.

Just because the triune had been directly handed down to the first-born daughter in *my* family didn't mean a woman whose connection to us was distant or indirect wouldn't be able to use it if we all died out. If I was killed, Vincentia and then my aunt would be the next in line. After that, the triune would fall into the hands of whoever was our next closest living female relative.

"How's she positioned?" Sgott said. "Can you see any obvious signs of injury?"

I swept the light up her body. She was wearing jeans and a thick hoodie, the latter pulled up over her head so that her hair was hidden. Her build was indistinct thanks to the bulkiness of her clothes, but she appeared to be reasonably tall—at least my height, if not more. "She's face down, but I can't see an injury yet."

"Check her pulse but please, be careful."

I edged forward cautiously. When I was absolutely positive she wasn't about to jump up and attack me, I squatted beside her and felt for a pulse. Her skin retained some warmth, but there was no beat of life.

"Anything?" Sgott asked.

"No pulse, but I don't think she's been—" I stopped, suddenly spotting her right hand.

A hand that was stretched out in front of her, as if pleading for help or perhaps even mercy.

A hand that was missing two fingers.

Horror bloomed through me, and I instinctively pushed away from her, landing with a grunt on my butt several feet away.

It *couldn't* be Vincentia.

Couldn't be.

She was under the rule of the red knife. It was impossible for her to have left the defined boundaries of their home and prison. The magic simply would not have allowed it.

"Bethany?" Sgott said urgently. "What's wrong?"

I swallowed to ease the dryness in my throat and somehow said, "I think it's Vincentia."

"Impossible."

"Yeah, I know, but here we are."

He swore. "Don't touch her. I'll get Frankie up here to record the scene and then we'll roll the body over."

Frankie, if I remembered rightly, was one of the wolf shifters who worked for Sgott. I nodded, even though he'd already disappeared back down the ladder to make the call, and slowly rose. I didn't look at the body of the woman who might well be my cousin, moving instead over to the old wood heater. The Codex remained in the flue's hidden compartment. Now that I was closer, I could feel the pulse of its presence through the Eye.

I left it where it was, walked over to the skylight, and peered up. Clouds drifted slowly across night, concealing stars that were rarely visible thanks to the city's light pollution. It was a necessary part of life in any city, big or small, thanks to the Annwfyn.

A soft, scratchy sound had my gaze snapping to the left edge of the skylight. I couldn't see anything up on the roof, of course, and for too many minutes the sound was not repeated.

Another couple of scratches, closer to the skylight this time. It sounded for all the world like the scrape of tiny claws against the slate. Not rat claws, but rather bird. It wasn't likely to be an owl, and most of the other night-loving birds tended to be migratory and not really about in winter.

Which meant we more than likely had a shifter on the roof.

I hesitated, tempted to just jump up there and confront him or her, but common sense got the better of instinct for a change. I walked across to the loft ladder and squatted down.

"Sgott," I said softly, "have you got anyone on the roof?"

He glanced up sharply. "There's someone up there?"

I nodded. "A shifter, I believe. It's not making enough sound to be human."

He immediately made another couple of calls. Two men were dispatched from the lane and a bird shifter called in. Whether any of them would be in time to catch our intruder was debatable, given he was already on the move.

Footsteps vibrated through the floor below. Sgott's people appeared, one of them Frankie. Cynwrig wasn't visible, but I knew he was in the kitchenette. I hoped he was putting the kettle on. Or, better yet, readying a dram or two of whiskey.

I moved back to allow Sgott's people room to climb in, then walked back to the open skylight. There were no repeats of the scratching on the roof, and I had no way of knowing if our shifter remained up there. Grand old oak beams might support the roof structure, but the slate was a dead zone. If he didn't make a noise, I wouldn't hear him.

"Ms. Aodhán," Frankie said. "Would you mind coming over to ID the body?"

I jumped slightly, then nodded and walked over.

"You ready?" she said, when I stopped a few feet away.

I crossed my arms and nodded. She and another woman rolled the body over onto her back.

It *was* Vincentia.

She'd been stabbed multiple times. There were wounds all over her chest and across her stomach, suggesting she'd been the victim of a murderous frenzy rather than a controlled and deliberate action. There was blood on her clothing, blood on the floor where she'd lain, but no further spread, suggesting the killer had indeed used some sort of containment bubble.

There was also nothing to suggest she'd been taken by surprise. Nothing to suggest—at least from where I stood —that she had in any way fought back. Which was odd, because if they'd been close enough to stab her, she'd have been close enough to use pixie control on them. Had the restrictions on her personal magic held even if the boundary ones had failed? Or had her murderer been an elf and therefore immune to control?

That was likely, given the Looisearch were all elves—at least as far as we knew—but that didn't explain the lack of defensive wounds. At the very least, there should have been slashes across her hands, arms, and even legs. If someone had come at *me* with a knife, I could sure as hell guarantee I'd be kicking the bastards long before they got within chest-stabbing distance.

"Bethany?" Sgott said softly. "Is it her?"

I sucked in a breath and tore my gaze away from the bloody mess that was her body. "Yes."

He grunted. It was an unhappy sound. "I'll ring the pixie council and see how the hell she escaped the red knife's restrictions. It shouldn't have been possible."

"Unless she was never officially placed under the knife. She was in hospital when Lugh and I handed down the council's judgment, remember."

"She was under guard. If she'd escaped, I would have been informed."

"Except the Looisearch seem to have fingers in every pie, so maybe there's been a deliberate delay in telling you."

"I wouldn't have thought so, but I'll check." His phone rang, and he answered it. After a few minutes, he growled, "Fine. Remain up there and keep an eye out, Joode."

I walked over. "I take it the person on the roof has gone?"

"Yes, though I suspect he or she hasn't gone too far. The problem with all these fucking old buildings is there's too many damn places for a small shifter to hide."

I smiled. "Which is why you have rat shifters on the team."

"Yes, but that doesn't mean I have to be happy about the other side having them."

I laughed, as he'd no doubt intended. "I guess not. Do you need me up here anymore?"

"No, you can come on down."

I climbed down, then walked across to the kitchenette. Cynwrig didn't say anything, he just wrapped his arms around me and hugged me for what seemed like forever. Then he stepped back and gave me a whiskey.

The man was definitely a keeper.

Shame that I couldn't.

I took a sip of the whiskey and moved over to my chair to sit down. He followed, propping on the chair's arm then draping his arm around my shoulders.

"Did they find the Codex?"

"No."

"That's something."

"Yeah."

I remembered the banner bag and looked around. It wasn't sitting where I left it, which most likely meant our skylight escapee had grabbed it without looking inside. I would have loved to have seen their faces when they opened the damn thing.

"The thing I don't get is, why kill Vincentia?" I took another drink. "Surely the fact she could catch my thoughts when she was close should have made her a valuable asset."

"Doesn't the red knife prohibit all contact?"

"Yes, but thoughts aren't contact."

"Depends on the definition placed on the word when they placed the restrictions, I'm thinking. The pixie council were aware of the link you formed when you magicked her, so it's possible they included it."

"Maybe but that still doesn't explain why they killed her."

"I suspect *this* might have something to do with it," Sgott said.

I glanced around and saw that he was holding what

looked to be a piece of paper in an evidence bag. "What is it?"

"A warning. To you."

I held out a hand, and he grimly gave it to me. The handwritten letter was short and sweet. *Give us the Eye or she won't be the first to die.*

I frowned. "Why on earth would they demand the Eye and then kill the one person who could have used it for them?"

"Your aunt can use it, can she not?" Cynwrig asked. "The red knife might block her ability to hear wood song or to leave her property, but it would not inhibit psi talents."

"Using the Eye is more than just a psi talent, though, and my aunt knows that. Besides, why would she want to help the very people responsible for maiming—and now killing—her daughter?"

"I think it likely Riayn blames you for that rather than her daughter's less-than-optimal choice of employer," Sgott said.

Given Vincentia had never been able to do any wrong in my aunt's eyes, that was possible. "That doesn't negate the stupidity of her murder—or why they'd still want the Eye when they can't use it. Riayn is being watched, remember. They wouldn't be able to access her without permission."

"Maybe they intend to destroy it rather than use it," Cynwrig said.

"That makes no sense. Not when it's basically the only hope anyone has of finding the remaining Claw."

"Have you any other relatives who could use the Eye?" he asked. "Someone who might be sympathetic to the Looisearch's cause?"

"No one direct, but they'd have to kill both me and my aunt first before that even became a possibility." I offered him the bagged note. "I don't suppose you recognize the writing?"

He took the bag and carefully studied the note. "It could be Rosin Morrisa's. He has the same sort of flourish when finishing words."

"Is he in any way connected to Seryn Morrisa, Vincentia's contact?"

"Husband."

"Who has, of course, also disappeared, right alongside his wife."

"Got it in one." Cynwrig handed the note back to Sgott. "I'll head back to the compound and reinterview their kin. One never knows, they might have something new to say."

The compound in question was called Dorcha Dearg. It was the main Myrkálfar encampment in the area and situated on—and in—the Peckfort Ridges to the west of Deva. Though I'd never been there, I'd seen plenty of photos of the weighty but wondrously exotic buildings that ran the length of the ridge. It had become something of a tourist attraction over the centuries, although most folk were constrained to a viewing platform some distance away. Very few were given permission to enter the external buildings, and even fewer were allowed underground.

Someone who had somehow gotten inside—in more ways than one—was my grandmother. She'd not only regaled me with stories of how incredibly light and beautiful the underground areas were but had also extolled the benefits of having a dark elf lover. And she certainly hadn't been wrong about that. Of course, whenever I'd mentioned that dark elves never allowed outsiders into their inner compound, she'd laughed, patted my knee, and said it depended on who you asked and how sneaky you were.

I suspected that no matter how prettily I asked the man

sitting next to me or how sneaky I was, I would never get to see Dorcha Dearg's inner light.

"Surely even their closest kin wouldn't be that willing to risk prosecution—or your wrath—to protect them."

"My wrath will never match the need for revenge, or the sympathy it engages." He shrugged, a movement I felt across my shoulders more than saw. "Remember, we Myrkálfar have suffered more than most when it comes to the dark gates, as we are not only the gate monitors, but the only ones capable of closing them down after a break-through."

But not capable of closing them *permanently*. The fracture between our worlds seemed to prevent it, although no one was sure why.

It was why the Looisearch had gone after the Claws. The death of Morrisa's daughter had been one death too many.

"This is the first time there's been a concerted effort to do something about it though," Sgott was saying.

Cynwrig glanced at him. "Yes, but we are not mages, and that means there has to be a greater power behind this plot."

"Ah, the ever-mysterious puppet master who somehow sees all, knows all, but reveals fuck all about himself." I wearily rubbed my forehead. It had been a long day and I was starting to get a headache. "It's damnably frustrating not knowing even the slightest bit about him. Or her, as the case may be."

"Every villain makes a mistake eventually," Cynwrig said. "Especially when they're getting desperate, as these people appear to be."

"Not sure where you get that idea," I grumbled. "Right

now, from where I'm sitting, they seem to be at least a couple of steps ahead of us."

"We have some of their names, we have the mother of the daughter they just killed, and we have something they want—the sword," Cynwrig said. "They will come after it and when they do, we'll get them."

"I like the confidence with which you say that." I yawned and then grimaced. "Sorry, it's been a long day."

Cynwrig squeezed my shoulder gently then downed his drink and rose. "I'll head back to the compound and start organizing the interviews."

"Let me know if you uncover anything new," Sgott said.

"Indeed." Cynwrig bent and dropped a sweet kiss on my lips. "You should get some sleep. I'll ring you in the morning."

I watched him walk away then returned my gaze to Sgott. "I need to speak to Aunt—"

"You can't. Ring your brother and warn him of the threat."

"I will. And if I approach the council and explain—"

"If you approach the council, they might hand down their judgment for your actions with Vincentia."

"She's now dead, so it shouldn't matter."

"Her being dead won't change a thing and you know it."

I scrubbed a hand through my hair. "Aunt Riayn isn't going to talk to anyone else."

"And she's *definitely* not going to talk to you. She revoked your kinship, remember."

"That was before Vincentia was murdered. I believe it'll change things."

Sgott snorted. "You have far more faith in your aunt than I do."

"And perhaps I'm stupid for doing so. Doesn't change

the fact that I need to at least try."

He sighed. "I have to contact the pixie council to request permission to go see your aunt and break the news about Vincentia's murder. I'll make a plea on your behalf as well."

"I'd appreciate that." And if it was an official request from the IIT, they might be less likely to hand down their judgment on the spot. "But why face-to-face? Can't you just tell her over the phone?"

"It's not the sort of thing you can do over the phone. I dislike the woman, but she deserves to hear this sort of news in person."

There was a part of me—a very minor, but still very angry part—that thought she actually didn't, but I held my tongue. There was enough bad blood between me and her. I didn't need to be adding to it.

"Are you staying here," he added, "or heading over to Lugh's?"

"Would it be a problem if I stayed?"

"Not if you can sleep through all the noise, but we'll be here for a good few hours yet."

I nodded. "Can I repair the stairwell doorframe before I fall into bed? Or do you need to dust it for prints or something?"

"I think—given the fact her killer obviously employed some form of magic to prevent arterial spray—the only prints we'll likely find is that of a boot when they kicked the door open, so feel free to fix the frame."

"If they were using a containment bubble, they should have just magicked open the fucking door." I drained my whiskey and rose. "You'll lock up when you leave?"

"I won't be leaving until you wake, lassie. As Cynwrig said, you still have something they want, and I'll be doing my best to make sure they don't get it. Or you."

I smiled, walked over, and kissed his bristly cheek. "You're the best stepdad I could have ever asked for."

"You are a darling girl," he said softly, "as dear to me as my own blood."

I knew that. I'd always known it.

I smiled and headed downstairs to make repairs. Once back up in my room, I lightly wove the door and frame together, just on the off chance someone got past Sgott and all his people, then tried to ring Lugh. He wasn't answering, so I sent him a text, then stripped off and fell into bed.

And once again dreamed. Not just of that lake and its unholy treasure chest, but of a hand reaching into a storm and drawing forth the sword.

If the dreams were to be believed, we were running out of time.

I was running out of time.

And I wasn't entirely sure whether that meant death had already fixed her hungry eyes on me, or it was just a warning that she lay in wait if I wasn't very careful.

The sharp ringing of the phone woke me. I fumbled around for the thing on the bedside table, then pried open an eye to glare at the screen.

Lugh.

And it was barely six.

I hit the answer button and said, "You'd better have a fucking good reason for ringing at this ungodly hour, brother mine."

"You're usually awake at this hour, so don't be getting all grouchy at me, especially if you've spent the better part of the evening sexing rather than sleeping."

"I only spent half the night sexing. The tavern was broken into again last night, and Vincentia was murdered."

"*What?*"

"Yeah, and the latter came with a warning to me."

"I saw the text you sent, but you forgot to mention the warning was found on her body."

"Sorry, but I figured that sort of news was better said in person." Or at least over the phone.

He grunted. Whether that was in agreement or not, I couldn't really say. He and Vincentia had never really been close, thanks to the age gap between them. "The threat was obviously aimed at me, but it isn't the first time my life has been put on the line, and it won't be the last. They'll learn soon enough that we Aodhán pixies are rather hard to kill."

That was apparently the result of a godly blood infusion given to both the Aodhán and Tàileach lines when we'd been tasked with protecting the old gods' relics. The same blood had also given both lines our height.

But it hadn't saved Mom.

And it certainly hadn't saved Vincentia.

"Killing her makes no sense, though," Lugh was saying. "She's the one decent link to us that they had."

"From what I saw, it was more a murderous venting of fury than a planned death."

"Which means we must be getting close to them, and they're started to panic."

"I think you're reading too much into their actions."

"Maybe. Did they take anything?"

"Yeah, the banner bag containing your hiking poles. But they were up in the loft looking for the Codex."

"Why on earth did they think it was up there?"

"Because it was."

"But how did they know that? And how did they even

find—" He paused then answered his own question. "Vincentia."

"She must have remained connected enough to the Codex after I performed the ceremony to feel its presence when she was close."

"I take it from the lack of panic in your voice that they didn't get it?"

"No."

And that suddenly struck me as odd. If she'd been able to sense its presence in the loft, she should have been able to pin its location.

So why hadn't she?

Had she realized the danger she was in? Had she finally seen past the urbane veil most elves wore and realized that no matter how useful she was to her employers, she would in the end be rewarded with nothing but death?

Possibly. Vincentia had been many things, but she certainly had never been dumb.

"It does mean you're probably not safe to remain alone at the tavern," he said. "If they're getting desperate, they'll keep hitting it until they get what they want."

"I don't get *why* they're desperate, though. Winter is drawing to a close and Annwfyn crossovers usually decrease over the spring and summer months." I threw off the bedcovers and padded over to the door to unmesh the wood. "Besides, wouldn't it make more sense to simply lay low until some of the investigative heat dies down?"

"Grief makes people behave in strange and sometimes incomprehensible ways," he said.

I guess it did. I mean, here I was, absolutely refusing to grieve for my mom until her killers were caught.

"In the meantime," Lugh continued, "maybe you should move in here for a few weeks. It'll be safer."

"Not if they hire more dwarves to tunnel in."

He laughed. "I got Morris to ramp up the protection spells. Neither a dwarf nor indeed a dark elf will break into this place now."

Morris was a local witch locksmith who ran a profitable sideline on protection spells. He was responsible for the spells that currently protected the tavern, including a recent addition that rejected any attempt at fire-bombing. Which wouldn't stop someone setting the place alight from the inside, of course, but they did first have to get in.

"Won't me moving in cramp your style?"

"I have no style to cramp."

I snorted. "Yeah, I know, but not through lack of trying on Darby's part. Did you see her last night?"

"I did, and things are progressing nicely."

My eyebrows rose. "Is that a polite way of saying you finally had sex with the woman?"

I could almost see him rolling his eyes. "Normal sisters would not ask such a question of their brother."

"I'm not a normal sister, and Darby will tell me if you don't."

He sighed. It was a very put-upon sound. "Fine, yes. And yes, it was bloody fantastic, and yes, I should have acted on her advances far earlier."

I whooped. He gave another one of those sighs. "Can we just drop the whole matter now and let me enjoy my fledging relationship with her without getting the third degree from you every other second?"

"Sure. But you didn't answer my original question."

"No, it will not cramp my style, because the walls are soundproofed. It might cramp Darby's style, though."

I laughed. "Darby's a light elf. They don't have any hang-ups when it comes to sex."

I knew *that* for a fact, having spent ten years with Mathi.

She was also from the forester class of elves—which was basically the middle class in the three tiers of elven society and included professions such as medics and arborists—rather than highborn. From what I'd seen over the years, they tended to marry for love far more. Their reputation for straying once married wasn't as fierce, either.

Which was a relief, even though I was well aware she would never do anything to emotionally hurt him or me. It just wasn't in her nature.

"It's sorted then," he was saying. "Do you want us to come and pick you up?"

Meaning she was still there. I couldn't help my delighted grin. "No. If I don't do the accounts today, the staff and suppliers won't get paid, but I'll give you a head's up when I'm on my way."

"That won't be necessary," he said, voice dry. "I do have to work today, remember?"

"Oh yeah. Say hello to Eljin for me."

"Why? Aren't you seeing him tonight?"

"Yes, but we've been away for five days, and he might have forgotten our date."

Lugh snorted. "So just ring the man and confirm."

"I do not want to come across as desperate."

He did that eye-roll thing again. I still couldn't see it, but it was definitely happening. "Fine. Talk to you when I get home."

I said goodbye, then tugged on my sweatpants and a wooly sweater and headed out. Sgott was making himself a hot drink but turned as I appeared. "Coffee or tea?"

"Tea, thanks. How did things go? Did you find any useful evidence?"

"A few fibers, a couple of dark hairs, and a solitary footprint in the blood that isn't Vincentia's."

"So, we have a possible lead in the hair?"

"If we can find a DNA match on file, yes, but that's not always guaranteed with dark elves."

Because they had centuries of experience when it came to avoiding the law. "No murder weapon, I take it?"

"No, but we did find a partial message."

"Really? What sort? Another threat?"

"It wasn't a threat, and it was written in blood."

My eyebrows shot upwards. "*Seriously?*"

He nodded. "We discovered it under Vincentia's body. It's been smeared, either by her weight or by her attacker, but we can only make out a couple of letters—EIN."

"The name of the person who killed her, perhaps?"

Or, better yet, the name of the person behind the Looisearch?

It was probably too much to hope for, but hope I did.

"Hard to say. Forensics are going to see if they can sharpen the image."

"Fingers crossed that they can."

"Indeed." He made my tea then poured his coffee into a travel mug, then added, "I'd best be going. I need to write up the reports before I head to a meeting with Ruadhán later this morning."

"You don't want a toastie? I'm just about to make some."

"I'm good. Thanks all the same, lass."

Once he'd left and the toasties—baked beans and ham, which was an abomination according to my brother, who preferred the more traditional, and in my opinion more boring, ham and cheese—had been made, I put everything onto a tray and headed down to the office to start doing the accounts.

The tavern's crew came in an hour or so later and started preparing for the day. It was close to two when Ingrid popped her head around the door.

"Mathi is here to see you—shall I send him away?"

I leaned back in the chair and wearily rubbed the back of my neck. "No, it's fine. We're friends these days."

She snorted. "Light elves ain't ones to keep females as friends unless they're still fucking them, and I thought you had more sense than that."

I grinned. "Oh, he definitely wants back in, but it's not going to happen."

"Good, but I'll keep within shouting distance in case he decides to get handsy."

She obviously wasn't going to believe he was capable of behaving himself, so I simply said, "Thanks."

She nodded. "I'll let him in, then."

"You locked him out?"

"Saw him approaching from the lane when I was down in the storeroom." She shrugged. "Didn't want him in here hassling you unless you were warned and ready."

I laughed. "Good to know you've still got my back."

She nodded and headed back down to the ground floor to let him in. He appeared a few minutes later but didn't step all the way into the office—it was a tiny space, and even though he fell more on the lean and sinewy side rather than possessing Cynwrig's magnificent mass, by light elf standards he wasn't exactly small, either.

He crossed his arms and leaned casually against the doorframe, his golden skin and hair contrasting sharply against the darker wood. He was wearing a sweater the same summer blue as his eyes, but rather than his usual crisp black pants and shiny shoes, he was in jeans and well-worn brown leather boots. While I'd always loved it when Mathi went for a more casual look, I knew he only ever did so when there was "less than savory business" at hand.

Which sometimes meant nothing more than a trip to one of the many forest plantations the Dhār-Val family owned. They were one of the largest silviculture businesses in the UK thanks to their formidable ability to manipulate the energy of flora to triple its growth rate. Mathi, despite the fact he was the son of a second son, was the group's director, thanks to an uncle who'd retired some eight years ago without male issue.

Of course, sometimes jeans and old boots meant darker deeds were afoot. The Myrkálfar might have the reputation for criminality, but the Ljósálfar were hardly angels despite the fact they looked like them.

"Good to know that some things never change," he said, warm voice amused. "Ingrid still hates me."

"Don't feel maligned. She hates most light elves."

"Then why work here, in a place that is favored by the foresters?"

"We pay good wages," I said. "It makes up for her having to deal with your lot on a regular basis. Why are you here, Mathi?"

He raised a pale eyebrow and somehow made the motion look sexy. "Aren't I allowed to visit an old friend?"

"In the middle of the day and dressed like that?"

He laughed, a sound that ran warmly down my spine. I might have broken up with this man, and I might want nothing more than friendship from him, but my hormones still hungered for his touch.

My hormones needed to be bitch slapped.

I mean seriously, they not only had Cynwrig to play with, but the possibility of a very eligible pixie on the horizon. They needed to get over the past.

"I admit it," he said, "I'm here to ask a favor."

"What sort of favor?"

"One that could be beneficial for us both."

The twinkle in his eyes suggested he knew exactly where my thoughts immediately went, but I didn't bite. "Meaning?"

"Meaning, I have a lead on Aram, and I believe we should go investigate it."

"'We' meaning my knives rather than me."

"Given your knives cannot wield themselves, you are just as important as them."

"Good to know where I stand," I said, voice wry. "And in case you need reminding, the last time we went after Aram, his office exploded, we were almost killed by the blast, and his remains were subsequently found in the burned-out shell."

"It wasn't his body. The autopsy came back this morning and confirmed it."

"Has Sgott been informed?" Surely if he had, he would have said something—although maybe that was what the meeting with Ruadhán was about. "And your father is breaking all sorts of rules by sharing that information."

He shrugged. "As you said, that blast almost killed us. He understands my need to track down the perpetrator. Which reminds me—did Nati ever contact you about the blue dust sample you asked her to trace?"

Tracers like Nati—who was a friend, even though we hadn't caught up for a couple of years—could not only analyze and unpick the spells connected to both gold and blue pixie dust, but also trace its origin. Which wouldn't give us a name, but there were only two lines who used the dust, and each bloodline had specific magical tells. It was a starting point, and better than nothing.

"No, I actually forgot all about it."

"Too busy spending time with Cynwrig, I suppose." It was evenly said but there was an annoyed light in his eyes.

"No, I was in Scotland trying to get rid of the goddamn sword."

"You didn't tell me that."

"Because you and I are no longer an item, and even when we were, you had no need or right to know all my movements."

He sniffed. It was a disparaging sound. "The four of us —five if you count Darby—are a team, remember? We're supposed to be sharing information so we can find the Claws and bring these people down."

Most people would have called them bastards, but Mathi, like most light elves, considered swearing to be the purview of the coarse and uneducated. He'd spent a good part of our ten years trying to wean me off the habit, with little success.

"True. Sorry."

"No, you're not."

I grinned and didn't deny it. "Did they manage to ID the body?"

"It was Peadar Bhàsa."

"Who is?"

"Jalvi's husband."

Shock rolled through me. "Has Cynwrig been informed?"

"I would imagine my father has done so by now." He shrugged. "Cynwrig or indeed his family are unlikely to grieve for the man."

I frowned. "Peadar was kin by marriage—"

"And his *kin* almost killed his sister. He *will* seek revenge. He is not what he appears on the surface, Bethany."

"No elf is," I said dryly.

"I am, of course, the exception." A smile teased his lips. "On the surface, I'm a virile and extremely sexy manwhore, and that's exactly who I am underneath."

I snorted and shut down the computer. "I will grant that you have a little more depth than that."

He gave me a mock bow. "I am honored that you think so."

I rolled my eyes. "Where are we going?"

"Earl's Court in Curzon Park."

Which was a very posh area on the other side of the river. Rogan lived there, but I wasn't sure if it was Earl's Court or not. He wasn't only secretive when it came to his love life, but just about everything else outside of work.

Of course, he *did* live for work. More so than Lugh, in fact.

"How can a second-rate mage afford to live in a place like that?"

"He wouldn't have been employed by the Looisearch if he was second-rate."

"Not true, given the quality of some of the thieves they've sent against me."

"I suspect they were underestimating you. I also suspect they are no longer doing so."

I suspected he was right, especially after last night's events. Sgott might have found some trace evidence, but they'd gotten in and out very quickly, despite finding time to murder Vincentia. That suggested they were—for the moment, at least—doing their best to avoid another confrontation with me.

It wouldn't last. I felt that with every inch of my being.

"I take it there's no official record of him owning this posh place, so how did you—or your father—learn about it?"

"An informant." He shrugged. "More than that, I do not know."

"A trusted informant? Because the suspicious part of my brain is instantly thinking trap."

"My father said the source was reliable."

"So why isn't he sending his people over to check it out?"

"Because I expressed a desire to investigate." Though his expression didn't change, ice crept into his eyes. "They have tried to kill me twice. There will be no third time, Bethany."

I believed him. I also believed that the Looisearch would never face the courts or sentencing. Not the legal courts, anyway. Cynwrig and Mathi were one in that aim, even if Mathi hadn't yet admitted it.

I pushed to my feet. "I'll have to go upstairs to grab my coat and keys. You can stay here."

"I have no intentions of seducing—"

"And tonight, the moon will fall from the sky and never rise again."

His smile was decidedly wicked, and my pulse rate did its usual dance. "One day, you will give in to the fire that remains between us."

"You just can't accept the fact that I was the one who made the break, not you." I made a shooing motion. "Back away so I can get out."

He made a somewhat aggrieved-sounding sigh—which

was muted by the glimmer in his bright eyes—and obeyed. I ran up the stairs, hastily collected my knives, coat, and a credit card in case I needed money, then grabbed my phone and sent a quick text to Lugh. If there was one thing I'd learned over the past few weeks, it was that I needed to let people know where I was going. If things went wrong—and they often had—then at least they'd know where to start looking.

I clattered back down the stairs and met Mathi at the bottom. "Are we walking over there?"

"In this weather? You jest."

I glanced toward the front windows in surprise. Though they were protected by the first-floor row, it was absolutely pelting down in the street beyond.

"I had no idea it was even raining."

"That's what you get for having your eyes glued to a computer screen half the day."

"It's called work, Mathi. You should try it occasionally."

He grinned. "I was there yesterday. They don't need me there today."

I rolled my eyes and waved him on. "Lead the way then."

"A gentleman never walks in front of a lady."

"Given I'm no lady and you're no gentleman, that shouldn't be a problem for either of us."

He laughed, and we headed out. His driver was waiting at the rear door with a couple of umbrellas, so the dash to the car wasn't as wet as it might otherwise have been.

The traffic was light, so it didn't take us all that long to get across the river. Earl's Court was a wide, leafy street filled with a mix of old and new housing stock, with those on the right side of the street possessing million-dollar views over the park and river.

Aram's place was a handsome, red-brick period townhouse on the river side of the street. There were no cars in the driveway, but the electric gates were open.

Mathi's driver pulled to a halt on the opposite side of the street and, after telling him to wait in the car, Mathi climbed out. I hastily followed suit, tugging up my coat's hood as I ran across the road after him.

"So we're just going to walk up, bold as brass?" I said.

"Skulking around in posh neighborhoods is never advisable, as it tends to be noticed. Far better to act as if you belong."

"And you do."

He glanced at me, eyebrow raised. "I do not have a house here. You know this."

"Yes, but you are posh. More so than me, anyway."

"Ah. True."

I nudged him. He laughed and pressed the doorbell. The chime echoed for ages but drew no response. He stepped back and motioned me forward. I pressed my fingers against the doorframe and lightly connected to the building's fabric. The song was surprisingly faint, and it took more effort to slip deeper into the stream and catch the information about the building's fabric. I couldn't hear anything unusual in the echoes coming from the two floors above us, but the ground floor and the basement—if there was one, and most buildings this age did have them—were basically dead zones. I wasn't entirely sure why, but usually when the music was so faint, there were two main causes— ill care, or renovations that involved the original flooring being ripped up and replaced, thereby breaking the connections within the building's fabric.

"There's no one moving about on the top two floors," I said. "But I'm not getting anything useful on this level."

He motioned me to step back, then retrieved his lock pick from his wallet and went to work. He had the door open in quick time—one of the skills he'd learned while hanging around the various crims being processed at the IIT in his youth, apparently.

He ushered me in and then closed and locked the door behind us. The entrance hall was a good size, with high ceilings, dark slate floors, and light gray walls. A large abstract painting adorned the far wall above the stairwell that wound down, and there were two doors, one to the left of the stairs and the other up a couple of steps to our right.

I walked over and pressed a hand to the frame, but the wood's song remained muted.

"Still nothing," I said. "But if anyone was here, surely they would have come to investigate."

"Your knives? Any response from them?"

"None at all." Which was odd if this place did belong to Aram. Given his business dealings weren't exactly above-board, surely the first thing he'd have done was protected the place he lived.

"Let's go check the basement first, and we'll work our way up from there."

I nodded and followed him over to the stairs, placing one hand on the banister as I walked down. The wood wasn't particularly old, and its music was strong but forlorn, thanks to the fact it had no real connection to the wood in the rest of the house.

We headed down into the darkness, the gentle hum of a refrigerator audible over our footsteps—mine rather than his. Elves tended to walk so lightly that even on gravel surfaces they made little to no sound. As we neared the last step, I dug out my phone and switched on the flashlight, sweeping it across the shadows. The room was long but not very wide. There was a washer and dryer along the wall to our right and, down the far end, a fridge and a couple of chest freezers. Cupboards and shelves lined the remaining wall.

"Nothing here," Mathi said.

"Nothing obvious here," I corrected. "But that freezer is overly large for a man who lived alone."

He glanced at me, amusement evident in his bright eyes. "Have you been watching too many horror movies again?"

I grinned. "Bodies are always found in freezers like that. You know this."

"Not in this neighborhood."

I raised my eyebrows. "Those living in posh neighborhoods probably have more skeletons in the closet than the rest of us. You're a prime example."

"There're no skeletons in my closet. Might be a few buried under other properties though."

Part of me suspected he wasn't kidding, despite the twinkle in his eyes. "A gentleman would do the right thing and just check."

"You're going to harp on this until I do it, aren't you?"

"I am."

"Why? Is intuition kicking in?"

"No. I just want to be sure something doesn't crawl out of it and chase us up the stairs."

He rolled his eyes, then walked over, flipped the freezer latch, and dramatically thrust the lid up.

And froze.

"Don't tell me," I said, voice dry. "We have a body."

His gaze came to mine, and my amusement died.

"Not just any body," he said softly. "But Aram himself."

CHAPTER FIVE

"How can you be sure it's him?"

"I've seen the file the IIT have on him."

Meaning Ruadhán had once again ignored legalities and given his son access. Which really shouldn't have surprised me, given Mathi was his only son. I shoved my hands into my pockets and walked over.

Aram had been a large man, with russet-colored hair and blue eyes that were wide and starey, matching the shock that was now forever frozen onto his face.

He'd known his killer, I thought. Trusted him.

"He was hit from behind and placed in here not long after his death," Mathi said. "He's also been in here for at least four or five months."

My gaze shot to his. "How can you tell?"

"For a start, the back of his head has been caved in, and it was still bleeding when he was shoved in here. Then there's the freezer burn on his extremities."

"He can't have been dead that long," I said, doubt evident in my voice. "He only broke into the tavern last week."

"We won't have a proper ID until an autopsy is done, of course, but if this *is* him, then it was someone else at the tavern."

Someone who was very good at magic. "Kaitlyn hired him, though, and she would have seen through any sort of concealing spell."

Kaitlyn was a half-elven broker of goods and services, some legal, but most not. She ran an antique shop over on Falkner Street, and she and I had clashed after Aram and his crew had stolen a moonstone from me.

"He was working with the Looisearch, as was Maran Gordon," Mathi was saying, "and *she* specialized in body morphing and concealment spells, remember."

"Yes, but no matter how good the concealing spell, they all have one flaw—they only work well if you're dealing with someone unfamiliar with the person you're impersonating. From what I could gather, he was one of Kaitlyn's regular contractors."

"If she dealt with him on a professional level, she might not have noted any inconsistencies in his personal behavior."

I guess. Plus, if he had been killed and replaced by someone he knew and trusted, that person was probably familiar enough with his foibles to get by, short-term.

I rubbed my arms, chilled more by the thought of a murderous acquaintance than the air.

And I could only hope like hell *that* wasn't second sight delivering a sly warning.

"I suppose it's pointless searching the rest of the house," I said. "Whoever did this wouldn't have hung around, even if he did steal Aram's identity."

"If he wanted to maintain cover, he might have had to."

Mathi pulled out his phone. "Why don't you do a quick check upstairs while I call my father?"

I nodded and returned to the entrance hall, first checking the door next to the stairs—which turned out to be a cloakroom—before moving into the kitchen-living area. It was a large, open, and very modern space featuring lots of grays—not to my taste at *all*.

I continued to explore, finding a snug, and then an office that held little more than a chair and a desk. I tugged a sleeve over my hand and quickly checked all the drawers, but all I really found—aside from the usual assortment of pens, paper-clips, and random single staples—was a stack of bills, the last of which had been paid back in September. If Mathi's conjecture about the time of Aram's death was right, this bill might have been the last one Aram had dealt with before his death.

What there wasn't was a computer, modem, diary, or anything else that came with running a business from home. Granted, Aram had had an office in Elsmoot, but it was rare for someone who was self-employed not to keep at least *some* records at home.

Did that indicate this house had been a rarely used bolt-hole? Perhaps someplace he could lie low until ill winds had blown over?

Maybe, though our discovery downstairs suggested that at least one enemy had known about this refuge.

I moved up to the next floor. There were three bedrooms and a bathroom here, and none of them appeared to have been used. There were no personal items on the bedside tables, no clothes in either the drawers or the closets, and there was a stale mustiness in the air that came with the stillness of a locked-up, poorly ventilated house.

I continued on to the loft, expecting to find more of the same. Instead, I found chaos. The bed had been stripped, the mattress pushed off the frame and resting at a wonky angle against the rear wall. The wardrobes tucked in under the roof line had all been opened, their contents pulled out and either smashed or thrown in untidy piles all over the floor.

This wasn't untidiness. There was too much destruction here to be mere untidiness. This was someone searching for something.

I pressed a hand against the doorframe, but the wood held no echoes of what might have happened. But then, wood song very rarely held on to memories of events unless they had impacted them directly.

I picked my way through the mess, heading for the bed at the far end, but was barely six feet in when I found the bloodstain.

It wasn't large, but the size and shape of it matched the wound on the back of Aram's head. I scanned the surrounding mess but couldn't see a weapon. There wasn't even a blood trail, and there should have been if Aram had been carried down to the freezer almost as soon as he'd been killed. Maybe the killer had somehow staunched the flow of blood long enough to get him downstairs—though why he or she would bother given they obviously hadn't bothered concealing the fact this room had been searched, I couldn't say.

This mess might explain why there was no laptop or other records down in the office, though, and even why Aram's office had been blown apart. Our spellcaster obviously had something his killers had wanted.

The question was, did they find it?

I stepped around the stain and continued on over to the

bed. The pillows had been tossed across to the window, and the lamp had been swept off the bedside table, and I rather suspected both were done in fury.

Whoever had murdered Vincentia had also possessed a temper—did that mean they were one and the same person? It was possible. More than possible, really. Coincidences did happen, but not all that often.

I carefully opened the top drawer, which was as empty as the ones in the office, although this time it was due to the fact the contents were on the floor. It was actually surprising the drawer remained in place—why bother doing that when everything else had ended up thrown out of the way? I checked the other drawer in this unit, then tugged my sleeve over my hand again and did Lugh's trick, checking the back for hidden things.

Sadly, I didn't find a lever to open a secret door, but I did find an envelope. It had been taped to the back of the bedside table, and unless you physically reached past the back of the actual drawer, you wouldn't have discovered it.

I carefully pulled it free, my pulse rate accelerating. Nothing had been written on the front or the back of the envelope, but it had been sealed. I carefully slid a nail underneath and opened it. Inside was a neatly folded, single sheet of paper.

The soft song of the floorboards underneath my feet altered their cadence slightly. I looked up as Mathi appeared in the doorway.

"The IIT will be here in five minutes." His gaze dropped to the envelope. "You've found something?"

"Aside from this mess and a bloodstain on the carpet between the bed and the door, this was stuck to the back of the bedside table."

He skirted around the stain without really looking at it and stopped next to me. "What is it?"

"I haven't had a chance to look yet." I carefully tugged the paper free and then unfolded it. Inside was a small black-and-white photograph.

"Whoever took this certainly wasn't a photographer." I turned the photo around in an attempt to figure out what it was. "Is that a person? In front of a gravestone?"

Mathi plucked the image from me, got out his phone, and took a picture. After giving me the photo back, he enlarged the image on his phone.

"It was definitely taken in a graveyard," he said, after a moment. "You can just make out a couple of other gravestones behind that first one."

I peered closer at the original but couldn't see anything more than a couple of darker blobs. "Why would he have kept something like this at the back of the bedside table?"

It wasn't like you could see the figure's face, as he had his back to the camera, and there certainly wasn't anything identifiable about his clothes or body. If there was some sort of memoriam on the gravestone, it wasn't visible in this image.

"It has to be of some value to his killer, otherwise this room would not have been torn apart."

"Presuming this is what he was after, of course." I wrinkled my nose. "I don't suppose you recognize the graveyard, do you?"

"The Ljósálfar do not bury their dead in such grim places."

"No, but I dare say you've buried a few non-elves in them."

Amusement warmed his eyes. "Possibly, but it's not one

I recognize. It looks too unkempt to be Deva's main center, though."

"It does." I turned the photo around. A date had been written on the back, and there was a series of numbers underneath. I had no idea what the latter were.

"That date at least explains the photo's condition," Mathi said. "The photographic stock they used back then tended to degrade rather badly over time."

"What about the numbers underneath? Any idea what they might be?"

He shrugged. "Could be an old phone number or coordinates or anything, really."

"If it was coordinates, wouldn't they have used a directional marker, such as north, east, whatever?"

"Not if they're using degrees, minutes, and seconds."

"Huh." I stared at the numbers for a few seconds, but enlightenment didn't happen. "I wonder if the date is of any importance?"

"I can't remember anything significant happening in that year, but I'll run a check through IIT's records and see what I can find."

I glanced at him, eyebrows raised. "*You* will?"

He grinned. "I've long had access to my father's computers. He's aware, of course."

"And does this access have anything to do with the bodies you mentioned earlier?"

"Of course not."

"Liar."

He smiled and didn't deny it. "We'd better head back down. The IIT will be here any minute now."

He'd barely said that when the wail of approaching sirens broke the silence.

I grabbed my phone, took a quick shot of the front and

back of the photo, and then carefully tucked it into the envelope and gave it to him. It was pointless putting it back where I found it, as our fingerprints were all over it.

As we headed down, the IIT were coming through the door. I let Mathi deal with them and sent a text to Sgott, letting him know what we'd discovered. He'd no doubt get an update from Ruadhán, but he'd be less annoyed at our breaking-and-entering actions if I was upfront about it.

By the time our statements had been taken, nearly an hour had passed. The rain had eased to a drizzle, but the day had definitely gotten colder. Mathi opened the car's rear door, ushering me in before slipping in next to me.

After directing his driver back to the tavern, he shifted in the seat and said, "What's your next course of action?"

I wrinkled my nose. "To be honest, I'm not sure. We need to deal with the sword, but we also have to find the ring."

"Is it truly wise to be searching for it now? Would it not be better to put that search on hold until the Looisearch are found?"

"They won't stop looking even if we do."

"The only reason they found the first two Claws is Vincentia. They've quite literally erased *that* advantage, so unless they can find another Aodhán pixie to do their dirty work, they're stuck."

"If they get stuck, they'll come after me, Mathi."

"There are enough of us to prevent you getting kidnapped again."

I hoped he was right, but I suspected he wasn't. I forced a smile. "I can't quit now, Mathi. Would you?"

"My position is somewhat different to yours. I'm an annoyance to them rather than a viable asset. They'll not kill me unless it is absolutely necessary, simply because they know such stupidity will bring the full wrath of my father and the IIT onto them. And *he* does not have the same views on the law and punishment as Sgott."

Something I'd always suspected, but it was still rather shocking to hear it said out loud.

"The longer the search is drawn out, the more dangerous it becomes," I said. "Hiding won't alter that fact."

"Hiding would be sensible, and we all know you often suffer a lack of that." Despite his wry tone, his expression was surprisingly serious. "I don't want to see you dead, Bethany."

I couldn't help smiling. "Only because you'd have no chance of getting back into my bed if I were."

"You cut me to the core."

Which wasn't an actual denial.

As the car slid to a halt at the top of the lane that ran down to our tavern, I said, "You'll contact me once you know anything about the photo or get confirmation of our victim's ID?"

"Only if you promise to keep me similarly updated."

"I will."

He nodded. "Remain vigilant. Don't be taking any undue risks."

I resisted the urge to kiss his cheek goodbye—old habits were surprisingly hard to shake—and climbed out. Darby rang as I started walking toward the tavern.

"Hey," I said. "Congrats on finally getting Lugh into bed."

There was a slight pause. "*He* told you? I'm shocked, given the riot act he read me about saying too much. Well, riot act might be too dramatic, but you know what I mean."

I did. "I know exactly which of my brother's buttons to push. Glad he's finally woken up to the good thing you are."

"So am I." I could hear the laughter bubbling through her voice. "Not sure how much longer I could have hung around waiting for the man to get a clue. What time are you coming over?"

"I've still got stuff to do at the tavern, so I'm not sure yet. Why?"

"I need to know whether to make dinner for two or for three."

"I have a date with Eljin tonight, remember?"

"I obviously hadn't, but excellent news all the same." She paused, and I could almost hear the wicked wheels turning. "So, is tonight the night you sex that man senseless?"

I laughed. "Depends on how well the dinner goes, I'm thinking."

"Given you've already met the man for coffee and for after-dinner drinks, you must have some idea on whether he's a worthwhile pursuit."

"You make him sound like a piece of meat."

"Cynwrig's the meat, and a juicy piece he is too. But while dark elves are sexual heaven, they will never be long-term. Eljin, however, is a very different proposition."

Very true. "There's definitely chemistry between us, but I'm torn between taking it slow and jumping into a relationship feet-first, so to speak."

"As someone who has suffered through an extremely long build up to a relationship, I suggest feet first all the way."

I laughed. "I wasn't intending to string him along for years, just a few weeks."

"Why?" she asked bluntly.

"I don't know."

"You do. I know you do."

I sighed. It was pointless lying to her when she'd known me for so long now that she could tell a lie sight unseen, from just the sound of my voice.

"I jumped straight into a relationship with Mathi and I'm doing the same thing with Cynwrig. I just thought maybe it would be better to take a different path with Eljin."

"Again, why? *When* you have sex doesn't matter in the long term. What does is whether you're compatible in bed *and* out. You might as well enjoy yourself, my friend, while you're discovering the latter."

"True enough, I guess."

"Then go out there and fuck that man so senseless he won't even think of bedding the many other desperate pixie women hunting him down."

I laughed again. "I'm thinking you just don't want me home too early this evening and spoil your seduction plans."

"I'm thinking more of your brother. He's still adjusting to an elf's lack of modesty and inhibitions."

"I'll ring the doorbell when I'm coming in, just to give you—or rather, him—fair warning."

"Excellent. But if you're here before midnight, I will be very disappointed. And you're not to spend all that time simply *talking* to the man. I mean, you're an Aodhán pixie. Get it together, woman."

And with an evil sort of laugh, she hung up.

I shoved my phone away, punched in the rear door's keycode, and headed into the tavern. Ingrid glanced around as I entered the main bar. "There was a woman in here looking for you earlier."

"Who? Did you get her name?"

"No, but she was short and very untidy looking. Seemed to have a bird nest in her hair."

I grinned. It could only be Beira, and she probably did have a nest. She was certainly well past caring what we mere mortal folk thought of her.

"Did she leave a message?"

"No, but she muttered something about you needing to pay more attention to the wind and that she would be back."

Which would undoubtedly have been said in a threatening manner. Beira didn't have much patience for politeness. "Thanks. I'll see if I can contact her, but if she happens to drop by again, tell her I'm staying over at Lugh's for the foreseeable future."

She nodded. "Probably wise, given what's happened upstairs and everything else that's been going on. I'm surprised Mathi didn't offer his bed, though."

I laughed. "I daresay he would have, had he even the slightest hope of it being accepted."

Ingrid's grin was a toothy thing. "You keep that determination. You deserve better than the likes of him."

Yes I did, but right now, the supply of good men definitely outstripped demand. Which reminded me... I glanced at my watch. It was close to five, which gave me just over two hours to get ready for my date.

Plenty of time.

I really, *really* should have known better than to tempt fate like that.

I was halfway up the stairs when the Eye surged to life, its pulse of power so fierce and unexpected that I stumbled, hitting my knees hard on the next stair nosing. I swore, pushed back up, and somehow made it the rest of the way up the stairs before the force of the vision became so strong, it picked me up and washed me away.

To where was a question I couldn't answer. There was nothing but darkness and a vast unending feeling of emptiness. And yet this place was not uninhabited. There were forces here, forces that were both of this world and not. It reminded me a little of the confluence and perhaps even the library, both of which existed in a place beyond ours, but there was a fiercer energy here, and it was one that spoke of the unbridled fury contained within storms.

I received your message.

The voice was low but thunderous, as sharp as the crack of lightning and yet as soothing as summer rain.

This was the master of all storms. The being who stood above all the other gods and goddesses whose elements were the wild winds and weather.

You are a godling rather than a full blood, it continued. *You will never fully house that which you can call down. Your flesh is not strong enough.*

Which is basically what Beira had already said. *Then why was I told to seek the confluence if control was never possible?*

It was said perhaps a little too sharply considering who —what—I was facing, but I was getting a little sick of being sent on useless quests.

Especially when my own were going nowhere fast.

The word impossible never entered my vocabulary. Curb your impatience, young godling.

I didn't reply. The last thing I needed was to be booted back into reality before I got any sort of answer.

It will be no easy road you undertake, and it will be dangerous. This I understand you have already discovered.

I certainly had. If not for Beira leeching the heat from my body, my insides would have boiled away.

The answer will lie in using a conductor to both call down and disperse the storms.

But how do I disperse it? I asked. *Why does the heat of lightning remain within me even after I have redirected its force elsewhere?*

As one of flesh, you would need to be earthed, otherwise that which has not been dispersed will remain within.

How do I earth myself? Is it simply a matter of being barefoot, or is it more involved than that?

Being shod or not will make no difference, and you already possess the means with which to earth. Practice, young godling, and never call down more than you can safely disperse.

With that warning ringing in my ears, I fell back to the real world, finding myself on the floor and shaking so hard my teeth rattled. I drew my knees up close to my chest and hugged them close, trying to slow my breathing and ease the painful pounding of my heart.

It took what seemed forever.

Eventually, I pushed upright and walked over to the kitchen to pour myself a large whiskey. It burned all the way down, but I definitely felt better mentally, if not physically, afterward.

I glanced at my phone to see how much time had passed and swore loudly. Conversing with the master of storms might have seemed to have taken only a few minutes but I now had less than twenty to shower, dress, and get over to the restaurant where I was meeting Eljin.

I was, needless to say, late.

The Grill was one of the newer restaurants to enter the already fierce battle for Deva's dining elite, and its twist was using wild and farmed meats and goods from within the region. It was yet another one I'd been meaning to try and hadn't gotten around to, although it wasn't necessary to book months in advance, as you had to with some of the more established ones these days.

The maître d' took my coat, handed me a ticket, and then led me through the warmly lit room decorated in rich woods and deep greens.

Eljin rose as we approached, his gaze slowly skimming my length and coming up appreciative. Darby's words had definitely been ringing in my ears when I'd chosen this outfit. Though the dress was a simple silk the same frosty green as my eyes, it lovingly skimmed my curves before gently falling to my feet. The appearance of modesty, however, was voided by the high splits either side that were only a couple inches away from being indecent. But in this lighting, it didn't matter.

"You made it." His voice held just enough of a French accent to be sexy. "I was beginning to wonder if I'd been stood up, despite what your brother said."

The maître d' pulled out the seat opposite Eljin. I smiled my thanks, tucked my dress underneath me, and sat down. "And what did he say? I dread to think, especially after all the years I've spent attempting to set him up with my best friend. He sees your arrival as an opportunity to get some revenge."

Eljin's laugh was warm, rich, and decidedly sexy. "He has no need to push me into dating you, Bethany, and I would hope you feel the same."

A smile teased my lips. "You do know there's a dearth of eligible pixie males in Deva, don't you?"

He laughed again. "Yes, and it has made for some interesting conversations."

"Women throwing themselves at your feet?"

"Twice, in fact. The machinations have been fascinating." He leaned back in the chair, the soft light behind him setting his longish mahogany hair ablaze. "It would not be an understatement to say some have been far more blatant about what they wish to do with me than others."

"And do you find women who are forthright about their wants a turn-off or turn-on?"

"Oh, definitely the latter." He paused, the darker specks in his golden eyes making it appear as if they were flickering with heat. "What about yourself?"

"I'm afraid I'm not into women, so if you're having visions of a ménage à trois, you're going to be disappointed."

His smile was decidedly rakish. "Not a thought that had crossed my mind."

"Happy to hear that."

The waiter reappeared with menus. After a brief discussion, we decided on a lovely pinot noir and then ordered our food. The waiter collected the menus and disappeared again.

I leaned forward and crossed my arms on the table. It was a position that revealed perhaps a little too much of my breasts, but if I was worried about showing too much skin, I certainly wouldn't have chosen a dress designed for seduction. If the hungry gleam so visible in his lovely golden eyes was anything to go by, it was definitely working.

"How was your first day at work? Did Lugh give you any guidance, or did he drop you feet first in the thick of things and walk away?"

Eljin smiled. "Would it surprise you if I said the latter?"

"Not at all."

He waited until the waiter had opened our bottle and

poured our drinks, then added, "Monsieur Rogan is an odd man, don't you think?"

"He's very dedicated to the museum, to the detriment of all else."

"Obsessive," he said, with a nod. "Has there been some trauma in his past?"

"Not that I'm aware of," I said, a little surprised. "Why?"

He hesitated. "I mentioned, did I not, that my sister had second sight?" When I nodded, he continued, "While I unfortunately don't possess that particular gift, the men of our line do have the capacity to 'read' people. Its strength works to varying degrees, depending on who is being read, but it generally allows us to get some sense of their past, their dreams, their character, and their motivations. In Rogan I sense a great sadness, one that he has never recovered from."

"You couldn't tell what caused it?"

He hesitated, frowning a little. "He lost someone, but it was a long time ago. I wasn't close enough long enough to feel out more."

Interesting. "So, it's a form of telepathy?"

"Nothing as concrete as that. Your thoughts and your mind are perfectly safe from me."

"But not my body, I would hope."

His eyes gleamed and he raised his glass. "May that which already sings between us develop into something exceptional."

Amen to that. I lightly clinked my glass against his. "What do you read about me?"

He didn't immediately answer, but his gaze burned into mine and became a little unfocused.

"There is a fierceness within you that is almost otherworldly, something rare and beautiful, but seen by too few." His gaze deepened, drawing me in, making me feel like I was drowning in a shimmering pool of gold. "You hunger for answers but also fear them. You want what you cannot have, and you are haunted by sadness that remains unacknowledged. You also fear that you will never be as strong or as happy as your mother once was."

Which was a fucking accurate reading. Almost scarily so.

He blinked and refocused. "How did I go?"

"It was a little too close to the bone, in many respects."

He raised an eyebrow. "Why so?"

"I barely know you, and yet you have the inner me pinpointed almost perfectly."

His slow, sensual smile had desire trembling through me, though it was perhaps accompanied by a touch of nervousness. Which was weird, given I'd had no such reaction with Cynwrig, and he definitely *had* been a stranger when I'd fallen into bed with him. At least Eljin and I had taken the time to know each other first.

"Perhaps," he said softly, "we could take a step or two toward solving that inequity tonight?"

I licked my lips a little nervously, a movement his gaze followed, and then nodded.

He smiled again and the conversation moved on, flowing easily over dinner and dessert. It was close to ten when he leaned back in the chair and said casually, "Do you wish coffee here, or would you like to come back to my place and have a nightcap?"

He was giving me an out if I wished one. I didn't.

I nevertheless pretended to think about it for a couple of seconds first. "A nightcap would be lovely."

He immediately motioned for the bill, and once it had

been paid, we collected our coats and headed out into the blustery night.

"Can you walk in those heels, or shall we catch a cab?"

I smiled. "Walk. It's not that far from here, presuming you're still in the same apartment."

"I am, because I've not been able to find something that suits my needs as well." He shrugged lightly, a move that was somehow elegant and sensual. "I have in fact approached the owner with an outrageous offer, and I'm currently waiting to hear if they've accepted it."

He caught my hand and we casually strolled along the street, Deva alive and noisy all around us and yet having little impact on the comfortable bubble of silence that surrounded us.

His apartment was the penthouse suite of a lovely old red-brick church that had retained all its beams and original windows when it had been converted into five apartments a few years ago. It was located within walking distance to the river and the museum, and also happened to be close to the tavern.

Which would be handy for both of us if things progressed as I hoped.

Eljin punched in the door code and then led me up the chrome-and-glass staircase to the top floor. Once inside, he took my coat and hung it in the closet.

"Would you like a coffee, sherry, or port?"

"Port, please."

"Excellent choice." He smiled, pressed a hand against my spine, and gently ushered me into the main room. It was a large, double-height expanse, with the lovely old oak trusses painted white to give the room an even airier feeling. Their song, though muted, was rich and warm, a consequence of being one of the few churches that had undergone major renovations without major destruction. On the street side of the building there were two beautifully simple stained windows and, at the other end of the room, a compact but well-equipped kitchen. Beside this was a chrome-and-glass staircase that wound up to the loft bedroom.

"I can see why you want to buy this apartment," I said. "It's truly beautiful."

"But not as beautiful as the woman who now stands within it."

"Smooth," I said with a smile.

"But true, nonetheless."

He raised my hand to his lips, kissed my fingers, then released them. "Please, take a seat while I make our drinks. Would you like some music?"

"Yes." I sat down on one of the two-person sofas and crossed my legs, revealing an indecently long length of leg.

His gaze slowly skimmed upward, then rose to meet mine. He knew, as I now knew, how this night would end.

While he put on some music—something soft and bluesy—I sent a quick text to Lugh, telling him not to worry if I didn't appear tonight. He knew I was with Eljin, of course, but better to confirm the fact I was safe than having him worry I'd been kidnapped after dinner or something. Darby did not need her man distracted when she'd only just snared him.

He handed me a port, then sat down beside me, close enough that his left leg pressed the length of my right. I couldn't help but wish it was skin-on-skin contact and that we were doing more than merely pressing thighs.

We sipped our drinks slowly and chatted about all manner of inconsequential things. Once the glass of port had been finished, he took it from me, placed it on the table, then rose and held out his hand. "Dance?"

I smiled and let him pull me to my feet. He slipped a hand around my waist and pulled me close, his body warm and hard against mine as we slow-danced around the room. It was both exquisite and torturous, and by the time his hand finally slipped to my rump and pressed my crotch against his erection, I wanted him more than I'd wanted any other man in my life.

Except, perhaps, for Cynwrig, but that was to be expected. He was a dark elf, after all. Animal magnetism was an essential part of their nature.

I tilted my head upward, an unspoken invitation to be kissed, and he obliged. For very many minutes, there was nothing more than a gentle dance of mouths and tongues, teasing, tasting, and exploring.

Eventually, he slid his fingers back up my spine and undid the dress's zip. Then he slipped his fingers under the shoestring straps and slid them from my shoulders. The silk shimmered to my feet, and I stepped free. Aside from my stilettos, I was naked. Eljin didn't move, but his gaze consumed me, the heat of it prickling across my skin, leaving me breathy and wanting.

Then he sighed and, with a soft "Magnifique," silently undressed. He was, as expected, also magnificent, his lean body perfectly muscled and without an ounce of fat.

He caught my hand, pulled me close once again, and we continued to dance, our bodies pressed close, heated skin sliding easily—wantingly—against heated skin. For the longest time, we did nothing more. It was a seduction unlike any I'd ever experienced before, and it was as glorious as the man.

When he finally whispered, "Are you protected against pregnancy," I was slick with wanting.

"Yes, I am." It came out husky, thick with need.

"Then shall we take this dance upstairs?"

"I believe we should."

His smile was that of a cat who was about to consume all the cream.

And consume he did.

It was glorious. Utterly, mind-blowingly glorious.

Needless to say, I didn't make it back to Lugh's that night.

But I did dream.

CHAPTER
SIX

I SAT UPRIGHT IN BED, MY HEART A FIERCE DRUM THAT reverberated through the silence and a scream dying on my lips.

Eljin was holding my hand, speaking words I didn't understand, words that nevertheless sounded both soothing and concerned.

I drew in a deep breath and scrubbed a hand through my tangled hair. "Sorry. Didn't mean to scare you like that."

"That is of no concern," he said, switching to English. "I take it you dreamed?"

I nodded. "Oddly, I can't remember of what."

"Is that unusual?"

"Very."

"Then perhaps it was nothing more than the unspoken worry of sleeping in an unfamiliar bed with an unfamiliar man."

It was teasingly said, meant to draw a smile, and it did. "I hardly think you could be called an unfamiliar man. Not now."

"It is indeed a truth that our explorations were very

thorough." His smile remained warm, but concern nevertheless dominated his expression. "Would you like a drink? Perhaps a cup of tea to soothe your nerves?"

"That would be lovely. Thanks."

"Wait here, then, and I shall prepare it."

He slid off the bed and padded naked down the stairs. As he rattled around in the kitchen, I cupped the Eye and felt the answering flicker of energy roll through it. No visions rose, but I could feel the lingering ghosts of one haunting the outer edges of my mind. They were filled with an odd sense of betrayal, a warning to be careful, but of who or what, I couldn't see.

I sighed, released the Eye, and then rose. According to the clock on the bedside table, it was close to five, so I might as well get up. There was, after all, a sword to destroy and a ring to find, and I couldn't laze about in bed with a sexy man, as enticing as that always was.

Eljin glanced up as I appeared. "Seeing as we're both now up, would you like something to eat? Perhaps a croissant? Or some crusty bread and cheese?"

I nodded and perched on the stool, watching him prepare a small platter of fruits, cheeses, and bread to share. "You do know that if you keep treating me this well, I might not want to leave."

"How do you know that isn't my exact plan?"

I smiled. "There is another man in my life."

"I would be surprised if there wasn't." He paused. "Serious?"

"No, but fun."

"Meaning I have my work cut out for me."

"Indeed, you have."

"Excellent. I shall make it my mission to lure you away from him."

I laughed, though there was a light in his eyes that said he wasn't joking. "May the best man win, then."

"Oh, he will," he said, with all the confidence of a man who had just sexed a woman senseless.

I smiled but didn't reply. While I could easily envisage spending a lifetime with Eljin after only one night, a long road remained ahead for us. And I had no intention of giving up Cynwrig until I knew for sure my heart—and Eljin's—were a match.

We chatted easily over breakfast, shared a shower and another glorious session of sex, then we got dressed and he walked me back to the tavern.

His kiss goodbye was long and lingering, filled with promise and warmth. "Ring me soon?"

I smiled. "Yes, though I have stuff to do with Lugh and another date with the competition."

"Ah, but the competition obviously isn't a pixie, given the previously mentioned dearth of them, so I have no doubt my wiles will eventually become more alluring than his."

"His wiles are pretty damn impressive," I said with a grin.

"Then I will need to up my game. Call me tonight?"

When I nodded, he stepped back, blew me a kiss, and walked away, his hands in his coat pockets as he whistled a cheerful tune.

I smiled and headed inside, only to discover Beira waiting for me.

"Well, it's about fucking time you showed up." Her voice was guttural and unpleasant, absolutely nothing like the dulcet tones I'd always imagined goddesses would have.

She was also dwarf short, but slender, with sharp

brown features and an aura that echoed with the ferocity of a storm threatening to break at any moment.

And there was *definitely* a bird's nest in her wiry gray hair this time round. I had to stop myself taking a closer look to see if there were any inhabitants.

"Sorry," I said evenly, "but the last few days have been rather hectic."

She harrumphed. "If you have time to satisfy carnal urges, you have time to take the calls of an old woman."

"You have something against carnal urges?"

"Only when they prevent you hearing me."

"I've heard the wind raging, but I couldn't hear your voice in her. Unless, of course, that raging was you, and if so, you need to calm the fuck down and speak a little slower. I'm new at all this, remember."

She muttered something about inconsiderate young-sters and followed me over to the bar, perching on one of the lower stools designed specifically for dwarves and small pixies. They were the magical equivalent of gas lift chairs, and automatically adjusted the height of the stool to the size of whoever sat on them. They were high maintenance, thanks to the need to regularly replenish the spells, but they kept the customers happy, and that was the main thing.

I poured a triple whiskey and slid the glass across. She accepted it with a nod and quickly downed it. "Now that eases a few aches. More exist, however."

I took the hint, refilled her glass, and left the bottle on the counter so she could help herself. "So, what was so important that you were screaming into the wind at me?"

"You pulled your punch up on the mountain and now you must deal with the consequences."

I frowned. "I didn't pull any—"

"You let him live."

I stared at her. I knew the gods had a bloody bent, but still... "I'm not going to kill someone just because they get in the way."

"Then you will pay the price, now and in the future. That wasn't a mere weather witch you faced at the confluence but rather a storm mage. One with the ability to seek what storms hide."

I frowned. "I didn't think there were any true mages left."

There were certainly plenty who used the name as a means to signify their superiority over "common" witches, but true mages were born within the elements they controlled and were in truth neither human nor a god, but somewhere in between.

"They are rare finds here in England," she replied, refilling her glass one more time, "and I don't believe this one is element born. But his skills are nevertheless as strong as any true mage, and you will not best him in a straight-out battle. Not at the moment."

"Well, thanks for the confidence."

"I'm not here to mollycoddle but to impart realities."

I snorted. Beira and mollycoddling were not two words I would ever have used together. "It does at least explain the dream I had of a hand reaching into my storm to claim the sword."

"If you're dreaming that, he's too close to the sword for comfort. You had best destroy it, as you were supposed to."

"Which is a hard thing to do when you don't know how. You gods aren't exactly forthcoming with information, you know."

"You have the Codex. You don't need anything else."

"The Codex library is also somewhat lacking when it comes to specific details."

"You can't be expecting us to be doing all the leg work for you. We wouldn't be needing your help if that were the case." She drained her glass then slipped from the stool. "There're too many eyes following me these days, so I'd best be going. You need to stop fucking around and get that sword destroyed."

"Yes, ma'am," I said, with a light salute. "Immediately, ma'am."

"Don't you be sassing me, young woman." Lightning crackled through her aura, but its threat was tempered by the amusement dancing in her eyes.

I watched her walk out, then recapped the whiskey and headed upstairs. The door remained off its hinges, and the living area held a decided chill. I did a quick check to ensure no one lay in wait, then headed into my bedroom, exchanging my coat, dress, and stilettos for much warmer clothes. After filling up the kettle and readying the teapot, I went up into the loft. I might not have been able to remember last night's dreams, but the fear of them combined with Beira's dire warning sure as hell said I'd better concentrate on doing something about the sword.

Once in the loft, I retracted the ladder and then shoved the bolt home to ensure no one could reopen the thing from below. With the stairwell door in pieces, this was probably the safest place now to be using the Eye—especially when the Eye tended to sweep away any awareness of my immediate surroundings.

The section where Vincentia had been murdered remained taped off, with Mom's chair a forlorn island in the center. Fingerprint dust covered the various books, shelves, and the skylight winder, but the log fire remained untouched. I walked across to the wood heater and retrieved the knives and the Codex. My fingers tingled when I touched the latter, and the Eye pulsed in response. There were visions to be had.

I walked over to the cushion-adorned sofa that dominated the wall opposite Mom's chair. After Gran had bought her own place, I'd spent many an afternoon up here on this lovely old leather sofa, propped up on those same cushions, reading books or watching movies on my computer. And sometimes Mom had come up during her breaks, and we'd sit here, reading and enjoying each other's company in comfortable silence.

Gods, I missed her. Missed her tuneless singing in the mornings and her warm laughter drifting up from the bars at night. Missed the kisses she dropped on my cheek when bidding me goodnight and the random hugs she gave for absolutely no reason at all other than it being a chance to say how much she loved me or how proud she was of me. Tears stung my eyes, and I blinked them fiercely away.

Once I started to cry for her, I would not stop.

I grabbed a cushion to clean away the layer of dust that now covered the leather, then sat cross-legged with the cushions behind me, supporting my back, in much the same manner as I had all those years ago. My gaze rose to Mom's chair again, and I could almost see her there, her wavy red hair shining in the lamplight, her lovely features glowing with pleasure as she reread one of her favorite romances.

This was why I didn't come up here much anymore. There were too many memories. Too many ghosts.

I blinked again, then placed the knife and Codex onto my lap. I'd already gotten what information I could from the Codex's otherworldly library, so it was probably better not to visit it again—especially given the librarian's warning that overuse—or overstaying—could be dangerous. But the triune was designed to work in unison, so maybe having the Codex and knives close when I was using the Eye would help me control the direction of the vision.

It wasn't like I had anything to lose by trying. And while Lugh said he'd run a search, he obviously hadn't found anything, as he hadn't yet gotten back to me about it.

I fixed the images I'd seen in the Codex—a malformed limestone rock formation that rose high above the edges of a disused quarry and the jagged slit in the cliff face that sat behind it—in my mind, then wrapped my fingers around the Eye, holding it tightly enough to ensure the stone touched skin despite the cage. The Eye pulsed in response, the jagged lightning that cut through its center sending a bright beam of purple shooting past my fingers and across the room. It was something that hadn't happened before, and it reminded me a little of a lighthouse beam, one that was seeking rather than warning.

Then the room disappeared, and I was spun into another place—one that was lush and green, filled with red-tiled rooftops on one side and patchwork fields on the other. Dividing the two were ribbons of white interspersed with random dots of greenery. The image wheeled closer, and I realized it was the quarry I'd seen in the Codex. Which was no real help at all, other than confirming that what I'd seen in that place did actually exist in this. I frowned and tried shifting my focus to an area that looked to be a viewing platform close to the crooked and rather twisted limestone column.

Once again, the vision shifted so abruptly it made my head spin. Then I was staring at a sign that not only named the rock formation—The Devil's Chimney—but gave me a brief history and an actual location.

Using the triune in unison had goddamned *worked*.

The elation was short-lived, however, because the minute I released the Eye, the trembling hit. I rested my head back against the sofa and spent several seconds breathing slow and deep in an effort to control my erratic heart rate.

Would using the Eye ever get easier? Had Mom ever suffered this sort of aftereffect?

It was both sad and annoying that I just didn't know. While I did understand her decision not to teach me about the Eye and its use until there was a solid indication my second sight *would* develop, that reluctance was now costing me dearly.

Of course, she hadn't exactly foreseen dying so early, either. If she had, why would she have gone alone into the tunnel where betrayal and death had found her?

Maybe the nature of your own death was something those gifted with second sight were incapable of seeing. If that were true, then maybe the sacrificial death *I'd* seen might not be mine.

Of course, given that I was apparently using the Eye in a very different manner to Mom, it probably was.

I sighed, picked up the knives and Codex, then rose and walked back to the ladder. I was just about to unlatch it when I heard a soft noise downstairs.

I froze for several seconds, but the noise, whatever it was, was not repeated. I knelt and pressed one hand against the floorboards. The rich timbre of their song flooded my mind, and it took several seconds to swim through its wash and find the thread I needed.

Someone moved through the room immediately beneath me.

Someone who had somehow gotten past Ingrid and the kitchen staff without challenge.

It didn't feel like either Cynwrig or Mathi. Aside from the fact that neither had reason to be here, they would have called first, given they were both aware that I was temporarily shifting to my brother's. They'd also have announced their presence as they came up the stairs. As much as I kept needling Mathi about his seduction intentions, his manners would never allow him to enter a lady's home or indeed bedroom without invitation.

Of course, once given, it was all bets off.

But it wasn't Darby or Lugh, either. The wood song would have acknowledged my brother's presence, given he'd spent a good part of his life here.

I tucked the Codex behind a nearby crossbeam, then dragged out my phone and sent a quick text to Sgott, explaining the situation and asking if he still had people watching the place outside.

His response was quick and to the point. Stay put, his people would be there in minutes.

Relief was fleeting. The ladder made an odd sound, and it took me a minute to realize someone had pressed the release switch downstairs.

Thank *gods* I'd slid the latch across.

I pressed my fingers against the floor again. The stranger stood directly below me, and though I couldn't see him, I had an odd sense that he—or she—was staring up at the ladder, as if willing it to unfold.

Then my knives came to life.

He wasn't willing the ladder down. He was magicking it.

I dragged my knives from their sheaths. Light flickered down their lengths, but it wasn't particularly fierce, suggesting the spell caster fell more to the "light" rather than the dark. But that was neither here nor there, given that up until this point, the knives had really only reacted when the magic would cause me harm in some way.

Obviously, the witch below *didn't* intend to share a cup of tea and a quick chat.

I quickly took off my slippers to maintain skin contact with the floorboards, then I placed one knife against the edge of the latch to stop the magic sliding it back and the other against one of the hinges. As long as I kept a hinge and the latch in place, the ladder would remain exactly where it was, no matter what the caster tried.

For several seconds, nothing more happened, then the knives flared and there was a brief, sharp retort that almost sounded like a gunshot. A foul, almost eggy scent started staining the air, catching in my throat and making it burn. I somehow stopped the urge to cough, not wanting to confirm my presence up here even though he or she pretty obviously knew where I was.

The burning moved down my throat, hitting my chest and making it difficult to breathe. I couldn't stay here and keep breathing in this muck. It would end badly if I did.

As I pushed upright, I heard the footsteps.

On the roof.

Fuck.

My gaze jumped to the other side of the room. Was the skylight shut? Had it properly locked? The wire dangled rather than being secured to the crossbeam, but Sgott's people wouldn't have known what it was there for simply because Sgott wouldn't have known it was necessary.

Why the fuck hadn't I thought to check it myself? Especially given I'd known they'd already used it as an exit if not an entry point.

The wood song altered, telling me several people were now running up the stairs from the ground floor. Sgott's men, I presumed, which meant the witch down below would soon be dealt with.

What Sgott's people wouldn't know about was the person on the roof.

The cough finally escaped, and it was so damn bad it left me dizzy and gasping. The pulsing in the knives sharpened, as did the scent of foul eggs.

Move, instinct said. *Now.*

I left the knives where they were and thrust up, my footsteps vibrating through the floorboards but not loudly enough for anyone other than a pixie to hear. The person below wasn't a pixie—none of us were capable of regular magic—and wouldn't know I'd moved. Unless, of course, I coughed again.

The noxious scent eased the farther away I got from the loft ladder, and though my throat still burned, breathing became less difficult.

The stranger on the roof had reached the skylight and stopped. I hurried over... just in time to see the flat edge of a crowbar appear between the frame and the sash.

I glanced around and spotted the rarely used metal fire poker leaning against the wall behind the skylight. I hurried over to grab it, keeping out of the shifter's direct line of sight. The poker was decades old, as heavy as fuck, and had—according to Gran—been designed more as a weapon than a poker. When I'd asked if she ever had used it as designed, she'd simply given me an inscrutable sort of smile. But its placement close to the dodgy rear skylight rather than the wood heater certainly suggested intent if not actual use.

The skylight opened, and the crowbar angled across the corner edge, presumably to prevent it being closed. I hefted the poker and waited for the stranger to appear.

He didn't.

Not in human form, anyway.

As the night-dark feathered form arrowed in, I swung the poker hard. And missed.

The momentum behind the blow was enough to spin me around and throw me off balance. A second later, something thumped into my back and sent me flying.

Somehow, I managed to keep hold of my weapon as I flailed the other arm to keep upright. The shifter was on my back, tearing at my clothes and skin with talons and a needle-sharp beak that dug into my neck and shoulders. I swore and reached back with one hand, trying to wrench it free, only to get bitten hard enough to draw blood. It shifted shape, wrapped an arm around my neck, and then hit me in the solar plexus hard. As my gut spasmed and pain rolled through me, the arm disappeared, and the needle-beak was pecking at my neck again.

I tried to swear; couldn't. Couldn't even breathe really. But I nevertheless threw myself back, trying to crush the shifter against the wall. At the very last minute, it flew upward, out of the way.

I swung the poker again, and this time, it scraped across the shifter's underbelly, sending black feathers flying and drawing blood. It flew high into the rafters, dripping blood as it circled around, and then snapped its wings closed and arrowed down. I hefted the poker and waited.

At the last possible moment, it flicked a wing, changed direction, and went for the skylight.

"Oh no, you don't, you bastard."

I lunged forward, grabbed the dangling cord, and yanked the skylight down. The crowbar prevented it from fully closing but it didn't matter. The shifter crashed into the glass hard enough to crack it then fell in a heap onto the floor.

Its form shimmered, rolling back from bird to human form, revealing a small, thinnish woman with hair that initially looked black but had a shimmer of purple and green when she moved. A common starling rather than a blackbird shifter.

I pressed the poker against her stomach. "Move, and I'll fucking break both your arms."

She stared at me, her eyes glazed and sweat popping out across her forehead. Shock, I thought, which was no real surprise given she'd crashed into the glass hard enough to not only mash her nose, but also split her mouth open.

I warily stepped closer and then, when she made no move to attack, bent and gripped her hand. She automatically tried to pull free, but I held on tight.

I called to the pixie controlling magic and said, "You will answer all my questions honestly and you will not move until I tell you to. Understood?"

She licked bloody lips and nodded. Her gaze was unfocused, suggesting if I didn't hurry up, she'd be unconscious.

"Why were you sent here?"

"I was to question you about the location of the Eye and relieve you of it if it was here."

"How were you meant to question me?" Few shifters were telepaths, so she couldn't have read my mind. Even fewer were magic capable. "As shifters go, you're on the small side, and unlikely to overwhelm me physically."

Although she almost had.

"I was supposed to fly in and dart you once you'd gone to bed."

Which meant whoever had told her about the broken skylight latch didn't truly understand the deep connection pixies had with manufactured wood. No matter how easily she had entered the loft, she couldn't release the ladder without attaining human form, and her sudden weight on the floorboards would have altered their song enough to alert me.

"Then why use the gas?"

"I didn't."

"No, but your friend downstairs did."

"I have no friend. It was a solo contract."

Then who the fuck was the mage downstairs? Hopefully, Sgott's men had caught the bastard. The knives were no longer reacting, and the wood song was a confused mess right now thanks to the number of people down there, and while I could sort it out, it would take deeper immersion, and I simply didn't have the time. Or the inclination, to be honest. Either he'd been caught, had concealed himself, or scarpered, and no matter what option he'd chosen, Sgott's men were more than capable of dealing with it.

I returned my attention to my prisoner.

"Who gave you the contract?"

"Kaitlyn."

Which meant either the stupid bitch obviously *hadn't* taken the warning to broker no contracts involving me or Lugh to heart or the payment terms were simply too high for her to ignore. Either way, she needed to be dealt with ASAP. As much as I'd have loved to have been personally involved in that, she was half elf, and therefore immune to my controlling magic.

But there were other ways to mute someone.

Sgott might not be so inclined—he was the IIT night chief after all and restricted legally with what he could actually do, even if Ruadhán seemed to have no such qualms—but there were other means of making someone listen. One of those was to threaten the thing they held most dear.

In Kaitlyn's case, that was her business and her reputation. I might have only met the woman once, but it had been pretty obvious in that short space of time just how vital both were.

And while Lugh did have some "gray" contacts who could possibly make life hard for her, Cynwrig's family basically controlled a good chunk of the black market. It was unlikely he'd destroy anyone's livelihood on my say so, but the Looisearch had made the fatal mistake of attacking his sister. If he realized Kaitlyn was still accepting contracts from them, she wouldn't know what had fucking hit her.

In fact, it was surprising she hadn't already faced his fury, but maybe Sgott had warned him off.

"Have you taken any other contracts regarding me recently?" I asked. "Have you been tracking my movements from on high?"

"No. My contract was for this specific job, nothing else."

Someone banged on the top of the ladder, the sound reverberating, making me jump. "Ms. Aodhán? It's Harry Preston—I work with Sgott. We've met."

His voice matched what I remembered, although that didn't mean anything in a world where electronic and magical modulators existed. "What happened to the mage?"

"Gone."

"Are you sure? Because it's possible he used some sort of

concealment shield to get in here. He would have been stopped before he got near the stairs, otherwise."

"No matter how good light and dark shields might be, they can't conceal scents. He went out the window as we were coming up and ran along the Row's roof to escape."

"You couldn't track him any further?"

"The rain was heavy enough to disperse his scent, and that makes tracking more difficult."

I glanced up and saw the raindrops dancing across the skylight. Could feel the rumble of thunder in the distance and the electricity held within in. It was a little surprising I hadn't noticed earlier, but then, it wasn't like I'd had a whole lot of time *to* notice. I glanced down at my captive. Her eyes were beginning to roll back. "You'd better call an ambulance. I've an injured intruder up here."

"Will do. You need to open the loft so we can assist you and deal with your captive, Ms. Aodhán."

"Just give me a couple of seconds to make sure she can't escape." To my captive, I added, "What were you supposed to do once you got the location of the Eye?"

"Retrieve it if possible."

"And give it to Kaitlyn?"

"Yes."

"And if for some reason you couldn't retrieve it?"

"Hand the location information over."

"And she would then inform the contractor?"

"I presume so. I have no idea how the system works higher up the food chain."

Few contractors did, I imagined. It was safer for all involved. But the fact remained, Kaitlyn was still a problem and needed to be immediately dealt with... but as much as I'd love to be involved in taking the bitch out, my priority *had* to be the sword. Once it had been destroyed, the probability of the world being turned into a ruinous wasteland by these idiots would be reduced, even if they could still cause untold damage with the crown and the ring.

"Were you to ask any other questions?"

"No."

"You weren't supposed to kill me or anything else?"

"Not kill, but they told me to..."

Whatever else she was going to say died on her lips. She was unconscious.

Which was damnably frustrating given she obviously *was* supposed to do something else. I guessed we'd have to wait until she gained consciousness to find out.

I pushed up and walked back to the ladder. The eggy smell had all but dissipated, but my throat nevertheless itched. After sheathing my knives, I undid the latch, released the stair lever, and then stood back, just in case this was a trap.

The head that appeared a few seconds later did indeed belong to Harry, and I relaxed. Two other people followed him up. He directed them down to my captive and then said, "Are you all right, Ms. Aodhán? Your voice sounds unusually harsh."

"The witch released some sort of gas that burned my throat. Any idea what it was?"

"Hydrogen sulfide smells like rotten gas, but that in itself isn't immediately dangerous, especially at such low-density levels. It *is* mixed with another gas, but I couldn't say what without getting a sampler up here." His gaze shifted to my captive. "I take it you used pixie obedience magic on her?"

I nodded. "She said she'd accepted a contract from Kaitlyn and that she was supposed to dart and then question me. She denied working with our witch. I couldn't get much more than that, because I was lucky to get any answers from her at all, given she'd all but knocked herself out when she tried to escape."

He cocked his head sideways, obviously listening to something beyond my hearing range. "The ambulance is almost here. Go get checked, and we'll take your statement after that."

I retrieved the Codex from behind the crossbeam and then headed down the ladder. The medics soon arrived and, after a quick examination of the various abrasions and beak wounds, declared I should go to hospital to get a more thorough examination and to ensure there were no unseen consequences of the gas. When I refused, they tried to change my mind, but eventually suggested sipping warm water with honey and a dash of ginger to ease the soreness in my throat and once again emphasized the need to go to hospital if symptoms got worse or I felt unwell.

Harry reappeared and, once he'd taken my statement, said I was free to go. I sent a text to Sgott to let him know I was okay, even though he probably already knew it. He sent a reply a few minutes later saying that whatever I did next, I was not to do it alone, and to always keep him informed. Emphasis on the NOT and ALWAYS.

I smiled, sent him back a kiss emoji, then headed into my bedroom, packing a large suitcase of regular clothes and shoes, and a smaller one of evening wear. People might be out to dart and maybe even kill me, but I'd be damned if I'd let that totally void my social life now that I finally had one again.

And hoped like hell I hadn't just jinxed said social life.

Neither Lugh nor Darby were home when I arrived at Lugh's, but that wasn't surprising given both had to work. I let myself in and dragged my two cases into the spare bedroom. Once I'd unpacked everything, I made a pot of tea and then settled down to google Devil's Chimney. The first one that came up looked like the right one, which made a nice change. It was located just past Cheltenham, meaning it'd be a good two-and-a-half-hour drive to get there, if not more, depending on the motorway traffic.

I glanced at the time. It was still early enough to make it in daylight, but only if we moved fast. The last thing I really wanted to be doing was exploring a damp and probably dangerous cave inhabited by all sorts of critters in the middle of the night.

I grabbed my phone and called Lugh. He might be working, but that shouldn't stop him from accompanying me, especially if he informed Rogan it involved a lead on one of the Claws.

"Hey, sister mine," he said, in an extremely cheerful manner. "I'm thinking a very good time was had by all last night given Eljin is walking around whistling spritely tunes."

"And by all, I'm thinking you need to be including yourself in that. You're not exactly all sad and gloomy sounding."

My voice was wry, and he chuckled. "To what do I owe the honor of this call? Has something happened?"

"You could say that." I gave him a quick update. "I've found the Chimney, but I can't go—"

"You certainly can't," he cut in brusquely. "Give me half an hour to sort things out here and clear it with Rogan, then I'll be home. It might also be worth contacting Cynwrig and even Mathi to see if they're available to accompany us."

"Yeah, because putting those two in the same car isn't asking for trouble at *all*."

"They're adults. They can handle it."

Yes, but I wasn't sure *I* could. They might not argue, but the bristly distaste they'd radiate at each other might quickly get overwhelming in a small space.

"I can understand asking Cynwrig, given we might need his skill at manipulating stone and earth, but why Mathi?"

"Muscle," Lugh said. "He may not hold Cynwrig's mass, but the man can fight."

My eyebrows rose. "You've seen this?"

"He's a Dhār-Val." Lugh's tone was dry. "In underground circles there's a saying—better to cross the devil than a Dhār-Val elf."

While I'd long known the dark reputation light elves had, I'd never witnessed any actual violence from Mathi. And yet, the casual way he sometimes spoke of retribution against those who crossed either him or the family businesses certainly suggested he was no stranger to it.

"I'll give them both a call and ask them to meet us here if they're available."

"Good. See you soon."

He hung up. I immediately called Cynwrig. The phone rang for what seemed forever, and I was just about to give up when he finally picked up.

"Bethany," he said, his tone breathless. "Sorry, I was otherwise occupied and didn't hear the phone until it was almost too late."

"Is 'otherwise occupied' code for being in bed with a lovely young woman?"

He laughed. "Sadly, last night's companion had to leave at an indecently early hour. I was lifting weights. This bod does not maintain its magnificence by sex alone, I'm afraid."

I tried to ignore the sliver of... not jealousy, but maybe something akin to it at the confirmation that he *had* been with someone. Our relationship was a casual, open, no-strings-attached deal, and it wasn't like I'd been home alone twiddling my thumbs.

But understanding all that and not being affected by it *emotionally* was a whole lot harder than I'd presumed.

"What can I do for you?" he added.

"I'm just wondering if you were free today."

"The council called a meeting for later this afternoon, but I've no plans aside from that. Why? I take it this is *not* a booty call. Unless, of course, the lovely Eljin proved to be not so... satisfactory in bed."

Was there a slight edge in his voice when he said that? I'd have loved to believe so, but in truth, it was extremely unlikely.

Elves did *not* do jealousy. Dark elves did have a reputation for falling hard and fast once they met the right woman, but unlike their golden kin, apparently did *not* fuck around once the relationship got serious.

Whether that was true or not I couldn't say, and it wasn't like I'd ever find out.

Not until he met his true love and either ditched me or not.

Of course, it wasn't like I'd be his bit on the side if he *did* find his heart's desire.

"Oh, the lovely Eljin was *extremely* satisfactory," I replied. "Not only did he live up to expectations, but he exceeded them."

"I'm pleased for you."

He didn't sound pleased, but then, it was becoming more and more evident that this man did not like sharing 'his' women. Not that he'd ever admit something like that. Not even to himself.

"So am I," I said cheerfully. "Finding one hot man who

not only knows what a clitoris is but where it hangs out is rare enough, but two? The gods have definitely taken pity on me for the long months of celibacy suffered after my breakup with Mathi."

He chuckled softly. "Not something I have ever faced."

Or ever would. "I believe I've found the cave that hides the forge where the Claws were made, but given neither Lugh nor I are cavers, I'm thinking it might be wise to—"

"Have someone along who can read and manipulate stone and clear any rockfalls," he finished for me.

"Yes." I hesitated. "Lugh also suggested Mathi come along. He feels we might need the additional muscle given the Looisearch have ramped up their attacks on me."

"There's been another?"

"Unsuccessful, obviously, but yes."

He swore. "At Lugh's?"

"No. Home. I went there this morning to collect my things and head to Lugh's."

There was a bit of a pause, suggesting he hadn't missed the implication I'd stayed the night at Eljin's. But all he said was, "As much as I hate to say it, it's probably a good idea. Mathi can handle himself *and* a weapon extremely well. How far away?"

"It's over near Cheltenham way, so it means you'll be away most of the afternoon."

"That isn't a problem."

"But what about the council meeting? They won't be happy about both you and Mathi missing it."

"They want the people behind these thefts and the death caught, so again, it won't be a problem. I'll contact them now, give them an update, and send our apologies. When are we leaving?"

"Can you get here in half an hour?"

"To Lugh's? Yes. See you then."

He hung up and I called Mathi, basically repeating the conversation without the whole Eljin thread. He didn't have the right or the need to know I was dating someone aside from Cynwrig.

"You want me armed or not?" he asked. "I'd prefer the former given the number of times they've caught us unawares thus far."

Carrying a gun wouldn't actually guarantee we wouldn't be caught unawares again, but it'd still make me feel better if at least one of us had a weapon. The wind and my knives could only do so much.

"I take it you are cleared to carry?"

I could almost hear his smile. "I've special dispensation on a case-by-case basis. I'll let my father know what we're doing so that if things go wrong and someone gets shot, we're covered."

"You really aren't averse to using your father's position for personal benefit, aren't you?"

"Not just personal. Family too."

Which only made me wonder what other shady dealings Ruadhán had turned a blind eye to.

And whether Sgott knew.

I hung up, tucked my phone into my pocket, then walked over to the sash window and slid it up. The wind whisked in, thick with the promise of heavier rain. There were no voices to be heard within her, no screeching caterwaul to suggest Beira was trying to contact me, but I nevertheless had a sense of her presence. She continued to keep an eye on things, even if a distant one.

But there was also something—or rather, some*one*—else in the wind now. It was little more than a distant tremble of wickedness, but it made my skin crawl. If that tremble was the storm mage, he was *not* on the side of the angels.

I stuck my hand out the window, letting the wind play through my fingers as I envisaged the front that held the sword safe within its stormy heart. Once I'd "caught" it, I sent it skittering toward Cheltenham. Given the recent attacks, it really wasn't safe to call the sword down and physically keep it close right now. I'd have to do so once we were ready to enter the cave, of course, but until then, it *had* to be safer where it was.

Lugh appeared twenty-five minutes later.

"Any problems with Rogan?" I asked, as he stripped off his coat and hung it on one of the hooks near the door.

He shook his head. "Other than wanting a few details, he practically pushed me out the door."

No surprise given how desperate he was to get his hands on the Claws for the museum. "How is he going to react when he discovers we actually intend to destroy the Claws rather than allow the museum to display them?"

"In a perfect world, he won't discover it. I certainly have no intentions of mentioning that particular fact."

"Rogan's not stupid. He's going to figure out something is wrong sooner or later."

"It wouldn't be the first relic hunt that has amounted to nothing." He shrugged. "Can you put the coffee on? I need to change out of my office gear."

His office gear—jeans, a shirt, and a woolen sweater—wasn't all that different to his civilian clothes—jeans, T-shirt, and a long-sleeved fleece—but I nodded and headed over to the brand-new coffee machine. Darby had a serious love for freshly ground coffee and had obviously installed this as a replacement for Lugh's crappy one.

Mathi and Cynwrig arrived within a few minutes of

each other. After making coffee for everyone, we sat around the kitchen counter and discussed the various scenarios of attack and how we could counter them.

I hoped we'd done enough to be safe.

I suspected that we hadn't.

But maybe that was my natural pessimism coming to the fore. Things hadn't exactly gone our way so far, although at least we'd managed to keep hold of the sword this time.

We headed out twenty minutes later. The traffic was relatively light and the conversation surprisingly easy and without tension. It was close to one by the time we turned onto the narrow lane that led up to an empty parking area. According to Google Maps, there was another one farther up the main road, with a path that led to the lookout I'd seen in my vision, but this one meandered around the quarry's base. There wasn't much in the way of photos of the old quarry itself, but the limestone cliffs appeared steep enough that accessing the cave from above wasn't practical and probably unsafe, despite all the ropes and harnesses we had with us.

Once we'd parked, I grabbed my credit cards and license from my purse and slipped them into a card holder attached to the back of the phone. With all the other shit we had in our backpacks—climbing gear, headlamps, water, and protein bars—I wasn't about to carry anything more than necessary. Besides, with the way our luck had been running of late, the car would get broken into while we were in the cave, and I didn't need the hassle of trying to replace all my cards on top of everything else.

I was about to shove the handbag under the front seat when instinct twitched. I retrieved my purse, pulled the Eve token out of the coin section, and tucked it into my pocket. I had no idea why instinct was insisting I take it with me, but I wasn't about to gainsay her.

I climbed out and glanced skyward. My storm hovered almost directly above the Chimney, although it looked no different from any of the other rain-laden clouds currently threatening to unleash winter hell upon us.

I could feel neither the mage's presence nor Beira's in the wind but that only tightened rather than eased the inner tension.

If our mage *had* been tasked with finding the sword, there should have been some sense of him in the approaching storms. Of course, maybe it was simply a matter of me not being *capable* of finding him, especially if he'd taken steps to conceal himself. My storm-born abilities remained very raw, and the only real training I'd had was Beira's quick tutorial on how to create "storm storage."

That, and a warning not to call down the lightning again until I had a means of heat dispersal.

"Is there a problem?" Cynwrig asked.

"No." I hesitated, my gaze drawn skyward again. "I'm just wondering if we're being watched."

"By shifters?"

"By anyone. I'm not sensing anything untoward, and that's worrying me."

"Would you sense a shifter on the wind?" he asked.

"I have before."

"If we *are* being watched by a shifter," Lugh said, "we can't do anything about it."

"Actually, I *could*." And it would give me the greatest of pleasure to catch the shifter with a sliver of wind and toss it across the country. But I had no sense of a flighted watcher. No sense of anything at *all*.

And it just felt wrong.

"Surely our main problem will be the mage," Mathi said. "If you can't sense him, maybe he's simply not around. It's not like he can fly in at a moment's notice, is it?"

I gave him my best "don't be daft" look, which only increased his amusement. "If one can control the wind properly, one can ride it."

"That will be a handy skill if you ever get a handle on your own abilities," Lugh said. "It'd surely beat spending hours driving from one location to the other."

"As the librarian noted a number of times, I'm a godling not a god. I might never achieve the level of control needed for that sort of thing."

Not to mention the likelihood that even if I *did* manage to gain some level of control, my strength would probably fail at the wrong moment, and we'd plunge to our deaths from a very great height.

Pessimism, thy name is Bethany.

"Control is learned not gifted," Mathi said, in a solemn tone totally voided by the deepening amusement in his eyes. "Practice is the key to all talents, though I'd suggest that in this case, you do so somewhere that provides a soft landing."

"Except for the fact that, if the velocity is high enough, a 'soft' surface will probably do as much damage as a hard one."

I didn't wait for a reply. I just slung my pack over my shoulder and headed down the gravel path toward the quarry's basin. The wind played through the trees, rustling the barren branches and teasing the evergreens. There was no sign of anyone else in the area, even though this was something of a tourist spot, and still no indication that anything was wrong.

Yet the conviction that something *was* grew.

I flexed my fingers and resisted the urge to draw my knives. As much as I'd feel better with their weight in my hand, knives were a poor substitute against guns. If they *were* watching us, they'd most likely be armed this time around. Given how wrong previous attacks on *me* had gone, I suspected they wouldn't risk confronting three large and very capable men without a weapon.

We finally reached the base of the limestone rock formation that was the Chimney. I stopped near its base—which had been shored up with rocks after what looked to be either erosion or storm damage—and scanned the nearby cliff face, looking for the crooked slit that marked the cave's entrance. After a moment, I spotted it behind a curtain of green.

I struggled up the steep and very wet grass slope, the cliff face looming above me, gray against an even grayer day. Rocks littered the slope as we neared the cave's entrance, though I had no idea whether the rockfalls were recent.

I swung my pack off, pulled out the flashlight, and turned it on. It didn't really illuminate much more than a few feet inside the cave, but that was enough to reveal the rough and ready nature of the walls. This crooked fissure was natural, not man created.

"Well," Mathi said, peering over my shoulder. "That's going to be fun to get through."

"I can widen it if necessary," Cynwrig said. "But it's only the first sixty feet or so that'll be tight. It opens out after that."

I glanced at him. He had one hand against the limestone cliff face, his expression distracted and gaze inward as he listened to whatever the earth was telling him.

"Any indication there's a forge inside?" I asked.

"No." He paused. "There is, however, an unnatural heaviness about a mile in. The stone around it is not responding."

"A mile huh?" Lugh said. "I've done worse."

"As long as there's no bats," I muttered. "I can't handle bats."

Cynwrig pushed away from the rock and flexed his fingers. "I thought it was only rats you hated?"

"Bats are just winged rats, in case you didn't know."

"No," Mathi said. "That's pigeons."

I snorted and returned my gaze to the cave. "If we're ready to go in, I'll call down the sword."

"Why can't you leave it circulating until we discover if there's a forge or not?" Lugh said. "It'd probably be safer."

"Probably, but I'm not sure what sort of control, if any, I'll have over the wind that deep underground."

Lugh nodded and motioned me to proceed. I pulled on my silver-lined protective gloves, then raised a hand and called to my storm, asking her to release the sword into the wind's grasp and deliver it to me.

Black metal arrowed down, accompanied by a high-pitched scream of fury wrapped in the wind. The sword, expressing its displeasure.

It had barely slapped into my hand when the mage attacked.

CHAPTER
SEVEN

THE WIND ROARED AROUND US, SO LOUD IT SOUNDED LIKE A JET plane. Air tore at the sword in my hands, trying to wrench it from my grasp. I held on tight, countering the invisible fingers of wind with my own, tearing them off my skin and the weapon as fast as they were placed.

Thunder rolled, a deep and resonant sound of displeasure, and lightning split the sky, striking the earth not far from where we were standing. Stone and dust flew skyward, and the fierce air swept toward us, the sharp shards tearing into our clothes and cutting flesh.

I raised a hand, trying to counter, trying to create a shield of wind to at least ease the force of the mage's attack but as soon as it was created, it was torn apart.

As we would be if we didn't find shelter soon.

"The cave," I shouted. "We need to get inside the cave."

My words were torn from my lips and tossed away, but Cynwrig obviously had the same thought. He lunged for the cave's mouth, pressed a hand against the side wall, and forced the rock apart to give us greater access.

"In," he shouted. "I'll seal it once—"

He got no further. A whirlwind caught him, raised him, and tossed him away. As I sent air chasing after him with the order to cushion his fall, Mathi was yanked off his feet and tossed in the opposite direction. I sent more wind after him.

Then Lugh rose.

I wasn't going to lose my brother. No way, no how.

I jumped forward, wrapped my arms around his legs, and caught the edges of the mage's whirlwind, sending it spinning away. My own wind swept in under it and I quickly arrowed us into the fissure.

Too fast, too high.

We crashed into a wall six or so feet in, slid along it for several more, and then fell in a tangled and bloody mess on the ground. The sword slithered from my grip and skidded toward the entrance almost of its own accord. I swore, detangled myself, and lunged after it.

But just as my fingers touched the hilt, the whirlwind picked it up and tore it skyward.

I sent wind chasing after it, but it was already too late. The mage, his storm, and the sword had all disappeared.

I punched the ground in frustration. All that did was bruise my hand. I turned and scrambled back on hands and knees to Lugh. He was conscious and sitting up, but more than that I couldn't say because I couldn't see. I swung my pack around, dug inside for the headlamp, and put it on. Given I'd crashed on top of my pack, it was a damn miracle the thing even worked. Its bright beam chased the immediate darkness away, revealing the tunnel's rough walls and the odd patches of moss that hung from the ceiling and dripped down the walls.

Just the sort of place bats loved.

And that was fine. Perfectly fine. As long as the bastards stayed out of my hair, we wouldn't have a problem.

Lugh had a deep gash down the right side of his face that bled profusely, and his jacket sleeve was shredded. Mine was similarly shredded, and moisture oozed, so we'd definitely at least skinned our arms when we'd crashed and slid down the wall.

I retrieved the first aid kit from the pack and carefully opened it. There wasn't much more than saline, antiseptic, painkillers, and bandages, but that was all we immediately needed. Darby could heal us both easily enough once we got home, although if we kept injuring ourselves every time we went out, she'd start insisting on coming with us.

I raised my gaze to my brother's. "Anything broken?"

Nothing *looked* broken, but given his tendency to ignore such things and just carry on, one had to ask.

"No." He raised a grimy hand and pushed the hair from my face. "You've a nasty gash on your cheek."

"You can deal with that once I deal with yours."

"What about the sword?"

"The mage snatched it away when we hit the wall."

He swore. Violently. "Cynwrig and Mathi?"

I shrugged. "I sent air chasing after them in an effort to cushion their fall. Hopefully, it worked."

Hopefully, they hadn't become little more than two bloody stains on the landscape.

A sick sense of doom rose at that thought, but I pushed it back down. They'd be okay. They *had* to be okay. I didn't want to lose anyone else I cared about...

Lugh grimaced and dragged his phone out. "I'll see if I can contact them."

While he tried, I took care of the cut on his cheek. It was deeper than it looked and full of grit, some of which I just couldn't remove. I applied antiseptic and a sticky plaster, then said, "Any luck?"

"No, although whether that's because we're underground or there's simply no signal in this area, I couldn't say."

"What do the little signal bars say?"

He squinted at the screen. "Can't say. There's too much damage to the phone's face."

I dragged mine out of my pocket and was greeted by a similarly smashed screen. Face recognition wasn't working, which could have simply been a matter of there not being enough light rather than a result of the smashed screen, so I keyed in the code. It, at least, worked. The signal strength indicator on the home screen wasn't showing anything, but I nevertheless attempted to make a call. There was no dial tone, no connection. The phone might still be functioning, but its ability to connect to the network's cell towers had been broken.

Which would have been bad news had one of us been seriously injured. The best we could have done was run down to one the houses further down the hill for help—and to be honest, I'd have had serious doubts about the safety of such an action, given we had no idea if the Looisearch remained in the area. Just because the mage had apparently fled on the wind didn't mean the rest of them had.

Presuming there was a "rest of them," of course.

"There's one more thing I can try."

I tugged the Eye out from under my clothing and wrapped my fingers around it, pressing its cage hard into the palm of my hand so that the stone met skin. Then I closed my eyes and envisioned the two men, trying to get some sense of them. Energy stirred through the Eye's dark heart, and I had a sense of life, though it was very distant.

"Anything?" Lugh said.

"They live. More than that I can't say."

"At least that's something."

Something *wasn't* all that comforting when they could still be broken and bloodied. Once again, I pushed the thought away and handed Lugh the first aid kit and the water. While he'd stoically borne the discomfort of getting patched up, I did *not*.

When he'd finished torturing me, I shoved the kit away then sat back on my haunches. "Now what do we do? Retreat and regroup? I'm sure one of the houses down the hill would have a phone we could borrow. Or we could just drive to one."

"I think our time would be better spent heading into this cave to confirm the forge exists. After that, we find the fucking ring before the Looisearch can get their grubby hands on it."

"The problem being, they're not actually looking for it. They're just waiting for us to find it so they can steal it. In fact, it might be safer to simply sit on our hands and do *nothing*."

"Do you honestly think that'll be an option?"

"No. But—"

"These people have shown a propensity to kidnap and kill, Beth. If we do nothing, they *will* react. Badly."

He was right, of course, and not just because of the Looisearch. Beira had also warned that this task was mine and that no matter how I might wish otherwise, there would be no escaping it.

I scrubbed a hand across my eyes, smearing grit in the process. "What I don't understand is how they even knew we were here. Even if we were followed, they wouldn't have been able to get the mage here *that* quickly. Not by a car, at least, and if he'd ridden in on the wind, I *would* have sensed his approach."

My talents might be raw and untrained, but surely even *I* wouldn't have missed such a deliberate and direct movement of clouds and air.

"Given how quickly the mage attacked once you'd called the sword down," Lugh said, "there's only one real possibility—they knew our destination beforehand."

"But no one outside Rogan knew we were coming here."

"Eljin knew because he was there when I was talking to Rogan about it, but it's doubtful he was in any way involved. Aside from the fact he's only just arrived in the country and hasn't the contacts, I'm still getting him up to speed with everything Nialle was involved in. I haven't yet mentioned the Claws."

"Rogan wouldn't have said anything to anyone, though —not with how desperate he is to get his hands on the Claws for the museum."

"Unless, of course, he *does* suspect we plan to destroy them rather than hand them over."

"Why would he suspect that? You haven't said anything, have you?"

"No, but he did come into the office when I was searching for 'the Forge of the Gods.' It wouldn't have been hard to jump to the right conclusion." Lugh grimaced. "Personally, I'd rather believe his office is bugged than think he'd go to this extreme to get the sword before we could destroy it."

"I guess it would depend on what he valued more— you, or having the Claws for the museum." I paused. "Do you actually think the council would allow them to be displayed, given how dangerous they are as a package?"

"Who knows with our fucking council." Lugh pushed to his feet and offered me a hand. "Shall we continue to search this black and undoubtedly dangerous slice through the earth?"

"Sure, but I give you fair warning—if bats divebomb me, I will scream." I let him haul me upright. "What about Cynwrig and Mathi?"

"If they're not too badly injured, they'll probably make their way home—"

"No, they won't. They'll be coming here to check what the hell happened to us."

Lugh hesitated and then nodded. "It'll still take them time to get here. Time we could be using to check whether this is the tunnel we're looking for or not."

And time was something that was rapidly running out for us all. He didn't say that, but it nevertheless seemed to hang in the air.

He pulled on his headlamp, then ordered me to put on a harness. Once we were roped together, we started down the narrow tunnel, the lamps highlighting the jagged edges of limestone and glimmering off the larger calcite crystals.

It was tough going, as the passage was narrow and the footing an inconsistent mix of rubble and smooth, slick stone, meaning we had to watch every step. I scraped my shoulders more than once. Lugh, who was far bigger than me, had just about shredded his jacket by the time the tunnel finally gained some width.

Lugh stopped and pulled a flashlight from his pack. The beam was far brighter than the headlamps, and it illuminated the narrow but high cavern we'd entered. Water trickled through the center of the floor below and dripped from the stalactites above.

I couldn't see an exit point, but Lugh headed left, walking along the narrow ledge that circled the cave's basin until we reached a particularly large stalagmite. The passage continued behind it.

"How the hell did you spot that?"

My voice echoed loudly and, from the darkness above, leathery wings rustled. I shuddered and quickly followed Lugh in.

"I have a gift for finding exits in tight situations. It's come in handy a few times, let me tell you."

"One of these days, you really are going to have to stop going into godforsaken places to find relics. Rogan isn't paying you enough to risk your life like that."

"It's never been about the pay, Beth."

"Mom basically said the same thing once when I asked her why she went after relics without a guaranteed paycheck. She said that there are more important things in this world than money."

"Indeed, but there is a difference to what she did and I'm doing."

"She worked for the Gods; you work for the museum."

"That's not what I meant." He slid sideways past a large outcrop of rock before continuing. "She had responsibilities that I don't. She should never have risked her life in the service of the gods while you were little."

"I wasn't little when she died."

"No, but that's a moot point."

I sucked in a breath and did my best to squeeze past the outcrop without scraping my chest. "She might not have had any choice. Old gods and goddesses have never taken no for an answer, and they're not above threatening the people or things that you love to get their way. You've said that multiple times about Beira."

"At the very least, she should have informed someone where she was headed," he growled. "If she had, she might still be alive today."

"And have us—or Sgott—possibly stepping into a dangerous situation? There's no way she'd have ever risked that, Lugh."

He glanced briefly over his shoulder, almost blinding me with the headlamp. "Another instance of 'like mother like daughter,' I'm thinking."

I half smiled. "Have I not been keeping you updated on my movements lately?"

"Yes, but please keep it up. You're the only family I have left, and life wouldn't be the same without your nagging and sometimes annoying presence in it."

"Ditto, brother."

We walked on in silence for what seemed like forever. The descent got steeper, the ground wetter and more dangerous, and the air thick and stale, making it increasingly harder to breathe. I knew enough about old caves and fouled air from the various things Lugh had said over the years to understand that, while there was no immediate danger, the longer we stayed, the more carbon dioxide would collect in our bodies, and the greater the chance of aftereffects.

Hopefully we'd find the forge before we had to worry about getting disorientated and dead.

Eventually, the path evened out and we stopped heading down. The tunnel walls switched from limestone to a faceted mirror black that didn't appear in any way natural. Our lights danced across its surface like hundreds of tiny stars, making it appear we were walking high in the sky rather than deep underground.

Though the air remained still and foul, there was now an odd sense of... weightiness... coming from up ahead. It was as if whatever lay hidden by darkness had been there so long it was unable to support expectation or hope.

Then the darkness swamped us, and the starlight died. The headlamps weren't having much luck penetrating the unnatural thick curtain, so Lugh got out his flashlight again and turned it on. It had no more luck than the headlamps did.

He raised a hand and cautiously stepped forward, feeling for a wall that was obviously there even if we couldn't yet see it. His fingers were briefly swallowed by black ink and then rejected.

"It appears we have a magical barrier rather than a physical one," he said. "You feeling anything?"

I shook my head. "The knives aren't reacting, so if it *is* magic, it's not the dark kind."

He nodded and kept pressing his fingers against the wall, exploring its dimensions. As expected, it covered the entire passage, preventing us from going any further.

"If the gods' forge does lie behind this thing, then maybe it's not human touch that will raise the barrier. Maybe it needs to be godly."

"I can't imagine the old gods would have ever used such a narrow and dangerous damn tunnel."

My voice was wry, and his smile flashed briefly. "Well, no, but it's also unlikely they'd have forged the Claws and all the other artifacts themselves, either. They would have had human help."

And making the help traipse through deadly tunnels on a daily basis would be right up their alley.

"If that's true, then this barrier was probably raised *after* the Claws and whatever other artifacts had been made here were finished," I said. "Presuming, of course, it is the forge on the other side and not a cave troll or something."

"Cave trolls only exist in fiction."

I snorted. "I assure you they don't. Just look at the current crop of parliamentarians."

He laughed, a sound that was weirdly muffled in the thick atmosphere. "There has to be a way past it. You wouldn't have been shown the forge if it was impossible to access it."

"Except I didn't actually ask if it *could* be accessed. I just asked where it was."

"Surely they'd have said something if it couldn't be."

"No, because that wasn't part of my question. One needs to be very specific, I learned."

"While they do have a well-deserved rep for being petty and manipulative, I'm thinking that's not what is happening here. It's more likely a case of me not having the right bloodline: i.e., of direct godly descent."

I raised an eyebrow. "Why would they have created a barrier only I could raise? Not even the old gods could foretell the future that far in advance."

"Not you specifically, but definitely a godling whose existence was no accident," he said. "Think about it—your conception was unlikely to have been a mere whim. Nothing the old gods ever did was ever without intention, even if that intention was chaos. You use the knives in a manner Mom never did. You are the first Aodhán in a very long time to blood bond the Triune and use it as designed. And *that* happened not long after the Claws gained attention and a major hoard went missing. Intent, Bethany. That means you should be able to open this barrier."

I drew in a deep breath, momentarily forgetting the foulness, and coughed so badly my head spun. Lugh handed me some water, and I gulped it down to ease the fire in my throat.

"Remind me never to do that again," I croaked.

"Don't ever do that again," he said blandly.

I swiped at his arm, then, before I could think too much about it, raised a hand and splayed my fingers against the invisible barrier. I'd expected it to be cool and slick, much like the black walls around us, but instead it was warm. Unnaturally so.

For an instant, nothing happened. Then the tips of my fingers sank into the wall, followed quickly by the rest of my hand. The air stirred, gently sweeping away the dark barrier away, revealing our tunnel. One that reflected our lights so brightly, we were once again surrounded by stars.

"It appears I was right," Lugh said, with just a touch of smugness.

"And as a reward, you get to lead the way once more."

I grandly waved a hand, and he bowed and did so. But we'd only gone a dozen or so feet when the passage opened out onto a wide flat platform that jutted out over an enormous cave. There were no stalactites here, no moisture, no bats. The twin beams of light from the headlamps had starlight dancing all around us but couldn't penetrate the deeper darkness below.

Lugh pointed his flashlight down... and spotlighted a set of bellows so big it surely had been used by giants. The forge was similarly massive, the wall so high that had I been on ground level, I wouldn't have been able to see over it. There were various hammers and tongs on the rock shelf behind the forge, once again all overly large. I couldn't see the hammer I'd been shown in the library, but I had no doubt it would be here somewhere.

"Did giants ever actually exist?" I asked. "Because no human could have used this."

"Maybe the answer lies in the name—the forge of the gods."

I snorted. "When have the gods ever done the dirty work themselves?"

"Good point."

"Then here's another—there's no way known we'll be able to get this thing going."

"I'm thinking that if you were advised to destroy the Claws here, there's going to be a simple means of starting the thing."

"I'm hoping said means is magical, because we're not getting coal down here very easily."

"No." He swept the light along the walls closest to us and then headed right, following a narrow path that wound down to the cavern's floor. The forge looked even larger, the bellow arms thicker than my waist. The forge itself was made of stone the same shiny black as the walls and floors. I pressed a hand against it; it was glass smooth and surprisingly warm.

Lugh continued on, looking almost dwarven compared to the size of the forge. "There're steps over this side. Human-sized ones."

"Considerate of them," I said, heading around.

He was already halfway up. I scrambled after him. The steps were relatively narrow and steep, but the rim of the forge was a good two feet wide.

I stopped beside him and stared down. Deep in the heart of the vast forge was a faint orange glow.

"It awaits," Lugh said softly.

"Yes." I shoved my hands into my pockets. "It's some pretty powerful fuel they're using if heat still lingers after eons of disuse."

"Old gods' magic is some powerful shit, let me tell you. There's a lever over there—" He waved a hand toward the edge opposite. "Shall we go see what it does?"

"Do you really think that wise right now?"

But I was already speaking to thin air. I hurried after him again. The knee-height wall dividing us from the edge of the forge gradually rose until it neared shoulder height. The lever was as thick as my arm and made of a metal I suspected had once been silver but was now tarnished black. Lugh gripped it with both hands and hauled it back.

Or tried to.

The thing didn't budge.

He shifted his weight and tried again. Still nothing.

"Maybe it works the other way," I said. "You generally pull something toward you to close it, don't you?"

"Depends on the country," he said but nevertheless changed his grip and shoved all his weight against the lever.

It shot forward so suddenly, it dragged Lugh with it. I lunged forward and grabbed his jacket—totally forgetting about the rope that bound the two of us—and hauled him back to safety before he could tumble over the furnace's edge.

The stone under our feet began to vibrate, and a deep rumbling filled the air. Within the forge's heart, the glow changed from orange to white, then spread out rapidly, until the entire base glowed white-hot. Then, with a fierce whoosh, fire exploded into being, the force so great it knocked us off our feet and sent us tumbling to the ground.

I landed on my back, knocking the air from my lungs.

For several seconds, I simply remained there, staring up at the mirror-black ceiling, watching the flickering reflection of flames as I battled to breathe but *not* too deeply. I did not want to throw myself into another fit of coughing.

Behind us, the bellows moved independently of touch, the vague shadows they cast and the whooshing air they produced giving me vague visions of a dragon breathing.

"Well," Lugh said, sounding a little breathy. "I guess that answers the question of how we start the thing."

"It also explains the chest-height wall." I accepted his hand and let him haul me up. "I'm guessing it's meant to be some sort of fire shield."

"It was built for midgets if it was," Lugh said. "We'd better head up and shut it down again."

I nodded and once again followed him up the steps. The closer we got to the rim, the fiercer the heat became. Sweat poured down my face and trickled down my spine, but in all truth, it wasn't as bad as it could or should have been, given the sheer size of the firepit. That was no doubt due to the air that now stirred around the forge, creating a gentle vortex that swept the worst of the heat upward.

In the pit itself, the flames shimmied and danced in almost joyous delight, seeming to follow us as we walked carefully around the rim's edge. Once we reached the lever, I remained behind the half wall while Lugh walked on. The rope that tied us together played through my gloved hands; this time, I was ready to react if something happened. He had to lean over the flames to grab the lever, and just for an instant, the circling air caught and lifted him. As I yanked him back, he grabbed the lever and then made a hasty retreat.

Once again, a shudder went through the stone underfoot, then the flames whooshed out, leaving only the softly glowing coals far below. The bellows wheezed to a stop, sounding somewhat like the last breaths of a dying animal.

"Well, at least we achieved *something* today," Lugh said. "Now we've just got to find the ring."

"And somehow get it here without it being snatched away."

The former might be easy enough thanks to the clues we'd gotten from the library, but the latter was definitely going to be problematic, given the storm mage could keep track of all my movements through the wind. Which in truth was a guess on my part, but how else could they be tracking us?

Maybe I needed to talk to Beira. She was the goddess of storms, after all, even if she was stuck in human form. Surely she could do something about the man.

Although given she was the one who'd warned me of his presence, maybe not.

"Let's worry about one thing at a time," he said. "I haven't the brain space for anything more right now."

"You're a man, so that goes without saying."

He snorted and nudged me lightly. "As penance for such a blatant lack of respect for your older and much wiser brother, you may lead us out, sister dearest."

I smiled and took the lead. It didn't take us long to reach the exit out of the cavern, but the tunnel was all uphill and as slippery as fuck, so it took us even longer to reach the outside world than it had to get in. I was hot, sweaty, and more than a little weary by that time.

I stopped several yards beyond the tunnel's exit and breathed deep, trying to drive the lingering foulness from my lungs. The sky was full of clouds, though the storms that had threatened earlier had come and gone. The air was still, giving me no means to investigate the surroundings or to check whether anyone was about watching us.

And no means to check whether Cynwrig and Mathi were nearby.

I dragged out my phone and tried once again to make a call. I had no more success this time than I had the last. I shoved it back into my pocket with a little more force than necessary. "Perhaps we need to buy an emergency phone and keep it in the car for situations like this."

"Good idea. I'll grab one tomorrow." Lugh paused and glanced at his watch. Surprise rippled through his expression.

"What?" I immediately said, my voice sharp.

His gaze met mine, green eyes holding a hint of disbelief. "It's only been three hours since we were attacked."

I stared at him. "Are you sure that thing is working?"

"Positive." He twisted his arm to show me the watch. "We must have gone through some sort of time slip."

"Do you think that's what the barrier was?"

"Maybe, although it would have taken at least a couple of hours for us to reach that point, and more to return. Somewhere along the way, time actually stopped."

Which should have been impossible, but it was becoming increasingly obvious that when you were dealing with the old gods, there was no such thing as "impossible."

We were halfway down the slope when I noticed the chimney's absence. I stopped abruptly and only then realized it was deep, old forest that lay below us rather than a scrappily treed quarry.

"Toto," I said softly, "I've a feeling we're not in Kansas anymore."

Lugh stopped beside me. "Well, fuck. It would appear

that not only did time stop, but the tunnel configuration was altered to redirect us."

"Wouldn't we have felt the movement through the stone if reconfiguration had happened?"

"Not necessarily. Not if magic was involved."

He turned and pointed his flashlight back up the mountainside. It definitely *wasn't* the same cavern. The entrance to this one was pointed and angular, with jagged rows of rocks running along its upper rim that made it look like an animal readying to take a bite. I hadn't noticed the "teeth" when I'd walked out, probably because I'd been too intent on escaping the gloom and getting fresh air into my lungs.

"I don't suppose you recognize where we are?" I asked.

He swung the light around in an arc. "Nope, but that forest below us feels ancient, and there's not many of them left in the UK these days."

I frowned. "The only truly ancient forest near Cheltenham is the Forest of Dean, and that has to be at least twenty-six—or more—miles away from the Chimney. We certainly didn't walk that far."

"Perhaps not, but if the magic can reroute us without us noticing, why couldn't it also jump distances?"

I guess that was no more impossible than anything else that had happened. I scanned the area, looking for some sign of civilization. Beyond the swath of lovely old trees, lights twinkled, distant and inviting.

"How many hours do you think it'll take to get there?" I asked, pointing.

"Only one way to find out," he said cheerfully, and walked on.

I sighed and traipsed after him. I might have the godly blood, but he definitely had godly energy.

We entered the forest ten minutes later, and it felt like we'd come home. The music of the trees was rich and vibrant, their song so powerful it vibrated through every part of my being, making me feel alive in ways I couldn't even begin to describe. It was heady and enriching, and I could have walked through these ancient woods forever and not complained.

It was with more than a little regret that we left the warm chatter of the trees and followed the road into the village—Staunton, according to the signs. We found a small but lovely old inn on its outskirts and Lugh launched into a wild tale about us taking an off-trail shortcut, getting lost, and falling down a ridge to explain our less-than-pristine condition. By the time he'd finished, the innkeeper had not only given us his best rooms but arranged for our clothes to be washed and dried overnight and ordered a couple of pizzas for us.

After a long, hot shower, I wrapped myself in one of our borrowed dressing gowns then reapplied the antiseptic and stuck a wide plaster onto the messy scratch on my face. Which hurt like hell after said hot shower, but all things considered, we'd both gotten off relatively lightly. The speed of our impact could—should—have caused far worse wounds.

I scooped up my clothes and shoved them in the laundry bag, leaving it outside the door as ordered, then grabbed the first aid kit and followed the scent of pizza into Lugh's room.

He was stretched out on the bed, talking softly into the room's landline. Though I couldn't hear the person on the other end, his general demeanor suggested it was Darby. I tossed the kit onto the end of his bed, motioned for him to use it once he'd finished yakking, then grabbed one of the pizzas and headed back into my room to give him some privacy.

And to make use of the landline in my bedroom.

After all but inhaling the first slice of pizza, I dialed Cynwrig's number and waited, my breath caught in my throat as it rang.

It wasn't caught for long.

"Bethany?" he said, relief riding his rich tones. "Where are you? Are you okay? Why aren't you answering your phone?"

"We're in Staunton, near the Forest of Dean, and the only things that are damaged are our phones."

"Both of them?"

"Yeah. I got a little enthusiastic when I was tearing us out of the mage's grasp."

"But you're okay?"

My heart did a happy little jig at the concern still riding his voice. My heart was insane. We were friends and lovers, but in truth we very much remained strangers. I could not let the deep connection I felt with this man overwhelm common sense.

"Other than being bone tired, yes I am."

"So how did you get over in Staunton when Lugh's car remains in the parking area? It's too far to have walked, and I didn't think you had enough control of the wind to use it."

The fact he knew the car remained in the parking area meant he was there.

"The whole question as to how we got here remains a mystery, though we suspect a time slip happened somewhere along the line. What about yourself? How far did the mage toss you?"

"Quite a distance, but thanks to that pillow of air you

sent, I came away with little more than a few bruises and scratches. We'd probably both be dead if you hadn't."

"I could hardly let you get dead, as I haven't finished playing with you yet," I said teasingly. "I take it Mathi's also at the quarry with you?"

"Indeed. As is a caving crew. We were just getting ready to go in after you. Figured if you *had* escaped the mage, that's the first place the two of you would have gone. Did you find the forge?"

The man might not have known either of us very long, but he'd certainly gotten our measure when it came to predicting our actions.

Although I guess even a complete stranger could have probably predicted us going into the cave.

"We did." I gave him a quick update and then said, "The one piece of good news is that the Looisearch and their cohorts likely won't be able to destroy the forge, because it takes godly blood to enter and godlings aren't exactly thick on the ground these days."

"Or at the very least, are harder to find," he said. "I doubt the gods have entirely given up their cherished sport of messing with the various layers of humanity."

Neither did I, to be honest. In many respects, my existence bore that out. As Lugh had pointed out, it was unlikely to have been an accident.

"You want us to drive over and retrieve you?" he added.

I hesitated. I might have told Mathi hiding wouldn't alter the danger we were in but, right now, he and Cynwrig were the only people who knew our current location. It seemed silly not to take advantage of the brief moment of respite it gave us. Whether we did some serious research into the Ring's location or just grabbed some much-needed rest didn't really matter given both were vital right now.

"It might be better if we all lay low for a day or so. I've a bad feeling things will really hit the fan if we don't."

He snorted. "I've a feeling it'll hit the fan regardless of what we do."

"Undoubtedly, but I'm in no condition to deal with it right now."

"Ah," he said softly, the understanding in his voice making my stupid heart quiver. "Then find a hotel, take a long hot shower, and give us a call when you're ready to step back into battle, dearest Bethany."

"I will. Thank you."

I bid him goodnight, then hung up and called Eljin. I said I'd call him, so I'd better, especially if I did want to deepen our relationship.

Which I did... didn't I?

I swiped the silly thought away and listened to the ring-tone. After a few seconds, his lovely voice informed me he was currently busy and to leave a message. I did so, then grabbed the pizza box and headed back into Lugh's room. He was in the process of making tea for us both.

I plopped down on one of the chairs at the small table and munched into another slice of pizza. "How's Darby?"

"She's at the encampment, checking the babe's progress."

The babe in question was the grandly named Ruairí Veon Talein Riagáin, who was her brother's first son *and* the first male to be born in the current generation, an event that took the pressure off Darby to marry within her own race and produce an heir to carry the family's genes forward.

"Is she staying there the night?"

"Yeah." He wrinkled his nose. "It's a bit of a hike to get

back to the city from there, and to be honest, given everything that's happened, it's probably also safer."

The light elf encampment lay to the east of Deva and was in truth only twenty minutes away in good traffic. But I totally understood his sudden need for caution.

"Cynwrig offered to drive over and pick us up," I said. "I told him we were staying the night and that it was probably safer if we lay low for a couple of days."

"So they're both alive?"

I nodded. "The cushions of air I sent chasing after them worked, apparently."

"Good." He slid a cup of tea across the table to me then sat down with his own and opened the pizza box. "If we *are* laying low, we'll need to replace our phones and grab a computer as a matter of priority. I'll need to be able to access my search results and files."

"Will that be safe, given the likelihood someone at the museum is working for the enemy?"

"Should be. No one else has access to my files—"

"Passwords are easy enough to crack these days."

"They won't be cracking mine easily, and I routinely change them anyway."

"What about Rogan? You're going to have to explain why you'll be absent from the office again."

"Yes." He paused. "It might actually give us an opportunity to confirm whether or not Rogan's office has been bugged."

"Or whether Rogan himself is involved." I hesitated, remembering what Eljin had said. "Do you know if Rogan has ever lost someone close to him?"

"If I have no idea what his current status is, relationship-wise, I'd hardly know something like that." He raised an eyebrow. "Why do you ask?"

"Apparently Eljin has a psi talent that allows him to emotionally read people. He said there's a great sadness in Rogan, and that it was a result of a loss that happened a long time ago."

Lugh shrugged. "It would certainly explain his reluctance to get emotionally involved with anyone else now, but I can't see how it would connect to our current situation."

"Could it have made him a target? Could the Looisearch be manipulating his loss to aid their cause? Or blackmailing him, even?"

"I guess if he was somehow responsible for the death of the person he lost, the latter is a definite possibility." He picked up another slice of pizza and bit into it. "It's certainly an angle worth researching."

"And here's another." I retrieved my phone from my pocket and turned the thing on. The low battery warning came up, but all I needed it to do was bring up the photos I'd taken at Aram's place. They were easy enough to find, given they were the last things I'd photographed, but the state of the screen made for difficult viewing. I handed the phone to Lugh and added, "We found this photo when we found Aram's body. There's a date and a series of numbers on the back—any idea what the latter might be?"

He squinted at the screen, moving it around in an attempt to find a better view through the myriad of cracks.

"It's too long to be a phone number." He changed the angle of the phone again. "It could possibly be a location coordinate though. Write these numbers down."

"Hang on." I walked over to the bedside table and grabbed the pen sitting next to the phone. "Right, go."

He reeled off a series of numbers. I jotted them down, then tore off the sheet of paper and walked back, handing it to him. "We're going to need working phones to do a search."

He nodded. "We'll head out tomorrow and grab everything we need, including a hire car. Did you tell Sgott about the photo?"

"Yes, and we gave it to the IIT. Mathi said he was going to investigate the date and see if there was anything significant about it."

He nodded. "It's not ringing any bells with me, but it's more than possible I was on a hunt. I tend not to take too much notice of the news when I am."

"You tend not to take notice of anything," I said dryly. "Even calls from your mother and only sister."

"*That* is a lie. I always called back."

"Usually days or weeks later."

"That does not moot my point."

"Says the man who not so long ago said that if Mom had kept us more informed, she might be alive today."

"You always knew where I was, Beth," he said gently. "But I nevertheless get your point, and promise that in the future, I will do my best to respond more quickly."

"Excellent." I paused and couldn't help adding, "I'm sure Darby will appreciate it, too."

He rolled his eyes. "You're not going to give up until we're married with dozens of kids, are you?"

"All I want is to see you happy, whether that's with Darby or someone else. I know you've been avoiding long-term relationships because of your job and how dangerous it can be, but loneliness doesn't sit well on you, brother mine."

He caught my hand and squeezed it gently. He didn't say he loved me or that he wanted the same for me, but he didn't need to. It was all right there in his eyes.

He released me and returned my phone. "I'll contact Rogan in the morning and give him a false location."

"We'd need to keep an eye on said location to confirm whether he's the leak or not, and it wouldn't be practical for us to do it." Not if we want to concentrate on finding the ring. "It probably wouldn't even be wise for either Cynwrig or Mathi to be involved."

He nodded. "Which is why I suggest you give Sgott a call, tell him what we're up to, and see if he can spare a couple of shifters to keep an eye on the place."

"You've a location in mind?"

"Cwmorthin. It's an old slate mining town that's been abandoned for a long time now. Aside from the buildings, there's a deep network of caverns and tunnels, many of which were too unstable for exploration. He's aware I was running a search through the mine research society's records and the industrial heritage listings, so it's a believable starting point."

"And you're sure there's no chance of it being the actual location? Because that would be pretty ironic."

"Not one hundred percent sure, but quarrying at the site began in the early 1800s and no relics of any kind were ever found there, even during the archaeological explorations that happened much later."

"And how do you know all this? Were you or Nialle involved in a dig?"

"No, but I did date one of the archaeologists involved in a more recent exploration for a while."

I drained my tea and then rose. "I'll ring Sgott in the morning and request a watch be placed, then. What time are we leaving?"

"I ordered breakfast for eight, and the innkeeper said

our clothes should be ready by then, so I'm thinking about eight-thirty?"

"I don't suppose you thought to ask about car hire?"

"I did indeed, and I even have an address."

"I applaud your efficiency, brother mine, especially after the long day we've had."

"The ability to adapt on the fly is all part and parcel of what I do," he said in a dry sort of voice. "So it's not surprising I'm thinking a little clearer than you right now. Go get some rest, Beth. We'll plan the finer details in the morning."

I bid him goodnight and headed into my room. To say I was asleep almost as soon as my head hit the pillow would have been something of an understatement.

I woke just before seven-thirty. Our clothes were pressed and hanging on a little hook in the corridor next to our doors. I grabbed mine, had another shower in an attempt to wash the lingering tiredness from my limbs, then made my call to Sgott.

"Glad to hear from you," he said. "I was getting a mite worried, especially given both Mathi and Cynwrig were at the hospital in the early hours of the morn."

Alarm flicked through me. Cynwrig had said there'd been no major damage, but maybe he simply hadn't wanted to worry me. "Did you see them? Talk to them?"

"I didn't see them; I just got the reports. Mathi had a broken arm, Cynwrig a broken wrist. Both had multiple cuts and scratches, but they were healed and released after a couple of hours. Cynwrig went home, and Mathi went straight to Ruadhán's office. He's been scrolling through IIT archives."

A smile twitched my lips. "Undoubtedly thinking you are none the wiser."

"Undoubtedly," he said, voice wry. "Both he and Ruadhán have a tendency to underestimate my reach in this organization."

And did so at their peril, I suspected.

"Do you know what he was researching?"

"No, but I gather it has something to do with the photo you and he found at Aram's place?"

"More the date on the back. Can you remember if anything major happened in that year?"

"I don't believe there was anything out of the ordinary, but it was a while ago and the memory isn't what it used to be."

His memory remained as sharp as a tack, and anyone who thought otherwise was a fool.

"What about Aram? Did you get the coroner's report on him yet?"

"Too early for blood and tox results, but initial findings confirm death occurred as a result of a blow to the back of his head. He's probably been in that freezer for four or five months, at a bare minimum."

Which was basically what Mathi had guessed and all but confirmed the Aram who'd attacked me at the tavern was indeed an imposter.

"Have you talked to Kaitlyn about him?"

"Yes. She said she hadn't noticed any changes in his mannerisms and behavior over the last few months."

"And wouldn't tell you if she did."

"Indeed. I currently have people doing a very thorough search of both her official and her unofficial offices and stores. If she *is* hiding anything, we'll find it."

"Good." If nothing else, it would disrupt her business for a few days. That, more than anything else, might make her think twice about brokering another contract involving me. "What about the bird shifter?"

"She remains in a coma. We have her under twenty-four-hour guard and will speak to her when—if—she regains consciousness."

I frowned. "I hadn't thought she'd hit the skylight hard enough to end up in a coma."

"Many bird shifters have thinner skulls, much the same as their feathered counterparts."

It still seemed odd to me. "I don't suppose they did a blood screen on her?"

"Yes," he said. "And I have requested the results be sent to us once they are through."

I should have known he'd be a couple of steps ahead of me. "What information did Kaitlyn have about the contract and the person who placed it?"

"That it came through secure channels, no names attached."

I snorted. "As if she wouldn't have the means to trace them if they defaulted on payment."

"She always takes a security bond before any contract is advertised."

"And she can't trace that back to the originating account?"

My disbelief was evident, and I could almost see his smile. "Oh, she most certainly can, and she's currently in the process of assisting us."

I couldn't help but wonder if Kaitlyn's reputation and business would survive the "assistance." And whether Ruadhán would step in and protect his "source," subsequently risking the anger of his nighttime counterpart.

"And the witch who tried to gas me?"

"We have a partial print but otherwise, there remains no trace of him."

"You're running the print through the system?"

"Of course, but if he hasn't got a criminal record, we're unlikely to get a result."

Dead ends—that's all we seemed to be hitting at the moment. I sighed. "Lugh and I are planning to lay low for a couple of days."

"That's the first sensible thing I've heard you say for weeks," he said, tone dry. "But I'm guessing it really just means you won't be telling any of us where you are."

I smiled. "I refuse to answer that question on the grounds I may incriminate myself."

"Just remember what happened to your mother and be careful. You and Lugh both."

"We will. In fact, caution is one of the reasons why I'm ringing."

"Meaning you need IIT help in regard to a distraction?"

I smiled. The man knew the workings of our minds very well indeed. "The attack on us yesterday was more or less proof someone at the museum is working with the Looisearch."

"Rogan?"

"Possibly, although we're not sure if he's a willing participant or being blackmailed in some way. But we're going to tell him we're heading to Cwmorthin, and we were wondering if you could send a couple of shifters up there to intercept whoever might turn up."

"Easily done. I can run a background check on him, too, if you'd like."

"You might have to do it off book, because it's likely the Looisearch have sympathizers within IIT, and we can't risk warning them."

"I've been doing this sort of thing for a very long time now," he said, with just a hint of amusement. "I don't need a whippersnapper to be telling me what to do."

I laughed. "Sorry."

"No, you're really not." The amusement was stronger. "By the way, I have permission from the pixie council to go see your aunt. You do not, which is just as well given your decision to lay low."

I hesitated but couldn't help asking, "Did they say anything about their decision on my punishment?"

"No. But they wouldn't, as I'm not a pixie."

"There's a bit of me that wishes they'd just hurry up and get it over with." Even if the more sensible part said the longer the better.

"No council works with any sort of speed."

"They did with the red knife."

"That was an entirely different matter—they had Deva's council riding their asses."

Which suggested Deva's council did have some sway over ours. I wasn't sure why, but that news had all sorts of trepidation stirring through me. "Just be careful when you're talking to my aunt. She's unstable enough as it is, and this might well break her."

"I have the council's protection and blessing, lass. She can't and won't hurt me."

Which didn't mean she wouldn't try. "Are you going to run a search through Vincentia's things?"

"I've warrants to search her two properties—we might turn up something there."

"One of those properties was recently blown up."

"Yes," he said, in a heavy sort of way. "You wouldn't happen to know anything about that, would you?"

"You've read the reports, surely."

"Yes, and that did not answer the question."

"Because there are some questions that are better left unanswered."

He harrumphed. "You've still got my private emergency number, haven't you?"

"Yes."

He'd given it to me when I'd first started dating, with strict instructions that I was only ever to call if I felt threatened or needed immediate help. I'd only used it once, back when I was eighteen. I'd gone to a weeklong "school's ending" celebration, and a half elf I'd been semi-keen on had herded me away from the rest of the group. He'd wanted a whole lot more than the kiss or two I was willing to give and had been so angry at my rebuff that he'd locked me up in a dingy room and said I could rot there until I complied.

Unfortunately for him, while he'd taken my purse to ensure I couldn't ring for help, my phone hadn't been in that purse. Sgott had broken land-speed records to get me out of that situation, and the elf had gotten the book thrown at him. Last I heard, he was doing a couple of years in jail for breaking and entering.

"Use that to send me updates on what you're doing," he said.

"I will, just as soon as we get new phones—we smashed our other ones."

"Deliberately?"

"No. It was a consequence of hitting a wall a little too hard."

"You're all right otherwise?"

"We've a few minor cuts, but yes, we're fine."

He grunted, a disbelieving sound if ever I heard one. "If you're still in the Cheltenham district, I can give you the name of a retired elf healer who is the soul of discretion. Just in case the minor cuts aren't."

I smiled, reached for the pen and paper, and jotted down the nurse's name and address. "We'll head there once we hire a car. That way, she can ease your concerns."

"I'll let her know to expect you this morning, then. And do please be careful."

"We will. Thanks."

He hung up. The smell of bacon and fresh toast hit my nose, and I quickly headed into Lugh's room. He was just placing the stacked tray onto the table. I filled the kettle and readied the cups for our tea.

"Sgott's given me the name of a retired healer," I said. "I think that should be our first stop once we grab a car."

He nodded. "It'll be easier to avoid attention if neither of us look like something the cat dragged in."

"It'd have to be a pretty big cat to drag you anywhere, brother mine."

He grinned. "Not necessarily. There was this lovely feline in Egypt who—"

"Details are *not* necessary," I cut in.

"*That* would have to be a first."

I grinned, and we got down to the business of breakfast. Once we'd gathered our few meager possessions and paid our bill—giving the owner/manager a good tip for all his additional help—we caught a cab down to the car hire place. After nearly an hour of faffing around with paperwork, we drove to the healer, who was ready and waiting for us. She was a lovely woman who insisted on us staying for tea, cake, and a chat after she'd healed us. I rather suspected she was lonely, as there wasn't an elf enclave nearby and, according to what she'd said, her family had all moved overseas.

By the time we got to Coleford and purchased phones, clothes, and a computer, it was close to one. We found an out-of-the-way cafe with free WIFI, ordered something to eat and hot drinks, then started plotting.

But fate hadn't quite finished with us yet.

I'd barely inserted my SIM into my new phone when several messages came through—one from Eljin, and one from Sgott.

I opened the latter and read it with a growing mix of disbelief and regret, then raised my gaze to Lugh's.

"What?" he immediately said.

"It's Aunt Riayn. It appears she's been murdered."

EIGHT

"*Appears*?" Lugh said. "What does he mean by that?"

"They haven't found her body yet, but there's evidence of a fight and blood in the kitchen. They're currently doing a line search through her property."

Lugh leaned back in the chair and scrubbed a hand across his bristly jaw. "Why on earth would anyone want to kill Aunt Riayn? She has no connection to the search for the Claws—"

"She's Vincentia's mother, and probably knew a whole lot more about what her daughter was up to and who she was working for than she ever admitted."

"Yes, but she was under the red knife. She couldn't have talked to us—and wouldn't have, given she severed all ties with us."

"The Looisearch wouldn't have known that."

"The pixie council would have informed Deva's council. A red-knifed pixie can't receive any visits without permission aside from those supplying vital goods or services. If the Looisearch *do* have council connections, they'll have known she was no threat."

"They're not exactly the type to take any sort of risks. Vincentia was protecting their asses until the very end, and look where it got her."

"The manner of her death suggests fury rather than intent. She must have said or done something to trigger the attack."

"Or maybe she did nothing more than refuse to give them the Codex."

"Her connection to it was more than likely severed when you performed the blood ceremony," Lugh said. "She probably boasted she *would* find the Claws once the Codex was back in her hands, and when she couldn't even find *that*, found herself on the wrong end of a sharp knife."

"Except she *did* lead them to the loft—"

"The two of you spent plenty of time up there as youngsters," he cut in. "She'd have known you wouldn't risk hiding anything *that* important in the beam storage cavities, so the loft was the next likely location."

All of which was not only logical, but probably the truth. Yet there remained a bit of me that couldn't help thinking Vincentia had—when it was all too late—seen the true danger of the situation and tried to do the right thing.

"None of which explains the attack on Riayn," I said. "And why kill her, then hide her body? That makes no sense at all."

"We're dealing with people who'd risk wrecking our world in order to gain revenge. I'm thinking sense isn't playing a major part in their thinking right now."

"I guess not." I took a sip of tea. "Still, if they want to use the Eye to find the ring without the hassle of going through me, why kill the only other person who can assist them?"

"Perhaps they think the Eye can be used by anyone. Either that, or they're simply not intending to kill you off."

Which, if true, only accelerated the danger I was in.

"Hopefully, once we find and destroy the ring, they'll stop coming after me."

"Or maybe," he grumbled, "they'll just decide to erase you out of spite."

Maybe, but there wasn't a lot we could do about that, and I already had enough to worry about. "Are we staying in Coleford for the night, or holing up elsewhere?"

Lugh hesitated. "I think it would be better to head up to Gloucester. It's easier to hide in a large city than a village or town."

I nodded and sent a message to Sgott, telling him where we were going and asking if he'd keep us updated. Then I opened Eljin's message and read it with a growing smile. I mischievously answered in kind, although I was far less cryptic about what *I* intended to do to *him* the next time we were together.

Text sex—who knew that could be so much fun?

Not me, but then, Mathi had always been a man of action rather than words when it came to sex, and I'd certainly never been left wanting during our time together.

Once we'd finished our meal, we climbed back into our hire car and headed into Gloucester, opting to spend the night in a two-bedroom apartment with parking and free Wi-Fi near the Cathedral. Once we'd dumped our new clothing purchases into the bedrooms and transferred the files from our old phones to our new, I headed out to get some essential groceries—tea, coffee, milk, chocolate— while Lugh booted up the new laptop and started going through his various search results, looking for mines that matched the one I'd seen in my dreams.

On the way back, I spotted a witch's spell shop and, on impulse, headed in. A wiry, ginger-haired woman with brown skin and fierce blue eyes came out from behind a curtained doorway.

"Afternoon," she said, in a voice that was warm and welcoming, "how can I help you today, young lady?"

I smiled. "I have what I believe is called an Eve token. I was just wondering if you could tell me a bit about it, or perhaps even who might have made it?"

Her pale eyebrows rose. "And why would you be needing to know that? Was it used on you, or perhaps someone you care about?"

"My brother. He's a little too embarrassed to come here himself because he was a little too chatty with the woman when it came to bank details."

Which was an embellishment of Lugh's story but held enough of the truth to ring true. It wasn't unusual for a witch running this sort of shop to have a nose for false-hoods, even if they weren't psychic.

The woman laughed, the sound bawdy. "Hope he at least had a good time before he was scammed."

"Best six hours of his life, apparently, even if it cost him a fortune."

She laughed again. "Either your brother has the stamina of a bull, or the token is not a run-of-the-mill one. You got it on you?"

I put the groceries down then tugged the token from my jeans pocket and handed it to her.

She sucked in a breath. "*This* is no ordinary Eve token. There's some major magic behind the creation of it."

"I thought all Eve tokens took major magic?"

She grimaced. "Depends on what's required. This

particular token has two prongs of attack—seduction, of course, but there's also a sound bubble spell."

"Meaning it ensured no one could hear them beyond the limitations of the bubble, or that *he* couldn't hear anything beyond it?"

"The latter. It's an odd choice, really, as most people using Eve tokens generally prefer to keep their trysts secret. Whoever used this was more concerned about her victim hearing what else might be going on than of being seen or heard."

Which is exactly what had happened. The question was, what had they been looking for? Had they found it? Was that why he was killed? Or was his death truly an accident?

"I don't suppose you can tell where the token originated? Or perhaps even who cast it?"

"Possibly." Her gaze swept me shrewdly. "What are you intending to do with caster once you find him?"

Him, not her. At the very least, she knew that much. "Ask him if he has the record of who he crafted the token for. My brother wants the woman and his money, not the witch responsible for the token. And he'd rather avoid getting the cops involved—getting scammed like this wouldn't go down well at work."

She laughed again. "I can understand that." She paused, flipping the token over to study the runes on the back. "I can do a reverse search on the few magical threads that remain, but it'll be costly."

"Not as costly as the sum he lost in this mess, I'm thinking." I paused, though mainly for effect. "How much are we talking about?"

"An even grand should do it."

Wow. She certainly *was* taking advantage of the situation, given the cost of tracking spells—or at least the ones I'd seen advertised—generally hovered around the two hundred mark. Still, I couldn't exactly blame her, given it was winter and tourists—who were generally the main trade for shops like this—were thin on the ground.

"If I'm going to be tattling on a fellow caster," she continued, obviously having seen my reaction, "I'm going to be well paid for it."

Which was also fair enough. "Are you able to try now?"

"Well, it ain't like I'm being rushed off my feet right now. This way."

I picked up my groceries and followed her through the curtained doorway. The small room beyond was filled with all manner of witchy items, and the floor and ceiling covered in arcane symbols. I had no idea what any of them were, but a deep sense of well-being and safety infused the air—a feeling amplified by the fact my knives didn't react.

She motioned me to sit opposite her at the table, then placed the token in the middle of an intricate circle inked into the wood.

I put the shopping on the floor and resisted the temptation to run my fingers across the table; there was an odd, almost otherworldly energy emanating from it that suggested it wouldn't be a wise idea.

She pressed a finger lightly against the token and began what I presumed was a spell. I couldn't understand any of the words, but energy rose, the power strong enough to nip at my skin. Again, the knives didn't react. Her magic might sting but it wasn't designed to harm. It also meant that, unlike so many witches who ran these sorts of shops, this woman was the real deal.

Once again, instinct or second sight or whatever the hell that inner voice was had not led me astray.

The token began to glow lightly, and the woman's eyes became slightly unfocused. I watched her, waiting, as the token pulsed under her finger and the energy nipping at my skin increased, until it was all I could do to remain still and not scratch. Then the light died, the biting faded, and the woman sat back in her chair with a sigh.

"Any luck?" I asked.

She nodded. "The craft behind the spell has the resonance of the Einar line, who these days hail mainly from Cambridge."

Einar? My pulse rate accelerated. Would it be too much of a coincidence to believe that the person who'd created this token was the very same person whose name Vincentia had written in blood?

Were we finally getting a decent break?

I did my best to hide my excitement. "I didn't think there'd be much call for witches in a place like Cambridge."

"Are you kidding me?" She laughed. "Humans are always looking for a way to cheat the system or gain an advantage over others. Being a university city doesn't alter that."

"I guess not." I hesitated. "Is the caster who created this in Cambridge? Or somewhere else?"

"Definitely not Cambridge." She picked up the token and studied it through slightly narrowed eyes. "It came from a seaport, and not one that's close by."

That flicker of hope died again. "Elsmoot?"

Aram had had an office there until it had been blown up, almost taking Mathi and me with it.

"No, closer than that." She turned the coin over, her eyes narrowed as she stared at the symbols on the back again. I had a feeling she wasn't really seeing them, but rather plucking whatever fast-fading images remained

209

from her spell. "It's definitely a seaport, but in Wales not England. If I was guessing, I'd say Swansea but mainly because the Einar line originated down that way. If you want some certainty, I can place a homer spell on it, but it'll cost an extra five hundred."

If the token had been created in Swansea rather than Elsmoot, then we probably weren't dealing with Aram—unless of course he had offices elsewhere. But that left us with one other problem—why would someone purchase an Eve token in Swansea if they intended to use it in Scotland? It was the other end of the country, for goodness sake, and it wasn't like Scotland didn't have any capable witches of their own.

"Will the homer lead to the witch who crafted the token or simply the place where it was created?"

"The latter, but that should also give you the former."

I nodded and motioned her to proceed. She placed the token back onto the table, pressed a finger on top of it, and once again began to spell.

It didn't take all that long. Once she'd finished, she picked up the token and handed it to me. I'd expected energy to run across my skin, but it felt no different than before.

"Once you're ready, you can activate the homer spell by gripping it and saying, 'take me home.' Then place the token on a flat surface and it'll act like a compass, with the circled snake being the directional pointer."

"Brilliant. Thank you."

She nodded and rose. "How you paying? Card?"

I smiled. "I'm not in the habit of carrying *that* sort of cash around with me."

"Probably wise. Pickpockets around these parts generally aren't a big problem in winter, except on event or festival weekends, but it never hurts to be safe."

I picked up my shopping and followed her out into the main room. Once I'd paid the bill, I pocketed the receipt, thanked her for her time, and headed back to our apartment.

"I was just contemplating heading out to search for you," Lugh said as I came through the door. "What happened? Did you get lost, or were the shops packed?"

"Neither." I dumped the shopping bags on the counter and began putting everything away. "I visited a witch."

His eyebrows rose. "Why?"

"Remember that token I found? Thought maybe she might be able to tell me a bit about it."

"And did she?"

"Yes indeedy." I told him everything she'd said and then added, "If Aram—or whoever is now impersonating him— is behind the token, it's not going to help us much."

"It's still worth following up, though the ring has to be our priority."

I nodded, put the kettle on, and handed him the receipt. "Figured you could claim it on expenses and reimburse me. You had any luck with the mine search?"

He nodded and tucked the receipt safely into his wallet. "There's a half dozen likely candidates."

"Meaning they all have underground lakes?"

"The majority have, yes. Most are open to the public, a couple are partially open, and there's one that's only open to experienced cavers."

"You think that's our one?"

He nodded. "It's near the Blaenau Ffestiniog slate mines in Gwynedd. They've become a major tourist attraction—

there are even zip lines across one of the pits, apparently—
but this particular mine hasn't been developed as yet."

I crossed my arms and leaned back against the counter.
"Why do you think it's the one we're looking for?"

"The Blaenau Ffestiniog mines are considered to be
the largest and deepest slate mines in the world and
consist of miles and miles of tunnels. Many of the more
ancient ones—including ours—broke into natural
caverns, which is what I think you may have seen in your
dreams. Most of these sections are sealed off to the public,
as aside from the flooding, there have been wall and roof
failures and multiple chambers that have collapsed
entirely."

"You make it sound so inviting."

He laughed. "Well, the good news is that the first five
levels are easily accessible by anyone who has the right
equipment. All we have to do is ring the custodians and ask
for the key."

"Easily accessible is not a comfort, given we'll be
heading down into the inaccessible parts. What about the
others?"

"There's one I think we need to check first, though it's a
cave more than a mine." He smiled. "Interesting tidbit,
apparently it was once used by the Chartist Rebels to stock-
pile their weapons."

I frowned. "What I saw appeared to be a mine rather
than a cave."

He nodded. "Excavations done a few years ago uncov-
ered a lower chamber with many passages leading off. It's
believed they link to a wider, deeper caving system."

"Which doesn't address the point—"

"*Some* of those passages and chambers show evidence
of exploratory mining. It's theorized one of the abandoned

mining operations might have broken through into the lower chambers and tunnels at some point."

What I'd seen definitely looked like a mine shaft, but it wasn't like we could afford to ignore any possible location. The minute we did, it would turn out to be the one we wanted. "Where is it?"

"A few miles north-northeast of the village of Trefil. We can check it out first, and then head on up to Blaenau Ffestiniog. It's a bit of a drive, so we might have to stop overnight somewhere."

I hesitated. "I know Swansea is a little out of the way, but could we kill two birds, given we might not be back this way for a while?"

"From what I saw on the maps, it's roughly an hour away from Trefil. That's workable depending on what we find and how long we're underground."

"You want me to book something?"

He shook his head. "Let's play it by ear. It's not like the place will be overrun by tourists."

No, not when we were zooming toward the coldest month of the year in this area. "It might be wise to grab proper caving suits if we're heading deep underground, just in case we end up having to swim."

He nodded. "We'll also need to call Cynwrig in. If something does go wrong underground, at least we'll have a means of getting out."

"What if he's being watched? The Looisearch are well aware he's looking for them *and* helping us."

"They can only watch him on the wing—anyone else he's going to sense through the stone."

"You're forgetting they likely have sympathizers in the encampment reporting his movements."

"Yes, but the Myrkálfar encampment literally has miles

and miles of tunnels through which they can move unseen. No one will find him if he doesn't want to be found. Mathi, on the other hand, will be a different matter."

"We really haven't a reason to call him in on this particular trip." Although *not* doing so would probably piss him off. "Besides, light elves really don't like being underground all that much."

"He seemed pretty happy to venture into the caves behind the Devil's Chimney."

"I suspect he simply didn't want to be shown up by Cynwrig."

Lugh laughed. "I can totally see that. The man is not at all accepting of your breakup."

"Light elves do *not* like to lose."

"Then he shouldn't have shared his wares with all and sundry."

I grinned. "Monogamy is another thing highborn light elves don't like doing. Even the married ones stray."

He shook his head sadly. "I don't know why you stayed with him for so long."

"Because, as I've said before, the sex was good. If he hadn't decided it was time to get married and reproduce, I'd probably still be in his bed."

Lugh grunted. "Well, at least there's finally a decent relationship prospect on the horizon."

"Speaking of which, do you think I should ask Eljin to do a more detailed reading of Rogan? It might be one way to uncover what—if any—secrets he might be harboring."

Lugh hesitated. "It's probably better not to. We've already dragged enough people into the situation. Besides, he hasn't really got a legit reason to be talking to Rogan."

I raised my eyebrows. "He works at the museum, in Rogan's department. How is that not a reason?"

"Because I'm in charge of Antiquities Retrieval—"

"But if you're not there, Eljin would report to Rogan, would he not?"

"Yes, but he has no reason to do so right now, and if Rogan *is* involved—willingly or not—then we can't risk any deviance in regular behavior in case it gives him—or whoever might be pulling his strings—warning."

"It was just a thought," I said, somewhat glumly.

"A good one, and if he'd been there longer than a few days, worth trying. But I won't risk the life of your future husband just yet."

"Just yet?" I said, ignoring the whole "future husband" jibe. "Does that mean you'll only do so once he's settled into the job?"

"Well, relic hunting does come with inherent risks."

As Mom's death had amply shown. Although in truth, it wasn't so much relic hunting that had killed her but trusting someone she shouldn't have. At least, that's what I'd sensed when I'd found Egeria's Coin, a good luck token that had been handed down through the generations in my family. Mom had never taken it off, so me finding it in the grit of a walled-off tunnel had been no accident. It was mine by right now, but I hadn't worn it yet. I couldn't. Not until her body was laid to rest in the ancient forests of our traditional homelands deep in the heart of Devon.

"When do you want to head out? Immediately?"

He shook his head. "I need to buy caving gear, given all of mine remains in the trunk of my car. Besides, we'll need all of our stamina for what will no doubt be a long and arduous exploration underground, so we should grab an early night and head out in the morn."

The kettle boiled, so I made my tea and his coffee, then broke open a packet of chocolate Hobnobs and plucked one free. "You want me to tell Cynwrig to meet us here or in Trefil?"

A somewhat devilish twinkle entered his eyes. "I'm guessing *that* would depend on how well you want to sleep tonight."

"You're the one that said we'd need all our stamina for caving tomorrow. While his presence here will undoubtedly mean I'll be a very *satisfied* woman in the morning, it's unlikely I'll be at peak stamina. The man has a rather large... appetite."

He laughed. "Trefil it is then. It'll take him at least three hours to get there, so maybe suggest around ten? In front of the pub?"

I nodded, finished my biscuit, and took another. "You might as well bring dinner home with you. I only bought the essentials."

"I noticed." His voice was dry. "We have a kitchen—you could have at least purchased steak and some chips."

I raised an eyebrow. "Were you going to cook them? Because this little pixie wasn't."

"If you had purchased, I most certainly would."

"Then there's a supermarket just down the street."

He rolled his eyes, drained his coffee, and then headed out. I rang Ingrid to get an update on what was happening at the tavern, then called Cynwrig.

He answered almost immediately. "Didn't expect to hear from you so soon—is something wrong?"

"You mean other than the possibility that my aunt was murdered? No."

He sucked in a breath. "When did that happen?"

"Sgott went up there yesterday to break the news about Vincentia, but he's not sure when it actually happened. At the moment, there's no body."

"Ah damn, Bethany, I'm sorry."

"So am I." No matter what had happened between us or what I personally felt about her actions, she'd been family. Her death not only brought our direct line that much closer to extinction, but also ended any chance of us patching things up.

Mom would have wanted me to at least *try* to do that, even if a few years down the track, once the dust had settled.

Of course, Mom was something of an optimist at the best of times. My aunt, on the other hand, could definitely hold a grudge.

"I take it that's not the reason you're ringing though?" he said.

"No." I quickly explained what we were intending. "We were wondering if—"

"Absolutely," he said, without waiting for me to finish. "Where shall I meet you?"

I gave him the directions, and our conversation flowed easily onto more inconsequential stuff. We were still talking when Lugh finally arrived home, one small shopping bag in hand.

I bid Cynwrig goodnight and hung up. "No luck with caving gear?"

"Plenty of luck, but I couldn't see the sense of hauling it all up here. It's in the car."

"Ah. Good idea."

"I'm full of them today."

I grinned. "Full of something, that's for sure."

He rolled his eyes and pushed a bottle of red at me. "Make yourself useful while I cook our dinner."

I poured our wine and then sat on a kitchen stool while he fussed about in the kitchen. Aside from the steak and chips, he'd also bought eggs, which really topped off what was one of our favorite meals.

Once I'd done the dishes—it was an old rule in our house that the cook never cleaned up—he did some more research while I scrolled through the multitude of TV channels, looking for something to watch. I gave up at about nine and headed to bed.

And really wished I hadn't been so pragmatic about conserving my strength for tomorrow. I had an unsettling feeling that the shit was well and truly about to hit the fan, and it would have been nice to have Cynwrig take me in his arms and tell me everything would be all right.

Even if we both knew the lie.

Trefil was located near the Brecon Beacons National Park and was reputedly one of the highest villages in the UK. Which meant, of course, it was damnably cold in winter, although at least there wasn't a whole lot of snow on the ground at the moment. Maybe the bitter wind was sweeping it away.

The pub was a cute, white-washed building with a slate roof and a big old chimney on one side, behind which lay an obviously later extension. There was a small courtyard out the front that held six tables and a smattering of chairs. Cynwrig sat at one of them, a coffee mug in one hand and his phone in the other. At his feet lay several backpacks.

As we pulled up, he slid his long legs free from the bench seating, gathered his packs, and then walked over to the car.

After throwing his gear into the trunk, he climbed into the back seat. "Asked the proprietor about the cave. He said to stop at the roadside car park at the junction of B4560 and Llangattock mountain road, and head in from there. He also said the cave can be difficult to spot."

Lugh nodded. "I have a map and a compass. We won't get lost."

That wasn't in any way said in a boastful manner. Lugh had used a simple map and a compass most of his relic-hunting life, and his ability to navigate with them rather than relying on apps had gotten him out of several sticky situations.

The parking area wasn't that far out of town and, once we'd all put on our weather gear and claimed our backpacks, we headed through the gate.

The moor was rough and wild, the fields dotted with lumps, bumps, and grasses. We came across the occasional memorial stone and some very old cairns, but for the most part, there was nothing but emptiness for as far as the eye could see. It was rather glorious.

We climbed steadily toward a rocky slope, eventually reaching the semi-domed entrance into the cave. The front of it was strewn with boulders and loose rocks, and the way appeared steep and rather wet. Once we'd donned our caving suits, Lugh handed us headlamps, and then, with a warning to be careful, led the way in.

I cautiously picked my way through to the entrance, then half slid down the narrow path leading into the main chamber. It was surprisingly large—at least a few dozen people could have fit in here—but despite the small pool of water gathering at its center, it wasn't what we were looking for. *That* lay far deeper and would undoubtedly be far more dangerous to reach if the two narrow tunnels I could see were anything to go by.

Lugh glanced at Cynwrig. "I don't suppose you can tell which one might be our target?"

Cynwrig smiled. "Well, you didn't bring me here for my good looks now, did you?"

"I did," I said lightly. "I might as well have a nice bit of ass to stare at as we're crawling through creepy tunnels. Keeps the mind off the dangers involved."

"Happy to be of service to you, dear Bethany, although I'm thinking said ass isn't all that impressive in this gear."

"Well, it's better than looking at my brother's ass, and far more appropriate."

"Concentrate, people," Lugh said, voice dry. "Otherwise we're going to be down here all fucking day."

Cynwrig's smile flashed briefly, bright in the gloom behind the headlamp's light. He tugged off his gloves, then placed a hand against the stone and closed his eyes. For several seconds, nothing happened. Then a very gentle vibration ran around the surrounding walls before leaping down our two tunnel choices. I watched him, half wondering if reading the earth and the stone gave him the same sort of feeling of oneness that reading wood gave me.

After several minutes he drew in a deep breath and opened his eyes. "The left tunnel leads to some sort of underground lake, but it's a fair way down. It's also the most degraded. I'm not actually sure Lugh or I will make it all the way to the bottom—it's very narrow toward the lake end."

I frowned. "Can't you strengthen and widen those bits of the tunnel?"

"I can, but it takes time and strength, and against seriously compromised earth, there's no guarantee of success. I'd rather save my strength for when—if—the tunnel collapses."

"Let's just get as far as we can, and decide what to do then," Lugh said.

Once we were roped together, we headed in. The tunnel's entrance was low enough that we had to squeeze through on hands and knees, and it didn't get any better, the crawl space becoming tight enough to scrape shoulders in several places. We finally reached a lower chamber, and with a sigh of relief, I stood and looked around. There were multiple passages and rifts leading off this chamber, but everyone one of them was blocked by earth and rockfill—deliberately so, I suspected, to prevent the unwary and unprepared from going any further.

Cynwrig walked across the chamber and pressed his hands either side of a rather crooked-looking crevice. After several seconds, the gentle vibration started anew, and the rocks and earth filling the entrance vibrated free, running past Cynwrig's feet like water and pooling close to the middle of the cavern.

Once the crevice was free of muck, he glanced around. "This first bit we'll be able to traverse upright, but further down we'll be on hands and knees again."

Lugh nodded and motioned him to continue on. The tunnel was small, dark, and wet, the air thick and unpleasant. It took us forever to go what seemed like inches, and I was sweating profusely by the time we came out of the tunnel into a third, much smaller chamber. Unlike the others, this wasn't natural—there were what looked to be pick marks on the walls and the rusty remains of mining tools on the floor.

"Well," Lugh said. "It looks like the theory about a breakthrough were right."

"Why the hell would anyone be mining this far down?" I flicked the bead of sweat dribbling down my face away with a grimy gloved finger. "Aside from the fact it would be damnably difficult to take anything back up to the surface, weren't they mining limestone around this area rather than precious metals?"

Lugh shrugged. "The known lack of valuable substances in an area has never stopped someone from looking for them."

"And," Cynwrig added, amusement evident in his voice if not his expression, "there're plenty of gold rushes started by people digging in areas most claimed would be a desolate waste of time."

He walked over to what looked to be a largish foxhole and squatted down. I walked over and then did the same.

"Please don't tell me this is our next tunnel."

"I'm afraid so." He glanced at me, one eyebrow raised and eyes bright in my headlamp's light. "You want the good news or the bad news?"

"Definitely good news. I've had more than enough bad recently."

"Well then, this tunnel is short even if it's steep, and it comes out at a shelf above an underground lake."

"I'm guessing the bad will be the fact neither Cynwrig nor I will be getting down it," Lugh said.

Cynwrig glanced up. "Indeed. There is one other major concern though—the pulse of the earth dies about twelve feet this side of the tunnel's exit point."

I frowned. "Is that usual?"

He shrugged. "It can happen in industrial regions, where the earth is so fouled, we cannot retrieve it, but it's rare in a region like this, despite its mining past."

"Could it be caused by magic?" I asked. "You not being able to read it, I mean."

My knives weren't reacting to anything, but maybe

that was because we weren't close enough. If they *did* react, I was going to be in trouble, because I'd stupidly kept them strapped on *under* the caving suit rather than over.

Of course, if I could call them into my hands from an underground cavern miles away from where they were, I could certainly do so when they were strapped to my legs.

He hesitated. "Possibly. Either way, you'll have to tread warily, because I'm not going to be able to feel the indications of a collapse *or* respond to it."

"Unless there's an island in the middle of that lake, I won't be journeying more than a foot away from the exit, trust me on that."

I pulled my backpack off, grabbed the flashlight, and shone it into the tunnel. Water dripped from the ceiling and ran down the walls before following the downward slope toward the lake I couldn't see or smell. The rocks were slick and shiny, and I had a suspicion going down face first would only end in me faceplanting on the shelf. But it wasn't like I could go down backward. I needed to be seeing where I was going.

"Are you really sure you want to do this?" Lugh said, peering over my shoulder in the narrow confines of the tunnel.

"I'm really sure I *don't* want to do this," I replied. "But I really don't want to back away now only to find out later it was the right goddamn lake."

Lugh nodded and glanced at Cynwrig. "You'll keep the tunnel secure?"

"I have no intentions of losing her to earth and stone, Lugh, you can be sure of that."

"Good." Lugh sat behind me and braced his feet against the wall either side of me, then disconnected the short rope that bound us all and tied on another longer one. "Ready when you are, Beth."

I tucked the flashlight into my caving suit to use when I reached the next cavern, then, before I could think about it too much, carefully edged into the tunnel's narrow entrance. It was tight. *Real* tight. My shoulders scraped the rough, wet walls, but thankfully the suit took the brunt of it even if I was likely to end up with bruises tomorrow. The bigger problem was the steepness of the slick descent, which made trying to get any sort of traction—even with gloves on—difficult. The only thing preventing me from toppling forward was the tension on the rope Lugh was carefully feeding out.

The deeper I crawled into the narrow space, the closer the walls pressed. Each breath was a harsh rasp of fear that echoed all around me, feeding my nerves and heightening the tension. About halfway down there was a semi-collapse, and while I knew it had to be secure given Cynwrig would have mentioned it otherwise, I nevertheless took extra time to squeeze sideways through the narrow gap. I seriously hoped there wasn't anything nasty waiting up ahead, because I was going to be in no state to deal with it.

Eventually, the tunnel widened enough that I could wriggle through without scraping my shoulders and hips. Air stirred gently past my nose, though it was flat and stale, containing no life or sound. A few yards on, the unyielding weight of stone gave way to a feeling of space and a deep, dark emptiness.

I retrieved my flashlight and slowly climbed to my feet. The bright beam pierced the darkness, dancing across the dark water that lay below the platform and gleaming off the stalactites high above.

"I'm out of the tunnel," I said, hopefully loud enough for the two men behind me to hear. The noise echoed through the still darkness, and in the distance, something stirred. Something that didn't quite feel right.

My knives didn't react, but my fear levels nevertheless ratcheted up.

"And?" came Lugh's faint response.

"There's definitely a lake." I swept the light across the water again. At the very edges of its reach there was an odd, almost box-like shape poking out of the water. "There is something here, but I'm not close enough to see what. How much rope have I got to play with?"

"Still a fair bit, but don't you dare unclip if we run out," came his distant reply.

"I won't." Mainly because if I did somehow manage to damage myself, it was the only means they had of retrieval.

"Also remember that the earth is dead where you are," Cynwrig said. "If something goes wrong, you need to get back into the tunnel before I can help you."

"Understood. I'll be careful."

More so than normal, given the creeping sense of wrongness.

I flexed my fingers, then warily moved to the right, following the three-foot-wide ledge that hugged the wall and sloped down to the lake. My footsteps echoed softly, and my light continued to dance across the still water, gleaming off little waves that lapped at the edge— The thought froze.

Why were there waves?

The air wasn't still here, but it also wasn't anywhere near enough to be causing waves. At all.

I swept the light across it again. There was nothing to see, nothing to explain the movement in the water. I glanced toward the shape, but it wasn't any clearer than before, even though I was now much closer.

I shivered, torn between the desire to retreat and the need to confirm whether that shape matched what I'd seen in my dream. Right now, I very much suspected it wouldn't, if only because it appeared far bigger than the chest I'd seen and there were no luminous skeletal fingers crawling around it. But I couldn't leave on a suspicion. Besides, it was possible the fingers would only appear once I tried to open the chest, just as they had when we'd found the sword.

I continued on, but I'd only gone a few more yards when a gentle shudder ran through the stone under my feet. I stopped immediately, my heart a sharp tattoo of sound that echoed across the silence. The shudder was not repeated, and there were no signs of cracks or fissures or anything else that might explain the brief movement. There was nothing. My gaze went back to the water. Those waves were getting stronger...

I retreated a step and then stopped again. I couldn't leave until I knew for sure what lay ahead. The last thing I needed was to leave now, only to discover at a later point that this *was* what I'd seen in my dream. One journey through the shitty tunnels was more than enough. There was no way I was going to do it all over again.

But I also couldn't risk continuing without some means of protecting myself.

I held the torch with my teeth, directing its beam over the water toward the still undefined shape, then unzipped the caving suit and half shrugged out of it so I could reach my knives. Once I had them both, I shrugged back into the suit, zipped everything back up, and continued on, the flashlight's thin barrel pressed against the hilt of the knife in my right hand. Its light made the blade glow an eerie silver blue that somehow jarred against the surrounding weight of darkness.

I finally hit the reach of the rope. I was briefly tempted to disconnect and move on, but quickly slapped that stupid thought right out of my head. I was far enough away from the tunnel's exit that they probably wouldn't hear me now if I did get into trouble, but it remained my sole link to them, and I wasn't about to lose it.

I shone the light across the water again. It still barely caressed the edges of shape—which was damnably odd given how much closer I now was—but the sheer size of the thing was evident, and it definitely wasn't a chest or an island. In fact, it appeared to be the top of some sort of stone structure—an arch of some kind, perhaps. One that was more squarish than rounded.

Though why would an oddly shaped arch be here, in the middle of a lake, in a cavern deep underground where no structure should even exist?

Was something else going on here?

Something that explained the increasing feeling of wrongness and the need to just get out of here?

I swept the light back across the water. The ripples flowing through the middle of the structure and fanning out across the rest of the lake were increasing in depth and velocity.

A deep sense of doom hit.

I had to get out of here. *Now*.

I turned and retreated, fighting the urge to run, not only because any hasty movement could be dangerous but also because it might incentivize the unseen threat in the water. As I moved back up the slope, the rope connecting me to my brother fell loosely to the ground. I briefly debated gathering it up as I went, but that would mean sheathing my knives and the looming sense of danger suggested that would not be a good idea.

The motion in the water increased. Waves surged, hitting the edge of the ledge, and splashing into the air.

I swung the light across the water again.

That's when I saw the eyes.

Huge, round eyes in a skeletal face that possessed weirdly elvish features and gills at its neck.

Fear hit, so fierce and strong I could barely breathe.

The structure was a fucking gate, and those eyes belonged to Annwfyn.

Aquatic Annwfyn.

CHAPTER
NINE

FOR TOO MANY SECONDS, I COULDN'T MOVE, COULDN'T THINK, couldn't do anything more than stare at the three nightmares who bobbed lazily in the water.

Then the larger of the three surged toward me, and adrenaline flooded my limbs.

I bolted for the tunnel, my feet flying over the slippery stone and my heart a rapid drumbeat that echoed through the darkness. The intensity of the waves hitting the narrow platform increased, the dark water splashing high enough to hit my legs. I didn't look around. I didn't dare, lest I lose my footing.

But I could feel them.

Hear them.

Their verbalizations were a series of clicks and whistles, reminding me a little of the sounds made by dolphins and whales.

Initially, there were only three, but as I ran further up the ramp, more joined in, quickly becoming a chorus that filled the chamber and would have drowned any attempt of mine to shout a warning to Lugh and Cynwrig.

Surely, they'd hear the noise.

Surely, they'd realize something was wrong and start retracting the rope.

My light bounced erratically across the darkness, one minute gleaming off stone, the next darkly luminous eyes filled with hunger.

These Annwfyn had not hunted—or tasted flesh—in a very long time.

I ignored the rising tide of terror and concentrated on not falling, on reaching the exit before they could grab me. Then the rope lying on the ground ahead started snaking back to the exit. Hope surged, even though a retracting rope meant nothing in the scheme of things. They couldn't actually help me until I was inside the tunnel.

I could get there. I *would* get there. These fishy bastards were not going to dine on my goddamn flesh. No way, no how.

The clicks and whistles behind me swelled, somehow managing to convey both anger and consternation. Then the rope still trailing behind me snapped taut, and I was yanked back, falling on my butt hard enough to send a shiver of pain up my spine. The flashlight slipped from my grip and rolled down the slope, spotlighting the webbed claws of the creature who held a loop of rope and the sinewy, gray-skinned form that climbed out of the water.

I swore and did the only thing I could—I slashed the rope from my harness, then scrambled upright and ran on.

A huge wave hit the wall in front of me. As it bled away, it revealed another Annwfyn. Its thin lips peeled back from its mouth, revealing double rows of needle-sharp teeth. Then, with a sharp clicking sound, it leapt.

I dove under it, raised a knife as it flew overhead, and

gutted it from neck to genitals. As blood and gore rained around me, I scrambled upright once again and ran on.

I wasn't far away from the tunnel when I heard the footsteps behind me. The thick air stirred weakly, containing the faintest of warnings. I ducked and swung around. The claws that would have ripped through the back of my head flew inches above it instead.

I lunged forward and slashed at the Annwfyn's bony legs. Dark purple light rolled down the fullers of the two blades and seemed to add extra force to my blow. Their razor-sharp edges cut through flesh, muscle, and bone as easily as water, and the Annwfyn fell backward, its body totally separated from his limbs. Black blood sprayed across my face and hair, and I gagged, but once again turned and ran on. More water splashed, this time behind me. Multiple pairs of feet slapped wetly against stone. I didn't stop, didn't look around. I just kept my gaze on the tunnel entrance, determined to reach it before any of them could grab me.

As the air stirred again, I scrambled into the tunnel, then wasted a precious second to sheath the knife in my right hand, even though it meant slicing through multiple layers of protective material. It wouldn't matter; not if I didn't get the fuck out of here.

I wrapped the rope around my right wrist and screamed, "Lugh, get me out of here! Now!"

I was immediately dragged forward over the slick ground but had only gone ten feet or so when something grabbed me and I stopped abruptly. Pain flashed, red hot, through my foot and knifed up my leg. I screamed, the sound echoing all around me.

"Beth?" came Lugh's shout. "What's happening?"

"Caught," I somehow replied. "Wait."

I looked down my body. In the headlamp's pale light, the Annwfyn who filled the tunnel seemed huge. He had one claw lodged deep into my foot and his lips were already retracting, his sharp teeth luminescent. Panic surged and I twisted toward him, trying to reach him with my knife, trying to slice its hand or its face or do something— anything—to get free. But my shoulders hit the side of the tunnel and no amount of shoving, twisting, and cursing could get me close enough. So I did the only thing I could— I drew back my other leg and booted his thin features with every ounce of strength I had left. The blow was strong enough to shatter teeth and snap its head back, but his claw remained. If I didn't dislodge it, I'd be in trouble. I kicked the Annwfyn again and again, desperate to get free. Every hit had the claw in my foot moving, causing waves of nausea to roll through me. I bit my lips in an effort to hold back the screams, the bile, and the pain, and kept booting the bastard. Blood dripped from his shattered face, and he was making a series of gargled clicks, but that claw remained in my foot.

Then a sinewy arm shoved past the waist of the first Annwfyn and, with a sharp downward motion of its needle-sharp claws, severed the lower part of its companion's arm.

I was free.

"Go," I shouted.

The sudden upward movement in the rope had it briefly slipping through my grip. I clasped it tighter and slid through the dark and narrow tunnel with dangerous speed, but the relief that had briefly flared just as quickly died. The Annwfyn whose claw remained in my boot was torn from the tunnel and another appeared, scrambling swiftly after me.

It was fast.

Fucking fast.

I twisted around, preferring to see what I was careening toward rather than what careened after me. The tunnel was narrowing, the walls becoming sharper and much rougher, but there was nothing I could do now other than hang onto the rope and hope like hell Lugh could pull me up faster than Annwfyn could scramble.

But it was now so close I could hear the rasp of its breath.

Damn it, I didn't want to go out like this. Didn't want to go down without a fight. But there was no room to move, let alone fight, in this goddamn tunnel.

Then, with a roar that sounded almost human, the tunnel walls began to shake violently. The amount of water running down them increased, splashing almost eagerly onto the tunnel's floor, deftly splitting around my length before rejoining just beyond my feet and rushing on.

Only it wasn't water. It was stone. *Liquefying* stone.

Cynwrig.

I'd obviously reached the "live" portion of the tunnel.

I glanced down again, and saw in the headlamp's weak glow the dark wave hit the Annwfyn. It swirled up his arms and across his skeletal features, solidifying almost immediately, freezing him in place even as it turned him into stone. Making him a statue that totally blocked the passage.

Relief hit so hard, it left me shaking and weak.

I took a deep, shuddering breath, and then shouted, "Ease up. I'm safe."

The frantic upward pace immediately slowed, and my shoulder felt better for it.

"What happened?" came Lugh's question, still

sounding far too distant for my liking. "Cynwrig said it felt like Annwfyn."

"It was. There's a gate under the water."

"They were aquatic?"

"Yeah."

"Fuck."

"Yeah."

I shoved the other knife into its sheath through the caving suit, then concentrated on the ascent, letting them pull me up but helping where I could through the tricker, narrower sections.

As I neared the exit, Cynwrig reached in, slipped his hands under my armpits, and gently dragged me out. Lugh released the rope and then pulled me out of Cynwrig's arms and into his. He didn't say anything. He just hugged me fiercely for several long seconds, his shaking body and the frantic beat of his heart telling me everything I needed to know.

After several minutes, he dropped a kiss onto the top of my head, then pulled away and quickly scanned my length. Alarm flashed through his expression when he got to my boot and the partial arm that was still attached to it via the claw.

"Hate to say this, but I don't think removing that thing would be a wise move right now."

"On that, we agree," I muttered.

The claw hadn't just sliced through my boot and foot, it had gone right through. There was a good inch of its needle-sharp point sticking out of the sole. While I was definitely bleeding—the wetness of my sock was testimony to that—I knew enough about first aid to understand that the claw might be acting as a temporary plug, stopping me from bleeding to death.

"We'll need to pack that foot to prevent too much movement before we do anything else," Cynwrig said.

He appeared on my other side and swung off his pack. His face was drawn and his cheeks hollow; all magic had its costs, no matter what its source. For those able to control living energy, be it earth or flora, that cost was our strength. It was utterly possible for an elf or pixie to use so much personal strength in their quest to alter or reshape their element that they had nothing left to live on.

"Packing it isn't going to make it any easier to walk on," I said. Especially when even twitching my toes had warmth flooding my boot and pain shimmering up my leg. Of course, I guessed I should be thankful I *could* wiggle my toes; it meant nothing vital had been severed.

"You'll be crawling through most of it, so your foot shouldn't be impacted too much as long as you can keep it raised," Lugh said. "The bits we can stand up in, we'll assist you."

Keeping the foot raised was going to be problematic given the long ascent ahead, but he knew that as much as I did. I returned my gaze to Cynwrig. "Is there any record of a dark gate in this area?"

He pulled a first aid kit from his pack. "Do you honestly think I would have let you go in there alone had I known?"

His reply held the bite of annoyance, and I grimaced. "Well, no, and I didn't mean to imply that you would."

He nodded and glanced at Lugh. "Hold her foot still for me. Beth, this will probably hurt, but I'll try to be as gentle as I can."

I automatically clenched my fists though he hadn't even started yet.

"To answer your question, yes, there are records of dark gates around this region." He looped the end of the bandage around my ankle and heel then retrieved a number of bandage pads, placing one either side of the bit of claw poking out of my foot. Then, carefully, he wound the bandage in a figure eight around the two of them and my upper foot. "The majority of them have been inactive for decades, however, and the one that isn't lies over near Swansea."

That made sense. The gates tended to follow the ebb and flow of the human population, the older ones going offline while new ones formed. Not that, as far as anyone knew, the latter had happened for eons now.

I sucked in a breath as the claw moved fractionally. Cynwrig gave me an apologetic look but kept on wrapping and padding.

"Is there any record of aquatic Annwfyn?" I asked, when the pain eased enough.

"Not that I'm aware of."

"It's damnably frustrating we still know so little about them," Lugh growled. "Even after all this time and all the lives lost to them."

And the little we *did* know came from the very few men and women who'd been taken as breeders—in the same way humanity used sheep and cattle to ensure a steady supply of fresh young meat—and had somehow escaped back into this world. They'd never been the same, of course, their minds and bodies destroyed by what they'd been through, but the government had nevertheless employed telepaths to pluck what information they could from them.

"You know, there's a big part of me that actually sympathizes with what the Looisearch is attempting to achieve," I said. "If it didn't mean wrecking our entire world —if the power of the Claws could be used to solely target the Annwfyn—I'd be stepping back and wishing them good luck."

"It would indeed be tempting," Cynwrig said. "But the genocide of an entire race because we do not like their actions is, in the end, unjustifiable."

"That hasn't exactly stopped anyone in the past."

"Yes, but it doesn't make it right."

I suspected there'd be far more who'd agree with me rather than him. Which still didn't make it right, of course.

"Right or wrong," Lugh said, "it is a pointless argument. Until we can find a means of permanently closing the gates, the Annwfyn will remain a fact of life."

Given we hadn't figured out how the gates had formed between our worlds or even if the Annwfyn were responsible for the closure of some and the reactivation of others, permanent closure was unlikely to ever happen.

Cynwrig finished packing around the claw and tied off the bandage. Then he pressed a hand down onto the stone near my foot. A shudder went through it and, a heartbeat later, thick fingers of black rock rose, looping gently around my entire foot and ankle before forming a thick platform underneath.

"A rock moonboot," Lugh said. "Genius."

"Walking still risks moving the claw and causing further damage," Cynwrig said. "But I've made it as secure as possible."

"Thanks," I said.

His smile flashed, warm despite the worry in his eyes. "Can I borrow a knife? Cutting that arm off will make things easier."

I drew a knife and handed it to him hilt first. He carefully sliced away the surplus section of limb, then returned the knife. Once I'd sheathed it, he grabbed both my hands and rose, drawing me up with him. I balanced on one foot, a little wary of putting any sort of pressure on my injured one, even with the moonboot. Lugh handed me a couple of painkillers, which I suspected wouldn't do a whole lot, then picked up both our packs and led the way out. Cynwrig slipped his arm around my waist and all but carried me.

The next few hours were something of a nightmare as we slowly ascended. Darkness had well and truly fallen when we finally reached the entry cavern. Cynwrig, who was sweaty and gaunt with exhaustion, nevertheless swept me up into his arms and carried me the rest of the way.

Which was just as well. Despite the boot, despite the painkillers, I was close to passing out. Only sheer bloody determination kept me going.

Lugh's mapping skills got us through the moor and back to the car quickly and safely. Cynwrig gently deposited me in the back seat, and it was all I could do not to flop across it and just let go.

"The nearest elven healer is in Merthyr Tydfil." Lugh glanced at me. "You able to hang on until then?"

I raised an eyebrow. It was an effort. I really, really just wanted to let go. "Like I have a choice?"

"No, I guess you don't. Cynwrig, keep an eye on her for me."

He climbed into the car and, as Cynwrig settled beside me, punched the address into the GPS and drove off. Cynwrig wrapped his arm around my shoulders, and I leaned into him. His weariness was a blanket that washed over me, but underneath it ran a core of unyielding stone that made me feel safe. Protected. Cared for.

My eyes drifted closed, and the pain washed me away.

I woke to the familiar warmth of arms wrapped around me, but this time, it was in a bed rather than the rear seat of a car. Cynwrig's powerful length was pressed against mine, his soft breathing stirring sweetly past my ear. I remained still, not wanting to wake him. Darkness held the small room captive, but the clock on the nearby side table said it was 5:00 AM. I had no idea whether that meant it was the following morning or if I'd skipped an entire day.

They'd obviously found the healer, even though my memory held little more than a vague blur of faces and continuing waves of pain. My foot was no longer bandaged, the claw was gone, and I could wiggle my toes without blood gushing. I'd been extremely lucky in that cavern. The Annwfyn could have easily munched down on my foot rather than securing it first with his claw, and no healer, no matter how skillful, could replace a lost limb.

The fingers resting gently against my stomach twitched as sleep gave way to awareness. He stirred, pressed a kiss against my shoulder, and then said, in a voice that was husky with sleep and oh-so-sexy, "How are you feeling?"

"Better." I turned to face him. His erection grew between us, pressing against my stomach, a heat I suddenly ached to feel more intimately. "What happened after I lost consciousness?"

"We found the healer and convinced him to work on you immediately."

I raised an eyebrow. "Meaning he was initially reluctant?"

"It was after midnight, and he'd been in bed." His silvery eyes sparkled with amusement. "Let's just say Lugh made a convincing argument that it would be in his best interest to treat you. Immediately."

"Lugh can be quite persuasive when he wants to be."

"Oh, there *was* nothing persuasive about his actions or his words. It was a straight-out threat."

I laughed softly. "How long ago was all this?"

He shifted fractionally to glance over my shoulder at the clock. "Just over twenty-four hours. The healer did warn you'd probably sleep that long."

"So where are we?"

"A hotel in Merthyr Tydfil."

I had a vague memory of Lugh mentioning that city but didn't reply, more than a little distracted by the fingers trailing delight down the curve of my body toward my hip. When he reached that point, he slid them between my legs, and lord, it felt so good I couldn't stop the groan of pure delight escaping.

He chuckled softly and continued to caress and tease.

I licked my lips, determined to concentrate on the conversation rather than the havoc his clever fingers were causing.

"What have you and Lugh been doing in all that time?"

"Lugh said he was going to do some research, and I was here, sleeping right alongside you."

I arched an eyebrow. "For twenty-four hours?"

"Turning stone to water is no easy task, you know." His voice was dry, and I smiled.

"But you're recovered now?"

"You can't tell?" he said, in a lazily sexy sort of way.

I chuckled softly, slipped a hand around his neck, and claimed his lips. For several minutes, there was no sound, no thought, nothing more than exploration and pleasure.

When desire became so great that the air burned with it, he gently pressed me onto my back and slid on top of me. I shifted my legs to allow him access, but he didn't immediately move. He simply stared at me, his gaze consuming me, filled with warmth and wanting. But running deep underneath was something else, something that was almost... proprietary? As if in this moment, with this act, he was somehow claiming me as his.

Which was ridiculous, given this wasn't our first time and we could never be anything more than mere lovers anyway.

Then he slipped slowly inside and began to move, and thought was swept away by the rising tide of pleasure.

Not just the once, but twice more over the next few hours.

If he *had* intended to claim me, he certainly did a proper job of it.

After we'd showered and dressed, I called Lugh to let him know we were finally awake and arranged to meet him downstairs for breakfast. I was just pulling my spare boots on when my phone dinged, the sound telling me it was a text. There was only one person outside the two men I was with and maybe Mathi who had any reason to be texting me, and the latter would rather call than text. He'd once said that seduction was harder over the phone. He was very wrong.

I hit the message and quickly read it, a laugh of delight escaping.

"Something funny?" Cynwrig walked into the room, the towel wrapped around his hips not covering a great deal.

I really *did* love the often too-small towels provided by smaller hotels. At least in situations like this.

"Just a message from Eljin."

"You haven't told him where we are, have you?"

It was sharply said, and I raised an eyebrow. "You have a problem with me receiving a text?"

"I have a problem with too many people knowing where we are."

He tossed the towel aside to dress, and I enjoyed the view. He really did have a magnificent physique. "And perhaps with the fact that I have another lover?"

He met my gaze at that. "We both do, so no."

I dropped my phone on the bed then walked over to him, amusement bubbling through me as I cupped his face in my hands. "Is that a hint of jealousy I'm hearing?"

"I have no reason to be jealous."

"No, but it would nevertheless warm my lady bits if you were."

Amusement twitched his lips. My words were basically an echo of what he'd said after one of his lovers—newly returned from overseas—had tried to steal him away from me during our dinner date at a swanky restaurant.

"I think your lady bits get more than enough attention."

Another echo. My amusement grew. "Says the man who has at least six women—if not more—tending to his cockles."

His laugh was warm and deep and sent delight skimming across my skin. "But my cockles *adore* the attention."

"As do my lady bits. What is good for the rooster is good for the hen."

"Then I thank the gods that credible competition in the form of eligible pixies is in short supply. I would not appreciate being relegated too far or too often down the lover line."

I laughed and kissed him. "Let's get downstairs before Lugh starts getting antsy."

"I would rather we go back to bed."

"So would I, but I'd rather not spend the day with an annoyed brother."

"Took you long enough," said brother grumbled when we arrived in the dining room a few minutes later. "How's the foot? You're certainly walking better on it."

"I am." A lingering ache remained at the point where the claw had entered my foot, but I suspected that had more to do with the tightness of my spare boots. "Did you spend the whole twenty-four hours researching, or did you actually catch some sleep?"

He gave me the look. The one that said "don't be daft." "Of course I slept. And before you ask, I did also ring Darby."

"Good. But those eye baggies are looking pretty fierce, and you *do* have a habit of forgetting self-care and then lying about it when you're nose-first in a computer or some dusty old book, looking for clues."

He rolled his eyes. "Do you want to hear what I found or not?"

I promptly sat down opposite him. "I'm all ears."

"No," Cynwrig said, pulling out the chair next to me and then sitting down. "That would be me."

Lugh groaned. "Seriously? Can we not make farcical attempts at comedy before coffee has even arrived?"

The waiter obviously heard the mention of coffee, because he hurried over to take our drinks and meal orders.

Once he'd gone, Lugh continued. "Remember those coordinates you found on the back of that photograph? They pinpoint an abandoned village called Pynwffynnon, about twelve miles outside Swansea."

I frowned. "There's tons of abandoned villages all around Wales—what makes this one special?"

"The fact I couldn't find *anything* other than the

mention of a foot and mouth outbreak in the area just before the date on that photo."

"Foot and mouth did—and still does—cause untold damage to many communities, so that's not exactly odd."

"No, but being unable to find anything else about the place is. It might as well have been erased from history."

"Maybe it's just a boring little village in which nothing interesting happens."

He gave me that look again. My grin widened.

"Or," Cynwrig said, "the mention of foot and mouth followed by deep 'radio silence' might have been a diversionary tactic. Governments back in the day sometimes used a so-called 'outbreak' to stop the wider public becoming too curious about what was happening in a particular area."

Which wouldn't work these days—not with the proliferation of smartphones—but back then TVs were brand new, expensive, and not something most people could afford, which meant they relied on newspapers and gossip for both their local and wider news. If the government wanted something covered up, it would have been fairly easy to do.

"Which is why," Lugh said, "I called Mathi and asked if he'd seen any mention of the village while he was doing the date search through IIT's records."

"Wouldn't it have been easier to just call Sgott?" I asked.

"*If* he was in the office, yes," Lugh replied. "But he's not."

My eyebrows rose. "He's still up in Scotland? Why?"

"Because they haven't found a body yet, and he's waiting for cadaver dogs. He wants to be certain she's not on the property before he begins a wider search."

I blinked. "How could she not be on the property? The red knife would have prevented anyone removing her—"

"Not if she's dead," Lugh said. "The restrictions end when life is extinguished, remember."

"Yes, but why would anyone kill her there and stuff her body elsewhere?" That made no sense at all. "What about the woman who was renting a room? The one installed by the Looisearch to keep an eye on her?"

"She's also disappeared."

"From the house, or more permanently?"

"They suspect the latter, as her stuff remains in the bedroom and a search at her listed home address showed no sign of recent use."

"So no one came to retrieve her after we'd given Riayn the red knife?"

"No."

Meaning maybe I'd done *too* good a job of restricting her movements. But surely if that were the case, someone would have contacted me about it. Or had she simply been forgotten in the rush to restrain and punish my aunt?

The waiter reappeared with our drinks. I smiled my thanks and then said, "I take it Mathi *did* find something about the village, then?"

Lugh nodded. "Annihilation."

"Annwfyn?" Cynwrig asked.

Lugh took a sip of his coffee, then winced and reached for the sugar. "Much of the report he managed to access was redacted, so we may never know with absolute certainty, but apparently there were only three survivors —a seven-year-old who had gone down into a cellar, a cop who was out hunting for a lost hiker, and a teenager who was found unconscious in an underground cold store."

"And how much are we betting one of them now leads the Looisearch charge to destroy the Annwfyn?" I said.

"I would think the odds on *that* would be extremely short," Lugh said. "Their names were amongst the stuff that's been redacted, but Mathi's put in a request for further information."

"If he sends me the file number, I'll chase it further up the line," Cynwrig said. "I know he's accessing his father's computer, but my father will have more pull when it comes to classified government files."

A suggestion Mathi was unlikely to appreciate simply because of who was making it. I poured my tea then added some milk. "Why was a media embargo placed on the attack though? It's not like entire villages haven't been destroyed by Annwfyn before."

In fact, before electric lighting became a reality in *all* cities, towns, and villages, they were a somewhat regular occurrence.

"From what Mathi could glean, it happened the same day they were testing something called Awbrey's Key on a gate that had been inactive for centuries."

My eyebrows rose. "What the hell is Awbrey's Key?"

"It was supposedly a means of permanently locking the dark gates," Cynwrig said, voice heavy. "Keelan Awbrey—who touted himself as the world's greatest auditory mage —came up with the idea."

"Supposedly?"

"The man was a scamster and his proposal dangerous. It was rejected by both the House of Lords *and* parliament."

"So why do you know about Awbrey and the key, but can't remember the annihilation?"

"Because after the rejection of his proposal, my father tracked Awbrey down and threatened to personally shove him through the nearest dark gate if he ever made and used his key."

"And yet he obviously *did* get approval from someone in government to do just that," I said.

"Obviously," Cynwrig said. "But it was never officially sanctioned, as it would have gone to the House for review. It never did."

"So why was your father against the key?" Lugh asked. "Given the toll monitoring and closing the gates continues to have on your people, why was your father so reluctant to take a chance on the project?"

"Because Awbrey believed that to permanently close the gates we simply had to choose the correct sequence of sounds and vibrations. He was convinced this is how the Annwfyn open them, so it was therefore reasonable for us to close them in the same manner."

"How do you know he wasn't right?"

His gaze sliced to mine. There was anger in those smokey depths. Old anger, and older frustration. "You mean aside from the fact his theory was tested in Pynwffynnon, to the detriment of that entire village?"

"Yes."

I ignored the sting in his tone, picked up my cutlery, and started eating. And discovered I was absolutely famished, which wasn't surprising given it had been over twenty-four hours since my last meal.

"I never said he wasn't right, but in order to create a key that will close each gate you must first create the correct auditory sequence to open it."

"If the gate was inactive, that shouldn't matter."

"Just because it's inactive on our side doesn't mean it is on theirs. It simply means they are not, for whatever reason, currently using them." He began to eat. "Finding the right auditory sequence for the individual gates isn't truly hard, especially if you've been around them as long as the Myrkálfar. There are, however, two problems. One, certain frequencies can be very destructive. Two, gate activation from our side is a call to arms for them."

I stared at him for a second. "The Myrkálfar have tried auditory locks?"

"There is nothing we *haven't* tried. To date, our best offense remains fusing the gates to their structures and that, as we all know, does not last." He glanced at Lugh. "Did Mathi find anything else?"

"The dead were all buried in the local cemetery, and the government then bought all the surrounding farms and removed everyone from the area."

I frowned. "That's a lot of time and money spent covering up what could have simply been attributed to an actual Annwfyn attack."

"Yes, and it leads me to suspect something else happened there. Perhaps something to do with the Key." Lugh picked up his cutlery and began to eat. "Which is why I think we need to detour past Pynwffynnon before heading on to Gwynedd. If nothing else, we can try to find the gravestone in the picture and see if that provides us with any clues."

I wrinkled my nose. "That might not leave us much daylight to check out the mine, and I really don't want to be squeezing through impossibly small tunnels alone at night."

Cynwrig's fingers slipped over mine and lightly squeezed them. "You will *not* be going into any tunnel alone, no matter how small."

I smiled lightly. "I appreciate the gesture, but as you've already said, it would dangerously drain—"

"Yes," he cut in softly, "and I don't care."

My gaze met the heat of his, and my heart twisted. It would be easy, so very easy, to believe the emotions so visible in those silver depths were more than just the caring of a friend and a lover. But this is what the Myrkálfar did. They made you believe, made you *desire*, things you absolutely should not.

I pulled my hand from under his and reached for a piece of toast. "Maybe we should stay in Swansea and start out fresh in the morning. It'll give me a chance to try out the tracker on the token."

Lugh hesitated and then shook his head. "We'd have to backtrack to go to Swansea, and I don't think we can afford the time waste."

"It's not a time waste if it gives us information about the bastard in charge of the Looisearch." I studied him for a second. "Has Rogan been in contact?"

He grimaced. "Yes, and he's getting a little narky about our lack of progress. Apparently, he has a meeting with the higher-ups about next year's exhibition. I think he was hoping to make the Claws the main draw."

"That will never happen," Cynwrig said. "If they are not —or cannot be—destroyed, they'll be returned to the Tenebrous Hoard, from which they were initially stolen."

"Rogan isn't aware of our destruction intentions," Lugh said. "And he has had other hoard items on display in the past."

"Not from the Tenebrous Hoard, I assure you."

"From the Éadrom hoard?" I asked curiously.

A smile tugged at his lovely lips. "Even the Ljósálfar are not *that* slack."

They were certainly slack enough to allow someone to sneak in and steal the whole goddamn hoard from under their noses. That no items from the hoard had yet hit the black market wasn't actually comforting, because godly items sometimes had a habit of taking matters into their own hands.

I mean, how did someone like Gilda, the working-class elf Mathi had been fucking during our relationship, get hold of one of the rubies from the Shield of Hephaestus? The rubies held the power of fire and were so goddamn dangerous that even the Ljósálfar had stored them separately. Gilda had been thoroughly vetted before she'd begun working—and sleeping—with Mathi, so if there'd been any black-market links, they would have been found.

And yet the ruby was in her possession, albeit hidden where no one other than a pixie might have found it.

I doubted it was an accident. It would have come to her for a reason, and I was beginning to suspect it might have been a *godly* reason. The fuckers seemed to be waking from their long sleep and once again intent on playing games with humanity.

"Meaning they came from the third hoard?" I asked. "The one no one talks about?"

"Yes," Cynwrig said.

When he didn't elaborate, I raised my eyebrows. "Is there a gag order on it? Can we not even say its name?"

"It's advisable not to. Certain names have power, and certain powers can be woken on naming them. We have enough problems on our plate. We do not need to be adding more."

"The third hoard can't be too dangerous if its relics were on display at the museum," Lugh commented.

"They were neither the most powerful nor were they named. Each card simply gave a date and description of usage." Cynwrig reached for a slice of toast, then started mopping up the remains of his egg yolk. "The only reason they were allowed to be displayed at all was the time and effort the museum took to retrieve them. But these are very different times, and the risk too great."

I glanced at Lugh. "All this happened before you started at the museum, I take it?"

He nodded. "There hasn't been a major exhibition of godly relics since Rogan was promoted, and I believe it's one of the reasons he's so intent on getting the Claws. He's determined to achieve what no other hunter or curator has before he retires."

Which would never actually happen now if what Cynwrig said was true. "Does that mean he was responsible for finding the third hoard items?"

Lugh nodded. "The success of that hunt is part of the reason he was promoted, though from what I've been told, he was extremely reluctant to accept the position. It was only after he and the department were granted full permission to access *all* vaults and records—not just the antiquities departments—that he finally agreed."

I raised my eyebrows. "He wanted to stay in the field? Gee, I wonder who *that* reminds me of."

Lugh laughed. "I'm never likely to be promoted. I've a long habit of saying exactly what I think, and it's rubbed too many people the wrong way."

And, sadly for him, most of those people sat on the governing board. "Do you believe this determination to get another hoard exhibition is what lies behind his sudden urgency? Or do you think someone is pressuring him?"

Lugh grimaced. "Hard to say. He sounded genuine, but I just don't know anymore."

"Meaning our trap at Cwmorthin didn't amount to anything?"

"A lone photographer did appear, but he was questioned and was legit. Been staying in the area for the last week, apparently."

"Which suggests Rogan is neither bugged nor the source."

"Or that our bait simply wasn't taken." He shrugged. "Sgott is keeping his man at Cwmorthin for a few more days, just in case, but I'm not hopeful it'll amount to anything."

"And the background search he was going to do on Rogan?"

"Not a priority, I suspect."

Which was understandable, given everything else that had happened over the last few days. We got down to the business of finishing our meals, then once we'd paid our bill, we climbed into the hire car and headed for Pynwffynnon. It was well after midday by the time we turned into the dirt road that led down to the village, but we'd barely gone half a mile when we hit a roadblock—three large round boulders sitting in front of an uneven wall of dirt. Beyond that again was a high metal fence that held numerous warnings that the area was not only dangerous but also regularly patrolled.

Those signs did not look old.

Lugh pulled to one side, and we all climbed out.

Once I'd slung my pack over my back, I zipped up my coat and shoved my hands in my pockets. The wind was bitterly cold, but at least she held nothing more than the promise of rain. "Someone remains damnably determined that no one is getting past this point."

"The valley is well known for landslips," Cynwrig said. "The Myrkálfar have on numerous occasions been called in to stabilize the ground around various other villages in the area, but even we cannot fully stop the earth from destruction if she so wishes it."

"Do you think that's why this area remains closed?" Lugh asked. "Because whatever did happen here was a long time ago, and it seems strange it remains secured."

"Until we know what lies ahead, that is a question I cannot answer." Cynwrig walked through the boulders and pressed a couple of fingers into the soil. "This earth is from a slide that happened six months ago. The rocks were placed here decades ago, however."

I walked around the barrier and stopped near the gates. The fence to the right and the left was covered with deciduous climbers. The road that stretched away from the gate was full of potholes and rubble from past landslips, and quickly disappeared into the shadows of a gorgeous old woodland. Aside from the obvious evidence of landslips, there was nothing here that looked or felt particularly dangerous.

Lugh stopped beside me and studied the thick padlock. "It'll take a heavy-duty bolt cutter to cut that damn thing. Just as well we have the Myrkálfar equivalent."

Cynwrig snorted but stepped past Lugh and gripped the chain. Several seconds later, it lay in pieces on the ground. While all Myrkálfar could manipulate earth or stone to some degree, it took a lot of time and training to become proficient enough to manipulate each element with a degree of precision. The Lùtair line were one of the few who were not only masters of manipulating earth and stone, but also metal. According to Sgott, the IIT had been forced to develop special cells just to keep them contained. Not that the Lùtairs were often on the wrong side of the law. Or rather, they weren't often *caught* on the wrong side.

Cynwrig pushed the gates open but had barely gone

more than a few yards when he hit something hard enough to rebound a few feet.

Lugh, in Captain Obvious mode, said, "An invisible barrier. Whatever they're hiding must be pretty damn bad to go to this extreme."

I nodded. "It also means someone must know what is going on here, because barrier spells are not perpetual. They need regular refurbishment and strengthening."

"Its existence doesn't necessarily mean that the current crop of government bods are in the know," Cynwrig said. "It might simply be the result of a historical overlay order, which is funded and serviced without details as to why it's being released."

I glanced at him curiously. "Are there many of those in existence these days?"

"There's a couple, mainly in the locations that saw the worst fighting during the war of the races."

A war mankind won, with more than a little help from shifters and mages.

I raised my eyebrows. "That happened centuries ago—how could the magic still exist?"

"It doesn't, but before it faded, it changed the viscosity of the soil. You might as well try walking on water." He motioned to the wall we couldn't see. "Will your knives counter this spell? Or are they designed to only counter foul magic or spells designed to attack you?"

"I guess there's only one way to find out."

I drew a knife and pressed the point into the unseen barrier. A gentle pulse ran through the blade, a soft beat that suggested it had at least recognized the presence of magic. A few seconds later, the pulsing increased, and the barrier shimmered and peeled away from the knife's point, creating a hole a meter or so in width. Which wasn't enough to let me step through, let alone the two men beside me. When I pulled the blade away, the hole slowly closed.

"You know," Lugh said, "we came across a barrier like this once in Egypt. Our mage tried every spell he knew but couldn't break it. In the end, we used two silver blades to create a gap big enough through which to crawl." He glanced at me. "Your knives are silver. That's probably why it pierced the barrier without breaking the spell."

The fading pulse in the knife suggested they *had* applied some interference to the magic, but I let it slip. "What do we need to do?"

"You place one knife on the ground and hold the other diagonally several feet away. We slip through the gap, you follow, and then reclaim the ground knife."

I frowned. "If it was that simple, wouldn't other people have tried to get in here?"

"Who would really want to get in here?" Lugh countered. "Photographers and cavers perhaps, but pure silver knives are expensive, and most would not bother."

I'd gone out with a photographer a couple of times, and it had seemed to me that being legally restricted from entering a place had only fueled his determination to do exactly that. He might have been a rarity, of course.

I placed one knife on the ground, drew the other, then took two steps sideways, pushing it into the barrier just above my head. The air once again shimmered and peeled away from the blades, this time creating a somewhat angular "doorway" rather than a neat-looking hole. Once the two men stepped through, I followed then bent to pick up my other knife. The barrier chased my movement down, closing fully the minute my knife was free.

"Hopefully," Lugh said, "we haven't set off all sorts of

alarms and traps. That did happen in Egypt. Got interesting for a while there on that trip."

Cynwrig rolled his eyes. "*Now* he mentions it."

"Wouldn't have mattered anyway, because it wouldn't have stopped any of us."

Which was a truth neither Cynwrig nor I could argue with. I sheathed my knives and followed the two men down the road and into the lovely old forest. What immediately struck me was the silence. Woods like this were usually full of birdsong, even in winter, but there were no sounds here aside from the gentle rustle of leaves stirred by the wind. Did the barrier prevent them from entering? It was possible, I supposed, but overkill in the extreme. Unless, of course, whatever happened in Pynwffynnon was as dangerous to wildlife as humans.

Which made me doubt the wisdom of entering this place, but not enough to stop, of course.

I brushed my fingers along the low-hanging branch of an old oak arching gracefully over the broken road. Its song was strong and warm, but it resonated with such sadness that tears briefly touched my eyes. I blinked them away and brushed the branch of another tree. It too mourned for brethren lost. And yet both were surrounded by trees that were perhaps even older than them.

As we moved closer to Pynwffynnon, the road began to climb, and the forest fell to our left while the mountain rose to our right.

It was then we began to see the destruction. While there were plenty of newer trees whose song resonated brightly across the stillness, dotted amongst them were the remnants of what had once been lovely old oaks and birches. They lay on the ground in lines that fanned out in an increasing radius, reminding me a little of an image I'd once seen of a meteor strike that had happened in Russia in the early 1900s. That forest had also been flattened, the trees stripped of all foliage, their bare trunks lying on the ground in soldier-straight lines that led away from the strike point.

If Pynwffynnon was the strike point here, then its destruction did not solely lie at the hands of the Annwfyn. Their weapons were claws and teeth, not bombs, bullets, or even knives.

We finally reached the top of the long slope. Pynwffynnon lay below us, nestled in the small valley between two mountain ridges. Like many villages around these parts, there was one main street lined with buildings on either side, and a smattering of houses on the slopes around it. All of them were in a state of decay. Mounds of rubble surrounded most of them, there were very few intact windows, and most of the roofing had disappeared, though whether *that* was due to erosion or theft, I couldn't say. Slate was often repurposed, and if they'd had time to bury the dead, then they'd probably had time to gather slate and other reusable building materials.

Blackberries and other noxious weeds rambled over what remained of the buildings, and the forest had begun reclaiming the main street. There was even a poplar growing out of the engine bay of a rusted old car.

There were no soldier lines of trees here, though. No old trees or plants of any kind, in fact. If this village was the ignition point for the blast that had caused the damage in the surrounding forest, then there was no immediate evidence of it.

But maybe *that* was all the evidence we needed, given the cover-up that had obviously happened here.

Cynwrig dropped onto his heels and pressed his fingers

into the gritty soil. After a moment, he said, "There's no indication that the ground is in any way unstable up ahead."

"Any vehicle or foot movement?" Lugh asked. "I know the barrier remains in place, but the signs did say the area was regularly patrolled."

"Nothing whatsoever." Cynwrig rose and dusted off his fingers. "This town is as barren as the forest when it comes to life of any kind."

"Which is damnably odd," I said. "And rather creepy, to be honest."

"Look on the bright side," Lugh said, slanting me a sideways glance. "At least there'll be no rats."

I snorted and shoved him down the hill. He laughed and continued on, his pace not slowing until we reached the outskirts of the town.

This close, it was pretty evident that the destruction of the buildings was due to time, weather, and erosion rather than any calamitous event. The wind whistled through the lonely remnants, shivering through the shrubs that clambered over them and rattling various bits of loose tin. I cautiously stepped through the broken doorway of what had once been an old sweet shop. Dusty jars still filled with sweets lined the wooden shelves, and the old-fashioned register remained on the counter. There were even two brown paper bags of sweets sitting nearby, as if still waiting to be picked up by the purchaser. There was no evidence of a fight of any kind, though, which was odd if the Annwfyn were the reason this place was all but wiped off the maps. But maybe the place had been empty when they'd hit.

I turned to leave, then caught sight of the stain on the floor near the counter. Curiosity stirred, and I walked over. The dark stain's shape was oddly similar to the pattern we'd seen in the forest, containing an obvious blast point and splatters that radiated out from there. There were also fine scraps of what looked like hair. *Human* hair.

A chill ran through my soul.

If someone had been at the counter paying for the sweets, this was more than likely where they'd been standing. But it was insane to think this stain had once been a human. Bodies just didn't—*couldn't*—spontaneously explode, even if the splatter pattern here did resemble the one evident in the forest destruction.

I rose and walked around the counter, stirring the heavy layer of dust that covered everything. It danced lightly around me, catching my nose and making me sneeze. My gaze dropped... there was a second stain under the old cash register. Same pattern, but a few more scraps of hair in a much lighter color.

Oh *fuck*...

"Everything all right?" Lugh said, as he stepped into the shop.

I jumped a little then swallowed heavily. "What does that stain near the counter look like to you?"

He raised an eyebrow, but nevertheless walked over to examine it. "Blood," he said, after a moment. "Old, dried blood and what looks to be hair of some kind."

"Human hair?"

"Could well be." He rose. "Neither is unexpected if the Annwfyn did come through here."

"Annwfyn aren't this neat," I replied. "If they did this, there'd be blood and bones scattered all over the place."

"There might be blood, but there wouldn't be bones, given the government apparently buried everyone who died here." He paused and scanned the sweet shop thoughtfully. "We should check the rest of the buildings to see if the stains are repeated."

I followed him out. Cynwrig was just leaving the building opposite. "Did you find anything?"

"Yeah," he said. "Unusual blood stains. You?"

"Same."

We moved into the next lot of buildings. More blackened, circular patches. More human hair accompanied by the occasional scrap of leather or cloth that could have been remnants of clothing. If nothing else, it was concrete evidence that the people here had been caught totally unawares by whatever had happened.

I shoved my hands into my pockets again and tried to ignore the shiver that ran through my soul. I really, *really* didn't want to believe what I was starting to believe.

As Cynwrig came out of the last building, I asked, "Where's the dark gate from here?"

"It's in the old mine just above us. Why?"

I automatically looked that way, but the new growth forest was too thick to see the mine or anything else. "I was just trying to figure out if the center of the blast that smashed the trees was here in the village or up near the mine."

"It came from the mine," Cynwrig said. "There's a detectable difference in the ground that lies just below the entrance to what lies above."

I raised my eyebrows. "What sort of difference?"

He hesitated. "The ground immediately near the cave is unable to sustain any sort of life, but returns to some normality a few yards further down, though none of it— even the ground here—has the same capacity to hold water that the ground above the mine has."

"Suggesting whatever the blast was, it targeted the

water in the soil." I rubbed my arms. "Do you think whatever affected the soil could be responsible for the bloody stains we're finding? Human bodies are roughly sixty percent water, so it would feasibly be possible."

"Except that in an area as large and as open as this, there's no way sound waves could ever reach lethal levels," Lugh said. "They'd disperse too quickly."

"What if they didn't though? Remember, Awbrey was an auditory mage. Scammer or not, he obviously had enough power to convince someone in the government the key was worth testing." I glanced at Cynwrig. "You also said his idea was sound but dangerous—what did you mean? You never actually explained."

"The frequencies necessary to open certain gates had the capacity to alter the very nature of nearby earth and stone." Cynwrig's voice was grim. "We never found one capable of vaporizing human flesh, though we did stop when the dangers became obvious."

"It would appear Awbrey did not have the same sense of caution," Lugh said.

"But even if Awbrey's Key is responsible for this mess," I said, "that doesn't explain why the barrier remains in place around this area."

"Perhaps it is simply a matter of no one ever recanting the overlay," Lugh said. "Or maybe we simply haven't come across the reason yet. Shall we continue on to the cemetery?"

"Well, it'd be fucking pointless to come all this way and not check it out," I replied.

He grinned, and once again led the way forward. The cemetery was positioned on the hill above the town, giving it a prime view over the entire valley. The rusted metal entry gates creaked when Lugh pushed them open, and the sound echoed across the stillness, as sharp as any gunshot.

Maybe it was my overly active imagination, but deep in the heart of the forest above the village, something stirred in response.

I shoved said imagination back into its box, pulled my phone from my pocket, and brought up the image of the old black-and-white photo. The first thing that became obvious was the fact there'd been a lot of new growth over the years since it had been taken, and that would make finding the right gravestone difficult.

Lugh plucked the phone from my fingers and studied the photo for several seconds. After increasing the size of the image, he said, "There's the shadow of what looks to be some sort of cross to the right and behind the gravestone the figure is kneeling in front of. We just need to find that, and it should be easy enough from there."

He walked on without waiting for a response. The graveyard was surprisingly large, although a good portion of it wasn't used. We'd entered into the older section, but as we followed the somewhat meandering path, the gravestones became newer and the burial mounds smaller. Maybe the Annwfyn had finished what Awbrey's key had started, meaning there hadn't been all that much left to bury.

My gaze drifted across to the forest again, and I shivered.

"You cold?" Cynwrig asked softly.

I shook my head. "I've just got a bad, *bad* feeling the shit is about to hit the fan."

His gaze followed mine, and his expression became thoughtful. He bent and brushed his fingers across the ground. "I'm still not sensing any movement."

"Would you be able to if the earth in the mine is as barren and unreadable as that just outside it?"

"No, but if the Annwfyn were on the move, they'd have to cross onto fertile soil to reach us." He touched my arm in a reassuring manner that didn't actually help. "I'll keep monitoring."

I nodded, but my gaze kept drifting toward the forest, and the sense of danger increased with every step.

After a few more minutes of walking through the overgrown cemetery, we found Lugh's cross. From there, it was just a matter of walking down the three lines of gravestones in this area to find the one that matched the size and position of the one in the photo.

In the end, it wasn't hard to find, because it was the only grave here that was weed-free. In fact, roses had been placed in front of it rather recently, and that meant we weren't the only ones who'd figured out a way through the barrier.

I stopped in front of the gravestone and read the inscription. "Here lies John Einar, his wife Rosy, and their daughter Dona. Survived by son—" I stopped, my gaze darting to Lugh. "*Rogan?* You don't think it could be our Rogan, do you?"

"Only if he's changed his name, and why would he do that?"

"Maybe he was adopted," I said. "Or maybe he was forced to do so by a government who wanted no easy means of tracking surviving witnesses."

"And maybe it's just a coincidence. There'd be more than one kid named Rogan in this world. I think the more important factor here is the surname—isn't Einar the name Vincentia wrote in her own blood?"

"Yes, but if you ask me, all the little coincidences are

becoming too big to ignore." I wrinkled my nose. "We really need that background information stat."

"In other words, ring Sgott and give him a nudge."

I grinned in response. Lugh rolled his eyes, pulled out his phone, and then grimaced. "No reception. We'll have to—"

He stopped, horror widening his expression. "Is it my imagination, or is there something big moving through that goddamn forest?"

Cynwrig and I swung around. The trees were shivering back and forth, as if they were being attacked by a turbulent wind. One that wasn't associated with weather, but rather came with a large force moving at great speed.

Cynwrig bent and pressed his fingers against the ground. His face lost all color, and my heart just about seized.

"Run," he said. "*Now*."

CHAPTER
TEN

As one, we turned and ran across the cemetery, away from the gate and the village. *It* was too close to the forest, too close to *them*.

Lugh crashed through some shrubbery, then leapt over a partially fallen metal fence. His jacket caught one of the rusted spikes, but he didn't stop. The jacket tore, leaving behind a bright scrap of material that fluttered like a flag in the breeze. I grabbed the fence, clambered over it with a whole lot less grace than either man, then tugged the bit of material free. The Annwfyn hunted by smell as much as sight, but there was little point in making it easier for them.

We ran on, up the slope, through sparse forest and lines of fallen trees. Cynwrig made little sound, but Lugh and I might have well shouted our location, we were so damn loud.

It didn't matter.

The Annwfyn's howls now filled the air. They had our scent.

Terror flooded my body, lending my feet wings. I leapt

over a fallen tree trunk, stumbled a little on the landing, and then raced on.

But they were closing in.

Cynwrig slid to a stop. When I faltered, he flashed me an angry look and growled, "Keep going."

I obeyed. A heartbeat later, the ground began to shake, and I risked a look over my shoulder to see what was happening. Cynwrig had squatted on his heels and pressed both hands against the ground. The earth rose in a wave before him, its velocity and size increasing the further away it moved. It swept everything before it—trees, stone, fence, and even gravestones—as it raced toward the forest and the first few Annwfyn emerging.

I hoped it would be enough to stop them.

I feared it wouldn't.

I swallowed heavily and ran on. The ground grew steeper and rougher, and my pace slowed. My breath was now harsh rasps that seemed to hang in the air, and my legs burned. Lugh paused long enough for me to catch up, then grabbed my hand and hauled me on, making the climb a fraction easier even though his speed forced me to concentrate on every step. When I did stumble, he tugged me up and on.

The roar of the Annwfyn briefly stopped, and the ensuing silence was eerie. Frightening.

Cynwrig reappeared. "We have five minutes, if that, before they come after us again."

"And the barrier?" Lugh asked. "Did you sense its location through the soil?"

"At least four minutes directly ahead."

Meaning it was going to be tight. Real tight.

We ran on. Sweat trickled down my face and back, and

everything protested—not just my legs and my chest, but also my fingers from the tightness of Lugh's grip.

It didn't matter. Nothing would if we didn't get to that barrier before the Annwfyn got to us.

We reached the top of the ridge and swept down the other side into a forest that held little in the way of damage, suggesting we were nearing the barrier. Lugh slowed, but not fast enough, and we both body-slammed into the thing. It sent us staggering back and we would have ended up on the ground in a tangle of arms and legs had Cynwrig not somehow caught us both and kept us upright.

Behind us, the hunting howls of the Annwfyn started up again. Those who hadn't been swept up in Cynwrig's wave had caught our scent.

And they were close.

Far too close.

I cursed, pulled out of Cynwrig's grip, and drew my knives, stabbing one into the ground near my feet then stepping sideways to shove the other in the barrier just above my head.

The air shimmered as the barrier started to peel away from the silver, but it was too slow. Far too slow. I gripped the wind with my free hand, spun it around to form a whirlwind, then sent it scuttling back into the forest. It collected shrubs and tree branches on the way through, before disappearing over the ridge and beyond our line of sight.

I glanced back at the barrier. Almost big enough.

Behind us, the hunting roar of the Annwfyn changed note as my whirlwind smashed into them. Bodies were tossed into the air like confetti, but the wind didn't catch them all. At least half a dozen had crested the hill and were sweeping down toward us.

I looked at the barrier again. It was as big as it was going to get. "Lugh, go."

As he jumped through, Cynwrig bent and sent another wave of soil crashing toward the Annwfyn. Then he spun and dove through the gap. As I stepped through after him, the wind howled a warning, and I looked around to see an Annwfyn that had obviously escaped Cynwrig's second wave launch at me from some distance away.

Lugh grabbed my arm and yanked me back while Cynwrig lunged for the knife in the ground, pulling it free. The barrier began to close but again, it wasn't fast enough. Cynwrig raised the knife and, as the Annwfyn came through the shrinking gap, plunged the blade into the fucker's head. The blow was hard enough that the point came out between its eyes.

The Annwfyn was dead before it hit the ground.

The barrier closed over the top of its body, slicing it in two, leaving its top half on our side, the bottom on the other.

The remaining two Annwfyn hit the barrier harder than Lugh and I had, and rebounded even further. They scrambled up quickly and relaunched, their screams muted by the barrier but not their anger and frustration. It burned around us, as fierce as the hunger in their eyes.

"Well," Lugh said heavily, "I guess we know now why the barrier remains in place. Awbrey's Key must have locked the gate open."

"He was probably vaporized right alongside everyone else," Cynwrig said. "It would have meant there was no one alive to close the thing."

I glanced at him. "Couldn't the Myrkálfar have done that?"

He wiped the knife blade clean and then handed it to

me hilt first. "We were never asked and, given the deadness of the soil outside the mine, it's likely we wouldn't have succeeded. Besides, given how quickly the Annwfyn reacted to the slight bit of noise that gate made, any attempt at closure would have been too dangerous."

I sheathed my knife and studied the Annwfyn still tearing at the barrier. "Given how effective this barrier has proven to be, why haven't they been employed around all the dark gates?"

"It would be impractical, given the number of gates and the time and energy it takes to maintain them," Cynwrig replied.

"And I'm betting there'd also be few witches—or mages —willing to dedicate their entire lives to that maintenance," Lugh added, "because that's basically what it would take."

I nodded. It did make sense, though I couldn't help but wonder if these barriers were used in areas considered of "national importance," such as the Queen's various residences and Westminster. "Well, aside from uncovering what happened, we also learned something else—the Annwfyn are not affected by the sun. Or at least, these ones aren't."

"Fuck," Lugh said. "That didn't even occur to me."

"It's not all that surprising when you think about it," Cynwrig said. "Annwfyn is a reflection of our world—one that exists alongside but on a different plane—so it's logical there would be different races with very different capabilities and tolerances. But you're wrong in saying they are not affected—look closer."

"I'd rather not," I said, but nevertheless did.

And saw the fiery red rings beginning to dot their dark skins. They reminded me a little of the bright glow that appeared on the edge of burning paper, and they spread just as quickly, racing up their arms and across their faces.

The note of their screams changed from rage to surprise to pain. They turned and ran. One became ash before he hit the deeper swathe of trees along the ridge, but I had no idea what happened to the other.

I personally hoped they *all* became nothing more than tiny bits of soot.

I pushed to my feet, shifted my backpack to a more comfortable position, then followed Lugh through the trees. I had no idea where the car was in relation to our current position, but Lugh tugged his maps and compass out of his pack and had us back at the car a few hours later.

By this time, I was starving, and the evening's shadows were once again drawing close. While he did a U-turn and headed back down the road, I dragged out my phone and, once I had a signal, called Sgott.

"Hey, lass," he said, gravelly tones relieved. "Where have you been? I've been trying to call you for hours."

"Sorry, we didn't have any reception where we were. I take it you've found Riayn's body?"

"No," he growled. "We did not."

"Meaning someone has definitely removed it?"

"A question I'm endeavoring to answer as we speak."

"Well, she could hardly have walked out, given the knife restrictions."

"Death ends the knife restrictions," he commented.

"Death by necessity also ends life. That's hardly a good way to get out of them."

"That would depend on whether there's a healer present, wouldn't it?"

My eyebrows rose. "That's a big risk to take, given even elven healers can't work miracles."

"Your aunt might have well thought it worthwhile."

He sounded unhappy, and who could blame him. He didn't need to be dealing with this on top of everything else. Granted, this technically wasn't in his region or his crime to deal with, but he'd obviously taken over regardless. Maybe the local IIT division was reluctant to deal with the pixie council and a red knife restriction—and again, I couldn't blame them for that.

"I did contact the pixie council this morning," he continued, "to ask if a request had been made for a temporary stay of restrictions or even permission to scatter her ashes in the wood."

The wood he meant was Ysbryd, an ancient Devon forest from which all five pixie lines are said to have originated. While the other four had found home woods elsewhere, we Aodhán had not. Ever since losing the job of guarding the hoards, we'd mostly lived in human cities rather than forests. Knowing what I did now about our history, I had to wonder if that had been yet another form of punishment. Especially given the Tàileach branch *had* maintained their connection to their ancient woodland.

But Ysbryd remained important to the Aodhán. While none of us lived there in life, our ashes enriched and protected the soil, and our spirits roamed her ancient wilderness, even to this day. Scattering had never needed council permission, however. The only reason anyone *would* have sought it was because of the red knife.

"Vincentia is the only person who could have asked that," I said. "And she's dead."

"She is now, but she might not have been when her mother was murdered. *If* her mother was murdered."

"I take it our council haven't gotten back to you yet?"

He snorted. "Your mob do not work with any sense of urgency."

A smile tugged at my lips. "You're not going to see me complaining about that right now."

"No, but it's damnably frustrating when it comes to policing."

And that was undoubtedly deliberate on their part. Pixies by and large tended to walk their own paths and ignore what other fae *and* humans said, did, or wanted. That's one of the reasons why we didn't have a great representation on Deva's council.

"Was that the reason you were calling us, or was there something else?" I asked.

"No, I wanted to let you know I got the results back from the full background we did on Rogan."

"And?" I said, with a quick glance at Lugh. His expression didn't give much away, but I nevertheless suspected he knew exactly what Sgott was about to tell us.

"There's no criminal history, no misdemeanors, not even a parking ticket. The man has led a squeaky-clean life," Sgott said. "We did, however, undercover the fact that he was adopted when he was seven years old—"

"Don't tell me," I cut in. "The surname of his adoptive parents was Garnet, and his birth name was Einar."

Lugh swore, softly and violently, his knuckles white against the steering wheel. He might have been half expecting this result, but it had nevertheless hit him hard. He'd worked with the man for nigh on forty years and considered him a friend even if they'd never been particularly close.

"Aye," Sgott said, surprise evident in his rich tone. "How did you guess?"

"We've just gotten back from a graveyard that held

what we believe to be the rest of his family. They were slaughtered. In fact, the whole village was slaughtered— only three people survived, and a seven-year-old Rogan Einar was one of them. It's not exactly an everyday name, so it wasn't hard to jump to conclusions."

"Indeed," Sgott said. "And witnessing such destruction could easily damage an adult's mind, let alone a young child's."

"What it *did* do was send him hurtling down a revenge-seeking path," Lugh muttered. "Everything he's ever done —every relic he's ever found—could be nothing more than the result of searching for a weapon strong enough to bring destruction to those who wiped out his entire world. And Nialle and I fucking gave it to him."

"Neither of you were to know Rogan was a bad egg."

"I know that. It's just—" He paused and shrugged. "I didn't see this coming. There is a part of me that thinks I should have."

"None of us saw it," I countered. "Not even Mom, whose business it was to see the future and uncover the unknown or lost."

"You're not the only ones to be duped by the man," Cynwrig commented. "My family have been longtime supporters of the museum and of Rogan's work. It does explain how Jalvi and her family got involved though. Rogan knew them well."

"The minute I got the information," Sgott said, "I ordered a team to bring him in for questioning. However, he's not at the museum and he's not home. I've issued a warrant, but I'm thinking he's gone into hiding."

"He can't know we suspected him," I said, glancing at Lugh again. "We've been very careful to keep him updated on what we were doing without going into specifics."

"Maybe he thinks Vincentia lived long enough to pass on information," Lugh said. "Just because we presumed he was at the museum when he rang us doesn't mean he was."

"We talked to Eljin," Sgott said. "He hasn't been sighted for a couple of days, though he has been ringing in to ensure everything is proceeding as normal."

"Kind of him," I muttered. "I take it you've tried tracking his phone?"

"His phone was at his house. He must have a burner."

"He's using the same number though," Lugh said. "I would have noticed if he'd changed."

"He's likely only slotting the SIM into his new phone whenever necessary," Sgott said. "SIM cards can't be tracked in and of themselves. We'll be notified the next time he uses it, of course, but I wouldn't be betting on the fact we can get to the location before he removes the SIM and moves on. You on your way back to Deva?"

"Not yet. We're spending the night near Blaenau Ffestiniog and will be exploring one of the mines there tomorrow morning." I paused then added, "If you don't hear from us by tomorrow night, send in a search party."

"I will, but I'd much rather not have to."

"I'd much rather you didn't have to, too."

He bid me a gruff "Be careful" and then hung up.

None of us said anything. There was nothing to say, in all reality, though I daresay that would change if Rogan did crawl out of the woodwork and was somehow caught.

Night had well and truly settled in by the time we reached Blaenau Ffestiniog. We found two rooms in a lovely old stone hotel not far from the mine site, grabbed a meal—fish and chips and the best apple crumble I'd tasted in a long while—then headed upstairs. I was asleep within minutes of my head hitting the pillow. I didn't even have the energy for a lingering kiss goodnight.

Lugh had collected the keys and directions to the mine after dinner, which meant we could head out before dawn and didn't have to wake anyone at an ungodly hour. We'd parked in the designated area at the base of a mountain of discarded slate and were making our way up the steep incline toward the lake at the top. According to directions, the mine's entrance was located close to the waterfall that ran from one end of the lake and behind a recently refurbished old mine manager's office, which apparently was used by hikers to escape the rather changeable weather conditions. Thankfully, there was no hint of wild weather in the air just yet, but it was crisp and cold, and a deep frost covered everything. The ground crunched under our feet, and our breath hung like little clouds in the air.

Even so, I was overly warm by the time we reached the old mine manager's office. We moved around it, found the fast-flowing waterfall, and then finally the fenced-off area into the mine. The gate lay in the middle of the river's overflow and meant wading through knee-high icy water. Lugh unlocked it, tucked the key safely back into his pocket, and led us into the mine.

It was cold, wet, and smelled like mud. Fouled mud.

The one bright note was the fact there was plenty of water running down the tunnel. If it was this wet here, then there were likely to be lakes deeper down. Whether any of them were the one we were looking for was something we'd undoubtedly uncover.

I hoped it was. I really didn't fancy yet another journey into a dark, dank, and dangerous fucking mine.

We came out onto a wide, flat platform that formed a semicircle around a man-made cavern. Three tunnels ran off to the left, one to the right, and emptiness lay directly ahead. Near the edge of the ledge lay a coiled climber's rope that was attached to a thick metal anchor bolt that had been sunk deeply into the stone. I carefully stepped past it and pointed my flashlight into the pit's darkness. There was nothing to see. Nothing but black ink.

I could smell water though.

"According to the directions, the zip line will take us down three levels and land us in a shallow lake," Lugh said. "We'll then need to walk down two more levels, which will bring us to the limit of the approved caving routes. From there, sister dearest, it's up to you."

"Let's hope my second sight decides to play the game, otherwise we could be wandering around this wretched place for days."

My voice was glum. Lugh smiled and patted my shoulder. "I have every faith in your abilities. But just in case, I've brought along a two-day supply of beef jerky and chocolate."

"You couldn't possibly carry enough chocolate to last me two days."

"You can have my share," Cynwrig commented, smokey eyes bright with amusement. "I'm not that keen on the stuff anyway."

I cast him a look of mock horror. "That right there is grounds for breaking up."

He laughed. "I think we all know it's not my culinary tastes you're interested in."

"Well, no, but it's still a shocking revelation. I mean, that takes body chocolate right off my to-do list."

"Oh, there are much better things to paint a body with than chocolate, I assure you," he replied, his smokey tone sending my pulse rate spinning.

"Can you two quit the verbal foreplay for two seconds, and put the harnesses on?" Lugh grumbled.

I accepted said harness with a grin. Once it was on, he checked everything was done up properly, then attached the caving descender and said, "Do you remember how to use this thing?"

I nodded. Rock climbing wasn't really my thing, but I'd once been attracted to a man who was deeply into it and had joined his climbing club in an effort to impress. He wasn't, so I quit after my first climb.

I might not have had tons of lovers in my past, but I'd done some seriously dumb things in the pursuit of them.

Lugh double-checked Cynwrig's gear, then said, "I'll head down first."

"How do we know the rope is safe?" It looked okay from where I was standing, but that didn't mean there weren't frayed edges hidden by all the coils.

"The operators said it was checked and replaced a week ago," Lugh said, "and there hasn't been anyone else in here since then, apparently. It will be fine."

I nodded and crossed my arms, watching as he threw the end of the rope over the ledge, attached himself via the descender, and then cautiously made his way over the ledge. I crept closer and watched his headlamp slowly descending. It was barely visible by the time he stopped.

"Dropped into water, and it's thankfully shallow." His voice was distant and echoing. "It's a big old cavern with lots of mining leftovers and no hint of anything dangerous as yet. Beth, you come down next."

I attached myself to the rope, had Cynwrig double-check it for me, and then carefully worked my way over the ledge. My descent was long and slow; I could have gone faster but I was wary of losing control or the autostop failing. Lugh would have checked all the gear, I knew that, but my pessimistic streak had risen again.

I made it down safely. Once detached, Lugh shouted the all-clear for Cynwrig's to come down.

I glanced up, watching as the starlight twinkle of his headlamp appeared far above us, then swung around to study the cavern. The water was calf deep and a clear blue-green in the light, and the rough-cut walls a mix of grays with the odd splash of green. There were three viable exits, and one that was closed off by thick old timbers and a big "Danger, Do Not Enter" sign nailed to the front of them. I splashed across and pressed my fingers against the timber. Its song had been drowned out long ago by the darkness and the water.

Cynwrig made it down a lot faster than me. We left the harnesses on and followed a rusting set of narrow rail tracks into the middle tunnel. The descent was slow and the ground underfoot wet and slippery, but the tunnel itself was high and wide enough to walk unimpeded.

By the time we reached the final level of the legally accessible part of the mine, hours had passed. I perched on the rusted, skeletal remains of an old mine cart to rest and contemplated the three blocked-off tunnels. Like the one on the upper level, the barriers here were thick-cut wooden pit props darkened to almost black by time and moisture. No song help from them, I thought.

A cup of coffee and a small chocolate bar appeared in

front of my nose. I flashed Lugh a smile and accepted them gratefully. I wasn't particularly cold or even hungry, but better to consume both now, while I could.

And I had no intention of exploring *that* particular thought any further right now.

Cynwrig was listening to the ground again, but after a few more seconds, rose and wiped his fingers on his caving suit. "There's a large mass of water in the bottom reaches of both middle and left tunnels. Can't feel an island in either, but that might just be because it's magically protected."

I placed my coffee on the ground and tore open the chocolate bar. "What makes you think it's magically protected?"

He accepted the mug Lugh handed him with a nod. "Because of what happened with the sword."

"That had more to do with the properties of the sword itself than external protections." The Annwfyn attacking us at the same time was just a "fun" bonus. "The crown wasn't protected in any way."

"Aside from the Annwfyn, you mean," Lugh said. "We can't discount the possibility of their presence here, given what has happened the previous two occasions."

"Surely to gods we've had more than our fair share of Annwfyn attacks recently," I muttered.

"The gods," Cynwrig said, "have not been in a generous mood when it comes to handing out good fortune of late."

"Were they ever?" I asked wryly.

"For most fae, no," he replied. "But let's be honest here, Aodhán pixies have held the favor of the old gods more often than not."

I guess that was certainly true. At least until my ancestors had totally thrown a spanner in the works.

I finished my coffee and chocolate and handed the mug

back to Lugh. As he repacked everything, I unzipped my suit and tugged the chain holding the Eye from under multiple layers of clothes. It twinkled brightly under the light coming from my headlamp, the lightning that split its dark heart pulsating in readiness.

I clasped the stone, pressing it hard into my palm as I pictured the island and the treasure chest I'd seen in my dreams.

For several seconds, nothing happened.

Then, with a suddenness that had my stomach lurching, the images in my mind spun away and were replaced by new ones. I saw the chest, this time free of the incandescent green fingers, then the island, which was barren aside from rusting, rotten mining paraphernalia that acted like a fence. The dark water loomed, still and oddly luminous, then the vision picked up speed, racing into a wide horizontal mining shaft, out onto a narrow path that followed a fast-flowing river, then into another shaft that was narrow and full of twists and turns. Then it exploded through a barrier and suddenly I was seeing me, sitting down, my eyes closed and my face pale. But in this vision, my clothes were wet and torn, and there was a ragged, bleeding cut following my hairline from my right temple to just under my ear.

It felt so real that I swiped gloved fingers along the side of my face, fracturing the vision and returning me to the here and now.

I gulped and released the Eye.

"Any luck?" Lugh asked softly.

I nodded and raised my gaze to the tunnel directly ahead. It was whole, untouched by the explosion that had seemed so real in the vision.

I vaguely waved a hand. "It's that one."

Lugh immediately spun and walked across. Cynwrig squatted down in front of me, his gloved fingers so warm on my knees compared to the chill running through me.

"You saw something else, didn't you?"

"I think we'll be attacked down there, but I never saw by what. It's possibly the green fingers I saw in my original vision, but it could also be something entirely different."

"Annwfyn?"

I hesitated. "I don't think so, but please don't hold me to that."

He laughed softly. "I believe I trust your visions more than you do at times."

"Probably because I'm still battling to understand even the basics."

"You need to trust your instincts and stop second-guessing things," he said softly.

I half smiled. "Easier said than done, I'm afraid."

"Always is."

He rose and offered me a hand. I clasped his fingers and let him pull me up. He didn't release me, instead keeping hold as we walked across to the barrier Lugh was in the process of dismantling.

"The wood is so damn rotten, it's a wonder it kept anyone out."

As if to demonstrate, he kicked the middle slab of wood and it all but exploded, sending splinters spearing into the darkness beyond.

"I'm thinking there are very few who'd be tempted to destroy what was basically a very solid-looking bit of wood."

My voice was dry, and Lugh snorted. "When it comes to cavers, it's all about the buzz of being the first to step onto uncharted paths. If they'd wanted in, these barriers wouldn't have stopped them."

He got out his flashlight and pointed it into the darkness. The shaft's walls dripped with moisture and were as rough cut as I'd seen. This section wasn't particularly steep, but I knew from the visions that would change at the midpoint.

"We should rope together," I said. "Things get pretty hairy further in this thing."

Lugh nodded and walked across to his pack to grab the rope. Once we were tied to each other, we headed in. We'd barely gone thirty feet when the tunnel did a sharp right turn and closed in considerably. Lugh was constantly ducking, but I was eight inches shorter and fared far better. At least when it came to headroom. The boobs did present more of a problem when we had to squeeze sideways through narrower sections.

We seemed to be descending forever, and yet my watch kept insisting little more than an hour had passed. Obviously, time had no meaning in this place.

The slope steepened abruptly, and from directly ahead came the sound of fast-flowing water—the river I'd seen in my vision.

We came out of the tunnel into a natural-looking cavern. There were stalactites above us and a deep trench below. Lugh pointed his light left and right, but there were no paths leading away in either direction. There *was* a bridge directly ahead. A bridge that had no decking boards left, and whose long beams were supported by rusting chains secured to the cavern's ceiling high above us but not attached at either end. At least, it wasn't now. Metal stringers held the two sides together, and rusted chains acted as hand grips.

I hadn't seen it in the vision, but maybe it had simply careened past too fast for me to notice. "That thing does not look safe."

"The runoff on the walls isn't as bad here, so there's a good chance the beams are solid enough. It's the anchor points that worry me more." Lugh glanced across to Cynwrig. "Are you able to check they're secure?"

Cynwrig nodded and pressed a hand against the cavern wall behind us. The air tingled as his power rose and I shone my light up toward the ceiling. The stone around the anchor point about a meter in flowed like water around the circular peg, then solidified. I moved the light along the two lines; another peg at the halfway point was also locked back down, but there was no further rock movement.

"Good to go," Cynwrig said as he turned to face us again.

"I'm not sure I am," I muttered, eyeing the unstable-looking bridge uneasily.

"It'll be fine," Lugh said. "Besides, if you slip and fall, you won't go far because you're tied to both me and Cynwrig."

"I'm comforted. Truly comforted."

He chuckled. "Come along, sister dearest. We've a ring to find."

I motioned him to proceed. He gripped the hand chain tight, then bent and touched the left long beam. After a moment, he nodded, as if satisfied, then rose and carefully stepped onto it. He waited a second for the slight swaying to stop, then stepped onto the other one.

I bit my lip and watched him carefully shuffle forward. When the limit of the rope tying us together was reached, it was my turn to go.

I repeated Lugh's actions, stepping carefully on the first

beam before placing my full weight on both, then gripped the rusty metal chains and slowly made my way forward. I was halfway across when Cynwrig stepped on. The wood groaned alarmingly, and the swing increased, but there was no immediate sense of oncoming doom.

It was still a monumental relief when I reached the other side and accepted Lugh's help onto the ledge. Once Cynwrig was safely on solid ground, we continued on, following the narrow tunnel until it came out onto the ledge that snaked alongside the rushing river. It was even narrower than it had appeared in the vision, and it forced us to keep our backs pressed against the wall and edge along sideways. *That* would definitely be a problem if we had to make a hasty retreat for any reason.

Thankfully, it wasn't a particularly long section, and we were soon in the next tunnel. This sloped down sharply; with the slickness of the rock, we all but slid the final few yards. The only reason Lugh and I didn't careen straight into the lake was thanks to Cynwrig latching onto a stone near the exit and acting as our anchor point.

I drew in a relieved breath and studied the dark, still waters ahead of us.

This was it.

This was the right cavern, and the right lake.

And it would become our tomb if we weren't very careful.

CHAPTER
ELEVEN

I IGNORED THE DARK INTUITION AND DUG MY FLASHLIGHT OUT OF my pocket, shining it across the water. There, deep in the distance of the enormous cavern, was the island. I couldn't see the treasure chest, but that was no doubt due to the twisted mess of metal and wood—a barrier I suspected was not created by chance.

Lugh bent to pick up a stone and tossed it into the water. Bubbles rose as it quickly sank, and a trail of worms that shone the color of the moon swept from the deeper shadows behind the island and plunged after it.

"I have no idea what they are," he said, "but I'm thinking it might not be a good idea to enter the water."

"I'll make a bridge," Cynwrig said, "but it will by necessity be narrow. It'll take too much strength to construct anything wider."

And he might yet need said strength to get us the hell out of here.

I shivered and rubbed my arms against the chill traipsing across my skin. Things could go very wrong here.

Would go very wrong here, if intuition and visions were correct.

Cynwrig removed his pack, dumped it against the wall near the shaft's exit, then squatted next to the shoreline. Those glowing worms flowed toward him but didn't leave the water or threaten him in any way.

I suspected had any part of him entered the water, the story would be totally different.

He pressed his hands against the stone and closed his eyes. For several seconds, nothing happened. Then the ground began to vibrate, and the water stirred, gently at first but with increasing ferocity. The worms fled.

The shaking increased. Out in the water, foam-caped waves appeared, washing to the left and the right of the thin strip of stone rising from the lake's floor. It arched lightly across the water, forming a solid yet decidedly fragile-looking walkway connecting our shoreline to that of the island.

Cynwrig released the stone and sat back on his heels, drawing in deep breaths that racked his body. "That was harder than it should have been."

I squatted beside him and offered him water. "Why?"

He accepted the bottle with a smile and pointed with his chin toward the island. "There is a presence here, and it's not the worms."

Lugh's gaze swept the distant shore critically even though it was impossible to see anything more than the rusted mining bits and pieces. "Annwfyn?"

"Not Annwfyn. I've felt their weight through earth often enough to be sure of that. Whatever this is, it's neither dead nor alive."

"Oh great," I muttered. "It's a zombie or a fucking ghost. Just what we needed."

His smile flashed, but it was a wan echo of its usually robust self. "The undead are at least easy to deal with, and ghosts, as a general rule, do not harm the living."

"There are people out there who'd disagree with the latter part of that statement."

"People who have too much imagination, I'd warrant. Humans bury their dead underground, remember, and we Myrkálfar burrow through it. I have crossed the path of many a ghost in my time, and none of them have been in any way threatening."

"Said ghosts probably had more sense than to tackle someone who could make their bones disappear," Lugh said, amusement evident. "It's a shame the same cannot be said of the living."

"Indeed," Cynwrig agreed, voice dry.

My gaze went back to the island and a sudden reluctance to go there rose. Which was stupid. I'd never been afraid of ghosts—as Cynwrig said, they were rarely dangerous—and zombies were the work of fiction, not reality.

But there were plenty of other undead possibilities when dealing with magic and old gods.

I hesitated and then said, "Is it possible we could be dealing with something like a lich?"

Traditional folklore said they were powerful sorcerers so determined to live forever that they transferred their soul into a magical object that both trapped and protected it, keeping them in a living state well beyond the realms of a natural lifespan. But according to Mom—who'd apparently clashed with one on a hunt when I was a teenager—it wasn't life so much as half-life. The lich's body gradually shriveled to a skeletal condition but remained able to interact with this world as long as its soul was safe. They were generally sorcerers who'd crossed the old gods in some way, and who were forced into the lich state to serve whatever penance the god chose.

Given the skeletal green hands I'd seen, it was a distinct possibility. Though *that* would suggest a god had either been involved in the theft of the Claws or had at least engaged the humans who'd stolen them—though to what purpose if all they were told to do was hide them in random spots again?

Was this all part of some grander scheme?

"Lich are rare," Lugh said, "but at this stage, I wouldn't be writing any possibility off."

I took off my backpack, placed it beside Cynwrig's, then undid the little straps locking the knives into their sheaths. Unlike the previous caving event, I'd done the sensible thing and strapped them over my caving suit. If there was a lich on that island, every second I wasted getting the knives into my hand could be the difference between life and death.

I returned to Cynwrig's side and studied the bridge for a couple of seconds. "I'm not doubting your building skills or anything, but it *will* hold the weight of the three of us, won't it?"

"It was designed to support two and it will most certainly do that. I think it best if I keep a rear guard. That tunnel is our only exit point, and we need to ensure it remains clear."

That made sense given we had no idea what would happen when I found the ring.

If I found the ring.

I stepped up onto the narrow bridge and shuffled forward cautiously. The stone remained reassuringly solid, and after a few seconds, I increased my pace, making it to the island without incident. As Lugh came across, I shone my flashlight up and down the empty shore, then up at the barrier that separated us from the island's interior. It included the rusting remains of carrier trains, big sheets of metal that had come from gods only knew what, and long lengths of twisted train track. I did not want to know who or what had twisted them, but I seriously hoped we didn't encounter them.

Lugh stopped beside me and shone his light onto the wall. "Do we climb over that crap, or is there a path into it?"

"There's a path. This way."

I followed the curving shoreline around to the left until I found it. It was narrower than I'd thought and forced us to move cautiously through the rusting forest that tore at our clothes with sharp metal fingers. Whoever had constructed this was obviously determined no one was getting in—or out—easily.

I ignored the shiver that once again stole across my skin and ducked under an arch lined with metal teeth. The ground rose gently from where I stood, with the treasure chest its crowning glory.

The fact it was just sitting there, all shiny new and innocent-looking, had trepidation stirring. It seemed too easy to simply stroll up and open the thing, which undoubtedly meant it wouldn't be.

Lugh stopped beside me and swept his light around. There was nothing to see. Nothing other than bare ground and that treasure chest.

"I'm not liking the feel of this," he said after a moment. "I've seen too many people walk into too many traps that were set up just like this."

"Even if it *is* a trap, we really have no choice but to spring it."

"As is also often the case," he replied, in a sage sort of manner. "I suggest we draw our weapons before we go any further."

I raised an eyebrow. "I take it that means you've brought a gun?"

"No, I brought something even better." He put his flashlight away, reached into his pack, and withdrew two hefty-looking foot-long metal stakes. "Meet Jack and Jill, who are made of cold iron and silver with an iron core, respectively. Handy against all manner of hellish ghouls that often inhabit relic sights."

"You've named your metal stakes? *Seriously*?"

"A good workman always respects the tools that might save his life. Naming is part of that respect." He motioned with his chin to my still-sheathed knives. "You should give them a name—it will help the bonding process."

"They're knives. Magic knives, granted, but still just knives."

"No item ever made by an old god is 'just' anything. Mom never named them because she knew they were not hers to name. Gran once said the same thing. You use them in a manner neither of them could; I think it safe to say the naming rights are yours."

"And I have bigger things to worry about right now than thinking up names for two bits of metal."

"Indeed, but it still should be done. All powerful magical items should be named. It is the mage way."

"Says the mage himself."

"Says the mage who made Jack and Jill for me." Amusement tugged at his lips. "Of course, he wasn't too impressed with the monikers I gave them, but he never said they had to be *classy* names."

I laughed. "So why haven't I seen them before now?"

"They're always in my pack, but they're designed to counter supernatural forces and the occasional soul in the service of the dark gods. They're useless against Annwfyn and human attackers, mostly because you have to get too close to the bastards for them to be effective."

"A possibility of a metal stake being shoved through anyone's heart will surely give them pause regardless," I said wryly.

"You'd be surprised. Besides, that would kill them, and there are laws against that. You want me to lead?"

"Given your weapons can't counter magic and mine can, I think it best if I do."

He waved me on. I drew my knives and walked up the gentle hill with more assurance than I actually felt. Despite the water that surrounded us and the gentle dripping evident in the distance, not even the weird moss that seemed to thrive in wet underground environments had gained a foothold here. The place looked—and felt— almost alien, especially with the metal fence casting weirdly shaped shadows whenever our headlamps hit it.

I was barely halfway when lightning began to flicker along the edges of the knife blades. There was definitely dark—or, at the very least, threatening—magic here.

I slowed as we drew close to the back of the chest. The three metal straps that bound it together were thicker than my finger and a good hand wide. The wood was of a type I'd not seen before—it was black and shiny, almost resembling metal—and was untouched by the rot that ringed this island. Whoever had built this had obviously intended it to last. Or did it need to be this strong to contain the power it held?

I flexed my fingers around the knife hilts—a gesture that in no way eased the gathering tension—and walked around to the front. There was no lock, just a simple latch, which surprised me. At least it was until I pointed a knife at it, and the whole blade glowed even brighter.

I glanced at Lugh, more for reassurance than anything else.

He gave me a nod and a quick, "Do it."

I bent and pressed the knives against either side of the latch. The lightning that rolled down the blades jumped onto it then ran up the lid and across the chest. With jagged little fingers, it dug into the wood, splitting the fibers apart where it wasn't confined by the metal straps. Beams of luminous green light speared through the cracks, lending the shadows an eerie glow.

Lugh grabbed my arm and hauled me several steps back. Though my knives no longer touched the latch, the lightning continued to crawl across the chest, widening its cracks and lashing out at whatever lay within.

Then, with a powerful *boom*, the wooden chest exploded, throwing us both backward and sending deadly splinters spearing through the air. I landed hard on my butt several feet away and rolled into a tight ball, hugging the knives close to my chest as the wooden rain fell all around me. Several splinters hit my back, but the coveralls prevented them from spearing deeper into my skin.

After a few seconds, the wood rain stopped. I peered out cautiously and then unrolled and sat up. Lugh was several yards away but aside from a scrape across his right hand, appeared unhurt.

"Beth? Lugh?"

Cynwrig's voice echoed across the stillness, and though nothing stirred in response, my uneasiness increased.

"Both here, both unharmed."

"What happened?"

"You couldn't see?"

"Some weird green light appeared behind the barrier, and I couldn't see past it."

Was that the light that had come from the chest or had we triggered something else? I shivered and hoped like hell we hadn't even as the pessimistic part of my soul was totally convinced that we had.

"I defused the magic around the chest, that's all." I sheathed one knife and walked over to my brother to offer him a hand.

"Sounded more like you exploded the damn thing."

"Same, same."

Lugh shifted the stake in his right hand to his left and then clasped my hand and let me haul him up. "If an exploding chest is the worst thing we encounter, I'll consider this a win."

"Given a green mist now surrounds the island, I'm thinking it won't be."

"No, but it doesn't hurt to put some positivity out there."

It hadn't actually helped so far, but maybe he'd have more luck with that sort of thing than me. I turned and studied the chest. There was no wood left, but the straps remained and looked like shiny metal bones. Inside their ribs lay a glittering pile of jewels, ornate mazers, and even a few knives and hair combs. This was definitely a hoard of some kind, but the question was, whose? And had the owner realized what he actually possessed when he'd hidden the chest here?

Or was it simply a blind? A glittery means of ensuring the Ring of Ruin didn't stand out in any way?

My gaze rose to the emerald that sat on top of the hoard —an emerald as big as my fist and which glowed the same luminescent green as the light that now ringed the island and the skeletal hand I'd seen in my vision.

I pointed a knife at it. No reaction. I couldn't help but hope whatever spell lay on the chest was the only magic we had to worry about, but when the hell had anything in this hunt been that easy?

"I'm thinking it'll be in our best interests *not* to disturb that gemstone," Lugh said, "though that's not going to be easy if the ring lays directly under it."

"Which it likely will, given that's how these things generally go." I paused. "Maybe the Eye will be able to give us some direction."

He nodded and motioned me to proceed.

I tugged the Eye from under my clothes and warily approached the skeletal chest. Light flickered through the emerald's rich heart, but nothing else happened.

I pressed the Eye hard into my palm and concentrated on the need to see the ring. For several seconds nothing happened, then my vision lurched forward with sickening speed and suddenly I was "in" the middle of the glittering pile of precious items, surrounded by an eerie green glow, staring at a golden ring that resembled a snake consuming its own tail.

I released the Eye and sat back on my heels, drawing in deeper breaths to calm the cloying sense of approaching danger.

"Anything?" Lugh asked.

I nodded. "There's an ouroboros ring, made of gold with emerald eyes, sitting right under the bigger jewel."

"Damn."

"I think a stronger word would be more appropriate at this point."

Lugh laughed. "Did you get any sense of a spell?"

"No, but let's see what happens when I touch a knife tip to the emerald."

I did. Nothing happened, though the increased intensity of the crazy inner light suggested there was definitely something going on.

"So, no magic," Lugh said.

"None that the knives recognize, anyway." I frowned. "What do you actually know about lich?"

"Not a lot." He shifted and studied the emerald from a different angle. "Going on past experience with various other occult nasties, I'd say it's likely that nothing major will happen until we touch whatever it's meant to protect."

"Is that the entire hoard or just the Ring of Ruin though?"

"Question of the day, I'm afraid."

"Shall I do the honors?"

"Please, be my guest."

I smiled and swept my gaze over the hoard, looking for something easy to spear in an effort to avoid disturbing the emerald. I saw a ruby-crusted silver ring sitting off to the side of the emerald and carefully pressed the knife's tip through its center and lifted it up.

The emerald cracked, and air hissed out. Green air that coalesced into long, bony fingers.

"Which leaves us with only one choice," Lugh said.

With that, he grabbed the emerald, drew back his arm, and tossed it high and long. It sailed over the misty green barrier and disappeared behind the rusty fence—not in Cynwrig's direction but the other way. A few seconds later, there was a loud splash and green light speared up toward the cavern's roofline, glimmering across ghostly stalactites.

"I have no idea what you just did," came Cynwrig's comment, "but the lake is beginning to bubble and steam."

"Is it affecting the bridge?" I asked.

"Not yet, but the water is becoming acidic and eating away at the stone. I can only combat its effects for a limited time."

"We don't need long."

I returned my gaze to the hoard. The golden ouroboros sat on the very top of the pile, almost plain-looking when compared to everything else in the hoard. I touched the tip of the knife to it. Again, no reaction from either the blade or the ring. I hesitated, then warily picked it up. Nothing. This ring, unlike the sword, wasn't activated by touch.

I held it out to Lugh. "You take it."

He raised an eyebrow. "Why?"

"Our foes will be expecting me to carry it."

"Our foes aren't here."

"No but let's not take any chances, given the bastards keep turning up at inopportune times."

I thrust to my feet, then paused and scooped up an ornate medieval ring with a thick black jewel at its heart. It was basically the design I'd been half expecting, and that might be just enough to fool those who would be waiting for us at the mine's entrance.

Would, not might.

I shivered but shoved this insight aside too. I had to concentrate on getting out of this mine before I started worrying about an ambush.

I walked around the skeletal chest and followed Lugh down the hill, but we'd barely gone a few steps when, from behind us, came a muffled *whoomp*. I spun around. Water had plumed high, and dark droplets rained all around, hissing where they hit the ground and stinging when they hit flesh.

Lugh tugged on his protective hood and said, "Let's get the fuck out of here."

I pulled on my hood and raced after him. A low, haunting moan chased after us, raising the hairs on the back of my neck and sending a chill through my heart. I didn't look back. I didn't dare. The little pits being created in the ground were now sliding into each other, creating deeper, wider pits of molten soil. The whole island was melting away...

Lugh ducked under the arch and disappeared into the barrier. I followed him in but had barely gone two steps when a jagged bit of metal speared through a gap, missing flesh but snagging the arm of my coveralls. I stopped so abruptly a yelp of surprise escaped.

Lugh immediately turned around. "You okay?"

"Fine. Go."

I sliced the caught section away then, from the corner of my eye, saw movement, and turned to face the island. Blood drained from my face.

A figure stood there.

A figure that was green and skeletal, with overly long fingers that ended in razor-sharp nails.

A lich.

It was a goddamn lich.

I turned and ran after my brother, but any sort of real speed was almost impossible. Not only was the twisty path too narrow, but a constant barrage of metal spikes speared through the barrier, slicing through clothes and skin but thankfully missing anything vital.

We finally reached the exit, but the metal continued to attack. Big chunks were being lifted by an invisible hand and thrown toward us, hitting the melting ground with enough force to send it pluming into the air. We swerved constantly in an effort to make it hard to track us with any ease and kept running for the bridge.

The moaning got closer, louder.

I gripped my knife fiercely and concentrated on getting to the bridge.

The lich appeared, looming over the top of the barrier. Its fingers—its *claws*—extended beyond all reason as it reached for us.

I ran on. There was nothing else I could do. The knives weren't reacting, and I wasn't about to confront the lich with nothing more than two short silver knives. Especially when I had no idea if silver would have any effect on a being that was neither dead nor alive.

Cynwrig shouted something I couldn't hear over the rain of black acid and the rasp of my own breath, but Lugh immediately stopped and swung around. "Fuck, Beth, watch—"

I didn't hear the rest of it because skeletal fingers closed around my head, picked me up, and tossed me aside. I landed with a grunt half in, half out of the water, blood running down the side of my face where a claw had dug deeper. I shifted, trying to get up, but the soil had the consistency of glass, and I slipped back down. Heard Cynwrig shout again and snapped my head around. A thick mass of luminous worms surged toward me. I swore, thrust the knife into the island's bank, and used it as an anchor point to scramble out. The worms lunged for me; two managed to latch onto my calf before I was completely free of the water, and pain erupted. I gritted my teeth against the scream that rose up my throat and sliced the bastards away. Blood oozed from the tiny holes they'd drilled into my pants and skin. They were some kind of goddamn leech.

They were also the least of my problems right now.

I thrust upright and ran for the bridge. The lich was attacking Lugh with one set of claws while he'd extended the other and curled it around him, forming a cage that prevented him from retreating. Lugh countered the lich's unnaturally fast blows with Jack and Jill, but his coveralls were nevertheless torn, and blood oozed from a cut on his thigh.

I wrenched my other knife out of its sheath and ran toward them, vaguely aware the white worms were tracking my movements barely a meter from the shoreline. If I slipped, they would have me.

I didn't slip.

Lugh did.

I screamed and leapt at the lich, stabbing a knife through its skeletal head. It made an oddly wretched, disbelieving sound that rebounded off the walls with surreal strength and stabbed wildly at me with knife-like claws. I wrenched the blade from its head and dropped low. As the breeze of his blows skimmed bare inches past my hairline, I slashed the knives across his calves in a cross-scissor motion, completely severing them from the rest of his body.

He made that odd sound again and toppled, almost in slow motion. As grit rained all around us, I swung around and kicked him hard enough to lift him off the ground and throw him into the water. As he went under, I sheathed my knives and darted onto the bridge, dropping onto my knees to reach for my brother. There was blood on his face, blood in the water, and the worms were coming in fast. Panic surged but I somehow forced it down and helped him clamber back onto the bridge. He lay there for several all-too-precious seconds, sucking in air, his body trembling. Then he surged upright, grabbed my hand, and didn't let go as we ran dangerously fast across the narrow bridge.

A bridge that was now being attacked by not only the acid rain but also the increasing amount of rubble falling from the cavern's roof.

It wasn't just the island that was disintegrating. It was the entire fucking cavern.

Cynwrig knelt at the end of the bridge, his hands on the stone and his power singing through the air. Through me. I had no idea how that was possible and no brainpower to ponder it.

As we leapt off the bridge, the lich climbed onto it and strode toward us, seemingly unhampered by the fact he had no goddamn feet. Cynwrig lifted his hands, and his song of power fell away. The bridge went with it, sending the lich plunging back into the swirling pool of acidic water and luminous worms.

They didn't attack him. Instead, the little fuckers formed a living raft that raised him from the water and sped him toward us.

We turned and ran for the exit. Cynwrig swept up our two packs and tossed them to me.

"Keep going," he said. "I'll block the exit."

I felt the rise of his power again but didn't look around. I hoped his stone doorway would be enough to stop the lich, but I feared it wouldn't. The lich appeared to have just as much, if not more, control over its environment than Cynwrig did.

He soon caught up, and we pushed on, slipping and sliding on the slick stone. The tunnel walls trembled, and chunks of earth and rock fell from the roof, an indication the destruction was not confined to the cavern, even if the lich did remain there.

We came out onto the narrow ledge above the waterfall. Rocks bigger than my head plummeted into the river from high above, and the stone under our feet was fissuring. Cynwrig squeezed past us and continued at pace, but his hands were on the wall and his energy pulsed through the stone. The cracks didn't grow, and the path remained intact, but one man couldn't keep an entire mountain from caving in... not for very long, anyway.

We reached the bridge. The whole thing swayed alarmingly, but I followed Cynwrig onto it without hesitation. I kept my eyes on his back all the way, though, not daring to look either down or up lest the enormity of danger we were in overwhelmed me.

Lugh had barely made it off the bridge when a massive rock came crashing through the middle of it, wiping out that whole section.

I shivered, but there was no time to contemplate what might have been. Not if we wanted to survive. We raced on, Lugh in the lead again. Dust and debris swirled all around us, making it difficult to see and breathe. The headlamps barely made an impact, their light little more than a dim puddle against the increasing viscosity of the air.

Then from behind us came a sound not unlike that of a fast-approaching train. The cavern—and the mine shafts behind us—was collapsing, and it would take us with it if we didn't get the fuck out of here.

The dust and the force of air hitting our backs increased. I dragged my sweater over my nose in an effort to filter some of the muck, but it didn't seem to help much.

"We're not far from the exit," Cynwrig shouted, voice barely audible over all the noise, "but we won't beat the collapse. You keep going while I shore up this section of the tunnel and stop the bastard behind it."

I wanted to argue that it wasn't safe for him to even try, but knew it was pointless. In all truth, the only real hope any of us had was him stopping or at least delaying the mine's collapse long enough for us to get the fuck out.

I ran on, concentrating on the man ahead rather than the one we were leaving behind. The air began to smell fresher, and the dust and debris eased, allowing the lights to wash brightly across walls that no longer shook. Safety was *so* close... Adrenaline surged through my limbs, and I raced on with renewed strength. Then, barely visible past Lugh's bulk, I spotted the end of the tunnel and remains of the barrier. Safety, if my earlier vision was to be believed.

I all but staggered past the barrier into the middle of the cavern then spun around, waiting with clenched fists for Cynwrig to appear. For too many minutes, nothing but dust spun out of the tunnel, a thick brown cloud that spread unevenly through the cavern.

Then he appeared, and by all the gods, never had I been so glad to see someone who looked so bad.

I ran back and threw myself at him. He caught me with a tired grunt and laughed softly. "This is the kind of greeting a man could get used to."

"Don't, because if you ever put yourself in danger like that again, I will kill you."

"I was never in danger."

"Liar."

"I would never lie to you, Beth. Not about something as important as that." He paused, a tired smile flirting with his dusty lips. "Which does not discount the prospect of me simply not mentioning it."

I laughed softly, then caught his face between my hands and kissed him fiercely. He tasted of sweat and mud, and I didn't care. He pulled me closer and deepened the kiss, seeming to need it as badly as me.

Behind us, Lugh cleared his throat. "I appreciate that a near-death experience can be something of an aphrodisiac, but we aren't out of the woods yet, so to speak, and we need to get moving."

I broke away somewhat reluctantly and swung around to face my brother. "Not before I get a drink and some more of that chocolate you brought along. There's no way known I can ascend a rope on an empty tank."

He unzipped his pack and tossed me a bar of fruit and nut. I plopped onto the edge of an old cart—the image I'd seen in my vision—and started in on the chocolate. My stomach felt a whole lot better, even if the rest of me ached like hell.

Getting out was a slow and careful process. All three of us were bone weary, and that's generally when accidents happened. After surviving a fucking lich *and* a collapsing mountain, the last thing any of us needed was to be taken out by our own stupidity.

We were all cold, wet, and exhausted by the time we reached the exit a few hours later. Cynwrig pressed his hands against the ground, his gaze narrowed as his power rose.

"I can't feel any undue weight on the ground," he said eventually, "but that doesn't mean there's no one out there. I suggest we remain wary."

We moved out in single file, splashing quickly through the bitterly cold water. After relocking the gate, we made our way up the hill toward the old mine manager's office. The day had darkened toward night, and thin slashes of pink and gold lined the clouds that streaked across the sky.

The whole area was quiet; hushed. There was no movement, no sense of danger, and yet...

Something was wrong.

I stopped. "Cynwrig, could you check the ground again?"

He immediately did so, then glanced back at me. "I'm still not feeling anything untoward, though if there's an ambush party waiting in the hut, I wouldn't, given its foundations are wood, not earth or stone."

I scanned the building ahead uneasily but couldn't see anyone or anything that tugged at my instincts. Maybe it was just nerves. Maybe the inner pessimist just refused to believe we could so easily walk away from the mine after everything else that had happened.

"I think we'd better be ready for trouble," I said softly. "Something just doesn't feel right."

Lugh reclaimed Jack and Jill, then moved out. I gathered air around my fingers and followed the two of them up the steep slope.

Then Lugh slapped at the back of his neck, the sound echoing. He didn't seem concerned, but my trepidation nevertheless increased.

It wasn't the right season for midges. It was too damn cold.

When Cynwrig slapped at his neck a few yards further on, trepidation became certainty. The area might appear empty as far as the eye could see, but we were no longer alone here.

"Gentlemen, we have a problem."

"Indeed, we do," Lugh said, in a voice that didn't really sound like his. "That wasn't a midge—"

The words stopped. As did he. Alarm surged through me. My gaze jumped to Cynwrig. His expression was one of fury and consternation, and his movement, like Lugh's, ground to a halt.

I hurried over to my brother and pulled down the back of his coveralls. That's when I saw the dart.

Oh fuck...

I swung around and scanned the area above the waterfall, where the dart must have come from, but the fading light made it difficult to see anything. Then the air stirred gently around me, and I heard the steps. I turned again.

A figure stepped out from the other side of the mine manager's hut. He wore black from head to foot, which made the silver gun he held even more obvious.

I gathered the air around my fists but didn't unleash it. Until I knew what the two men had been darted with, I couldn't react with any sort of violence, no matter how much I might want to. The man ahead might or might not be able to tell me that, but he couldn't have been responsible for the darts, because the angles were all wrong. There was at least one other person here.

"You even twitch the wrong way, and my friend with the gun will take you all out." The blunt warning came from behind and above us. The waterfall, as I'd guessed. "I should also warn you that your companions, at best, have half an hour before the effects of the poison become irreversible."

It wasn't Rogan speaking, but that didn't really surprise me. He'd shown no propensity so far to be at any of these "interventions," so why would he do so now, even if he was aware we were on to him?

But the speaker wasn't a complete unknown, because I'd heard his voice in multiple visions. This was the man who'd discussed Jalvi's capture with an unknown woman.

The man who'd arranged the attack on Cynwrig's sister at the start of this whole mess.

"What did you give them?" I said flatly. "And what do you want?"

"Oh, I think that second question is a little superfluous," the stranger said dryly, "but the darts contain a variation of Dahbree that steals the ability to respond in any way. Given what happened the last time we tried to drug your mountain of a brother, we thought it best to be absolutely positive he could neither escape nor react against us."

Fury burned around said mountain, and his fingers twitched into a fist, but the drug was doing what it was designed to do, and it would kill them if I didn't comply.

Hell, it might kill them anyway. We were a long way from any sort of help.

"Dahbree is dangerous," I said flatly, "and I'm thinking your boss probably doesn't want either of them dead."

"He might not, but I'm ambivalent. However, I do have the cure to hand, but you only get it if we get what we want. Where is the ring, Bethany?"

"What makes you think we found it?"

"If I have to dart and search you, I will. Of course, that'll mean there will be no one left to administer the antidote, and I'm thinking you might not want to die just yet."

"Don't ever presume to know what I'm thinking."

He laughed. "I don't have to presume. I can see the turbulence around your fingers, and I have firsthand experience of what you're capable of after our confrontation on Ben Nevis. Luckily for you, my priorities lie with our quest rather than gaining revenge for injuries caused."

Meaning I'd unknowingly had one of the Looisearch's

generals up on Ben Nevis and had stupidly allowed him to escape. *Fuck, fuck, fuck!*

"What guarantee do I have that you won't kill us the minute I give you what you want?"

"There's never a guarantee in this type of situation, but my colleague believes it remains in our best interest to keep you all alive until we're positive the Claws can do what we wish, and on this I do concur."

I snorted. "You actually think we'll willingly help you find another weapon if the Claws don't work? You're both delusional."

"Oh, undoubtedly, but in my experience, people will go to great lengths to protect those that they love."

My gaze flickered to Cynwrig, but I didn't reply because it was nothing but the truth. Lugh was all I had, and I wasn't about to lose him. Not to something like this. To a man like this.

I dug the black stone ring from my pocket and spun a protective shield of air around it. He'd no doubt be able to break through the barrier, but it would take time and effort, and I rather suspected he'd be more inclined to play the game as long as it remained the easier option.

"Ah, excellent," the stranger said. "Put it on the ground."

"Give me the antidote, and I will."

"You're in no position to bargain, dear Bethany."

"You want the stone; I want my brother alive. It's a fair exchange."

He sighed. The sound rode the breeze, filled with a mix of frustration and annoyance. "I have already assured you—"

"Yeah, but you're a murderous son of a bitch who has also said he'd have no qualms killing me."

He laughed. "True. We shall do a swap?"

"I want to ensure the antidote works before I hand over the ring."

"I could simply kill you. It really would be easier."

"You could, but that would leave you without a seer to find an artifact that'll work against the Annwfyn if the Claws don't."

His annoyance thickened on the air, but after a few seconds, the air shifted, and a small first aid kit appeared between me and the two men. I opened it and saw two liquid-filled syringes. I mentally crossed all things that it *was* an antidote rather than something that would finish off what the Dahbree had started and injected the two men.

A few minutes later, Lugh's fingers twitched more strongly, and his breathing eased. I glanced at Cynwrig. He nodded fractionally and half opened his mouth, but whatever he was trying to say remained at the back of his throat.

"You have proof of life," came the stranger's comment. "Now give me the ring."

I spun a thick wall of air around the three of us to ensure that if the shadow shot at us, the bullet would be torn away, then cast the ring toward the speaker.

Thick fingers of air immediately snatched it away.

"Thank you, Bethany." He paused, and then added, "Expect us to be in contact if you have, in any way, deceived us."

"That is the ring I was led to," I said evenly. "There's no guarantee it's the one either of us was searching for, though."

He didn't reply, but the sound of his steps rode the breeze, getting ever more distant. I glanced toward the cottage. The black-clothed stranger had also disappeared. I wished we could, because I had no idea how long it would take for them to discover I'd given them the wrong damn ring.

I returned my attention to Lugh and Cynwrig and waited as they regained movement. The minute they could walk, we moved on.

"I take it the ring you handed over wasn't the Ring of Ruin," Cynwrig said eventually.

"It was part of the hoard the lich was protecting." I paused. "How the hell do these people keep finding us? Sgott was the only person who knew we were coming here, and it's unlikely anyone could have successfully bugged his phone. And I haven't spotted an airborne shifter."

"Maybe they're tracking your phone," Lugh said. "They've obviously got people working inside the IIT, so it would be easy enough to do."

"I turned my phone off before we came here this morning though, so it would have been near on impossible to pinpoint us so precisely."

"Perhaps it's not the phone they're tracking but you yourself," Cynwrig said.

I frowned at him. "How can you bug a person?"

He smiled. "In the old days, it would have been done via a small transmitter placed on or in an item of clothing. They've been replaced by bio trackers."

"Bio trackers are fucking expensive, though," Lugh said. "And they're extremely rare on the black market, aren't they?"

"They're rare because there's only one company that makes them, and they keep meticulous records, which makes them almost impossible to steal," Cynwrig said. "Of course, almost impossible is nothing more than an inconvenience to Myrkálfar."

And there were Myrkálfar working with the Looisearch. "So, what are they exactly?"

"In their original form, they send a low-level electrical current through specific parts of the body to measure resistance and determine whether the electron response is indicative of optimum condition."

A type of miniaturized internal medical scanner, then. "And the non-original form?"

"Every bio tracker can be adapted to use the body's natural electromagnetic field to fuel a constant, low-level but unique signal that can be tracked. If Jalvi or one of her kin accessed our stash, it's likely whoever that was atop the waterfall has the tuned receiver."

"Then we need to find and remove the tracker."

"It would have been injected under your skin. We'll need a proper scanner to find it." He paused. "Was there any point over the last few days where someone brushed against you a little too hard?"

"No, but I was attacked by a shifter, and the bitch was pecking at my neck."

"That's probably when it happened."

I raised a hand and brushed the back of my neck but couldn't feel any sort of lump or bump. "Is there any way to block the signal? Or at least weaken it and make it harder for them to track us?"

"Copper or even foil is good for blocking radio signals," Lugh said. "Might work for biosignals."

"Worth a shot," Cynwrig agreed. "We'll stop at the first open supermarket we see and grab some."

Lugh nodded. "And then we'll head straight for the forge."

I wrinkled my nose. "That's a good four-hour drive from here, which means it'll be well and truly into night by the time we arrive. It won't be safe to enter the mine, no matter how many lights we carry with us."

"We'll find a place to stay close by." He tossed me the keys. "You'd best drive, given we have no idea how long the drug will take to totally clear our systems."

We jumped into the car and got the hell out of there. We made two stops—one for fuel and food, and one to buy foil and tape and then apply it—but it was nevertheless after midnight by the time we neared Cheltenham. We found a hotel within easy striking distance of the chimney and grabbed a couple of rooms. I had a quick shower to clean the various cuts and scrapes, waited while Cynwrig checked the tape holding the foil across my shoulder remained in place, then fell into bed and was asleep within minutes.

An insistent ringtone woke me gods only knew how long later. I opened an eye and glared blearily at the offending object. It didn't stop. Before I could move or even swear, a body pressed closer to mine, and then Cynwrig reached past me and grabbed it.

"Lugh?" he said, sounding as weary and as sleep deprived as I felt. "What's up?"

Cynwrig held the phone close so I could hear Lugh's reply. "I just got a call from Rogan, wondering where I was. He did not sound happy."

"Maybe the foil is working, and he can't trace us," I said.

"Could be, but I suspect we're nevertheless running out of time. Up, lazy people, we need to get moving. I've ordered coffee and toast to go, and it'll be ready in five."

"Well, why didn't you just say that in the first place," I grumbled. "See you soon."

Cynwrig hung up, dropped a kiss onto my cheek, and then threw off the covers and rose. I was tempted to lie there and just watch all the muscular magnificence on display, but Lugh was right. We were running out of time.

I sighed and got up. The tape sticking the foil to my skin immediately started itching, but I'd put up with a whole lot worse if it stopped the signal getting out.

Once dressed, I did my teeth, then grabbed my pack and followed Cynwrig out the door. Lugh was already downstairs. He handed us a takeaway coffee cup and a brown paper bag containing what smelled like raisin toast, then led us out the door and over to the car. A thick fog hugged the ground, and the air was crisp and still. It was a good hour or so until sunrise, but some birds were already and rather too cheerfully greeting the dawn.

I climbed into the back seat and happily munched on my toast as Lugh started the car and drove off. We were on Leckhampton Hill Road, heading for the chimney, when a car rounded the corner ahead with its lights on full beam.

"Idiot," Lugh muttered, and briefly flicked our car's lights onto full beam in warning. The driver seemed to take no notice, accelerating at us with speed.

"Um, Lugh," I said, "I'm not liking the feel—"

The rest of the sentence ended in a yelp as we were hit side-on with enough force to crush the side of our car and send us tumbling.

Over the road, down into a ditch, into deeper darkness and unconsciousness.

CHAPTER
TWELVE

Waking was a slow and painful process. I was aware first of the stickiness that plastered the side of my face and the little men armed with picks chipping merrily at my brain. There was a fiercer ache in the lower part of my left arm, and it felt wrong. Heavy, though I couldn't immediately tell why without opening my eyes, and I didn't want to do that just yet. Not without understanding more of my situation.

As my consciousness continued to deepen, I realized I was lying on some kind of carpet that vibrated oddly.

A car. I was in a car.

Our car?

Probably not. Not given the ropes of moving air that bound my arms to my body.

Lugh, I suddenly thought. Where was Lugh? Were he and Cynwrig okay?

Almost of their own accord, my eyelids sprang open, only to be met by darkness. As my eyes adjusted, I saw a carpet-covered wall in front of me and metal above. It took a moment for recognition to kick in. I was not only in a car, but the goddamn trunk of it.

KERI ARTHUR

I tried to roll over to check what lay behind me, but the minute my weight hit my left arm, a scream rolled up my throat. I somehow clamped down on it, but sweat popped out across my brow, and for several seconds, all I wanted to do was throw up.

When I could, I looked down. It was bandaged and splinted from wrist to elbow, suggesting I must have broken it in the crash. I could still move my fingers, so there was obviously no muscle or nerve damage, and that meant I could still grip my knives... Fuck, my knives. Their weight was missing, and their sheaths were no longer strapped to my thighs. Which in truth was more an inconvenience than a real problem, given I could call them to me, but I nevertheless missed their comforting weight. I did at least still have the Eye—I could feel its chain around my neck and its thunderous beat of power against my chest. It appeared to be beating in time with my heart, but its energy was one of fury rather than fear. Which was odd—the Eye wasn't in and of itself a weapon.

I rolled back onto my right side and stared at the back of the seats. I couldn't hear anyone talking and had no idea how many people there were with me in the car. The storm mage was obviously present, given the airy ropes, but I had no idea who else was.

I tried to gather the air around my fingers, but nothing happened. I had no idea why—I was aware of the movement of warm air in the cabin beyond the back seats, could feel the heaviness of an approaching storm, but a barrier of some kind had been placed between us, preventing me from reaching them.

Was it a spell? Or had they used some sort of inhibitor? I knew there were drugs that could temporarily stop the use of certain psi talents, but my ability to call down storms was more than just a psychic talent... wasn't it?

Whatever the reason for that barrier, it meant there was nothing I could do—nothing other than scream for help, anyway, and that would probably achieve nothing more than my mouth being taped—so I closed my eyes and let the gentle humming of the engine lull me back into sleep.

The next time I woke, it was to the slamming of doors and voices. Two of them. The mage said something I couldn't quite catch, and a woman responded. Her voice was familiar, thanks once again to the visions. All we needed now was Rogan, and the whole damn leadership team would be here.

The trunk opened, and bright light poured in, momentarily casting the figure standing there into shadow. I blinked away the tears and studied her.

It was Jalvi. Or rather, an older version of her. This had to be Seryn, her mother.

"Out," she said in a clipped tone. "There's work to be done and no time to be stuffing around."

"You have all the Claws, so you don't need me to go about your business." I was a little surprised how evenly it came out. Given the incessant pounding in my head and the jaw-grinding pain in my arm, I'd expected something far scratchier.

"You're insurance, tree hugger. Now get out, or I'll fucking drag you out, and that won't be pleasant, let me assure you."

Tree hugger. I almost laughed. It was a slur I'd not heard in a very long time. "Given I'm insurance, that must mean my brother is alive."

"He was when we were going through his pockets to

find the real ring. That substitution very nearly cost you their lives." She stepped back and motioned me to get out.

"And Cynwrig?" Surely he had to be alive as well. Surely the gods had already taken enough from me...

"Battered and bruised but also alive. And before you ask, we left your knives with them." Her expression darkened. "This is your last warning. Get out or I drag you."

I swung my legs over the edge, then maneuvered myself upright without using or moving my left arm. Nausea nevertheless swept through me the minute my feet hit the ground, and it was tempting, so very tempting, to unleash the bile that rose up my throat all over her natty brown boots.

I somehow managed not to and instead looked around. We were back where it all started for at least one member of the Looisearch.

Pynwffynnon.

I guessed it did make tactical sense, given not only was the gate here unmonitored, it was surrounded by a barrier few could cross.

Rogan and his companions were obviously among those few.

I glanced past Seryn and studied the storm mage. Aside from the longish slate-gray beard, he was thin of face, with pale gray eyes and a rather startling mane of silver-shot dark gray hair that was tied back in a ponytail. At first glance he looked to be in his mid-forties, but the lines around his eyes and spots decorating the backs of his hands suggested he was a whole lot older.

"I'm extremely disappointed Rogan isn't here to greet me."

My voice was dry, and the witch smiled. "So, he was right. You did suspect him."

"It took us a while, but we did eventually put two and two together. Where is he? In Pynwffynnon or at the gate?"

"Pynwffynnon. Approaching the gate without proper preparation will be dangerous."

I snorted. "Trust me, the Annwfyn attacking will be the least of his problems. The Claws will kill him."

"A price he is willing to pay if it rids our world of their scourge."

"At what cost to the world though?"

He raised an eyebrow. "Meaning?"

"You don't know? That's rather—"

"Enough with the delaying chitchat," Seryn cut in with a glance at her watch. "We've half an hour before noon— we need to be at the gate by then."

"It's going to take us a whole lot longer than that to get there," I commented.

Her smile flashed, though there was nothing warm within it. "For the unprepared, it might."

She didn't explain what she meant, and I didn't ask. I'd find out soon enough.

The witch detached his airy ropes and freed my arms. "Need I warn you not to try anything tricky? Because I'll happily break the other arm if you do. Rogan might wish you kept alive until we know if the Claws will do the business, but there are quite a few variations of 'alive,' and I'm happy to apply one or more of them."

I had no intention of trying to escape, simply because I was the only thing now standing between this world and utter annihilation. It might be three against one, I might have a broken arm, but I nevertheless was going to do my best to stop these bastards.

Or die trying.

Pessimism said the latter was more likely than the former.

"Were you always such a charmer?" I said mildly, more because he seemed to be expecting a reply than from any real need to acknowledge his statement.

"Charm died the day the Annwfyn slaughtered everyone and everything I cared about. Move along."

I followed Seryn through the gate and down the path toward the forest and the unseen barrier. This time, two white stones stood on either side of the road where the barrier started, and were obviously doing the same thing as my knives had earlier. Two electric motorbikes waited on the other side. Well prepared indeed.

"Isn't it a little dangerous to be leaving a gap in the barrier like that?" I asked.

"We're too far away from the gate for it to be a problem," the mage commented. "The Annwfyn here have proven able to withstand some sunshine, but too much and they crisp just as nicely as the rest of them."

It was said with a relish that sickened me. It wasn't hard to imagine him deliberately luring them from the mine just to watch them burn.

We climbed onto the bikes—me and the mage on one, Seryn in the lead on the other—and motored through the trees, the soft hum of the bikes sounding a little like the whine of insects in the forest's stillness. Before long, we were sweeping down the hill and into Pynwffynnon.

Rogan came out of the sweet shop as we halted. Anger swept through me at the sight of him, and overhead, thunder rumbled. I glanced up sharply. The day that had started so crisp and cool was now thunderously electric. It was a power I could use, a power I could call down, if I could somehow break through the barrier they'd placed on me.

Rogan stopped and made a casting motion with his hand. I had no idea what he'd just done, but the barely audible sighing of the wind through the nearby bushes died away, seeming to suggest a sound bubble had been placed around us.

A welcoming smile touched his familiar features. "Lovely to see you again, Bethany."

"Go fuck yourself, Rogan." I climbed off the bike and glared at him. "How could you betray us like this? How could you betray my brother? I thought you were friends."

He sighed. "I do regret the necessary deceit, but in war, there are always consequences and casualties."

"We're not at war—"

"Try telling my people that," Seryn cut in. "We've spent eons protecting this world with little help from governments or other races, and it's time for it to end."

"Ending your so-called war will end this world. I've *seen* it. Seen what will happen if you combine the Claws and bring endless summer to this world."

"Except," Rogan said softly, "it is not *this* world I intend to bring endless summer to. It's *theirs.*"

I stared at him. In all the discussions we'd had about the Claws and what using them would mean for our world, it had never actually occurred to any of us that he'd unleash their power in Annwfyn itself.

It *could* work. *If* he got through the gate alive and *if* he was a powerful enough mage to unite the Claws.

Yes, it was morally wrong to attempt such wholesale destruction. Wrong to wipe out an entire race because their ways did not fit with ours. But there was nevertheless a tiny part of me that wished Rogan every success.

"They will destroy you the minute you step through that gate," I said. "You won't get the chance to use the Claws."

"You underestimate me, dear Bethany. But then, you and Lugh have been guilty of that for a very long time now." He glanced at Seryn. "Lead the way. Alan, keep an eye on her. Injured or not, she will try to stop us."

I would. I had to, if only because taking the Claws into Annwfyn might give them a weapon they could eventually use against us. As Cynwrig had noted earlier, we still knew so little about the inhabitants of our sister world, and our only real encounters were with the hunters. It was very likely they were but a small fraction of the wider Annwfyn community.

Seryn took the lead, Rogan a few steps behind her. Alan pushed me after them, and I stumbled a few steps before catching my balance. Unfortunately, the bastard wasn't close enough for me to land a boot in a painful part of his anatomy.

"Where are the Claws?" I asked as we moved up the slope toward the forest. The trees close by were young and strong, but their song was muted. It was almost as if they feared being too loud because of the past destruction that still haunted this place.

"They await us in the gate's cavern," Rogan said, without looking back. "It was the safest place to store them, given the Annwfyn would not touch them and few others can enter this place."

"I take it you were given special compensation from the government?"

Rogan snorted. "The government erased the whole situation from practical memory. This place doesn't exist. For all intents and purposes, neither do Alan nor I."

I glanced around at the man behind me. "Does that mean you're the teenager they found unconscious?"

"Yes. And my parents were never found and didn't even get the benefit of a tombstone. Many here didn't."

The anger absent from Rogan's voice vibrated through Alan's. And again, I couldn't help feel a sliver of sympathy.

"Why bring me here, Rogan? If you just wanted me for insurance against anything Lugh might do, you could have tied me up and left me in the car."

"Given your propensity to escape, that would have been unwise." He cast a glance over his shoulder, and there was something in his eyes—a disconnect or dispassion that I'd never seen before—that chilled me to the bone. "And who said your presence had anything to do with Lugh?"

That chill got stronger. I swallowed heavily and somehow said, "I don't understand."

"Now that," he said, almost jovially, "is a lie."

And it was. I fought back the rising tide of fear and said, "You don't need me as bait, Rogan. Seryn can open the door for you."

"I don't need her to open the door. It's already open—has been since that fuckwit tried to use his so-called auditory prowess to permanently lock the thing."

"Then what the fuck do you want with me?"

"Perhaps Lugh got both the brains *and* the brawn in the family." He shook his head. "As you have already noted, the Annwfyn will attack the minute I step through that gateway. So, a distraction will be needed, and you will provide that very nicely indeed."

"If you think I'm going anywhere near that gateway—"

"You won't have any choice. The drug we gave you has not only severed your connection to the wind but will also make you compliant to our will."

So, I'd been right—the wall between me and the storm *was* a drug. Question was, would it leave my system in time, or would I be forced to fight this battle without my biggest weapon?

"Did you kill Vincentia?"

He sighed. "Regrettably, yes. It is never wise to threaten someone when you don't hold the appropriate cards and prove incapable of even retrieving them."

Meaning the Codex, no doubt.

"And the singing bowl? Why frame Lugh like that when you needed us to keep researching the Claws?"

"That was not my doing, Bethany. As you said, it was not in my best interest, and I was as annoyed as you when the council called a halt to the Claws search. Luckily, your brother has a pleasing tendency to disobey such rulings."

Overhead, thunder rumbled again, a deeper, angrier sound. I filled my lungs with the storm's sharpness, and her energy, her power, rolled through me, making my skin and muscles tingle, and my heartbeat abnormally loud. Then it went deeper, blazing through my veins, chasing fire, easing pain. I hoped it would be enough. Hoped it would allow me to use my broken arm and grip my knife...

Then the wind snapped around me and brought with it a familiar voice. *The storm's force will burn the drug from your system, but it will take a little time. You must stop him regardless. He cannot be allowed to take the Claws into Annwfyn.*

I cautiously wrapped my fingers around the Eye. *If you and your fellow gods didn't want the fucking Claws in the hands of the Annwfyn—or anyone else, for that matter—you should have destroyed the damn things long ago.*

Some of us tried came her response. *But there are two sides to every game, and our opposition currently has the upper hand. It falls to you to stop it.*

And if I don't?

There is no don't. There is only do.

I was tempted to point out it was unfair to expect me to succeed where a bevy of gods had failed, but I suspected she'd simply ignore that.

The wind fell away again. I had no doubt she was keeping an eye on the situation and couldn't help but wonder if she'd provide any assistance if the situation went ass up.

We reached the mine's entrance. It was in reasonably good condition considering just how much of the country-side around these mountains had actually slipped.

Rogan stopped, held up a warning finger, and then began to spell. Or at least, that's what I presumed he was doing with all the finger movements and whisper-soft murmurings.

He made a casting motion into the mine and then, after a moment, nodded sharply. "Right, there's a secondary noise barrier in place over the gate, but if they linger nearby, they will see your body heat, so keep out of the direct line of sight. Seryn, I'll need you to monitor the ground and tell me if there's any movement. Alan, when I give the word, toss our bait."

Said bait wasn't going to go quietly, but I didn't say anything. Better they think I remained incapable of doing anything more than what I was told. Which might well be the truth, given I hadn't yet tried to do anything else.

Rogan turned and walked into the mine. Seryn followed. When I didn't move, Alan pushed me forward. Thankfully, we didn't have to go very far to find the gate. Its frame was large and ornately carved with symbols and what looked like glyphs, and it dominated the far wall of the manmade cavern. There was no actual door though, just a weirdly viscous blackness sitting within the frame. It was a void that led to hell itself—if hell was a realm where humans were treated like cattle.

The sword and the crown lay on the ground in front of the gate. Rogan stopped in front of them and rather reverently drew the serpent ring from his pocket, placing it beside the other two Claws.

Seryn walked past him to the left side of the gate, pressing one hand against the ornately carved stone and the other on the cavern wall. She closed her eyes and, after a moment, nodded.

Alan pulled me to a halt and remained close behind me. Bad move, I thought, but resisted the immediate temptation to kick him in the nuts. If I acted too soon, they would knock me out. If I moved too late, I would die.

Trouble was, lightning still burned through my veins, which suggested the drug remained active. And I couldn't risk calling my knives to me until Rogan had begun the ritual or spell or whatever the fuck he had to do to claim the Claws.

I flexed my fingers again, my left hand less responsive than the right, and tried to calm the growing sense of doom. Patience; I just needed patience.

But the gate's viscous center now stirred in a sluggish circle, and I couldn't escape the sudden notion that the Annwfyn were coming.

Rogan began his spell. The crown rose, lifted by invisible fingers, and was placed upon his head. The spell's power ratcheted up; dark purple fire ran down the fuller of the black sword in response. As it was lifted from the ground, I closed my eyes and reached for the knives. The Eye pulsed and a heartbeat later, the heavy weight of steel landed in my hands.

It hurt.

I didn't fucking care.

The sword lay in Rogan's hand and the ring was rising toward his waiting finger.

Time was up.

I dropped to my knees, spun around, and thrust a knife through Alan's knee, twisting it sideways and slicing away a good chunk of his kneecap in the process. He screamed and fell, but somehow gathered air and cast it at me, throwing me across the cavern. I hit the wall with a grunt, and felt the earth moving at my back as Seryn tried to encase me. I rolled away, a scream tearing up my throat as my weight rested briefly on my broken arm. Caught a brief glimpse of the ring sliding over Rogan's hand and knew time was up. I surged to my feet and ran straight at him, knife raised, ready to strike.

Air hit me again, lifting me up, moving me forward. Toward the gate, toward the Annwfyn gathering on the other side.

I screamed in denial and reached for the lightning that burned through my system. It erupted from my skin, a blanket of brightness that flung itself at the bleeding man behind me, covering him, binding him, burning him. He opened his mouth, but no sound came out, the flesh at his throat sloughing away, taking with it all ability to speak. His leash of air disintegrated, dropping me hard. I landed on my hands and knees and white-hot pain erupted, flashing up my broken arm and rolling through the rest of me, momentarily threatening to steal consciousness.

I sucked in air, fighting the blackness, fighting the bile that rose up my throat. Air whispered a warning, and I looked up. A massive boulder was coming straight at me.

I flung up a hand, made a fist of air, and knocked the

boulder to one side. It crashed against the cavern wall and exploded, sending razor-sharp shards flying through the air. I caught them and flung them back at Seryn.

She slapped the wall, and a river of stone wrapped around her, protecting her from most of the projectiles. Then that wall exploded, and the projectiles were heading back toward me. I cast a shield of air in front of me, forcing them to either side.

Movement, light, caught my eye. I twisted around, but not quickly enough. Lightning hit me, burned me, even as air grabbed me and tossed me forward. Past Rogan, past Seryn, toward the gate.

I screamed another denial and, as my feet and legs slipped into viscous blackness, stabbed wildly at the wall with the knife. It slid into stone as easily as it did flesh, and I stopped with a suddenness that just about yanked my arm out of its socket. On the far side of the soupy blackness, hands grabbed my legs—clawed hands, greedy hands, trying to pull me all the way in even as the heat of lightning arced toward me again. I raised the other knife, let the lightning hit its tip. Let it rip through the blade and into me, then turned it around and flung it back at the storm mage. It incinerated him in an instant.

My grip on the knife hilt slipped against the pressure the Annwfyn were asserting. I twisted around and pointed the other knife at the doorway and unleashed another bolt of lightning. It hit the wall and broke apart. Flesh could get through but nothing else, it seemed.

Then the stone around my anchor began to melt. Seryn. Fury hit, as deep and as dangerous as the storm that rumbled outside. I called to the air, grabbed Seryn, and tossed her into the blackness behind me, aiming her at whoever—whatever—had my legs.

It worked. The minute I was released, I jerked my feet free, yanked the knife from the stone, then dropped to the ground and rolled away from the gate. And for too many seconds, couldn't do anything more than simply suck in air and fight the blackness that threatened to consume me.

Everything hurt. Everything ached. Burned.

The lightning. It was once again trapped within my flesh.

The answer, the master of all storms had said, *will lie in using a conductor to both call down and disperse the storms.*

The knives... I thrust one into the ground and imagined all the heat, all the fury, that boiled through me leeching down into it. The knife began to glow a bloody hue as the heat was channeled from my flesh into the soil, making it uncomfortably warm.

The burning stopped, but it wasn't over yet.

I forced my head up. Saw a blur of light. Unnatural light. Light that burned with the force of the sun.

Rogan, running for the gate.

I thrust up and threw myself at him in a last-ditch effort to trip him up and stop him entering the gate.

I failed.

He simply leapt over the top of me and plunged into the blackness. I thrust to my feet but didn't move. I simply stood there, weaving like a drunkard, bound to the spot by the morbid desire to see what happened next.

For several minutes, nothing did. Then an invisible fist of power hit me, lifting me up and casting me backward. I had a brief glimpse of shredded black flags, of an impossibly airy tunnel, the bloody remains of a woman, and finally a ball of fierce white light in the middle of which stood a man. A skeletal man who wore a glowing crown and who gripped a black sword lodged deep into the earth and who screamed, endlessly screamed, while a golden serpent with glowing green eyes flowed around him, consuming the burning figures that threw themselves at the united Claws in a desperate attempt to smother and stop...

I hit the ground and rolled down the hill, deep into the forest, deep into the new growth. Heard the songs of the trees and felt soft layers of leaves and limbs wrap around me, cocooning me, protecting me.

I was safe.

I could let go.

Unconsciousness swamped me, and I knew no more.

EPILOGUE

I woke to a soft, rhythmic beating. I listened for a very long time, comforted by its presence and the fact that I still had a heart and pulse to beat.

That I hadn't ended up as nothing more than bits of chewed-up meat in some Annwfyn's stomach was a miracle in itself... Then the memories of those last few desperate minutes rose, along with one inescapable fact.

I'd failed.

Rogan hadn't.

He'd taken the Claws into Annwfyn and unleashed their power. I had no idea if it would indeed stop them or even destroy them... was it even possible to destroy a world that was a shadow of our own without affecting our own?

Only time—and maybe the gods themselves—could answer that question.

I opened my eyes. Lugh was asleep in a chair next to the hospital bed, his big feet propped on the end, his arms crossed and head tilted back. I had no idea how he could sleep soundly enough to snore in that sort of position, but as he'd no doubt say, he'd probably slept in worse.

If he'd been injured in the rollover, there was no sign of it. But given I was in hospital, it was more than likely that even if he had been battered and bruised, he would have been healed by now.

But he wasn't the only one in the room. Darby stood on the other side, checking and recording my vital signs.

"Hey," I said softly.

"Hey," she replied. "Glad to see you're finally awake."

I raised an eyebrow. "How long have I been out?"

"A couple of days. We fixed all the breaks easy enough, but it's taken longer to replenish fluids and nutrients. Whatever you did up there basically caused your body to waste away."

"I used the lightning."

"Didn't Beira warn you against that?"

"Yep. But it was either that or become an Annwfyn's lunch. How did I get here?"

"How do you think?" Darby motioned toward Lugh with her chin. "That big lug found you and brought you here."

"The big lug resents being called a big lug," he grumbled. He opened his eyes and studied me. "Well, at least you look less like a skeleton and more like your regular self. You had me worried for a while there."

I smiled and lightly placed my hand over his. "I'm going to be around to give you hell for centuries yet, I promise you that."

"I'll hold you to that promise, dear sister."

"Now that Lugh's awake, I best get back to my other patients." Darby squeezed my arm lightly. "I'll check on you again later, okay?"

She blew Lugh a kiss and then headed out the door. He

watched until she'd disappeared and then returned his attention to me.

"As to how we found you..." He smiled. "Rogan got rid of his phone so we couldn't trace him but he forgot the GPS in his car. Sgott tracked it to Pynwffynnon, and we all converged on the place."

"All?" I said, raising an eyebrow.

"Sgott and about a dozen of his people, Cynwrig and as many of his people he could gather from the immediate area, and of course me and Mathi. We came prepared for a fight and instead we found a goddamn disaster zone."

I frowned. "What do you mean?"

"The gate is gone, all that remains of the mountain is a crater, and Pynwffynnon is a smoking ruin. It's almost as if the place was hit by some sort of heat bomb."

I remembered the heat wave that had tossed me from the cavern. "Rogan got through the gate and used the Claws. It sent a blast of heat through both worlds."

"Ah," he said softly. "When we found you, you were wrapped in the limbs of multiple trees, and they were singing to you. I suspect it was their energy that kept you alive."

"I remember their song," I said. "They were determined death would not touch them again."

"And it didn't," he said. "I don't know how or why, but the forest wasn't affected by the heat that destroyed every-thing else. Mathi reckons the trees that survived or grew out of the destruction caused by Aubrey's Key have devel-oped a resistance to heat and magic."

More than a resistance, I suspected, given the way they'd enclosed me. "Speaking of Cynwrig and Mathi, where are they?"

"They were both called to a council meeting. Apparently, there's been a development with the missing hoard."

"They've found it?"

"I have no idea." He grimaced and levered his feet off the bed. "There has, however, been a secondary development, one that affects us directly."

I studied his expression and didn't for one second like the seriousness there. "They've found Aunt Riayn's body?"

"No." He reached into his coat pocket and pulled out a small red envelope. "It's this."

"Oh, fuck."

"Yeah," he said grimly. "The pixie council has reached a decision regarding your punishment."

"And they asked you to deliver it? Bastards."

"We haven't many living relatives left, so I guess they had no other choice. At least it's not a knife."

"I don't find that at all comforting."

"You should, because that option was probably on the table, even if not for as many years as Aunt Riayn."

He held the envelope out. I didn't take it.

"You haven't read it?"

"It's sealed with pixie magic. Only you can open it."

Which meant he had tried. I took a deep breath and then gingerly took the damn thing. Gold dust was pooled around the pointed section of the seal. I hesitated, then pressed my finger against it. The dust disappeared, and the rectangular flap opened. Inside was a folded piece of red paper.

I returned my gaze to Lugh's. "I killed two people in that mine—do you think they know about that?"

"No. As I said, there is nothing left. Besides, it was in self-defense, was it not?"

"Yes, but—"

"The curse doesn't apply, Beth. Besides, there's enough to be worrying about without adding the weight of that."

I hoped he was right even as I feared he might not be and glanced down at the envelope again. It was pointless delaying the inevitable. I tugged the note free and unfolded it. The message was short and to the point. I read it with a deepening sense of incredulity.

"Well?" Lugh said, with a touch of impatience. "What's the sentence?"

I lifted my gaze to his, unsure whether to laugh or to cry. "My punishment is being bonded to the Deva council for a period of two years."

He blinked. "What?"

"They've forced me to do what Mom wouldn't. They've made me the council's relic hunter. They want me to help them find the missing hoard."

He stared at me for several seconds, then a smile spread slowly across his face. "Oh, that's delicious."

"It is indeed."

I was now inside the inner circle. I now had direct access to the councilors and the records. I might finally be able to not only discover who had planted the singing bowl to implicate my brother in the theft of the hoard, but also start investigating who had betrayed my mother.

"Give them utter hell, dear sister."

"I intend to, brother mine. I intend to."

Also by Keri Arthur

Relic Hunters Series

Crown of Shadows (Feb 2022)

Sword of Darkness (Oct 2022)

Ring of Ruin (June 2023)

Shield of Fire (March 2024)

Horn of Winter (Nov 2024)

Lizzie Grace Series

Blood Kissed (May 2017)

Hell's Bell (Feb 2018)

Hunter Hunted (Aug 2018)

Demon's Dance (Feb 2019)

Wicked Wings (Oct 2019)

Deadly Vows (Jun 2020)

Magic Misled (Feb 2021)

Broken Bonds (Oct 2021)

Sorrows Song (June 2022)

Wraith's Revenge (Feb 2023)

Killer's Kiss (Oct 2023)

Shadow's End (July 2024)

The Witch King's Crown

Blackbird Rising (Feb 2020)

Blackbird Broken (Oct 2020)

Blackbird Crowned (June 2021)

Kingdoms of Earth & Air

Unlit (May 2018)

Cursed (Nov 2018)

Burn (June 2019)

The Outcast series

City of Light (Jan 2016)

Winter Halo (Nov 2016)

The Black Tide (Dec 2017)

Souls of Fire series

Fireborn (July 2014)

Wicked Embers (July 2015)

Flameout (July 2016)

Ashes Reborn (Sept 2017)

Dark Angels series

Darkness Unbound (Sept 27th 2011)

Darkness Rising (Oct 26th 2011)

Darkness Devours (July 5th 2012)

Darkness Hunts (Nov 6th 2012)

Darkness Unmasked (June 4 2013)

Darkness Splintered (Nov 2013)

Darkness Falls (Dec 2014)

Riley Jenson Guardian Series

Full Moon Rising (Dec 2006)

Kissing Sin (Jan 2007)

Tempting Evil (Feb 2007)

Dangerous Games (March 2007)

Embraced by Darkness (July 2007)

The Darkest Kiss (April 2008)

Deadly Desire (March 2009)

Bound to Shadows (Oct 2009)

Moon Sworn (May 2010)

Myth and Magic series

Destiny Kills (Oct 2008)

Mercy Burns (March 2011)

Nikki & Micheal series

Dancing with the Devil (March 2001 / Aug 2013)

Hearts in Darkness Dec (2001/ Sept 2013)

Chasing the Shadows Nov (2002/Oct 2013)

Kiss the Night Goodbye (March 2004/Nov 2013)

Damask Circle series

Circle of Fire (Aug 2010 / Feb 2014)

Circle of Death (July 2002/March 2014)

Circle of Desire (July 2003/April 2014)

Ripple Creek series

Beneath a Rising Moon (June 2003/July 2012)

Beneath a Darkening Moon (Dec 2004/Oct 2012)

Spook Squad series

Memory Zero (June 2004/26 Aug 2014)

Generation 18 (Sept 2004/30 Sept 2014)

Penumbra (Nov 2005/29 Oct 2014)

Stand Alone Novels

Who Needs Enemies (E-book only, Sept 1 2013)

Novella

Lifemate Connections (March 2007)

Anthology Short Stories

The Mammoth Book of Vampire Romance (2008)

Wolfbane and Mistletoe--2008

Hotter than Hell--2008

ABOUT THE AUTHOR

Keri Arthur, the author of the New York Times bestselling ***Riley Jenson Guardian series***, has written more than fifty-five novels–35 of them with traditional publishers Random House/Penguin/Piatkus. She is now fully self-published. She's won six Australian Romance Readers Awards for Favourite Sci-Fi, Fantasy, or Futuristic Romance & the Romance Writers of Australia RBY Award for Speculative Fiction. Her Lizzie Grace series won ARRA's Fav Continuing Romance Series in 2022 and she has in the past won The Romantic Times Career Achievement Award for Urban Fantasy. When she's not at her computer writing the next book, she can be found somewhere in the Australian countryside taking photos.

for more information:
www.keriarthur.com
keriarthurauthor@gmail.com

facebook.com/AuthorKeriArthur
twitter.com/kezarthur
instagram.com/kezarthur

Ingram Content Group UK Ltd.
Milton Keynes UK
UKHW010630140723
425136UK00001B/11

9 780645 303209